a novel

JUSTIN KURIAN

The Canticle of Ibiza

Produced and printed by Stillwater River Publications.

Visit our website at **www.StillwaterPress.com** for more information.

First Stillwater River Publications Edition

ISBN: 978-1-963296-06-8 (paperback) 978-1-963296-23-5 (hardcover)

Library of Congress Control Number: 2024901082

Names: Kurian, Justin, author.
Title: The Canticle of Ibiza / Justin Kurian.
Description: First Stillwater River Publications edition. | West Warwick, RI, USA : Stillwater River Publications, [2024]
Identifiers: ISBN: 978-1-963296-06-8 (paperback) 978-1-963296-23-5 (hardcover)
Subjects: LCSH: Upper class men—Travel—Spain—Ibiza and Formentera—Fiction. | Male friendship—Fiction. | Questions and answers—Fiction. | Self-realization—Fiction. | Salvation—Fiction. | Love—Fiction. | LCGFT: Magic realist fiction. | Action and adventure fiction.
Classification: LCC: PS3611.U73226 C36 2024 | DDC: 813/.6—dc23

1 2 3 4 5 6 7 8 9 10

Written by Justin Kurian.
Cover and interior design by Elisha Gillette.
Published by Stillwater River Publications, West Warwick, RI, USA.

THE CANTICLE OF IBIZA

ONE

The waiter wore only a magenta speedo and sparkling silver wig.

Not anything wrong with this garb necessarily, but not the usual one John was accustomed to from a service staff member. Or from anyone, for that matter. Apparently no one else worked here but this remarkably lithe man, and, considering the wrinkles emerging from his eyes, he might even be the owner.

Now the cafe itself was certainly nothing special—a few wobbly tables balanced on the dusty sidewalk, and a peeling white storefront housed a grumbling coffee machine suffering from bouts of indigestion.

This cafe, located on a side street in Santa Eulària, did not bother with such trivial details as a sign, so its name remained a mystery. Against all odds though, it possessed a certain charm. The lovely Mediterranean morning exuded warmth, with clean blue skies expanding above. Shockingly fresh air whisked off the sea, and one could bask in the view of this sea, only a short block away, from its rickety chairs. John would drink his tea here.

He sat alone, with no other patrons present.

His move to Ibiza just the night previous, directly from his pricey but chilly apartment in the Upper East Side of Manhattan, had left him dazed and confused. He had sold his apartment for the initial offer received a mere forty-two minutes after placing it on the market. His appalled real estate agent turned an off-green as he insisted they could get far, far more money by waiting—perhaps even double—but John was desperate to evacuate.

The harsh realization that he lacked any solid plans once he arrived on this island now slapped him with authority. He knew not a soul on Ibiza save Gunther, and he had not seen or heard from Gunther in fifteen long years. But rumors suggested Gunther lived somewhere on the island, and John needed to find him. Only Gunther ever had the answers.

As he sipped his milky tea, she stealthily arrived.

Her age and nationality were impossible to determine. Quite tan, she wore immense sunglasses that concealed half her face, and a sunhat that shrouded the remainder in shadow. The blazing colors of her flowing sundress distracted the eye. What part of her tan was genetic, and what resulted from the burning Spanish sun, was difficult to discern. Of the two remaining tables, she chose the farthest one from John.

After removing her hat and placing it on the table, then applying maroon lipstick several times, all movement ceased. Even the coffee machine stopped distressing.

Although her head was turned slightly away, John could not avoid the feeling that she studied him from behind those opaque lenses. A protrusion of her neck tendons made him suspect eyes were aimed at his person.

"Do you always behave so appallingly?" she asked in perfect English.

The words carried crisply through the empty street. He realized, with a jolt, that she addressed him.

"Me?"

"Well, I'm not talking to the owner."

"I suppose you're not."

"So do you always behave like this?"

"Like what?"

She turned to him. "So damned self-absorbed."

"I'm self-absorbed?"

"Absolutely."

"I am alone at a cafe on an abandoned street watching the tumbleweeds. Self-absorption tends to occur."

"No excuse."

"Would it help if I told you I was thinking of my kindly but deceased grandmother?"

She heartily laughed, tilting back and displaying an oversized column of flawless white teeth, gums prominent on top. "You are American?"

"And so are you."

She laughed again. "Now this is rare. We have the Dutch, Germans, English, and Scandinavians visiting this island, and of course the native Spanish, but Americans are far and few between. It's simply too far away."

Spindly green weeds peeking through the sidewalk cracks trembled from a sea gust.

He closed his eyes, allowing morning sunlight to warm his

lids, the inside view transforming from darkness to a balmy orange. The severe squeak of a chair leg roused him.

He stared in wonder as she collected her bag and approached. Her straw-scented hat plopped onto his table and a single beige drop trickled down the side of his disturbed teacup.

Without the least bit of hesitation, she sat directly beside him. He should say something, but found himself too astonished to speak.

The odor of coconut lotion dominated. Her peculiar tan, or perhaps sunburn, had a purplish tint. Veins along her neck, which he now realized was quite sinewy, revealed an older age, probably early sixties. She kept herself so tanned and obscured it was impossible to gauge. Images of aging actresses from the golden age of Hollywood flooded his mind.

The nearly naked proprietor served her an espresso with lemon peel. Before turning away, he winked at her, a conspiratorial grin spanning his tanned face. Although she ignored him, her subdued amusement and tension about her lips revealed she was repressing a confirmatory grin.

The hot rush of embarrassment now seared John, as he appeared to be the naive target of some sort of inside joke or set up.

"Now. Let's talk about you, shall we?" she said, seemingly settled in for a lengthy conversation.

Apparently, the social norms on Ibiza were a bit different than he was accustomed to.

"And what is there to talk about?"

"Your name, to start."

"I see you commence with extremely challenging questions."

She briefly smiled. "Name?"

He scoffed, finding her persistence amusing. "John."

"Last name?"

"Does it matter?"

"Last name?"

John laughed again. "Balkus."

"Strange. You appear Italian."

"I'm a little of everything."

"Well, you intrigue me, John."

"Oh? I don't know any reason why I should."

Her left eyebrow lifted, as she perhaps expected a more flattered response.

"I must confess something to you, John."

"Please don't feel obligated."

She paused again, studying him with curiosity, and then exploded in laughter, flipping her brown hair over her shoulder. "I must. I absolutely must. And do not let this frighten you."

"Okay."

"When I spotted you, I absolutely thought you were the ghost of my husband."

He had hoped for a better start on Ibiza. Perhaps it would not look too awkward if he fled right now? Although, summoning a plausible reason for his abrupt departure in such a lackadaisical atmosphere would not be easy.

"Have I frightened you?"

"We're getting there."

"You look just like him when he was your age. Identical. What are you, thirty-three or four?"

"Seven."

"Your dark, wavy hair—and you are tall, with a tan color," she said giggling. "And those khaki shorts and white shirt—just like him. Both of you attractive. Astounding! Fate at work, as I always do say. Fate at work."

"You said I look like the ghost of him?"

"Absolutely."

"Does that mean I appear a ghostly version of him, pale and haunted in appearance—or rather, does that mean something happened to him and I appear similar to him, but I must be a ghost in that he is no longer present?"

Her head shook side to side, clicking emerging from her gaping mouth, her glossy lips freshly licked.

"I see intelligence is not a problem of yours. Another similarity you two have," she said with a scoff. "The answer is: something happened to him."

"I'm sorry."

Her chair leg squeaked.

"Well, aren't you going to ask?"

"Ask what?"

"What happened to him. No need to play mister cool and pretend you are not the curious one."

He thought being polite was a more accurate description, but so be it.

"So, what happened to him?"

Her tanned legs extended beneath the table. "Hopefully heaven. He died at forty-three when we were based in Beverly Hills. I've been here ever since."

Still not a soul passed by. Ibiza certainly remained sleepy in late spring, a stark contrast to the mad rush he heard unleashes during the impeding summer.

The proprietor returned, and as peculiar as this might sound, he now positioned himself with his privates no more than two inches from John's face. He stood motionless and mute.

John remained frozen. And understandingly baffled.

An awkward moment, surely, under any circumstances. What to say escaped him, and certainly he did not dare turn his way to inquire. Life, evidently, had not prepared him for all situations.

After readjusting his nearly nonexistent bathing suit with a resounding snap, the proprietor placed a glass of red wine directly before John. The smell of crushed dark cherries overpowered.

"What's this?"

"Your wine. Enjoy."

Sunlight gleamed off the lengthy strands of his silver wig, making it impossible to discern his features. All was just white brightness.

"I didn't order this."

"Of course, you did order it, Señor."

"I didn't—"

"You must not be embarrassed by that fact."

"Embarrassed?"

"Yes. Do not be embarrassed by your order."

"What on earth? Why would I be embarrassed?" John turned to her in befuddled amusement. She simply shrugged her shoulders and looked away.

"Look, I didn't order this. I have my tea, remember?"

"Relax, Señor."

"But I am relaxed."

"You do not need to be so ashamed."

"Ashamed? What on—"

"Shame has no place here. You are on Ibiza now, not Kentucky. You would do well to remember that," he said, patting down the fluttering strands of his wig as he walked away.

John turned to her in disbelief. "What on earth is with that guy?"

She looked aside, dismissing his inquiry.

"Did you just hear him?" John insisted. "What is he talking about?"

"So, are you just visiting for a few days like all the others, or here to stay a while?"

She definitively ignored his questions with such a perfunctory air that he questioned whether he had actually asked them.

"This cafe?"

"No," she laughed playfully. "Ibiza."

John sipped his tea, ignoring the fragrant wine. "I'll be staying a while."

Her hands tensed. "Wonderful."

"Is it?"

"Why did you come to Ibiza?"

The orange dust coating the street and sidewalks glowed in the morning light.

"To try to begin anew, I suppose," he finally answered. "If such things are truly possible."

She smiled broadly, as his answer seemed to greatly please her. "How positive-minded of you."

"Isn't it?"

"What an American optimist."

Surprising to hear that label. Many years had passed since someone last deemed him an optimist. It was a common designation from his university days, but certainly not from the barren years since.

"But perhaps you are a liar, John."

He turned to her. "Oh?"

"Yes."

"And in what form is my current prevarication manifesting?"

"Just maybe, might I suggest, you came here to escape?"

"Escape?"

She leaned forward. His reflection, clear in her enormous sunglass lenses, appeared riddled with concern.

"In my nearly fifteen years of experience here, many journey to Ibiza to discover a new way of living. Their little, eager heads bursting with hope. Nowhere on our fair planet is a better destination for that search than right here."

"And why might that be?"

She appeared surprised, if not hurt, by his question.

"We are standing, after all, on the landing spot of the original hippies who fled the US in the sixties." She stomped the pavement, a gentle tangerine cloud arising. "Some disappeared to Kathmandu or Tangiers, but *here* was their prime destination. It is 1988, and yes, they are still living here. And like attracts like. So they have continually attracted other open-minded individuals from throughout Europe to create our entirely unique culture of Ibiza."

John nodded. That particular bohemian history had undoubtedly endowed this place with a novel atmosphere, but to what extent he did not know.

"But then, many also come to escape. To escape something haunting their past. Something searing and consuming them inside."

"Sounds uncomfortable."

"And unfortunately, it does not always work."

"You, for example?"

She laughed heartily. "I'm Angela by the way. And sadly, if I came to escape something, it was nothing particularly intriguing. Just the doldrums of widowhood in Los Angeles."

"Sorry to hear that."

"You don't get invited to the parties anymore; those uptight women fear you might prey on their ridiculous husbands."

"So did you?"

"Did I what?"

"Prey on their unwitting husbands?"

She halted, her chair emitting a stringent squeak. All jubilance drained from her face, leaving a sour, downturned mouth.

"Hardly," she said coolly. "I damn well respect a marriage, unlike most."

It appears he might have misstepped.

"There is nothing more sacred, I always say, than marriage. And," she said, striking the table with her forefinger, "I truly hope you feel the same as well."

This sudden solemnity was quite unanticipated. He still expected her to burst into laughter. Yet she remained deathly serious, and awaited his answer in pregnant silence. He best agree.

"I do. I certainly do."

Angela's sunglasses bounced as she began giggling.

"What is it? What's so funny now?"

"I'm not here to scare you, John. So don't worry."

Everything seemed askew. Slightly off-kilter. But he could not discern if it were the jet lag and exhaustion, or the people and place.

"I'll keep that in mind."

The weather was now warming at such an alarming rate that he consciously noted the change, something that had never happened before. He stood.

"Nice meeting you, Angela. Perhaps I'll see you around."

She popped up and fastened her hat. "Nonsense. Now, it's painfully obvious you are new here."

"Is it?"

Not only was it "obvious," but "painfully obvious" he was new to Ibiza? That certainly did not sound like flattery. And to think he believed he was fitting in just fine.

"Let me guide you around Santa Eulària a bit. Everyone needs some help, even you."

What "even you" meant was again ambiguous, although at least it implied he projected a decent level of competence. Unless, of course, it had been uttered in sarcasm.

Either way, he was well-accustomed in New York to having

each minute of each day precisely mapped out. No wiggle room. A protein smoothie smelling startlingly like manure began things at 5:20 a.m. Ceaseless work consumed the day, which ended with cardiovascular on the exercise bike, always alone, in his cavernous and rather bare Manhattan apartment in late evening. More work, then a brisk shower and bed. Up at bleak 5:20 a.m. to start again, with absolutely no hits on the snooze button. A strictly forbidden indulgence. Free time, as you see, was an alien concept.

Yet now, here he was, randomly wandering Ibiza, completely liberated of any plans or obligations. From one extreme to the other, which is never easy to manage.

Side by side, John and Angela strolled down the street to the sea, their common American heritage perhaps contributing to some solidarity, as he felt no need to converse. He leaned against the rapidly warming iron rail spanning the length of the beach.

The serenity of this sea struck deeply. Not at all the hardy Atlantic John was accustomed to, with its white-foamed waves and ominous green vastness. Here, the sea, a gentle blue, barely stirred. A faint seaweed smell rode the soft breeze.

"Are you married?" Angela asked.

An abrupt question from seemingly nowhere.

"No."

"Divorced?"

"Good heavens, you aren't shy."

"Shy? What gain is there in being shy?"

A few gains, perhaps, at least when it came to social situations. Such as not turning into an annoying mess too quickly. But probably best not to list them at the moment.

"No, not divorced. Long relationship, but recently ended that."

"Did she propose to you?"

"Don't men do the proposing?"

"Not always. Not in particular circles...like yours."

John shook his head at her acumen. "Not bad, Angela, not bad. And yes, she did propose. A 'merger' she charmingly called it. I was to be 'merged.' A few months ago. It took that offer to shock me into the painful reality."

"What reality?"

He cleared his throat. "The vapidness of my entire situation."

Her fingers clenched. "So why did you refuse her offer?"

"Does that matter?"

"Yes, it does."

"You certainly are curious."

Somehow her gaze consumed, even though her sunglasses were impenetrable.

"After four years, I didn't even know her preferred genre of film. The 'relationship,' and I use that term generously, was built on high society and money. Like my life. Either way, she started dating another high earner at my company two weeks later."

"Sounds like a great company."

The corner of John's mouth lifted. "I finally, after fifteen years, freed myself of them, too. Left it all behind, and a few days later, here I stand."

She scanned him from hair to toes. "Rather drastic of you."

He hopped onto the warming sand.

"Do you know I have not even touched the Mediterranean yet?"

He removed his sandals and approached the sea. The beach, a sandy curve in front of the tiny city, had only three sunbathers on the distant end. The water was utterly clear, and when he dipped his toe into it, he felt nothing. This water felt so wonderfully warm it was undetectable.

He tossed off his shirt and submerged into this pleasure.

Underneath astounded. A marvelous school of sapphire fish darted past. Ribbons of light filtered through the water. Everything so remarkably peaceful, so serene.

On the iron rail, Angela awaited.

"How was it?"

"A glimpse of heaven."

"Wonderful," she said, peering at the sky. "You're fortunate. You have come to Ibiza at the perfect time."

"Have I?"

She exhaled, faintly whistling. "Did you know that for nine months a year, less than one hundred thousand reside on Ibiza? That's it. And then, come summer, the population explodes to over one million."

"Ten times increase. That is a hell of a drastic change."

She waved her rangy fingers through the air. "In less than a month, hundreds of thousands of invaders will descend, seeking their simple summer pleasures. But you came at the right time. You have a chance to meet the genuine residents before the flood."

"I'm fond of the beach," John said, wryly smiling. "Maybe I'm just here for simple summer pleasures, as you say."

"I have a powerful sense you're not. And I'm gifted with the sixth sense."

The squawking of several black-headed gulls gliding overhead pierced the air. John forcefully shook his head.

"What is it?"

He pulled his shirt back on, squeezing salt water from his thick hair. Although on the verge of asking an elementary question, he found himself hesitating, as a trembling sensation reverberated throughout his innards.

"Angela..."

"Yes, John? What is it?"

"Angela, do you know a Gunther Djurgenson?"

She frowned, for some reason disappointed with his inquiry. "Gunther? No, I don't believe so. Why?"

"It's okay. Don't worry about it."

"Why?"

John scoffed, as he was amazed, if not aghast, at her persistence. But effective she was.

"I believe he is here. In Ibiza. Living somewhere on this island. I need to find him."

Deep lines creased her forehead. "Ever heard of Alexander Graham Bell? Inventor of the telephone? Or at least have you written a letter to this Gunther?"

"Antonio Meucci actually invented the phone in 1849," John said. "Graham Bell got the first patent in 1876 and took all the credit."

She viewed him with amused admiration.

He gradually exhaled. "But no, I have not had contact with Gunther in fifteen years," he said. "No information. The rumors are he is living somewhere off the grid on Ibiza. I need to search him out."

"Fifteen years? A tad long to wait to contact someone so important to you, no?"

John smiled. "A question that I have asked myself many times," he said, shaking his head wistfully. He scanned the sea, spotting a lone white sailboat venturing valiantly across the endless blue.

"Well? What happened?"

"You are curious, aren't you?"

"We've established that."

The sail billowed in the wind.

"Such charmingly altruistic plans to improve the world we once had, while best friends and fellow theology and philosophy majors at university long ago. He was brilliant. We planned on publishing a journal of ideas and dedicating our lives toward this project and its fruits."

"Sounds beautiful, John. Like a dream."

"Doesn't it?"

"Well, what happened?"

John laughed deprecatingly. "I flushed our beautiful dream down the toilet."

Her dark lenses focused on him. "And Gunther?"

His molars ground smoothly together. Might as well divulge.

"I'm not proud to admit, but my lovely, high-earning self with my new high finance job left our plans out to dry. Abandoned our collaboration. Abandoned Gunther...lied to him." He paused for a moment, collecting himself. "No clue what happened to him the last fifteen years. No clue at all. And things have not been quite the same ever since."

"How so?"

"Let's just say my life has been on a downhill journey since that time."

"Fifteen is a lot of years to be descending."

"I could not agree more," John said. "I discovered hell occupies one of the upper floors."

Angela stroked her tanned chin. "Maybe your Gunther ended up doing superbly. Having a grand life. Have you considered that?"

"Well, if not, it's all my fault. Perhaps I incinerated his bright future, as well as mine."

"You're a bit harsh."

"Nonsense. Everything is entirely my fault, and I have no inkling if he is even okay."

Angela, squinting, observed him silently.

"Unfortunately, I've discovered that not knowing is the most torturous of all human conditions. The gnawing guilt." Sweat beads emerged on his forearms. "To find him and to finally—"

She forcefully clapped, startling several lingering gulls.

"Ibiza, though not that large, is difficult to navigate," she said in an enlivened, business-like tone. "Ninety-nine percent of tourists only visit the two major cities: Ibiza Town or San Antonio. They experience nothing but their tall hotels and crowded beaches." She suddenly searched about in a circumspect manner, although not a person was in sight. Her voice lowered to a whisper. "But much, much more exists on this island. More than they will ever know."

"More?"

She squinted, gazing inland. "Out there."

Emerald patches dotted craggy hills in the distance.

"Out there is where it all begins." She waved her hand across the landscape. "Out there are isolated rural areas, where the most bizarre of cults are practiced. Villas tucked into the hills where unadulterated decadence is the norm. Hippie communes with their free-loving lifestyles hidden away in the mysterious North. And, beyond all that, even something...deeper."

This "deeper," although disturbing in its ambiguous sense, especially intrigued John.

"Odd. I've read a few books about Ibiza. Haven't read anything about all this."

"And why would you?" she demanded. Her hands now quivered. "Tourists never discover these places, so to the outside world, they don't even exist. Don't you see? Not a single mention of them, even in all your books. This, John, is the legendary secret Ibiza." She peered cautiously around the empty landscape once again, her eyes ricocheting in their sockets.

It dawned on him that perhaps she did not have a complete grasp on her sanity.

"To explore these worlds, you need a car and connections; it's impossible to penetrate otherwise. And you need plenty of time. Your cherished Gunther can be embedded anywhere in those secret areas."

"Sounds insurmountable."

He looked back out to sea, squinting in the bright light.

They had turned onto the Carrer de Sant Jaume, the main avenue in Santa Eulària's center. A stone piazza lined with stumpy palms formed this center, and a few drowsy cafes with deserted tables dotted its sides.

"But if I'm to help find him, you must reveal to me exactly what transpired to cause this rupture. All the details."

"Help me? Why on earth would you help me?"

She snatched his wrist. Her grip was unexpectedly robust as the tips of her nails burrowed into his flesh.

"I see the sadness in your beautiful eyes, John. And I remember being new and helpless on Ibiza years ago. Terrifying."

He tactfully removed his wrist from her vise.

"Almost all visitors fly home," she continued, "naive as ever, proceeding with their pathetically dull lives, without ever discovering the secret Ibiza."

"The 'secret Ibiza?'"

"Yes."

"And you found this?"

"Now I can help you discover it."

"I'm here to find Gunther, not this 'secret Ibiza,' as you say."

Light flashed off her glasses. "Aren't they the same thing?"

A tall man in white roller skates zipped by, heading toward the beach. The air smelled of wild strawberries. Atop his head sat a medieval magician's hat. His naked and rhythmically wriggling buttocks streaked toward the sunlight, as astoundingly, he wore absolutely nothing but a pair of headphones attached to a Walkman in hand. Angela did not appear the least bit fazed.

"Did you just see that?"

"What?"

"What?" John asked in exasperation. "What do you mean 'what?' That guy with the Merlin hat."

"So he has a hat."

"Forget the ridiculous hat. He's roller-skating down the street completely naked."

Angela shrugged dismissively.

Time would be needed to digest all of this, for he certainly could not grasp it at the moment. His mind, seasoned at analyzing enormous amounts of data, began to recognize factors abounding here that he could not quite identify.

"Angela, I should be going now."

She wielded a sleek black fountain pen and seized his right forearm. He observed in wonder as she scribed her phone number across it, complete with a forceful period that drew a drop of blood.

He whipped his arm free.

A slender crimson streak slithered down his skin. He assembled a few choice words, on the verge of reprimanding her, but curiously, she looked away nonchalantly, not seeming to notice. Or perhaps care.

"Call me."

"Call you? And what if I misplace your number?"

"Unlikely."

"Dismemberment is a growing problem."

She laughed, sunglasses rattling on the bridge of her nose. "A very good friend of mine will be holding a marvelous villa party next week. An Ibiza-style party. Far different than anything you have ever experienced."

"Are you so sure what I've experienced?" he shot back. His retort was entirely impulsive, as he was increasingly aware—with a mixture of dread and fascination—that she was most probably correct.

She unveiled a pitying smile, as if he were but a child claiming knowledge. "It's a private party with, how shall I phrase this delicately for your green ears...*all types* in attendance."

"All types?" John asked. "Now what exactly do you mean by that?"

"I can sneak you in as my personal guest, and start to make introductions."

"Thank you, but—"

"Very few outsiders get an opportunity like this, John. The stars, I can see, are finally aligning on your side. Roll with it."

The blood had caked into a serpent's form on his freshly tattooed arm.

"Thank you, Angela. Nice meeting you. Do take care."

"Call me," she repeated, admonishing him with a startlingly long index finger. "Do not be too hesitant. Hesitancy is a fatal trait that can cause the cream of life to seep away. Learn to seize your opportunities with zeal."

She turned and strode away.

Quite the curious first encounter on Ibiza, to say the least. But what on earth had he gotten himself into by venturing here?

And as for this Angela, she sensed hesitancy in his character? Well, he would have to consider that. For heaven's sake, at this desolate point in life he was open to considering anything.

Her figure, standing perfectly upright as if a book rested atop her head, shimmered and shrank in the rising heat as she drifted past squat white buildings lining the avenue. She faded away in a hazy mirage.

Her eyes...he had never seen her eyes.

TWO

Very few ever visit the most splendid beaches on Ibiza, which remain isolated and unblemished.

This might sound counterintuitive, as sadly we are accustomed to people—or more specifically, investors—ferreting out and ruthlessly exploiting all the gems. The lamentable fate of the Costa del Sol comes to mind. Yet a clear explanation exists for Ibiza's fortuitous situation. The most impressive coves and sandy strips on Ibiza are empty, except for a few residents, as they are concealed on the far undeveloped ends of the island with only twisting dirt roads, if any, approaching them. Many cloister dramatically beneath massive hills or cliffs. Mercifully, development is all but forbidden in these areas. This led to an island with a few crowded tourist beaches rife with hotels and turmoil, and a lost array of peaceful treasures that take effort and creativity to discover. An explorer's paradise.

The time had arrived for this exploration. To ultimately find Gunther, comprehending this peculiar island would be necessary. John must get out and observe, converse with individuals, and *understand* Ibiza so he could search with purpose. Sounds far more reasonable and easier than it actually is, of course, but hey, plans usually do.

He purchased an old Mercedes, which he had spotted for sale in front of a Spanish man's finca. The man's smile, visible through his noble gray beard, proportionally increased as John counted out bills of cash. Fortunately the cost was relatively low, for after listening to the engine wheeze as he pulled away, he questioned whether it was actually a Mercedes, or even a hybrid of a Mercedes and other salvaged parts. Yet the car moved with a determined pep which earned his affection. It would aid him on his quest.

Unsurprisingly, beaches pulsed as the heart of Ibiza. John had spent the last days scouring the severely limited literature about these beaches. Finding readings inadequate, he began randomly asking locals which might be the best ones to visit to obtain a feel for the island. One elderly Spanish man with leathery skin who was gnawing a stalk told him plainly: "A beach is a beach. Sand and water. Are you seeking eternity?"

Right before abandoning his seemingly doomed approach, fortunes turned.

On a lonely stretch of road, passing fields sleeping in the early morning heat, he spotted the first person he'd seen in miles: a shawled woman, peddling vegetables before the doors of an isolated white church. She smelled faintly of an extinguished candle. When he asked, she confidently answered, "Cala Salada," with a wink of her startling emerald eye. It was the single direct answer he had received.

As he pulled away, a sack of pimento peppers now serving as passenger, he noticed in his rearview mirror that for some inexplicable reason she strode directly into the middle of the street to study him driving away. Her legs were straddled in a perfect "v" shape, her black hair hung from the shawl's sides. Yes, no cars were in sight, but he repeatedly checked the mirror, with mounting anxiety, to see whether she left the danger of the street's center. She never did, she never wavered, and after a sharp turn, she vanished from view.

Considering that unnerving display, her Cala Salada beach in the northeast had undoubtedly earned the status as his quest's launching point. That, and having no other suggestions, of course.

A soft paper map grabbed from the airport provided his sole guidance to this Cala Salada. While glancing at it resting comfortably beside him, he roamed through the narrow two-laned roads of the island's bucolic interior. Not a single highway existed on Ibiza.

Certainly, the views enchanted.

He sputtered past bright orchards, their gray, stone, country houses surrounded by fields of trees glowing with peaches and apricots. White villas nestled in the dark green of the steep hills. Black Menorquín horses galloped across dry fields, leaving trails of reddish dust in their wake. Several small, white-washed churches, not far from the roadside, lazed in the shimmering morning heat.

Eventually, to John's dismay, the main paved road heading toward Cala Salada beach abruptly ended a quarter-mile from the coast and split in opposite directions parallel to the shoreline. Before him sprawled Balearic pine forests and hills, with no access to sea. His molars ground in disappointment. The map revealed nothing more than a massive green area devoid of roads to the sea. According to his map, Cala Salada was inaccessible.

He visualized all the dirt roads he had passed during his ride over, and plentiful they were, peeking out from forests or winding across arid fields. Scanning his map, he noticed not a single one inscribed.

The predicament became clear: no one had ever charted Ibiza's innumerable unpaved roads. Officially, these vital routes did not exist. Coming from the United States—and New York in particular, where every last pebble was neatly mapped and recorded and filed—this situation was downright surreal. Thus, for navigation on Ibiza, good old-fashioned exploration would be requisite.

And to think such a place still exists on our exploited planet! The thrill of limitless possibility, the one explorers of yore must have experienced, pulsed through him.

Auspiciously, after an impatient period of random hunting, he noted a narrow path that could be generously termed a "dirt road" breaking through the trees and heading in the coast's direction. Deliberation inevitably followed. Was this all foolishness?

Perhaps. But perhaps a healthy dose of foolishness was precisely what was prescribed.

He chose to drive on down this path. A few cruel turns and ditches followed, and an incline which his car would certainly not ascend in rainy weather. And to think he used to complain about a few potholes on the West Side Highway.

The trees finally cleared.

He switched off the sputtering engine on a flat area by a cliffside along the sea. Patting the hood affectionately, he approached the cliff's edge. A frail wooden sign, painted with simple red letters, read "Cala Salada." He stepped forward, the breeze gusting hair strands across his eyes.

Nothing prepared him for the astonishing view.

An expansive aquamarine bay spread magnificently below with a narrow opening out to sea. Stark hills cradled both sides of the bay, sumptuously completed by an empty, sandy beach gently curving on the shore. Positioned in the center of the beach, a rock formation separated it into halves and ventured out into the water. One could climb it and leap into the clearness below.

So, Eden found.

Guilt twinged at his conscience for having all this loveliness to himself, for as a New Yorker, privacy in a beautiful locale was a rarity. But no need to complain. Inhaling the pristine air, he gazed out at this magical cove, his limbs stimulated by the purity of beauty.

A trail crisscrossed down the cliff, consisting of crumbling red earth and sporadic flat rocks. It was steep, treacherous even, something that could never exist in his previous home or lawsuits would abound. But he found his quaking body descending with impetuous zeal.

Upon dropping onto the beach, warm sand massaged his feet. The refreshing scents of rosemary and salt gusted off hills and sea.

He climbed onto the rock formation in the beach's center, as its smooth, flat top jutted several meters out directly into the water. Attentively stepping to the end, he checked below; the clearness of the liquid stunned him. The tiniest cream cockle shell lucidly resided at the bottom. Seawater like this he had dreamed of, but never truly believed existed.

"Magnificent, no?"

His fingers tensed. Behind him, on the beach end of the rock, a tanned and wrinkled man sat cross-legged with an immaculately straight back. He had spiky, blond-and-gray hair and a beard with indigo and tangerine beaded braids dangling below his chin.

"It is magnificent," John said. "Yes, very much so."

Why had John not noticed him? Although in fairness, the man was approximately the same hue as the amber rock, and his lithe muscularity blended in with its grooves.

"Your first time here," the man said. "And how do you like it?"

Was his behavior or demeanor so revealing?

"I am astounded by the beauty."

The man smiled broadly. John's answer clearly pleased him. A golden ring hung from his right nostril, and a necklace of brown seeds draped from his sinewy neck.

"It's been a while," John said.

The man raised an eyebrow.

"Since I have appreciated, or even noticed, something like this," John said softly. Something about his widely set eyes, their benevolence, prompted him to continue. "I'm afraid I've squandered much time in my life. Lost my way."

He squinted to obtain a clearer picture of John; his expression then softened as he nodded empathetically. "Patience."

"Patience?"

"Yes. Time is needed to get to where you must now go."

John found himself, in addition to puzzled, curiously grateful for his words. Perhaps the compassion in his tone affected him, as he had not experienced an iota of this in the last dry decade. His throat constricted.

"You have arrived at the essential destination," the man said.

"I'm sorry?"

"On Ibiza, the most meaningful things one cannot readily see with the eyes."

"What does that mean?"

"Why do you think searchers have journeyed here for hundreds of years?"

"Why? I actually have no idea."

The man smiled fondly at his honesty. "Deep inside, they sense something here."

This was fast becoming most interesting. Yes, the subject matter intrigued, but this man, something was...ineffable about him.

"And these meaningful things you refer to; how do you see or partake in them?"

"Few do."

"Oh?"

"Very few."

John rubbed his warming cheeks.

The man's skin crinkled around both eyes. "I come here every morning." He pointed to the horizon. "For the rising sun."

"Might I ask where you are from?"

The man did not hurry his response. He chewed something with his left molars. "Are we not all from the same place?"

A challenging question to respond to.

"So thus, your question is answered," he said. "But if you desire to know where I lived in my earliest years, then your answer is Stavanger in Norway.'

He must have been here many years for a Norwegian to have a tan like that. His eyes closed, and an indistinct prayer seeped from his fastened lips.

This conversation was apparently over, although John would love to continue.

John turned back to the water. Time to jump in.

He moved to the edge of the rock, and peered below.

Tension struck from soles to crown, and he hesitated. At least ten feet deep, so there should be no danger leaping in. At least it appeared that deep. Should be no danger, right?

No use delaying.

But of course, he found himself doubtful again, peering once more into the sea. He repeatedly gauged the depth, for goodness knows how long.

Finally, exhaling, he dropped in feet first, as headfirst was far too risky, and sliced water.

Warmth encapsulated him, and fish flashed in every direction. All muscles momentarily relaxed, all tension dissolved. Silence underneath. A glimpse of lovely tranquility, an estranged old friend from long ago. Wonderful to be reunified, even if only momentarily.

And there it was. High above the water's surface glowed the golden sun, the giver of life. It shimmered high above, prized creation of the Most High, far, far away. So very far away and sadly, no matter the depth of his longing to join it, seemingly unattainable. As unattainable as fulfillment.

With three firm strokes, John burst above, spurting out saltiness. He backstroked to shore, the sun drying his stomach and face. On the beach, coarse sand massaged between his toes.

His pulse quickened and muscles tensed.

He realized he was burning to see and hear that inscrutable man again.

Exactly why, he was unsure, but for some reason he felt desperate to find him. Sometimes feelings precede the awareness of their origins.

He scampered back toward the rock, salt crystals already caking the sides of his arms. The temperature escalated. He rushed up the rock, breathing erratically, short of breath, in a complete panic. His tongue was sandpaper.

Not spotting him anywhere, he hollered out a "hello," his voice discombobulated. Never had he experienced this fervent a desire to speak to someone as he did now. An awesome and frightening sensation. So much he wanted to ask and to learn from him.

Frantically, he searched.

Yet only bare rocks remained.

THREE

John had already scrubbed Angela's phone digits off his forearm days ago. Although meeting her had been most fascinating, one encounter surely sufficed.

But after a few uneventful days, he admitted that she and her mysterious party offered an initial pathway to meeting others on Ibiza he simply would never have access to. Angela was correct; this was a rare and valuable opportunity. Calling seemed wise.

Unfortunately, the number now escaped him, unusual for someone with his memory capacity. Once again, he had hesitated and waited too long. Grand opportunity squandered.

Yet while seated on his balcony viewing the open sea at sunrise, the image of his Norwegian friend from the rocks flickered in the recesses of his mind. A glimmer, nothing more, but he shuddered, and his memory suddenly resurrected the essential digits.

Instead of extended logical deliberation, his standby behavior, he seized the phone and dialed. Gunther had always emphasized that he learned almost everything from interacting with others.

Angela answered after a half ring, seemingly waiting by the phone.

Her dry voice enthused the moment he inquired about what time he should pick her up that evening for the party, as she released her "Five, sharp" with aplomb.

He arrived ten minutes early.

Her single-story adobe house stood isolated at the end of a dirt road lined with ancient olive trees. A lonely, rather sad place. The smooth walls, chipped in various spots, were of a soft peach color. Wind chimes adorned with scallop and clam shells dangled above the porch outside her door, and this chorus clinked a mournful performance in the breeze as John stepped from his car and waited outside, surveying the house. Certainly, she had heard his tires popping along the rocky road, but she did not come out.

After these soporific tunes lulled him for what seemed to be several minutes, she emerged. A lengthy summer dress and sunglasses covered her, and dark hair flowed around an extended smile.

"Afraid to knock?" she said with a patronizing laugh.

A retort sat on the tip of his tongue, but he thought it best to hold it, especially since her observation, although slightly humiliating, was correct.

His appearance met her approval, for after surveying him she nodded emphatically before entering the car.

"The couple who own the place, both are very good friends of mine. So don't worry."

"Worry?"

"You must brace yourself, John. People are different on Ibiza."

Worried, he was not, only curious. Although, her latest comment made him wonder if some concern might be prudent.

Traveling eastward, they passed the old city of Ibiza Town, perched on the high hill, with its massive fortress overhanging the cobalt sea. From there they headed toward the rolling hills south of San Antonio.

"So, who exactly are we going to say I am?"

"Meaning?"

"Shall I just say we are the oldest of friends, going way back a few days, and that the extent of our friendship is that we spoke momentarily at a cafe?"

She laughed heartily. "Fear not, they understand."

Perhaps. Although what precisely they "understand" was shrouded at best. The need to "understand" a situation or a person implied an element of oddity or idiosyncrasy existed. Was this peculiarity about John, or about her?

After traveling through a savin juniper forest and turning sharply several times, the land cleared and they began driving alongside a massive wooden fence. They halted before imposing gates comprised of enormous, darkened planks.

"And so we have arrived," Angela said, licking her painted upper lip.

"What on earth is this place?"

"What does that mean? What does it look like?"

"Housing for King Kong."

Angela slapped her thigh, laughing.

"You know," he continued, "you've mentioned a few times how different things are on Ibiza."

"Yes."

"Anything in particular I should be prepared for inside these gates?"

She cackled. "Oh? So now Mr. Cool is suddenly concerned?"

Well yes, he was, actually.

"I'm asking if I should be prepared for anything."

"Like?"

"A felled UFO? Choirs of nude midgets?"

She laughed again, shoving John's shoulder. Her cackling continued for a curiously long time until sputtering out into silence.

"It's time."

Her voice sounded metallic. She stared at him with a grave expression emerging from nowhere, and nodded toward the bell.

He found himself skittish. No particular reason to be, as he was entering a private party on Ibiza and he should be delighted at the prospect, but he *was* skittish, and he could not shed the feeling.

The temptation arose to pull the wheel around and hurtle back to the safety and solitude of his apartment, to lock that wonderful door with a click and gaze out the window at the sea and daydream of grand plans long lost. He did not know the first thing about where he was about to enter, anyway. Looking it up in a comforting Michelin guide was not an option.

Yet, here dangled his golden chance to begin his mission. Hesitating and delaying were deliciously addictive but corrosive habits, as he well knew from experience.

He pressed the cream-colored button.

No sound, no movement. After what seemed like minutes, he reached again, but she intercepted his arm mid-flight. With a crack, the electric gates began gradually grinding inward until they emphatically clanged open.

He discovered his sandaled foot lingering over the gas pedal, calf muscles locked, and not due to any lactic acid accrual. His hesitation drew a condescending expression, but he pretended not to notice.

Time to proceed.

After exhaling through dilated nostrils, he pressed down on the accelerator and drove through the looming gates. They shut behind.

The property was surprisingly flat.

He had expected hills and valleys and shrouded areas. Not the case. A few palm trees and shrubs grew on the yellow, sunbaked land. An extended, single-story house with walls of gleaming glass stood by a sprawling swimming pool, and far in the background shined an immense white bubble tent like a half egg emerging from the earth.

Indian sitar music resounded, the leisurely chords floating seductively throughout.

Dozens of scantily clad people relaxed on cushions by a winding pool, conversing and laughing. Apparently public affection was not shunned here, as they lazily kissed and caressed. John found himself gawking, but came to his senses and looked away, at least attempting an air of nonchalance. Never want it to be too obvious that you are the outsider.

To say "all sorts" attended would not be accurate, because the missing element was the uptight types John had encountered at his previous Manhattan parties, the types that spoke only of their extravagant purchases and lavish but unimaginative vacations. This absence John did not lament.

A willowy woman drifted by completely nude, her straw-colored hair swinging below her waist. John did his best not to stare, failing miserably. Many wore loose, Far Eastern cotton shirts or torn t-shirts, and handmade jewelry and untamed hairstyles were omnipresent. Personal income did not seem to matter, for although this was a magnificent compound, all sorts seemed welcome. A lofty shirtless man with a lengthy goatee walked by with striped pants brushing the dusty ground. He seemed to tower over eight feet tall, if that were possible. Anything suddenly seemed possible.

Quite a collection. Long-dormant shreds of John subconscious were enlivened by this fascinating group. Before him thrived an esoteric world which seemed to be liberated from all the conventional rules of social interactions.

So, such places really do exist.

"Welcome to Ibiza," Angela hissed into his ear.

She strode away, heading directly toward the house. A brusque departure, which was rather surprising, as he had the impression she liked remaining close.

Although evening, a heavy heat ladened the air. Along a path lined with fragrant sage, a woman approached with flowers in her hair and a glazed expression. She displayed a tray littered with dozens of pills of various colors and shapes. He expected her to pass him by, but she halted and smiled. Those wet eyes were hypnotically far away. Apparently, she awaited some reaction—but what to say? She waited patiently and, after receiving no response, finally asked if he would like to partake. Whatever he desired was his. He politely thanked her, declining. The last thing he needed was to be under the influence of some pill. She leaned forward, deftly licking the tip of his nose, the cold steel of her piercing stroking him. He turned to her in shock, but she flowed on.

Three women wearing bikinis and black motorcycle jackets walked by with arms interlocked. They spoke in German and laughed hysterically. John felt a slap on his bottom as they passed—a crisp, resounding slap—but they never bothered turning back to witness his gaping mouth.

Up ahead, resting in the shade beneath a clump of palms, was a darkly stained wooden table with twisting legs ending in screeching gargoyle heads. Quite an uncommon piece of carpentry. Bulbous, beaded glasses covered the table, each filled with mint leaves and a cloudy fluid.

"Rebujito," a slender young man said.

A yellow, stringed bikini bottom comprised the totality of his outfit, and dark blond hair tufted his head. Innumerable hours in the sun had tanned his entire body.

"Lent's favorite drink. Always has them." He sipped from one as he began handing John a glass, and then halted mid-air.

"This glass doesn't offend you, does it?"

The fresh mint leaves chilled in the fluid.

"Offend me? No. But why ask such a strange question."

"I'm Yoopie," he said, passing the glass.

"Yoopie, you said?"

"Yes."

"John."

"John. What a beautiful name. I love the name John."

"Compared to Yoopie, it's a bit dull."

Yoopie laughed delightfully. "You are so charming, John."

"Better than appalling."

Yoopie laughed again, blushing. "Tell me John, do you like the ballet?"

"The ballet?"

"Yes."

"Well, I guess I do. Yes. But why do you ask?"

"You like it very much?"

"Well, I don't know it all that well. But I certainly respect it."

"So, you do not like the ballet, John?"

John paused. "I like the ballet."

"Just not very much."

John scratched his chin, examining Yoopie's earnest expression. What on earth was this man getting at?

Yoopie blushed. "Do you get upset easily, John?"

"Upset easily?"

"Yes."

"No. Not at all. But why ask—"

"I'm so happy about that John."

"Okay."

"And you don't get upset easily, do you John?"

"No."

"You don't seem like you do."

"Well, I don't."

"I find you so fascinating, John," Yoopie said, giggling. "You may not like the ballet, but you're not angry, and I admire that in a man."

He stared at Yoopie with puzzled fascination, working to process it all. Categorizing things he was always adept at, in order to make sense from chaos. But in truth, despite his valiant efforts, everything here remained nebulous. This was all something different, something...new.

"Let me return to the pool; they're all waiting for me,"

Yoopie said. "My friends are so demanding. I love them dearly, but they miss me so quickly sometimes."

"Yoopie, I'm glad you at least have friends to miss you. I can't say the same."

His eyes widened in surprise, his hand touching his heart.

"Stop by later and spend time with me, John. No need for you to be alone." He looked shyly to the ground as he kissed his index and middle fingers and pressed them against John's lips before departing.

John drank the sweet lemony fluid and tasted its sherry base as he watched Yoopie glide away. Quite an opening to the party. Slightly different than convening with fund managers tugging on loosened ties at a midtown Manhattan bar while they denounced their exorbitant alimony payments.

He tilted the chilled glass fully back, gulping deeply before depositing his empty cup onto the table. The enraged gargoyles below eyed him.

Mystical sitar music continuing to gently strum across the property. How utterly alluring this type of music could be in such a setting.

"Avoiding me?"

Angela stood behind him.

A tall, athletic woman with glossy black hair reaching her waist accompanied her. She could not be more than twenty years old. They tugged John away, each interlocking one of his arms into theirs. This young woman pulled forcefully and walked with perfect posture.

Angela evaluated them side by side. "May I introduce Eden, the host of this magical healing place."

John bowed majestically, and Eden flashed an abashed smile, looking aside at the dry earth. Her initial facade of bravado already revealed cracks.

They escorted him poolside. The sitar music, emerging from hidden speakers in the palms, grew louder by the water. This pool, with its richly colored mosaic surfaces and its tributaries wandering in disparate directions, resembled a shallow lagoon. Dozens of nearly naked people reclined on cushions, many with feet wading underwater. Some smoked hookah pipes decorated with psychedelic patterns or just gazed into the depths of the purple sky. The sharp odor of burning frankincense pervaded.

"Lovely smell," John said.

Eden perked. "Ancient Egyptians burned the frankincense. They ground the charred resin into a powder called kohl."

"For what purpose?"

Her speaking quickened with John's interest. "You must have seen kohl's usage as that distinctive black eyeliner on figures in Egyptian art."

"I have, but its source was unknown to me. Until now," John said. "Thank you."

Her cheeks flushed. "Would you like to meet my husband?"

Angela closely monitored his reaction.

"I would, certainly," John replied. "And thank you for having me over."

"Isn't she beautiful?" Angela asked.

Eden's smile revealed white teeth contrasting against smooth olive skin.

"I'm sure her husband finds her so. And finds her intelligent as well."

Angela cackled. "See how polite he is? Did I not tell you? So well-trained. He can't even acknowledge your beauty."

Apparently John was a hot topic of conversation when not present—interesting, since he thought himself irrelevant here.

"I don't believe she needs anyone to acknowledge it," John said. "It is obvious enough."

To his surprise, Eden lunged and hugged him tightly. Her thick hair, ensnaring him, smelled deeply of incense. He did not hug back or resist, unsure how to react, and he felt a bit of the fool. Eventually she released her grip and strode away.

"Wonderful job," Angela said.

"Oh?"

"You've impressed her. Now that's rare. She has the highest of standards. You are talented, John."

"My goal here is not to impress."

Angela stepped back, hand on her chest. "Oh? So impressing is beneath Mr. Highbrow?"

"Not necessarily."

"So what is your goal?"

"Do I need one? This is a party, is it not?"

"What exactly happened with your former girlfriend, John?"

He heartily laughed. "How did we segue into that?"

For the first time, Angela blushed. "You need to meet a woman, John. You're obviously lonely."

"Am I?"

"Very attractive, and lonely. Many wonderful women live on Ibiza, John. I can help you." She removed her sunglasses for the first time, and ordinary brown eyes studied him.

"I'm not here to meet women, Angela."

"Why exactly did you leave your girlfriend?" she insisted.

He shook his head in exasperation at her dogged persistence. "What is it you need to know?"

"Did she deserve it?"

"Deserve it? What does that even mean? She wasn't a bad woman; she was an attractive part of the society."

"I, alone, know the right person for you, John. Remember that."

Fortunately, Eden returned, cradling a towering man's hand in both of hers.

"My husband, Lent."

Angela stood atop her painted toes and kissed his cheek. John shook his massive, constricting hand, cringing at its grinding grip. He must have been seventy, a jolting revelation due to Eden's youth, and an age gap more often noted among decrepit rock guitarists and their waitress girlfriends. But Lent kept himself in remarkable shape. His swimmer's chest expanded and his muscled forearms pulsed. A sheen reflected off of his bald head, and his gray beard was closely trimmed.

He glared at John for several moments.

"So, I hear you can't help but find my wife extremely attractive," he announced.

All fell silent.

"Is that what you heard?" John asked.

Lent glanced at an impassive Angela, and then focused back on John, maintaining his incendiary stare. No one spoke. John held fast during these uncomfortable moments, waiting for Lent's next move. The sitar music gently strummed.

He exploded into laughter, slapping John's back. Quite a hit, one that might send someone's dentures flying, but John made sure not to flinch. Some dignity must be maintained amongst confronting males.

"Come with me, John, let me show you around. Any friend of Angela's is a friend of mine."

Lent stepped emphatically as they strode across the property.

They paused before an immense wooden deck, raised two feet off the ground. It was circular and clean in appearance, with planks precisely cut and stained a chestnut color. An accomplished piece of carpentry.

"Built it all myself." Lent overlooked his deck with a half-smile of satisfaction.

"That's a hell of a carpentry job."

Not noticeable at first glance, but painted in black on the center was a circle with a crescent resting atop it.

"So, you decided to paint the Wiccan horned god?" John delicately inquired.

Lent whirled, clearly surprised. His pale eyes gradually narrowed with a grin rising below. "Quite the observant man you are, John."

Innumerable hours studying theology and world religions, although long ago, still served him well.

"A special coven gathers here on this very space to worship every week," Lent said, with a hollow voice, as if speaking to himself. "Here, the spirits of nature surround us."

"You find this fulfilling?"

"Fulfilling?" Lent laughed condescendingly. "Fulfilling? Our dear earth is falling apart. In dire need."

"I see."

"The very fate of our entire earth, our beloved planet and all of the beauty of nature, may depend on this. On the spells that are cast right here," he said, emphatically pounding the wood with his gavel fist.

"I assume the Wiccan traditions are from the original New Forest Region of England coven. Witches still practice according to Gardner traditions—nude, with goose grease on their skin?"

He peered at John again. "Educated you are, I see. Not bad. No wonder Angela is so bloody fond of you."

Was she? Certainly, she had made no indication of this to him.

Lent stomped his size-thirteen foot on the deck with a thud.

Despite his coiffed appearance, his mangled toenails desperately needed trimming.

"Ibiza's warmth negates any need for the grease." He smiled to himself. "Our Ibiza allows many things that would be eradicated elsewhere. Here, they thrive. You would do well to learn this."

This concept was undoubtedly dawning on him.

"Well, that's a hell of a carpentry job. Those massive gates and fence surrounding your property are your handiwork as well?"

Lent brightened. "A businessman and carpenter back in England, I was. You name it, I can build it."

"What else did you construct here?"

"What else?" he asked in an enlivened voice. "See that?" The peculiar white bubble dome arose in the center of the dry field. "Designed and constructed that, as well. By myself. Come, let's go inside."

The door hermetically sealed behind them. Inside, only silence. To suddenly hear nothing struck loudly. Beneath the translucent, domed ceiling sat an octagon pool, its water glimmering in chalky light.

"Here, Eden and I do our aquatic therapy: Witsa."

"Witsa?"

"Deep healing. The compressive hydrostatic pressure and relaxation enhances lymphatic function. Helps with the most difficult orthopedic and neurologic conditions. The grace and power of water. We have clients from around the island."

"I've never heard of this type of healing."

"From the dawn of time."

"Is it effective?"

Lent laughed. "Effective?"

"Yes."

"We've helped or cured hundreds, understand? Why do you think we are in such high demand here?"

"Interesting. Shocking, actually. Never read of it."

"See?" he said with a hearty laugh. "You might be quite the educated man, but you're deprived."

"Deprived?"

"You can read everything in front of your nose, but you can't read what they prevent from going into print in the first place. People like you forget that."

John decided to let the "people like you" comment go, whatever that meant, as he was finding Lent, although a bit extreme, insightful.

"Who prevents this?"

"Who?" Lent's eyes narrowed. "The bloody corporate world and the bureaucracies, that's who. Think it over. Why would they want you aware of natural healing when they invested billions in pills and machines?" He began to pace around the water, planks creaking under his weight. "All of you know only what they damned well want you to know. You're just their unwitting little puppets."

His voice rose, his lecture fast becoming a vicious diatribe.

"Those corporate demons ruthlessly suppress our beautiful healing methods. Screw the suffering and needy! Can you imagine what it would cost the bloody pharma companies if the world found out about this healing?"

"I understand."

"You never heard of this healing?"

"No."

"And outside of Ibiza, you never bloody will."

His pale face had morphed into a bright red mask that appeared to bubble at skin level.

"I see."

"Wake up. Their entire way of life is at stake. Nothing more dangerous you can ever do than threaten their way of life. Remember that. Those people kill and wage wars to preserve for far less than that."

Lent exhaled shrilly as if a kettle releasing steam.

"Fortunately, we have our secret haven here on Ibiza. The one place in the world far away from all those bastards." He stared directly at John. "Here, we do exactly as we desire."

"It certainly seems so."

Lent, now deep within his thoughts, surveyed the waters of his pool, and John considered it judicious to allow him time to simmer. After a bit, he abruptly smiled, a thought startling him. In the pale light, the top of his head resembled an egg from the Cretaceous period.

"By the way, she's my fifth."

"Fifth? I don't understand."

"Eden," Lent said with a chuckle. He slapped John's shoulder, a slap which nearly sent John plunging into the Witsa waters to begin his therapy. "My fifth wife. The other four didn't work out, although I got a horde of great kids from them."

"I see."

"No more worry about that."

"Worry?"

"I've finally had the old tubes tied."

When John returned, three young men in ragged shorts clustered around Angela, laughing obsequiously at whatever she said. The men's long hair and longer necklaces swayed, their ropy eyelashes seemingly coated with mascara. She drank seltzer, and, for some reason, her audience fled exactly when he neared, like night creatures scampering from a floodlight.

The sun had set, and the sky was deep purple. The music

shifted to a pounding euro techno rhythm. A massive wood pile had been erected in a clearing, and a crowd encircled it.

A section of the crowd parted, and Eden, with a woman on either side, formally approached this pyre with roaring torches. They halted, simultaneously leaning forward at the waist, backs impeccably straight in a ritualistic fashion, and set it afire. A blaze arose and crackled, the piercing pong of burning pine needles wafting through the air. The music heightened, and dancing around the bonfire commenced.

John observed all this from the side in utter fascination. To think, but a week ago he was riding the five train in Manhattan while assiduously keeping his eyes to himself.

Dozens, clutching hands and howling, some wearing nothing, bounded from all corners of this compound to join in. Far more people were in attendance than he had realized. Everyone joined the dancing. It was encouraging to see, but something was...awry.

The way they danced. These people danced more in bursting, twitching, individual performances than with one another. And what performances! Eyes bulged, and tongues flicked. Bodies shook and limbs quaked. Bizarre, even grotesque displays. Lent dominated the scene, moving spasmodically on his legs and then swaying on all fours in the dust. As if a spider had taken to the dance floor. It was difficult to see clearly in the firelight, but his mouth appeared to be foaming.

Dancing like this, John had never seen anything remotely close. Not in any parties or clubs. Not in movies. He had never even read about such things. Perhaps Lent was correct, perhaps he was deprived.

Eden and Angela danced together nearby, stretching arm tendons to the limits as they swung each other in circles and screeched. Someone's limp form was repeatedly hurled high into the air by a group; it appeared to be Yoopie. Red embers rose from the fire and floated into the above.

John continued to observe, mouth agape, from the relative safety of the edge. No way he would dare to join in. No way. Firstly, because he would have no inkling what to do and would only make a fool. But, more relevantly, because he was too flabbergasted to move.

The ever-darkening sky revealed a glistening panoply of stars, and those beneath it continued to howl and pulse in contracting rhythms.

FOUR

he weekly Hippie Market at Es Canar was the best-known market on the island. Everyone involved with the arts made an appearance. Since June had just unfolded, crowds were still limited, but vendors rehearsed with their tables and goods for the impending deluge.

The market stretched gently alongside the sea, set among circuitous paths, palm trees, and decaying fountains.

To enter, one first passed through a white plaster gateway, and then the brilliant colors of goods for sale exploded throughout. In the hippie market, one could discover handcrafted earrings, shawls from Nepal, and gouache paintings created on the island. Healing solutions such as mystic crystals, aromatherapy, and herbal remedies were available to cure anything from arthritic big toes to disinterested lovers. Racks of tie-dye T-shirts were ubiquitous. The exotic odors of burning incense pierced the air and inspired radical ideas. Small cafes, serving Turrón with wild honey, were tucked into nooks and were occupied with thoughtful people sitting alone, contemplating the mysteries of life.

Yet, the most captivating part was not the goods, but rather the vendors themselves. From those in their early twenties to those in their nineties, all ages hocked their wares. Most did not aggressively beckon you in the tradition of markets around the world, but rather their magical goods did the inviting. Some of these deeply tanned vendors lived on Ibiza year-round, avoiding mainstream society for decades. This isolation showed, as conversing with them offered a unique experience.

"What does beberis help with?" John asked. Dozens of slender glass vials of herbal extracts from Ibiza, Formentera, and Andalusia lined the table.

A tiny woman nimbly arranging the vials, who uncannily resembled a mouse, stared at him for a time. She peered into his eyes, as if knowledge of his soul aided in answering his question. Her gray hair was braided in a lone strand to her waist, and she was so thin it seemed a gust would blow her asunder.

"Have you not heard?" she asked in her delicate voice.

"Heard?"

"Healing."

"Healing for what condition?"

"For the mind," interjected someone who advanced on him from the crowd.

The appearance of this new individual required a moment to unpack. She wore a flowing, saffron, Indian sari and cream-colored turban. Three orange stripes were painted across her forehead.

She was nearly John's height and solidly built. Undoubtedly, a sight to behold.

"I am Swami Satchidananda Bhagwani."

John checked over his shoulder to be sure she addressed him.

"What are you seeking?" she demanded.

Was that an Indian accent? Odd, because of her white skin and the sandy blond hair peeking through her turban. He had heard that although many genuine people populated Ibiza, charlatans roamed as well, and he sensed this swami belonged comfortably in the second category. He turned back to the vendor, with hopes that the supposed swami would move on.

"These plant varieties, I've never heard of most of them. Amazing. And it appears you have ones that can alleviate any condition."

"You expected your solutions from synthetics?" the herbalist said, sorting piles of dried leaves with her miniature hands.

"Synthetics?"

She nodded.

"Well, no. Not at all. I didn't really...I guess I don't really know."

A sympathetic smile spread on her face as he bumbled thoughts and words. He felt a bit embarrassed at her reaction, but it was not an entirely unpleasant feeling.

"If we are burdened with a problem, nature always provides the answer. Always. That is the balance of nature."

"What are you searching for?" demanded the swami in an intrusive voice. "Are you looking to improve your karma?"

Unfortunately, this swami had not departed. She stood uncomfortably close by, and her pungent body odor pervaded. Apparently, she had some sort of interest in him, whatever that might be, but the feeling was not mutual.

"I am just looking to look."

"I'm not affecting your looking."

He ignored her once again, hoping she would leave. Ignoring might be the wisest strategy. He employed the same technique when facing babbling bearded men reeking of vodka on the subways of New York, and it usually proved effective.

He selected an earth-colored vial of Laurel Berry oil. The glass cooled his palm.

"You are lost," the swami said, snatching it from his hand. "Are you seeking to join me in the Daśanāmi?" She inserted the vial between her breasts.

"What?"

"I can feel your desire to join me in the Daśanāmi."

"I really just desire to learn about her extracts."

"Forget about her," she replied with disdain. Her Indian accent wavered, dipping into a German one. "Do not be coy. It does not suit you."

"Oh?"

"Your rigid Western ways cause your sad condition."

Although this alleged swami clearly was not associated with this table, she dominated the vicinity. John wanted to ask the herbalist more about her fascinating collection of extracts, to learn from her, but he retreated to escape the swami's onslaught.

Up ahead, an array of gloomy sculptures created from chunks of sea wood and scrap metals covered a table. Behind sat a wiry man with a shocking mane of curly gray hair draping below his shoulders. His smooth, tan skin contrasted with his aged locks. With a pocketknife, he scraped away at wood. Quite a talented hand had fashioned these pieces.

"Where do you obtain the materials for all of these?"

The man perked, squinting in surprise. "American?"

"I believe so."

He smiled. "I always love your American comedians."

"Do you?"

"You are Italian background?"

"Why?"

"You look like from *The Godfather* movies. I always love those movies."

"Do you—"

"Does this art raise you to bliss?"

A domineering voice had interrupted. John turned to it with dread.

The swami. She had tracked him down and now stood but a foot away, the smell of her perspiration overpowering.

"Excuse me, but I'm busy speaking with him."

She did not even afford the sculptor a glance. "Don't worry about him."

Evidently, she did not appreciate him speaking to anyone but her, as she had now brutally interrupted his second conversation within minutes. Fascinating people populated this market, but the towering swami would strangle any conversation he dared attempt.

"Can I help you with something?"

"You? Help me?" She laughed condescendingly, as John peeked over to the sculptor in bafflement. "What could someone like you ever possibly help someone like me with?"

"Let's both agree the answer is nothing. So, you can go your way and leave me be."

"That I cannot do."

"Why?"

"Because you need me."

A disquieting answer, as it implied they must be together, for whatever reason. This was becoming difficult. The question was how to terminate the swami's pursuit, as ignoring her seemed only to spur her on.

"Oh?"

"Allow me to help your mind understand," she said, patting John atop his head. "I, Swami Satchidananda Bhagwani, have spent a decade living in the horrific poverty of the endless slums of Malabar Hill in India, meditating and renouncing. I have found myself."

"Congratulations."

"And I feel, through our universal connection, that you suffer."

"At this moment, I would not argue that."

"You need me."

"So you've said."

"You must learn from me, or you will continue to wallow in misery. I have discovered my true self through denial of my desires."

"Malabar Hill is actually the most affluent neighborhood of Bombay. A neighborhood for the very rich. Just a tip, so you don't continue to embarrass yourself on future presentations."

She froze, her gray eyes blinking erratically beneath the turban. Perhaps her brain, faultily wired, had short-circuited.

"You must learn to relax your mind," she said, snapping right back into form.

"That much might be true."

"You are an American, entrapped in rigid Western thought patterns that have ruined your life. Look how you run from me, terrified of change. You run from enlightenment." Her version of an Indian accent had returned in a heightened form.

The sculptor silently carved, but was listening intently.

"You must learn to break the cycle of Moksha if you are to ever reach Samsara," the swami said.

John began laughing good-naturedly, which startled her. He laughed despite her barrage of insults, due to both the absurdity of her theology and the ridiculous confidence with which she espoused inaccuracies. The sculptor peeked up in nervous surprise.

The swami's neck tensed, tendons straining. His finding of humor at her expense clearly did not please her. Whatever serenity she claimed to have found through fabricated trainings in India certainly were not on display at the moment.

"You find your inflexible Western ways humorous?"

"Perhaps," John said. "Perhaps I do, sadly. But I believe what you are trying to say, dear Swami Satchidananda Bhagwani, is that if you want to reach Moksha, the cycle of Samsara must be broken. You are a bit mixed up on the essentials."

She stiffened once again, her shoulders pulling back.

"I think we've established you have not been to India. Now, if you ever actually had a guru, which I also doubt, I strongly suggest you check his credentials."

The sculptor still studied his work, but his shock of gray hair vibrated with laughter and he could not rein in an enormous grin. He appeared downright euphoric. The swami observed his mirth with swelling outrage, pursing her lips as the pressure compounded like an overheating kiln.

John might have acted foolishly. Did this swami have any behavioral limitations? At this point anything could transpire, including her beating him about the market with her turban.

Fortunately, she simply skulked off into the crowd, the chants of a fictitious mantra left in her wake.

"Now that was great," the sculptor announced while laughing. "Just great."

"You know her?"

"Know her? No. Rumor is she was a corporate lawyer from Munich."

"Cut that out. You cannot be serious."

"I'm serious."

His somber expression revealed he likely was.

"Well, I feel sorry for her clients if she was presenting in court dressed like that."

He laughed. "They say she went off the deep end and wound up on Ibiza. For years now, she wanders the markets hounding men she fancies. You should be flattered."

"I'd hate to see what she does when I should be offended."

The sculptor smiled. "You even remembered her name. Impressive."

"Did you?"

"I've heard many different versions."

They shared a laugh.

"You were just great. Amazing."

"What was?"

"You are the first person I have witnessed that's been able to expel her like that. The first! Usually, she plagues someone like a demon."

For some particular reason, John's interaction, or tussle, had deeply affected him. He seemed inordinately impressed, as his hands trembled with nervous energy.

"In truth, I actually found the swami somewhat interesting. And unfortunately, her assessment of me wasn't that far off. But, my pleasure," John said, with a slight bow.

"You are from New York?"

"Yes."

"Born there?"

"Yes."

"I knew it. I just knew it."

"Oh?"

"In all the movies, New Yorkers are tough. Don't take any crap from anyone. Don't get pushed around. Finally."

"'Finally?'"

"I've been waiting for the longest time to meet a genuine New Yorker. I prayed it would happen. Finally."

"I don't know if meeting a New Yorker is a good or bad thing," John said, laughing in amusement. "But I did study world religions while at university, so I'm not entirely ignorant on her talks."

"Wonderful."

"Your name?"

"Andre." He raised a dark sculpture of a mortally wounded condor. "You like this one?"

This condor, grounded with flattened wings, appeared utterly miserable. "Oddly enough, I do."

Andre returned it to the table beside a coal-colored sculpture of what seemed like a person having an uncomfortable spell on a toilet.

"Do you mind if join you and sit?

Andre's eyebrows lifted in shock.

"Yes, sure. Please. Sit down. Why not?"

He scurried to brush off the spotless chair beside his, and returned to his seat. He seemed quite pleased—proud, even—that John chose to join him, but his face simultaneously flushed with embarrassment. This cocktail of emotions made him overwrought. Within the first minute, he inquired twice if John was comfortable, standing both times and offering to exchange identical seats. He handed John a coffee in a tiny paper cup which John refused, as it was Andre's only food or drink in sight, but Andre insisted he partake with such earnestness that he yielded.

John sipped the tepid brew and studied the crowds drifting by. Observing from the other side of the aisle was enlightening, as it tends to be. Potential customers, seeing John behind the table, began looking to him for answers. He redirected them to Andre. Yet, something quite peculiar was occurring before him.

This Andre would barely interact with a single customer, no matter their persistence.

Curiously, he had been far more talkative with John than anyone else. He ignored everyone who inquired about his works. And many did. Yet, even as they observed his sculptures with interest and attempted conversation, he remained mute. If pressed, he would look askance and mumble. Embarrassing. An excruciating display to witness, for he squandered many easy sales, as his original artwork garnered serious consideration. But bafflingly, Andre would simply not do the necessary, which was not much, to sell far more. Something unidentifiable held him back.

"You don't say much to these people."

He nodded.

"You could be selling triple if you did. Your works are quite good."

"I'm not from New York. I'm not as good a talker as you."

They laughed together, and John chose to let it go for now, but desired an explanation for this destructive behavior.

"So, Andre, you are not from Ibiza, are you?"

"The Netherlands. Father from Indonesia, mother was Dutch."

Thus his deep tan and exotic appearance.

"You might not believe it."

"What's that?"

"I used to have an excellent job working for Dutch Air in Holland. Manager. A clean-cut guy with a pressed suit. Hard to believe, no?" he said, stroking his long, gray hair.

"You are right, I don't believe it," John said, smiling. "So, you liked that life?"

"Good people worked there."

Apparently, this Andre enjoyed conversing with him. He wanted to reveal more about himself, and John was interested in his tale.

"And you were an artist, also?"

"Always sculpted. Won regional contests."

"Yet you left all of that success to come to Ibiza?"

"My mother was not pleased. Not at all," he said, shaking his head. "Said I was insane."

"Was she correct?"

He smiled. "Said I was insane to throw it all away and listen to my lady."

"So it was your lady who wanted to move here?"

"Oh yes." His eye contact with John was fleeting. "She would not stop demanding we move here, day or night. 'Ibiza, Ibiza.' My mother hasn't spoken a word to me since I left," he added, dismally.

"You are married?"

Andre mumbled dismissively.

"How long have you been on the island?"

"A long time. Seven years."

"You must know a lot of people."

"I've seen a lot from behind this table."

John sipped the bitter coffee, swallowing the grounds as a couple strolled by, swinging interlocked hands and laughing with pleasure.

"So that swami character. Why on earth doesn't she just return home to Germany? She remains here for years and wanders markets, spewing nonsense?"

Andre polished an iron rod puncturing the figure of a writhing body. "It's not that easy to get off the island."

"What do you mean?"

"You stay here a while, home fades away." He shook his head with a wistful smile. "People forget you exist."

"I suppose it's the same whenever you leave home."

"Maybe. But when you remain on Ibiza, you also forget them. You become relaxed. Sedated. It's this place, man. Your old self gradually dissolves."

A somewhat troubling assessment. What was Gunther's current condition on Ibiza?

"This happened to you?"

"Returning to the world becomes too daunting."

A shirtless man passed, strumming a worn Spanish guitar.

"You plan on staying on Ibiza?"

"Who, me?"

"Yes, you, of course."

For some unidentifiable reason, sweat now glistened Andre's brow.

"No choice. My daughter is here. She is almost eight."

"Fantastic," John said. "She lives with you and your wife?"

Andre began furiously whittling a piece of driftwood. "Live with me? No, no." He carved a smooth groove and blew the shavings out into a pale cloud. "She lives with her mother, my ex-wife, in my apartment. I'm out."

"Out?"

Just then, two svelte men inquired about a sculpture depicting a man pleading on his knees, his arms extended before him, palms up and fingers splayed. Andre mumbled a price, absurdly low, and after exchanging surprised glances they pulled out the cash. They thanked him and he barely nodded. He actually appeared disdainful they should dare purchase his work.

"What do you mean 'out?'"

He smiled abashedly. "She took my Ibiza apartment a few months after we moved from Amsterdam."

"Took?"

He peered at John a moment. The strands of gray hair covered his eyes like a musty curtain.

"She had convinced me to buy it after we just married in Amsterdam. She was obsessed with Ibiza. So I paid for it, as she never had a job." He shook his head, scoffing. "'The unenlightened work, the enlightened live' she would always tell me."

"But she made sure you worked?"

"Oh yes. Absolutely."

"Amazing."

"Then she forced me sign the apartment over, just a month after we arrived here."

John paused. "Sign it over to whom?"

"To her. Forced me."

"Forced? Meaning what, she put a gun to your head?"

Andre released a morose laugh. "Started screaming that it was better for our daughter that way. I tried to argue, but no use. She just would not stop shrieking in front of her. Day and night. Even when my daughter was crying." He shook his head. "Just kept screaming."

"Screaming what?"

"That she is a most deprived person. That everyone, especially other women, are jealous of her. That the whole world is conspiring against her." He paused. "That I wasn't a man."

John remained silent.

"She screamed that I wasn't a man down there," he said, pointing between his legs.

John exhaled.

Andre weakly smiled. "Never had a problem there. But when someone keeps telling you that, it makes you wonder."

"As you said, you are fine."

"She would not stop screaming unless I signed the place over to her." He shrugged his shoulders. "So, I signed it over."

"With nothing in return?"

"Nothing. Said our daughter needed that security since I am an unemployed bum. An irresponsible father."

This tale was utterly outrageous. John toiled to contain himself. "But you lost your manager job in Amsterdam *because* of your ex-wife," he said with raised voice. "She insisted you relocate and give it all up."

Andre nodded.

"All happened so fast." He displayed his callused hands. Knuckles protruded on his thin fingers like speared olives. "And then one evening, months later, while walking on the beach it dawned on me."

"What?"

"I guess I knew it before, but it all became clear that evening."

"What was it?"

"I was nothing. No home, no job, no money, no family. Nothing."

"Good heavens."

"At least I look the real hippie part now," he said with a morose chuckle, indicating his torn shirt and baggy shorts and sandals. "Tourists love to see that."

John found himself appalled by the tale. He was all too familiar with the phenomenon of letting your life slip away, in his own fashion. This shared misfortune magnified his fervor as he felt it granted him special license to lecture on the topic. But composure was needed here, not denunciation.

"So where is your family now?"

"In my old apartment. My ex and my daughter."

"You visit them often?"

His sandaled foot swept wood shavings across the dusty ground. "My ex doesn't like me there."

"And why is that?"

"Why is what?"

"You said she doesn't like you to visit there."

He continued sweeping, although nothing remained to clean. "Well, my ex's boyfriend lives there also. When she kicked me out, he moved in."

"How long after you left did he move in?" John asked, dreading the answer.

"Who?"

"The boyfriend."

"The first one?"

"There was more than one?"

"She goes through them pretty fast."

"The one who moved in when you left. How long after you left did he move in?"

"Oh. Pretty soon."

"Pretty soon?"

"The same day."

John shifted from any remaining uneasiness to outrage. For some reason though, Andre trusted him, so he did not want to appear too aghast and have him regret his confession.

"So when do you get to see your daughter?"

"I don't."

John swallowed.

"Maybe a few times a year in public."

"And where do you live now?"

"Me?" Andre said.

"No, Charlemagne," John said, with a slightly raised voice. "Yes, you."

He scoffed, gazing at the dusty ground. "In the forest."

"What the hell does that mean?"

"In a tent. In the forest."

"That is how you live, year-round? In a damned tent in the forest?"

"A pathetic case, no?"

"Well, that's not what I meant—"

"I'm pathetic. It's true."

"Well, we all—"

"Don't worry, John. I finally can admit it all now."

Just then, another vendor arrived with trays of hand-carved necklaces. She wanted to sell on Andre's table, at the far end; they must have an arrangement. John arose to offer her the chair. Digesting all that Andre revealed about his life would not be easy, as it was not a palatable meal. No wonder he was depleted of zeal when promoting his artwork; an element of self-loathing lurked.

He yearned to say more to this man who had been so gracious with him, to utter something sagacious. But what? Breathing became erratic as the burning desire to help Andre in some way, any way, overwhelmed him, yet to his horror he felt powerless to do so.

"Please take this to remember me by," Andre said. "And don't offer me anything for it. It's my gift to you." He lifted one of his sculptures.

"You've been generous enough with your coffee and time."

He ignored John's comment and handed him a wooden sculpture of a head, melting at the crown, mouth agape, and tongue protruding as he howled. John ran his fingertips over the smoothly polished wood and looked up at Andre.

"Take care, New Yorker," Andre said, with a faint wave. His eyes were glass.

FIVE

John realized something was amiss a few minutes into what was supposed to be a casual stroll.

The beach itself was a straight strip with a miniature cliff running directly behind it, not gently curving like most on the island. It was unnamed. Yet, these were not its most peculiar attributes. For before him, feet planted in the sand, stood three men in their sixties, and all were stark naked. Well, except for the sunglasses that covered their eyes and the substantial mustaches that covered their upper lips. They moved not, more sculptures gleaming in the sunlight.

It took time, and a few more au naturel exhibits, until the supposedly clever John deduced that he was deep within a nudist beach. It was not too crowded, but people posed and reclined here and there. Already he had ventured a fair distance down this beach, but he had been busy staring out at the peaceful water, not the garment-free population. Now he noticed, with shock, that everyone present, all men, were nude. And all wore sunglasses.

They reclined on blankets in the sand, or stood proudly, their oiled bodies reflecting the bright light. Many inspected him, ever so subtly, as he passed. A flash of teeth often followed. Yes, John did take a peek or two, as all are innately curious about dimensions compared to their own, no matter what they claim to the contrary. But he quickly moved on.

Boulders high enough to climb onto dotted the beach. From the flicking sand and darting views of interchanging heels and toes, as well as a few moans, it appeared carnal activities might be occurring behind them.

John wore only his bathing suit, and had no intention of disrobing. He was far from a prude, but the nudist scene never tempted him—not that he had ever encountered the opportunity to join one. Nude beaches, in his imagination, summoned bizarre appearing and acting sorts. The origin of these images was nebulous, but the naked man standing to his left, with a full beard and drum rolling a patriotic song on his chest beside pierced nipples, certainly did nothing to impugn his original theory.

John also understood he was not playing fair. Here lay a sanctuary for the nude, a place to experience that enthralling freedom of being amongst only your own. John's presence violated this delicate ecosystem. And these nudists might believe he came to observe them as if visiting an art exhibit or even a zoological display. This could be permissible, or even lauded, but for he did so while clad. How dare he! A cheating, clothed infidel amidst their bare-skinned lands. This should not, nor would not, be tolerated.

Whistling and clicking sounds began emerging from disparate locations.

A towering man with a handlebar mustache stepped forward and glared directly at John. He was an impressive individual by all metrics. His black leather biker's cap with silver spikes shined, and his hands defiantly gripped his hips. He appeared to be some sort of leader, as a few smaller men draped his sides.

This whistling and clicking increased with alarming frequency. A few more men collected to the flanks of their colossal leader. Were the troops rallying against his callously clothed self?

In moments would arrive the insurrection, as dozens of rabid defenders wielding fleshen swords would descend upon him to expel him from their lands.

Evacuation time.

And maybe he was a bit prudish after all, for it would not take much effort to simply disrobe and fit in. The assembling army would dismantle, just like that. But he could not get himself to pull down his bathing suit here. Instead, he veered and hustled alongside the water, hugging the waves. In other words, he retreated.

His tense body moved as swiftly as possible with tightened limbs. His gaze remained steadfastly seaward during the totality of his escape, as the ominous clicking faded into the background.

Mercifully, it was now quietness behind him.

"Are you ashamed of yourself?"

This female voice startled John.

It sounded like a targeted yell, so he turned. He suspected himself to be the intended recipient. A slender woman stretched out across a blanket, wearing an emerald bikini. Sunglasses rested on her thin nose, and her blond hair was tied back. A book, arched onto its pages, rested before her, half read. She said nothing and did not flinch.

He paused, awkwardly waiting for her to speak.

Was she staring at him? Her inviolable sunglasses prevented enlightenment. Finally, with the burgeoning silence too uncomfortable to bear, he jostled on. Maybe he had been hearing things.

"Are you ashamed of yourself?"

Her voice again. She must be addressing him.

"I'm sorry?"

"Don't be sorry. Just answer the bloody question."

She removed her sunglasses and appeared amused at his befuddlement. Her blue-green eyes startled, as they emitted an air of benevolence and shrewdness, a rare combination, indeed.

"I am not sure what you are asking me."

"You just paraded yourself proudly back and forth across an entire nudist beach while dressed to the nines. Left those poor nudists wondering what could be. So, I am wondering if you are ashamed of your privates."

John chuckled. "Not so far."

She smiled broadly.

"By the way, I noticed you are covered as well. What might be your excuse?"

"Apparently you don't know the beaches here. After you passed the heart-shaped rock back there, everything south of it is a normal beach," she said. "Or, as normal as you might find on Ibiza."

"Thank heavens."

"They like their nudity. I say, let them enjoy it."

A few hair strands fell across her face as she waited patiently for his response.

"I suppose you are right. And you cannot help but admire their intrepidness."

John was surprised to find himself prematurely waving farewell and turning away, as if he had no control over his own bodily movements. Not even a goodbye. Could a surge of shyness be propelling him into this horrific rudeness?

"What are you doing on the island?"

He turned back, grateful her voice rescued him.

She sat up. The windswept embrace of the long-haired man and woman on her book's cover revealed a romance novel.

"Spending some time getting things straight."

"That's about as bloody vague an answer as you can get."

He laughed. "Would you prefer I said 'stalking nudists on their beaches?'"

Crinkles formed beside her expansive eyes.

"I notice you like to read."

He was always impressed, even relieved, to see someone reading a novel, although he never quite delved into why. Perhaps from growing up in a world where reading was commonplace, and enjoying the rich discussions stemming forth from that pastime. In his last barren years, frost-bitten spreadsheets were the sole form of literature found on the tundra.

She glanced at her novel. "Never a single day goes by without reading."

"Really?"

"Never missed one day. For decades."

"Decades?"

"Yes."

He was unduly impressed. "But why?" he asked with a slight shrill.

She squinted, observing him with curiosity. He had questioned her a bit too desperately and she detected this anomaly.

"For the company. Novels afford me my connections to humanity. You don't ever want to lose that."

Realizing from her earnest expression that she was serious, he found himself deeply stirred. And as silly as it might sound, he wanted to cry. Memories of long lost and well-read colleagues from university times, filled with enthusiasm and burning hope for the future, suddenly inundated his mind. He had not considered any of them, due to his suppressing of those memories, for the longest time.

"That is just so comforting to hear."

"Oh?" She smiled with amusement.

"Absolutely."

"All I said was I like to read a bloody book," she said, laughing. Her London accent was most pleasing. "A lifetime habit picked up from dear mother."

"Wonderful. She has similar reading tastes?"

"Certainly. Half of our library in our Yorkshire estate is romance novels of some sort."

"Fascinating."

"And you?"

"*Middlemarch* was my kindergarten favorite."

She laughed again, delightfully, with a dismissive hand waive.

"I actually did enjoy reading very much."

"Did? Gone blind since?"

John smiled. "Slowly getting back to it. Unfortunately, I went astray for a long time. Although, I've always concentrated more on the nonfiction realm in my studies."

"Such as?"

How encouraging that she actually requested specifics, that she actually appeared curious. He sensed genuine interest.

"Philosophy and theology. Thomas Aquinas, Sartre, plenty more."

Her hands dropped to the sand. "Brilliant!"

"Oh? Why is that?"

"Father's exact fields of interest. Leather-bound *Summa Theologiae* in Latin was a prized possession of his. All of that subject matter is the other half of our massive library. Sadly, the ignored half since he passed years ago. But all his volumes are still dusted daily."

His answer had clearly pleased her, as she straightened her back and clasped her fingers. "Well, this is fast becoming most interesting."

"Is it?"

"To see an intellectual sort like yourself out wandering on your own, absorbed in pensive thought. As if wandering the cliffs of Dover, pondering a lost love."

"I was actually considering what to have for lunch."

She laughed heartily.

"Don't be offended, but usually someone as nice-looking as you doesn't engage in much higher thinking," she said, continuing to laugh. "Shouldn't you really be out in Ibiza Town or San Antonio, partying, or recovering from one, like all the rest of them?"

Her designation of serious party goers as "all the rest of them" certainly intimated that she did not have the most elevated opinion of that lifestyle.

"Not my scene."

"No?"

"Not at all."

"Then what is your scene? I think we've established it's not the nudist one."

He laughed while considering her question. "I would think one need friends and a regular social life to have a 'scene.' I'm afraid that rules me out."

Her eyes remained fastened to him with amused curiosity. Toes twitched as he began to feel self-conscious.

"Your name?"

"John."

"Come now. Life cannot be all that bad, can it, Sir John the Prude?"

"Certainly not at the moment."

She paused, squinting in the light with the slightest smile, studying him. "New here?"

"I've only been on the island a few weeks."

"Here to stay?"

"As much as I cherished every single moment of it, I don't want to remain on a nudist beach."

She roared in laughter. "Silly pants. I meant on the island."

John laughed along. "I'm living up in Siesta, in the hills above Santa Eulària. Delightful tiny town. Beautiful sea views."

"What a fabulous coincidence!"

"What's that?"

"I'm up there as well. Wonderful choice. I guess you choose your living arrangements better than your beaches."

She lived there also? He had never seen her, as he certainly would have remembered.

A surge of warm interest flooded him. What an absolutely exquisite person. He could not remember the last time he experienced this peculiar sensation. It was an intoxicating feeling that he would happily linger within.

Maybe he should ask her address; perhaps he could stop by some time and bring books. Yes, he could do at least that. Why not? She loved to read. Chances like this do not just come along. That would be quite forward of him, but maybe he—

"Who knows, perhaps we shall see each other around?" she said, returning her sunglasses to her face. She snatched her book, flicking sand off its pages with her slender fingers. She commenced reading, flipping a page within seconds.

Apparently, this conversation had ceased.

She did not look up again. Describing the end of this exchange as "abrupt" would not be unfair, as she was admirably adroit at terminating an interaction, a skill likely honed over years of fending off her impassioned suitors.

After enduring a few moments of uncomfortable silence, he waved farewell to the statue before him. A quite intriguing statue, nonetheless. He found himself not only reluctant, but disheartened, to depart. But he had no choice. His brief opening of wonderful opportunity had slammed shut. The chance was now lost forever. And thus is the cruel reality of how life responds to those fools who hesitate.

"Diana's my name. Diana Clarke," she said, not bothering to look up from the pages as he walked away.

SIX

Near Cala Boix and the ensuing peninsulas, the road was tortuous with radical dips and climbs. It made for a demanding drive. From atop these cliffs, one is inexorably drawn to peer between clusters of hibiscus and bougainvillea flowers at splendid glimpses of turquoise sea. Yet a dearth of attention, even momentary, could result in a far closer view than recommended. While John drove this road, he rolled down a hill a tad fast, and the car tail veered at the turn onto a dusty yard. He braked and exhaled in relief as the orange dust settled in his wake.

Setting the wheels straight, he noticed an antiquated orange VW bus in a humble alcove near the sea, replete with painted flowers and peace signs and "love" scripted across its middle. The only element missing from this psychedelic vehicle was wheels. On a wooden stool before it rested a cardboard sign that read: "Will accept donations for peace." A teacup, coated in dust and devoid of coin, sat by its side.

He exited his car and noted a tiny house behind this vehicle. The windows were curiously glassless, but the plaster front and Spanish tile roof were intact. A garden grew nearby lined with rows of trellised tomato plants and winding cucumber vines. The raw scent of the plants rode on a sea breeze.

A flash of movement, and he realized someone was present, kneeling behind the tomato plants.

This someone emerged, and to John's surprise, a boy came forth. He was at most eight years old, with blond hair dangling in long dreadlocks, which appeared peculiar on a boy of his age. John's presence did not alarm him in the least; he simply returned to pruning plants after momentarily observing him.

"Hello there!"

Behind John, in the doorway of the house, stood a shirtless man with dark blond hair in magnificent, matted dreadlocks reaching halfway down his back. Beaded braids dangled from his chin. He was wide, powerfully constructed, but not muscular.

"You seem like a person with good taste in art," he said.

"Do I?"

"Excellent taste. I sense it in your character."

"Are you so sure of that?"

He had undoubtedly been expecting far more acquiescing responses, and the corner of his mouth rose ever so slightly in amused admiration at John's immunity to packaged charm. "Would you like to see my art?"

"Why not?"

He shook John's hand and studied him with his green eyes.

For all the frenzy of his aspect, a steadied measuredness existed to his observation process as his eyes calmly focused.

Inside was a stark white room with round pillows lining the floor. A portable stove attached to a gas tank and a washing basin rested to the side. Standing beside these, a thin woman with short brown hair flashed a smile.

"I'm Klav. This is Natalia."

She turned away without a word and began tea preparations.

Klav motioned to the pillows. They had once exuded bright colors, but had now faded into a drab dustiness. John sat, and Klav hustled to the back room. He returned with what appeared to be an aged volume.

"Here it is," he said proudly, as he sat down.

The cushion beneath him gradually released a hissing squeak, comedic in sound, and as he slammed it with his left hand, it released a final dying squawk. Although irked, he regained composure within seconds. After patting the book's cover, he smiled magnificently. "The Book of Life," he announced, with a finality to the tone.

He did not elaborate, but studied John's reaction with his expectant smile still fully extended. He clearly was anticipating, and attempting to induce, a positive reaction. Natalia peeked over from the kettle.

After observing two rather disconcerting fluid stains on the purple cardboard cover, John opened the volume. Its assemblage of ragged pages were fastened together by twine. The collection contained sketches of drums and guitars, brief writings about love and harmony in English and Dutch, and hastily pasted collages formed from snipped magazine photos. This comprised the esteemed Book of Life.

"It is my finest work," Klav said. "'I've worked on it for seven years."

Upon seeing John's lack of reaction, Klav seemed bemused, but he remained calm. He vanished into the back room again, with slightly greater speed, and emerged with two collages mounted on common cardboard. One was adorned with chicken feathers and two clam shells randomly glued onto it, and the other consisted of dried palm leaves and a black-and-white photograph of a Model T Ford.

"Art is my passion," Klav said. "We can discover the dimensions of our souls through experiencing art." He studied John, once again waiting in vain for the reaffirming reaction he undoubtedly was accustomed to receiving after uttering this gibberish.

"You made all this?"

"I did."

"What else do you do?"

Klav brightened. "What else? I am a musician and a writer, and a singer."

Almost all the arts were covered. Perhaps he danced as well?

Now, John was not ignorant in the field of visual arts. He had been raised among the museums of New York City, and his uncle was a painter who brought him to exhibits years ago. While at university he vacationed in Madrid, not only frolicking, but viewing superb collections of artwork in the Prado and the Reina Sofia and Thyssen-Bornemisza museums. He enjoyed a few art history courses, too. So, not a moment passed before he reached his palpable conclusion: Klav's artwork was the worst nonsense he had ever encountered. It was a misnomer to call it "artwork," since artwork is produced by an artist. Klav was not an artist.

Klav licked a paper, deftly rolled it, and offered it to John.

He waved it away.

"Are you interested in the art?" Klav asked. "I only sell my works to specially gifted people with taste."

"Really? So, what's the going price for that Book of Life?"

Klav picked up the volume lovingly and displayed it in his large hands. "This is forty thousand pesetas."

John laughed.

Yes, he probably should not have, but he simply could not prevent it and thus he laughed, and continued to do so for some time. Natalia watched with widened eyes from the gas burner, stalling tea preparations. The smoke from Klav's joint rose steadily from his petrified hand.

"Look Klav, I like you. I do. You invited me into your house, and I met your wonderful family. And I thank you for that."

Klav silently listened.

"But you are not an artist, and both you and I know that. Those pieces are disasters. So let us relax and talk as friends."

Klav did not speak and his expression revealed absolutely nothing. Natalia glanced at him nervously while completing the tea. He took a lengthy pull on his joint. Gradually, he exhaled through his nostrils, loudly, while examining the burning end of the cigarette with what seemed acute interest. The ganja smoke filled the room in lazy clouds.

Eventually, he motioned with a nod, and Natalia slipped over with the tea. After she poured two glasses, Klav handed John one. The liquid was jade, with broken tea leaves afloat on the surface.

"Where are you from?" Klav asked.

"New York."

"Long way to come here."

"Do you make any money with that donations sign?"

Klav appeared confused, and then turned contemplative, squeezing the beads dangling beneath his chin. "Not much. Once in a while someone will drop something in. Two months ago we received a good donation. But it brings people inside."

He offered John the joint, and John waved it away.

"You are a businessman from America?" Klav asked.

"I used to work with money."

"Used to?"

"An endless cycle, dragging you downward."

Klav nodded, appearing somber. "If you must deal with money at all, you want to work for it, not with it. Money is an artificial invention of man's. Unnatural, like plastic or detergent."

"Interesting. I confess I've never heard that analogy."

"We are not designed to think about money that much."

"The miracle is I broke away."

Klav exhaled a rising cloud. "I'm glad you did. Those who remain bankrupt their souls." He extinguished his joint on the cement floor. "But the best is when we don't need to work at all," he said, winking. "My father boxed in Holland. He fought until his fifties. Made a good living on fights, but always said he boxed for the thrill and competition. If money followed, so be it."

Just then, the boy from the garden entered. His enormous eyes, green as his father's, stared expectantly at John.

"This is Toobee," Klav said.

"Hi," Toobee said, shaking John's outstretched hand with both of his. "I'm in charge of the garden, and I get water from the well down by the beach. I can show you."

"Well, you do an excellent job, Toobee," John said. "That is a wonderful garden."

"I do all of it. And I can get water, and I can also get beans from down by the beach if the man doesn't get angry and chase me."

John laughed. "And what year of school are you in Toobee?"

"School?" Klav interjected. "School? For what, so they can teach you to be a slave?"

John chose not to question this observation, for several reasons. Klav was obviously impassioned, and the comment was of the rare strain that both carried weight and was absurd.

"I school Toobee. Natalia does also."

"Doesn't the state require something?"

"The state?" Klav scoffed. "What does the state know of us? We don't even exist to the state. We are free."

As Toobee dashed out the doorway back toward his garden, John considered Klav's comments. It dawned on him that he did not fully grasp the entirety of the situation around him. Much was missing from the picture.

He began observing this house more scrupulously.

The wood framing around the doorway was rotting and about to drop. The water Natalia used for the tea came from a metal bucket and was collected elsewhere. Very little furniture. That odor...everything smelled faintly moldy. No lights. No signs of electricity at all, in fact.

They did not own this house, and he suspected they did not rent it either. They occupied it as squatters.

The dual thuds of car doors shutting jolted Klav; ashes dropped from his joint. He nodded at Natalia, and she refilled the teapot with water. He nimbly returned his creations into the back room. Everything that unfolded over the last few minutes was perfectly rewinding and resetting.

Within a minute, a man in his forties wearing a white-collared shirt and aviator sunglasses peeked his head inside with a dutiful hello. Klav invited him inside, and he was closely followed, or rather shoved, by a woman wearing glossy lipstick who smelled of expensive but disagreeable Parisian perfume

"Hello!" Klav announced. He instinctively directed his talk toward the woman. "You seem like you are blessed with fine taste in art."

"Oh, thank you for noticing," she said, blushing. "I'm Sophie. Well, I've always had an eye for good things. I've decorated all three of our homes personally."

Klav's left eyebrow rose, but he remained admirably composed. "Would you like to see my art?"

"That would be fantastic," the woman said. "As you mentioned, I've always possessed an eye for such things. I can't remember when I first learned. Natural ability. My mother was blessed with it also."

Klav seated them, and John nodded a brief greeting. John had spent years in countless meetings, often running them, so he well knew what was requisite and how to act. His role here, at least initially, was to remain quiet and function as scenery. He would then gauge where he was needed. For some reason, Klav already felt he could trust him.

"I sensed you were an artist. We both just adored your van when we spotted it," Sophie said.

"I believe in love and peace for all. Society pushes us in other directions, but we must maintain our beliefs. You seem like you are in tune to that."

Sophie's cheeks colored and she agreed fervidly about her immense knowledge of love and peace. She even spent time, besides decorating her three homes, listening to music focusing on love. She selected her entire wardrobe, two closets full, with her love of impressing others in mind. Yes, she knew all about the depths of love. She failed to detail any of her expertise on peace, but considering the caliber of her resume on love, it was probably best omitted. An adept listener, Klav nodded at the essential moments, and he did not interrupt once. Only when sure she had no more to say, did he maneuver.

"Here is my masterpiece," Klav said, displaying the volume

before her. "The Book of Life. I've been working on it for eleven years."

John could not help but notice that Klav's years of toil on the book had inflated by four in the ensuing few minutes.

Klav summoned his wife to bring the tea. He passed the book over to Sophie, while draping his hand over her left shoulder. Surprisingly soft fingers began ever-so-gently massaging. She cradled the volume, gasping in awe.

"Eleven years! I've never had patience to work on anything for more than eleven minutes," she said, shaking her head. Her husband, motionless until now, robustly nodded in agreement.

She perused the volume. Exhaling and tongue clicking and nods of appreciation followed. She even wiped a tear with the back of her bejeweled hand. Her husband remained quiet, but dutifully concurred with all of her affirmations. Although, admittedly, he hesitated slightly when she announced how spectacular the Book of Life would look in the center of their new sitting room in Rotterdam.

Sophie looked directly at John, for the first time. "And what do you think about this work?"

Everyone, including Natalia, turned to John. Silence pervaded, broken only by the meowing of a distraught feral cat in the distance. Klav observed John calmly, almost sleepily.

"A truly stupendous work. Amazing." John turned toward Sophie. "Discovering it here shows me that the most precious artwork in this world is hidden among the real artists, not in the commercial galleries of New York or Amsterdam. But I suspect someone with your savvy knew this all along."

Sophie squeaked in joy. "I told you," she told her husband, slapping his shoulder. His sunglasses trembled on the bridge of his nose.

Klav lit a tobacco cigarette with a glowing match, and Natalia brought over the tea.

Creases suddenly lined Sophie's brow, as her jaw dropped. Her expression transformed into pure terror, as if the grim reaper himself stepped forth. She veered to John.

"Were you thinking of buying this?" she shrilled.

The Book of Life crackled beneath her fingernails. Her small eyes failed to blink as she awaited the dreaded answer.

Silence once again. Klav pulled on his cigarette, gradually exhaling a lingering smoke cloud that appeared like fine cotton.

"I am. A unique work. It would look sensational in a glass case in my Manhattan apartment."

"Ohh." Her eyes bounced in their sockets, expression fraught with panic.

"A truly unique work," John added.

After convulsing, she seized her husband's fingers and began mercilessly squeezing. His hand was quite accustomed to this particular grip.

"I was going to pay one hundred thousand pesetas for it," John announced.

The husband did his best to maintain a placid demeanor. He gave it a sporting try, with only a single sharp cough sullying his performance, but he did not perform poorly, all things considered.

"Well," Sophie said, as her husband's fingertips whitened under her clutch. "We understand you like it. But we would be willing to pay more. It's ideal for Rotterdam." The earlier mirthfulness of voice and jovial camaraderie of spirit were but a memory. This alleged practitioner of love and peace had transformed into ruthlessness. Those tiny eyes stared coldly aside avoiding all contact with John, and her mouth, a thin line, did not budge.

John shook his head with a maudlin expression. "Well, I can try to offer up to one hundred and fifty."

"We can do one hundred seventy-five," she countered.

Fortunately, her husband had never removed his aviator sunglasses, so later, as he laboriously counted out the cash, he managed to conceal any harrowing emotions. Klav and John watched them walk back to their car, Sophie leading the way and cradling and cooing at The Book of Life as if holding a newborn.

Klav turned to John as they drove off. His crinkled eyes were moist.

"I never got your name."

"John."

"You are a talented man, John."

"It was my pleasure."

Klav was silent for a time as the sound of the car faded away.

"Come to Cala Nova Camping tomorrow night, John. Good fun."

"What is that?"

"We artists," he said, with a flicker of a smile, "get together there for singing and music by the sea. Do come tomorrow after eight."

As John pulled away, he checked his rearview mirror. All three were linked together, holding hands in front of the decaying doorway. Toobee was waving goodbye.

SEVEN

Angela took him to several more parties, all unusual in their own way. Each time, she insisted he pick her up at home and hold open the car door for her, a ritual she seemed to cherish.

One afternoon, she called with a frenzied voice, announcing she had a most special place they urgently needed to go. As usual, he must pick her up immediately, and so he did.

After twenty minutes of driving north, they arrived at Port de San Miquel, a massive inlet beach with terraced hotels growing out of the rocky harbor hillsides. The early summer crowd had finally arrived, as dozens of lounges coated with oiled bodies slotted across the sand.

Angela led John down the wide beach to its distant end, where an isolated wooden stand with four stools fronting it sat lonely on the hot sand. It appeared out of place, as if it had washed ashore from a shipwreck. A single blender and piles of colorful fruits revealed a juice bar.

"One of my absolute favorite places. Never crowded," she said.

She abruptly whipped toward him with jaw muscles pulsing, eyes narrowed. "So don't you go revealing my little secret."

"Reveal it? To whom?"

"To all those new friends you are so hellbent on making. To all those women."

He paused, startled. Veiled behind this bizarre raillery seemed an element of animosity which he could not account for. But perhaps, hopefully, it was in jest.

Behind the stand worked a young woman with spiked brown hair and thick-framed glasses. She shyly smiled at Angela when they sat, but made no eye contact with John. In fact, she entirely ignored him, as even his polite "hello" was disregarded.

The sweet scent of fruit, heightened by the heat, swathed the stand in pleasantness. Oranges, lemons, quince, apricots, watermelon, pomegranates, and strawberries were heaped in mist-coated mounds. After ordering some exclusive recipe by exchanging nods, Angela shifted on her stool to directly face him.

"Had sex with anyone already?"

A sharp laugh escaped him. The forthrightness of this woman made her, undeniably, a unique character.

"You really believe that's all people think about?"

"Perhaps not all."

The bespectacled lady behind the stand placed two glasses before them which were beaded in chilled water. She then retreated without words. The mixture was the color of a blush and carried an initial sweet flavor with a biting, sour finish.

"She puts the peels in," Angela whispered into his ear. "That's her secret."

One could not help but notice the heat. Already, in the weeks since his arrival, temperatures had increased markedly. It was a dry Mediterranean heat, not sticky, which came with a burning sun and brilliant reflections off of water and pale stone. The entire landscape glowed in a soothing manner, as if one had passed into the afterlife after a life well-served.

"So, any luck with finding your estranged Gunther friend?" Angela said. "Any updates?"

He sipped his bitter concoction. This line of inquiry was inevitable. In fact, she likely summoned him here today for exactly this. Angela's Unholy Inquisition had begun.

"Not yet."

"No?"

"I'm getting to know the island a little first. That's my opening strategy."

"Sounds reasonable."

It was difficult to discern if she were sarcastic. But in truth, he would welcome a little goading, as he well knew he was dragging his feet on his search.

"As I branch out and get to know more people, I'm sure to start finding leads. I'll—"

"So why, precisely, is finding him essential?" she interjected.

A marvelous question. "Does it really matter?"

"It does. Yes."

"Oh? And why might that be?"

She seized John's hand, squeezing his knuckles with impressive force, tears welling in her eyes. From somewhere, she pulled out a photo of a couple sitting on a chair by a tennis court. The grinning woman, perched on the man's lap, was vaguely familiar. Yes...that's who it was: a younger Angela.

She appeared surprisingly attractive in the photo. The man's longish dark hair hung to the sides of his broad smile. Most striking was his uncanny resemblance to John. So similar, mind you, that John found himself momentarily combing memories to recall if it was possible that this photo was of him.

"My husband," Angela said, intently monitoring John's reaction. "And that's me. He died two months after that photo was taken."

In the photo, Angela's lean arm draped over her husband's shoulders. Strangely, the photo was black and white, slightly yellowish with worn corners. It appeared to be something taken at the turn of the century.

"I'm so sorry."

"Don't be, John. It was all a long, long time ago. I don't want you feeling sorry for me."

That, he highly doubted.

"We need to move on in life," she continued.

"And have you?"

Her nostrils distended, as if a voltaic current passed through her. He had struck some sort of nerve. But she rapidly composed herself once again, and began guiding him down the beach.

"So why exactly are you looking for this Gunther?"

Heavens, she was persistent. Or pushy. He was yet unsure if he admired or despised that about her, although experience taught him both emotions could coexist. But his dolorous tale of Gunther had been bottled for so long, bottled and fermenting, that perhaps cracking the lid would grant a modicum of existential relief.

With horrified fascination he realized, for the first time, that he had never revealed an iota of his shameful story to anyone. That was quite the condemnation of the depth of his relationships from the last decades.

"Why? He was someone I greatly admired when we were university students," John said. "A creative thinker, a true philosopher. Of course a bit eccentric, but that goes with the territory. We always found ourselves engaged in random battles of trivia and knowledge. Became infamous for that."

"What happened?"

"What happened?" John scoffed again. "I was somewhat surprised to learn he was a remarkably kind and patient man. And no arrogance, despite his intelligence. We became best friends, as they say. Both of us had a passion for learning, and particularly philanthropy."

Angela nodded approvingly.

"And then one day we made a pact to launch an academic journal together after graduating, dedicated to social improvements. A shared dream of ours, nothing flippant. And we swore an oath to do it."

"An oath?"

"Oh yes. Hands on a leather-bound Bible and all that."

"Impressive."

"And so for three years, we dedicated countless hours of our free time researching our journal. Found contributing writers and grants. Inevitably bragged about it to our professors and colleagues. Hyped it up."

"I am sure it was a grand success?"

John shook his head, eyeing the coarse sand.

"The time had finally arrived to launch it. University had finished and we only had a few things left to do." John said. "That extraordinary feeling of infinite possibility pervaded, like the opening night of a play you dedicated yourself to producing."

"Sounds wonderful."

"Doesn't it?" John said with a dismal laugh. "But life sours quickly."

"What happened?"

"You really are curious, aren't you?"

"I am, yes," she said, placing her clammy hand atop his. "About you."

This Angela was indubitably an expert at squeezing information. She did so cleverly, gently, persistently. "Manipulative" might be a brusque, but more accurate description. He believed he could resist, but if she so deeply desired to know, might as well grant her an explanation. This was lovely Ibiza after all, was it not? Land of healing and renewal?

"I was back in New York that summer, finalizing the logistics for the journal. In October, we would launch. Gunther was arriving in a few weeks. And then it happened."

"You went to jail for fraud?" she asked with exasperation.

A fascinatingly random theory.

"No, not quite. But that July, out of nowhere, an old teacher of mine offered me a connection to a prime job in a top Wall Street hedge fund. He knew my abilities."

"So you took it?"

"I did. I confess I did," John said. "Nobody's fault but my own."

"But why, when you already had your journal?"

"The ridiculously high salary, that's why. Student debts plagued me. Secretly, I planned to endure the job for a single year and then flee like a bat out of hell. I believed I could juggle the journal and the job that first year."

"How went the juggling?"

"The job required twelve hours a day, six or seven days a week. And I was good at it. I could only choose one path. Sadly, I chose foolishly."

She sipped her drink. "And did the bat eventually flee?"

"The gates stayed shut. I naively believed it would be easy to leave. Oh no, no. When the ghouls behind the curtain witnessed the caliber of my work, how I was making everyone exorbitant amounts of money, you don't get to just go whistling your merry way."

He recalled the flash flood of ten-course dinners and all-inclusive trips. Wide-open doors at private, debauched lounges. The overpoweringly seductive smell of leather and cigar smoke. The exhilaration of power and sin.

"Contrary to instinct, sometimes it's perilous to be too good at your job."

"I see. And where was Gunther?"

A brisk breeze blew, sculpting low whitecaps across the bay's surface.

"He arrived in New York that August. Bursting with zeal."

"So you two had a fight over your taking a new job?"

"I wish. I wish we had fought."

John shut his eyes in an attempt to weather the harrowing memories, but closed lids were no match for their toxic onslaught.

"The truth is I was deeply ashamed about the nature of my job. Our upcoming project was a philosophical and theological journal with a humorous edge, focused on societal improvements. That was our altruistic dream. And now, yours truly toiled at a billion-dollar hedge fund, fattening multi-millionaires while dedicating zero time to any spiritual or charitable causes. I committed heresy."

"What you did is understandable."

"Is it?" John asked with a sardonic tone. "I believed I could delay things, and maybe in a year or two we could get back to the journal."

"So you avoided him?"

"To avoid the truth emerging. The entire time the poor

guy waited in New York, we only spoke three times. And each time, I lied. Concocted some garbage that I was busy working something temporary for the summer, managing a friend's new clothing store on the Upper East Side. Now I could have just told the truth and saved this kind man precious time and pain, but I did not have the decency to grant him that. Looking back, it doesn't seem so hard to just tell the truth, does it?"

Angela shrugged.

"Well in hindsight, things always look easier. But I dragged it out in a nebulous fashion for weeks until he wore down and surrendered. My Machiavellian plan worked."

Her brow furrowed.

"Because, as you see, in a literal sense, *he* quit the journal, not me."

"It wasn't your fault."

She seemed intent on making excuses for him, to exculpate him. Ironically, this infuriated him. He was culpable, and now needed his guilt declared as a royal decree over a teeming town square. He deserved a good, solid public lashing.

"The hell it wasn't."

"It ended like that?"

John swallowed the remnants of his drink, shards of peel sliding down his throat. "What was he to do? He finally decided to try to regroup his life and return to Germany to attempt graduate work. Never saw Gunther again."

"Don't blame yourself."

"No?" John said, eyebrows raised. "Who should I blame? The Dalai Lama?"

"You were busy, John. It's not easy in that field, the pressure. I know from my husband."

So apparently her deceased husband had been involved

in the same industry. Thus, her absurd tolerance for those in the field.

"A person makes time for what is important to him."

Her hand rested on his shoulder. "You're being harsh on yourself."

"The hell I am," John said bitterly, the burden of melancholy memories tenderizing his voice. "He actually sent me a letter six months after he returned to Germany, telling me about his newest discoveries on early heretical movements in the Catholic church. Asked if I had any fresh ideas for our journal. Still believed it might happen, bless him," John said, wistfully. "He, unlike me, put our mission and cause above all things."

"So you got your precious second chance."

"The peculiar thing is I kept his letter propped up on a mahogany table in the center of my study." Moisture dotted his palms. "Dust gradually coated the envelope. But I never wrote back."

John stroked his chin, remembering that stormy evening when he sat gulping whiskey and gazing at the letter as rain lashed his windowpanes. He recalled the rising anger, how he became incensed with his loathsome self, because he deserved it above all. An awful thing, to see yourself as loathsome. Awful. Another burning glass of whiskey fell. And then he railed against Gunther, for it was Gunther who made him feel loathsome, was it not? Why did he consider himself so damned high and mighty, anyway? He barely perceived the next rush of whiskey as the glass proceeded to shatter on the floor. After that, he became bitter with the entire foul world and every loathsome person inhabiting it. Nothing was really fair in this life, now was it? Everyone was blameworthy in their own cosmic way, did not the quantum sciences hint at that?

So he tossed that cursed letter right into the flickering fireplace, where it damned well belonged. Slowly the letter smoldered, bluish flames consuming into forever.

"And?"

Her voice startled him back.

"And that was the final time I heard from him."

The whitecaps unflinchingly traveled toward shore. They marched in uninterrupted series, row after row, with no end in sight.

"After that, I actually upped my workload. Made the discouraging discovery that most workaholics are not the dedicated beings they pretend to be, but are simply cowards seeking refuge from anguish."

"That's a bit—"

"And thus things only further deteriorated, as they tend to do. Anything reminding me of my former life, I forsook. Out the window went all the books, articles, and especially those infernal journals."

His spacious Manhattan apartment had never been mistaken for a beacon of hope all these last long years. That much is certain. The mahogany bookshelves, once teeming, idled bare, and not a single painting or photo graced any wall. Ceiling lighting only. Silence, except for peevish car horns honking futilely many floors below. A ghostly abode.

The froth atop the waves had thickened.

"Visitors would be appalled by the bleak sight of my place. That is, of course, if I ever had any."

Angela worked a well-timed sympathetic smile.

"I even switched to the offensive and began belittling all the former things I loved with acrimony," he said. "You would never, ever recognize that bitter wretch as the same starry-eyed man from my university years."

She nodded, remaining silent, fully aware that no further goading was needed. She listened patiently, nodding, raising her eyebrows, patting his hand with varying pressure at crucial moments. It must be acknowledged that Angela was a fantastic listener when curious.

"And now, as much as I need to finally face Gunther, a sizable part of me wants to avoid him."

"But why?"

"Why? The shame, primarily."

"That's it?"

"Not juicy enough for you?" John said, smiling incredulously. "Well, maybe the man eventually turned rancorous. Happens to the best of us. Maybe he's been patiently waiting fifteen years to bludgeon me with one of his oversized philosophy volumes."

"Stop that!"

"Okay, okay," he said with a light laugh. "But in truth, who really knows what he has become? I know all too well about my own downfall, but how about him? Roaming the wilds, clothed in animal skins, consuming locusts and wild honey?"

"That's absurd."

"Haven't you ever been horrified at a school reunion?"

"That is true."

"I find myself delaying the full search for Gunther."

"And finding this Gunther. Do you think this will solve any issues you have?"

He stepped toward the sea, a strong briny scent burdening the air. "I need to know he eventually did well. If anyone on this dire planet deserves fulfillment, Gunther does. Please dear God, I hope he is well."

She examined his distraught expression for a time.

"Is it possible you two could still work together and finally launch that journal?"

He looked up with widened eyes, astonished she would dare ask that question of all questions. A decade and a half of hard time had buried that redemptive hope under more layers of concrete than a New Jersey mafia victim. Hearing this galling inquiry uttered aloud was akin to having a bandaged wound ripped open.

"Could you?" she insisted.

Lukewarm queasiness flooded him. "A crumbled dream from the distant past."

Angela hugged his exhausted body, her wiry arms constricting his suddenly brittle ribs. They would momentarily shatter into dust.

"Well, you did break out of that life. Let's start giving you some credit. Can we at least do that?"

"Fifteen years later."

"Let's be honest here, John, hmm? Money is more addictive than cocaine. Successful people never, ever leave that industry. And yet here you are, free as a bird."

"Am I?"

Angela had guided them down the entire beach during her successful inquisition. Had divulging been a cathartic experience after all these years? That remained to be seen.

Eventually, they chided each other about politicians back in America, and some ignored independent films that sorely needed viewing. By the time they returned to John's car and headed south, breezy humor filled the conversation.

EIGHT

he following evening, John chose to pursue Klav's rather abbreviated invitation for a visit to Cala Nova camping area. Cala Nova was a beach on the Eastern shore of the island, and supposedly a campground thrived nearby. Nobody seemed to know much about it, as it carried a mysterious air, but Klav had claimed musicians and singers congregated under the stars on certain nights to celebrate their craft.

He pulled up early, around seven-thirty in the evening, eager to begin his adventure.

A warm, orange light swathed the landscape, and the campground was surrounded by a dark chain-link fence which provided clear viewing of the inside. A range of tents and teepees spread throughout the sunbaked land. He had not seen a teepee since childhood, and the amalgamation of these colorful cones rising from the sandy earth in the orange evening light endowed the scenery with a dreamlike feel. A few olive trees blessed the grounds, their pale green leaves wilting from the day's heat. On the southern end was a bathroom and shower area.

A superb arrangement, undoubtedly, but then it hit him.

The premises was empty. Complete silence. This location possessed all elements of vibrancy, except for the lack of a minor detail: the presence of human beings.

The let down was painful, as he had unwittingly hyped himself up for a bustling evening filled with live music and the precious opportunity to meet intriguing people. Lost social opportunities always carry a particularly nasty sting. Had he understood Klav correctly, or did Klav even know what he spoke of? It must be remembered that Klav was not a bastion of veracity.

A crestfallen John traveled down a deserted street to the nearby Cala Nova beach. Heaps of dark seaweed amassed on the shore. He reclined on a flat formation of rocks behind the beach to gaze at the sea views. His mood had shifted to cantankerous, which knocked his usual calm, methodical thought process out of whack.

It took not a second to detect the motion—swift, erratic movements, something scampering across the rocks. He sprang up in alarm, realizing dozens of small lizards were dashing about. They were gray, with black dots ascending their backs. When one tumbled in an energy burst, it revealed a garish fluorescent orange belly.

"Wall lizards."

A man stood but a few feet away.

When did this guy appear here? A wooden drum fastened

to a strap hung from his muscular neck, and his black hair draped to his shoulders. John's bewildered state appeared to amuse him. Creases, formed from years of unbounded smiling, climbed the prominent cheekbones on his face.

"Wall lizards. You are shocked by them," he continued, laughing good-naturedly. "Native to this island. If the tail gets cut off," he motioned forward with his fingers, "they keep going."

"They live here?"

"On the rough rocks. A wise choice, as no one bothers them," he said. "At least, not usually."

John glanced to see if he were the referenced offender, but the man tapped his drum while looking out to sea, producing a hollow sound. The exotic smell of incense now pervaded.

"Where do you do your drumming?"

"Where?" The man grinned with a hint of condescension, as if John had asked an infantile question. "Anywhere."

Lizards darted over to the clumps of seaweed on the shore.

"That seaweed is the most wondrous thing," the man said, focused on the dark mounds.

"The seaweed?"

"What do you think helps keep the sand on the beach?"

"Interesting."

"And it only grows in healthy water, so it is always a blessing to spot it," he said, smiling broadly.

Quite cheerful, this man was, quite cheerful. But someone's cheerfulness, after disappointment, can often induce irritation.

"You know, I came to visit the camping tonight. A major disappointment," John said with accusing bitterness, as if our chipper drummer bore responsibility for the camp's forsaken state. He detected John's sourness, as his left eyebrow arose in amused curiosity.

"Oh? But why?"

Now it was John's turn to view his inquiries as puerile.

"Why? Because it's abandoned. Not a soul there. That's why."

"Is it? Come."

"Come where?"

"Let us journey there together, as brothers."

Perhaps this man misunderstood him. Incessant drumming may have impaired the workings inside his well-carved head. And what did this "brotherhood" nonsense have to do with this issue at hand?

"It's empty. Do you understand me? Empty."

John's testy attitude did not dissuade him. He strode off, motioning for John to follow. And why not follow? At least John could prove his point.

They travelled a path directly behind the beach across soft sand dunes, and approached the camping area from the opposite end. The resonance of his random drumbeats resounded across the dipping dunes. The barefoot drummer nimbly stepped across the pale sand, leaving not a trace on the surface.

As they neared, John halted.

Could it be?

Yes, apparently it could. Dozens of people ambled about inside the camping ground, in and out of the teepees, strolling the grounds, relaxing by the picnic tables. The area teemed with life.

"But where did they all come from?" John feebly pointed to the front gate in the distance. "I came from that end, before."

"All depends on the path you take."

He rolled a beat on his drum, then bounded away through the gates.

John shook his head in bafflement while observing the

bustle. Some rational explanation must exist. Perhaps he had missed something earlier, or everyone had been off attending a mandatory teepee maintenance meeting.

Positioned in the very center of the camping ground was an elevated wooden stage with two microphones up front. Several shirtless men with ragged jean shorts—lean types, seemingly allergic to body fat—adjusted wires and stands with the spark and animation of those preparing for a brewing event. Not far away, a robust man with dark, curly hair struggled to push a double mattress inside a tent.

"You help?" the man hollered at John. "Or just leave me here to die?"

The harsh tone of this request, or accusation, originating from seemingly nowhere, had the effect of propelling John forward without consideration.

John strained as he shoved the back end of the cumbersome box spring mattress. Oddly, while this other man's hands did grip the opposite end, and while he did grunt mightily during the struggle, these were mere histrionics, as he entirely feigned his contribution.

Inside was a tiny gas stove, a blue cooler, and a few wooden crates for seats.

"Not so easy," the man said, wiping his dry brow with his hand. "Hungry?"

"I'm fine, thank you. I'll get going now."

"Sit."

Although he should have been at least slightly concerned at being commanded not entirely unlike a dog, John found himself obediently crouching on an empty crate.

The man opened the cooler and removed a salami encased with a powdery white coating. He began slicing it toward his chest, eyes bulging and teeth sinking into tongue, as thin pieces plopped into a rising pile on a metal plate. He tore a chunk of thick-crusted bread and dropped it beside the burgundy slices.

"Eat."

John sampled, knowing he had no choice in the matter.

"Genoa," the man said, winking in mischievous delight. "Don't tell the poor Spanish. They are deluded to believe their salami the best. Our Italian secret is not only pork, but veal."

"I'll say nothing."

"I'm Luigi."

Curiously, this Luigi turned his back and said no more. Conversation over. He felt comfortable with John inside his home, despite the fact they knew absolutely nothing of each other. Quite dissimilar to his former Manhattan scene, where a shining pedigree and a minimum of one year's acquaintanceship must be firmly intact before permitting someone to peek the tip of their nose inside one's residence.

Luigi became absorbed with organizing his belongings. John remained silent, as he felt embarrassed to be spying on this stranger inside his home, and hoped his silence afforded some respect.

While struggling to arrange cutlery stored in a stein, a fork dropped to the ground. A pregnant pause, and Luigi booted it against the tent wall, bitterly cursing. Tendons protruded from his neck. Within his frenzied diatribe, accompanied by wild gesticulations of the left hand, he referenced an impressive array of Italian saints. John was tempted to evacuate the site, perhaps more to save Luigi any humiliation, but in truth John's presence seemed an inconsequential detail by now.

Luigi eventually calmed and turned to a square, black case and made the sign of the cross. He gingerly removed a massive, dark instrument from the purple velvet inside. An accordion, polished to a high sheen. From the case's side, he pulled out a white, Venetian masquerade mask. He dawned the expressionless mask, thick eyelashes blinking behind the holes.

With an abrupt start, he began playing Vivaldi's "Winter," the trembling tent struggling to contain the sound. His head jerked back and forth, mask glistening, body moving in fitful passion to the notes. His gaze focused on the tent's ceiling, or perhaps far beyond. The exuberance of an entire orchestra condensed into his dexterous hands.

After finishing, he exhaled dramatically and sliced more unrequested salami, mask still intact. John, watching in awe, had not dared make a sound this entire time.

Luigi returned to playing his music, continuing with the progressing seasons.

Amidst the performance, the tent doors parted. A mass of gray hair entered.

"New Yorker!"

It was Andre from the hippie market, smiling magnificently

"But what are you doing here? You know Luigi?"

"He's feeding me."

Andre laughed affectionately. "He does the same for me. As long as it's of Italian origin, of course."

Luigi entirely ignored Andre's arrival. They settled in on wooden crates and relished the performance.

"So, what the hell is the story with this guy?" John whispered. "What's with the mask?"

Andre shrugged dismissively. Apparently, while on Ibiza, having a masked, accordion-playing Italian perspiring before you within the confines of a tent was not worth analyzing.

"You want we should look around the camping?"

John nodded toward Luigi, whose gaze remained steadfastly heavenward. "What about him?"

"Let him be. He does what he likes."

Outside, the cooler, soft evening air greeted them.

"What a character," John said. "I didn't know guys like that really existed."

"Oh, they do."

"He sure can play that instrument though. I don't believe I've ever witnessed such skill."

"Oh, yes. They say he, and another musician from Lithuania, are the two best accordion players in all of Europe."

"Amazing. And we get a private tent concert with Italian cuisine included. Only on Ibiza."

The stars twinkled in twilight. Burning pine wood infused the camping area with a pungent odor. An electric sense of excitement prevailed, that particular brand which exists when anticipating an imminent and favored event. Everyone milled about buoyantly, performing their evening tasks, whether toting buckets of spring water or trays of freshly picked tomatoes. Sun-dried laundry was collected off the lines. All worked in harmony. Children darted around, laughing and playing games. The sense of community pulsed.

"How did you ever end up in this place?" Andre asked.

"It's so strange that I'm here?"

"Few know about it. No tourists."

"You live here sometimes?"

"No, no. A monthly fee. It's not much at all, but I live in the forest."

"So you've said."

Andre's lamentable life story had been needling away at John since their first meeting, and he craved to address it. He would employ his talents and knowledge and get Andre's life right back on track, no problem whatsoever. All that was needed was the opening to ease in.

"I come for the music and company." He turned to John.

"You know, the way that you defended yourself the other day, against the swami in the market? Very impressive."

"You're still thinking about that?"

"I witnessed greatness."

"You have quite the low standard."

John secretly could not help but feel warm appreciation for Andre's recognition of his particular skills. These skills once, long ago, were actually applied toward noble causes. And his statement offered John the opening he sought.

"Speaking of defending yourself, considering your situation with your ex and daughter, perhaps your time for making a stand has arrived?"

A nervy line, as it directly challenged Andre's failing approach to his volatile private life. Most would "mind their business" and "not interfere." But John now felt willing to risk.

Andre raised open palms above his shoulders, eyelids stretched open, as if being robbed at gunpoint. "Me? I'm not the great talker like you."

"Sounds like you have found quite the convenient excuse."

Darkness had arrived. On the left side of the stage, three shirtless men sat on stools with wooden drums, randomly tapping with fingertips. Microphones were plugged in and ready to go.

Two tanned men, both with curly black hair, leaped onto stage with their guitars. One appeared a younger version of the other. They laughed and patted shoulders and bantered with the delighted drummers. This guitar duo exuded such a jubilant air that John found it contagious and began to giggle.

"Gino and Geerie. Great Spanish guitarists. They play solo concerts on the mainland, even in Stockholm and Amsterdam."

"What are they doing in this campground?"

"Ibicencos; born here. Here is one place where they are not

celebrities, as no tourists know about the camping. They can relax and explore and enjoy their music."

Gino and Geerie strummed their dark, rosewood, flamenco guitars, creating a more percussive and sharper sound than is produced from classical guitars. Their adroitness shown instantly through the raw speed of strumming, the variation of sounds, and the consistent rhythmic finger taps on the guitar's front.

People from all over the camping ground now assembled before the stage, sitting cross-legged on the fragrant grass and laughing among themselves. The sky overhead was heavy with stars. Riffs of music commenced. Many came and went to and from the tents, bringing drinks and smokes and bowls of stewed quince. Several women braided each other's hair, weaving in indigo beads and orange blossoms. Wine, served in goat-leather pouches, was passed and shared freely.

Other musicians took turns joining in. Voices were exquisite, and tunes ranged from Samba to David Bowie. A true treat for the ears. Exceptional musicians, real musicians. Many performed in concerts in diverse parts of Europe, but here they found their haven to relax and jam with brethren.

Several drumming performances broke out, with teams beating their wooden drums in passionate frenzy. John even spotted his initial guide, who had graciously led him across the dunes. From time to time, dancers swayed in the crowd.

Gino and Geerie returned to the stage, to everyone's delight, and began lightly strumming. The father, Gino, possessed deep affection for his son and took pride in him, for when they played he observed him with an adoring smile, and when they attempted something unfamiliar or risky, he nodded reassuringly. Geerie, a teenager, focused more on his actual playing, but he sensed whenever his father observed and he unfailingly acknowledged him. For John, after years of listening to work colleagues spew depressing anecdotes of family estrangements and bitterness, story after story of who refused to speak to whom for whatever inconsequential reason—how restoring it was to witness a quality father-son relationship, built off this common art form, and to see it thriving.

From seemingly nowhere, Klav slipped onto center stage.

His loose, green, cloth pants resembled pajamas, with trails of yellow stars running down the sides. He wore nothing else. Layers of beaded necklaces accumulated over his broad chest. It was an outfit Klav alone could make work. He stood inches before the microphone, gazing as if it were in desperate need of his love. His wife Natalia seated herself directly on John's left. She shyly smiled.

"You also know Natalia and Klav?" Andre asked in wonder.

"They invited me here. You know them also?"

"But how on earth did you ever meet them?"

Gino and Geerie strummed, waiting for Klav to commence his vocal. Their task was to seamlessly weave singers into a tune. Their cues came from the singer, and what speed and rhythms he required. No easy task, but for these two professionals it had been an effortless display so far. Yet Klav jeopardized this streak. He randomly hummed and warbled into the microphone for several minutes, hips moving side to side, occasionally pointing to the sky. Sometimes the guitars sped up, sometimes they slowed, trying to feel Klav and receive his signals, if such signals even existed. Geerie glanced nervously at his father, but Gino winked reassuringly and continued.

Eventually, after several more minutes of humming like a moribund mosquito, Klav enunciated for the first time, chanting, "Allah, Buddha," over and over. This appeared to be the extent of his book of lyrics.

It occurred to John that Klav had absolutely no clue what he was doing, for if his musical skills were akin to his writing or artistic talents, this would undoubtedly be the case. And only dear Klav was foolhardy enough to flamboyantly command an entire stage, in a solo performance, whether capable or not. The sheer audacity demanded admiration.

The velvety wineskins continued their rounds. John partook, holding the pouch at arm's length while squeezing, as the others did. He splashed the crimson stream on his shirt, and good-natured chuckles followed from men around him.

Fascinatingly, no one was bothered in the least by Klav's nonsensical performance. Everyone seemed content and carefree. Gino and Geerie continued playing as the intermittent "Allah, Buddha" chant persisted.

"What on earth is he doing up there?"

"Don't ask," Andre said. "He thinks he's a singer, so no one stops him."

"He can't truly believe that?"

"That, I'm not sure of. That's the gray area. But how he loves that stage."

"Shouldn't he be stopped? Pull out the old proverbial cane?"

"Why bother? He wants to feel good, so they let him. Everyone is here to feel good."

John found Klav's performance disconcerting, he had to admit that. He usurped time from all the superb musicians. But he ruminated on Andre's comment that all came simply to feel good. A rudimentary idea, but after all his years in the financial sector, quite a novel one. In that world, if something interfered with quality, it was exterminated; cold and simple. Yet Andre's statement, while seemingly banal, gleamed as a revelation. No reason existed to erect any quality control here. That ruthless mentality even pervaded his former social circles as well. When was anyone who was even the slightest out of line with their ideal model of a human allowed to visit the parties or outings he had attended? Never.

And perhaps more importantly, judging what qualified as harmful was an intricate matter that required sagacity, for, as Gunther always said, out of what seemed disaster often emerged profoundness.

Klav's humming and chanting swelled. Gino and Geerie detected the impending crescendo, as their strumming reciprocated with increased speed and volume. The crowd leaned forward. Klav swayed faster, his eyes stretched open to their limits, as if viewing the Second Coming. With a shrill explosion he exclaimed: "It's the Book of Life!"

He dropped the microphone as applause erupted.

Multiple times he bowed in exhaustion, waving to his audience.

Hopping off the stage, he joined them in the grass below. He hugged John, kissing both cheeks, and patted Andre affectionately on the shoulder. After squeezing the entire contents of a wineskin into his mouth in a continuous hissing flow, spilling not a drop, he mentioned to John just how much it meant to see him again. When he asked John if he appreciated his musical performance, John answered that he did, very much so. That was true in a sense, in that John appreciated witnessing an extraordinary event, and this certainly qualified. But also because, as Andre taught him, all came to feel good, and Klav assuredly, in his own way, contributed to that goal.

"Do you enjoy your time here?"

This delicate sound, whispered into his ear, surprised him. Natalia spoke. Come to think of it, this was the first time he heard her voice.

"I do."

"My son Toobee asks about you," she said. "You cared enough to help us that day."

"He's so responsible for his age."

She cradled John's hand between hers. Labor had coarsened her skin, but her palms emanated remarkable warmth. Light from somewhere flickered on her pupils.

"I love you."

John was petrified. What was that? He could not have heard correctly, could he?

"I'm sorry?"

"I love you."

Instinctively, he veered to locate the others. Klav was off embracing a joyous Gino and Geerie as the main concert had now ceased.

"You love me?"

"Yes."

What on earth? Perhaps this was some peculiar strain of Ibicencan jest.

"That's good," John pathetically attempted.

"I do. I love you. You know, here, on Ibiza, we are all free to express our love whenever we feel so." She stared into John's eyes. "That is our way of living."

This, he did not see coming. Strangest of all, she did not seem the least bit concerned with Klav chatting nearby. The man was arguably within hearing range and yet she spoke freely.

Could it be that this sort of thing might be a frequent occurrence here? Come to think of it, she had referred to a certain "way of living" on Ibiza. Good heavens.

"Do you feel love for me?" she asked, stroking his thigh with her nails.

"Do I what?" he asked. "Well, certainly I appreciate you

and the wonderful job you are doing, and certainly..."

Mercifully, Andre plopped down beside him. A window of escape, and John leaped through it by clumsily integrating him into the conversation. Natalia said nothing more, but wore an amused and even sympathetic smile as John awkwardly transitioned the discussion into the benefits of the Spanish guitar. She even giggled a few times at the drivel he was spewing. He discovered he felt like an embarrassed teenager for the first time since, well, since he was an embarrassed teenager. Eventually others wandered over, and John stood to walk with Andre.

"It's late, I have market in morning. I need to get going home," Andre said.

"Where?"

"The forest. A few miles from here."

"I'll drive you," John said as they walked. "By the way, what do you think of Natalia?"

"Natalia? She doesn't say much. Why?"

"Shall we go?"

Tiny campfires now flickered around the campground, the woodsmoke wafting lazily in clouds. The opportunity to say farewell to Klav and Natalia had passed, as they had melted into the smaller groups spread throughout. Although the main concert was over, guitar solos and singing accompanied by sporadic clapping and cheering seeped out from various locations. The sounds were distant, echoing, almost dreamlike.

Andre called and they exited the camp gate, the metal clanging behind them.

Momentarily gripping the gate, looking back, a pang of wistfulness reverberated through him as warmth of community and merriment was left behind. It now all seemed a faraway and unattainable Shangri-La.

After ten minutes of ascending dark hills, Andre requested they stop. The pines before them partially concealed a three-wheeled transport van, Andre's method for reaching his markets. Dents were visible, and it seemed quite weathered. Not the vehicle to pull up with when desiring to impress.

"You live here?"

"A tent. In those woods," Andre said, gazing at the black line of trees.

"How is it?"

"I'm not here to complain."

"I'm curious."

"Curious? Fair enough. In the winter, the rats gnaw through the tent. Devour my food, no matter how I hide it. Even if I store it in plastic bags. They're very clever."

"Quite."

"And it rains and rains. But summer is okay."

"Well at least the summers are fine," John replied sarcastically. He shook his head in consternation. "So where the hell does all the cash you earn in those markets go? Certainly, you can afford the little required to stay in that wonderful camping ground."

"Look at you. You New Yorkers get all worked up."

"So where does your market money vanish to?" John pressed, not to be redirected.

"My ex."

"Your ex?"

"Yes."

The trees formed charcoal silhouettes against the dark sky.

"You don't mean the same ex who ruined your career

in Amsterdam and stole your apartment and savings seven years ago?"

"That's the one."

"The one who barely lets you see your daughter."

"That's the one."

"You still give her money?"

"Yes."

"All of it you make?"

"Yes."

This man was utterly unbelievable. John must be misunderstanding something.

"So handing over all you owned to her once before was not enough to satisfy your appetite for destruction?" John worked to tame his voice, but was doing a poor job of it.

"It's not so simple."

"No?"

"She says I need to send the cash over for my daughter. Especially since I abandoned her."

"Abandoned her?"

"She says my daughter is the only fatherless girl in her class. And she's embarrassed at school around her friends. All because of my abandoning her."

"Abandoning? Your ex kicked you out of your own apartment and barred you from ever visiting there again."

"She did."

"And prevents you from seeing your daughter, even though you want to."

"Yes."

"I don't think that qualifies as an abandonment."

"Maybe not. Whatever."

"Whatever?"

"Does the past even matter now?"

"It factors in."

"Not when it comes to my daughter."

John shook his head in frustration.

"I'm caught treading water," Andre said. "Poor decisions I made. But once you're down, it's not easy to get up."

"Oh? What about in all those American movies you claim you adore?"

Andre weakly smiled. "I'm of no help to my daughter. She is the one who suffers for my stupidity. That's a bitter pill to swallow."

John shook his head in frustration once again, mumbling something unintelligible. This was not going well by any standards.

"You're a nice guy, New Yorker. You really are. But you must understand that things aren't always so simple."

"Well, does any of the money you give actually go to your daughter? Or is your ex out spending it?"

"She says I must hate my daughter for the way I've ruined her childhood." Andre exhaled. "Tough thoughts to dance around your head every night. So I keep just enough money to survive and give the rest."

"'Hate her?' Give me a break!"

John struggled to contain his exasperation. Sound, logical reasoning, always a dependable tool, was proving feckless. Andre was clearly tortured, but this was a trial of emotions, not intellect.

Nothing would be accomplished here, that much he knew. He asked Andre if he could meet Monday afternoon for lunch, and Andre dispassionately assented. They agreed to convene by the west end of the beach in Santa Eulària. Andre departed with a faint wave.

John felt toothless watching the figure with the sloping

shoulders slip away into the darkness. His unmitigated failure to help him in the least accounted for the disheartening sensation enveloping him like a shadow at dusk. Andre did not bother stopping by his hidden three-wheeled monstrosity, but melted noiselessly into the black forest.

NINE

As John jogged up the hill Saturday morning, he gratefully acknowledged the presence of sea air. The hills in Siesta where he lived were deceptively steep, opening with gradual inclines that led to precipitous finishes, and running up them was no easy task. By car these hills would barely be noticed, as one absentmindedly pressed the accelerator and let the engine toil away—but on foot, ascending was entirely another matter.

Small and pleasant homes, smooth, white, adobe buildings, nestled into the surrounding greenery of these upper hills. Here lay a tranquil and charming place, hidden away from the bustle. Most homes had flat roofs for enjoying the sun, and for hanging laundry, which dried in a matter of hours in brisk morning breezes.

John stopped a few doors away from home, exhaling and stretching calf muscles. Perspiration beaded his body.

"Are you going to perish?"

The voice came from above.

The elegant outline of a woman peered down at him from a rooftop. Although it was impossible to discern her features in the morning brightness beaming behind her, that voice struck him as familiar in a most stimulating manner.

"And why would you ask that?"

"The way you plodded and puffed up that last hill, I thought I would need to drag your carcass up the remainder."

Diana Clarke. She had mentioned she lived in this area.

"And I thought you only spent your time hanging around nudist beaches?"

She heartily laughed. "Come up for a tea?"

A surprise, certainly. A shock, more like it, seeing her again, which he never believed would happen after his failure at the beach. And now being invited up to her place.

He climbed the white side-stairway to her roof as his recently calmed heart began to quicken, and not due to the steepness.

Brightly colored dresses snapped in the breeze on a drying line, and alongside the roof's far edge a round table with a single wicker chair overlooked the distant sea. Diana stood beside it.

"Why don't you sit?" she asked.

He observed the empty chair. "And you?"

"You are the guest, are you not?"

She motioned toward the seat. Tall in a most elegant way, she stood barely a few inches shorter than John. A novel spread face-down on the table, with far more pages digested than remaining. Yet already a different book than from the beach, as her appetite for reading appeared insatiable. Her literary preference remained steadfast though, as its cover bore a depiction of another romantic interlude.

"I can't just sit while you stand there. That wouldn't be proper. Shall I fetch another chair for you?"

He must have said something right, for Diana grinned in amused admiration, although she declared he was a bit of a "bloody nuisance." She led him to the door and they descended to her kitchen. A wonderful sun-filled room glowed with pastel, Mediterranean plants spread throughout the counters and table. Refreshing lavender invigorated the air. A silver kettle awaited on the stove with an assortment of teabags in a case to the side.

"No need to stalk me in the house, now. Get back up to the roof with your beloved chair and leave me be."

She returned promptly with a tray covered by a teapot, porcelain cups, and cream pitcher. After pouring, she deftly added a tad of cream and stirred. Reclining in her chair, she looked out to sea with a contented expression.

"You live just two doors down from here."

John raised an eyebrow.

"This roof is a lovely place for spotting all things," she added, laughing.

He savored the Yorkshire tea and rich cream. Her delicately thin porcelain cups, seemingly too fragile to survive even a moment outdoors, served to enhance the tea's flavor.

"So, what are you doing here in Ibiza?" John asked.

"Isn't that always the question?"

"It seems so. But no one ever asks you that question elsewhere. Quite odd."

"I had a gig."

John's attempt to gently return his cup onto the saucer

failed, as the ethereal porcelain clinked sharply on impact. He cringed, but quickly moved on.

"Gig? What does that mean?"

"Deejaying. I have one gig a summer in Ibiza. Already finished. I stay on Ibiza for the rest of the summer."

"You are a deejay?"

"No. But I do suffer from a chronic condition that causes me to invade deejay booths late at night, often after a few glasses of sherry, and pretend my way about."

He paused, bewildered momentarily, and then both shared a laugh.

"Amazing."

"What is?"

"Your career. A deejay...but are you really?"

"For heaven's sake. I didn't claim to be a bloody astronaut."

"I know, but..."

"What did you expect me to be, a nurse?"

"I know plenty of nurses. Nice people."

She laughed lightheartedly.

"Amazing"

"What's 'amazing' you now?"

"Your career."

"Well, it used to be. Deejayed from here to Rome to Vietnam to London. Ran my own company, a dream of mine," she said. "Spent fifteen years doing that. A blast."

"And now?"

She smiled, looking out to sea. "Now the younger deejays are in. It's a young person's game, not some old fogey in their late thirties. But I still perform one or two gigs a year."

"Fogey? Hardly."

Crinkles formed beside her eyes.

"Do you miss the busier schedule?"

"Not at all," she said, sitting up. "Heavens, no. It was a blast for a time, don't get me wrong. But now, finally, I can relax more in life. And go to bed at a reasonable bloody hour. Mother is happy."

"Oh?"

"She was always shocked by it all. Said with our estate in Yorkshire and the London apartments and all the investments, I'm foolish to be working at all. Makes me look like a silly girl trying to prove a point. Said I should do a bit of volunteering if I was so bored."

"But you still did it."

Diana smiled. "Yes, I did. She called me the 'ridiculous rebel' back then."

"And now?"

"Oh, she has other names, don't you worry."

They laughed heartily together.

"I am deeply impressed."

She looked at John with curious surprise.

"Well, I assume that is not an easy field to succeed in. Ultra-competitive and extremely cutthroat."

"That's for sure."

"And especially as a woman in that male-dominated world."

She listened attentively.

"And you ran your own company successfully in that environment for fifteen years!"

"Wasn't always easy, especially at the start."

"You did this all alone?"

"I had mentors in the beginning. In Rome and Tangiers in the 70s, at expatriate clubs where I learned the trade. Well-known male deejays; they taught me. While, of course, trying to bed me the whole time."

"Did you hold out?"

She laughed. "Long enough to learn the trade and escape with virtue intact."

"And most importantly, your success came in a field you enjoyed."

"Absolutely loved it."

"Amazing."

"You have an apparent fondness for that word."

John smiled. "You had the resolve to pursue what you cared about, and let nothing sidetrack you. The rarest of all occurrences, so I've sadly learned in this world of zombies," John said. "I certainly cannot claim to have had the guts to do that."

"I'm sure you have done very well."

"By certain metrics, perhaps. But you, on the other hand, are very impressive, Ms. Clarke. Very impressive, indeed."

Color rose in her cheeks as she glanced at the white adobe floor. A truly marvelous combination of beauty and intelligence. And wit. From whence came such a person?

To his surprise, she invited him to visit her "great" friend that evening. He owned a French restaurant called La Grenouille in Santa Gertrudis, supposedly the finest on the island, if not in all of Spain. She did caution him though, with a plaintive head shake, that although brilliant, her friend could be "a bit of an ass" to certain people.

John accepted, nonetheless. He would have accepted a winter swim in a bog.

And this "friend" he could handle, as John was particularly adroit at dealing with the strain of personality given the taxonomic designation of "a bit of an ass."

After thanking her, and bowing with an impeccably straight back, they agreed to convene at eight that very night. She remained seated while observing him depart, the corner of her mouth raised in a thoroughly admiring smile.

After glancing at his combed hair for a third time, John suspected something amiss. All evening, he had felt skittish.

Although he wore shorts and T-shirts for the last weeks, only a more decorous outfit would befit this evening. A fine dinner out with Diana awaited him, after all. And as a French restaurant served as their destination, this necessitated a degree of formality. Let him not be the one to violate this universal code. Slacks and a button-down it would be. And of course, they would meet the owner, Diana's very good friend, whose temperament had received a less-than-ringing endorsement.

He strolled through the twilight to meet her. Clement oaks, heavy with acorns, lined both sides of the street. Bursts of purple from Clematis draped the white-washed buildings, and bright yellow from the Immortelle flowers arose from the dust.

There Diana stood, positioned atop the roof, looking down as he approached.

She informed him through cupped hands that she would be "right there." Evidently, "right there" meant twenty minutes, but when she finally emerged he was taken aback by her long, sleeveless and strapless dress, pale blue and white, free flowing. She had tied her hair into two pigtails, and smiled grandly.

Upon greeting her with an awkward kiss on the cheek, she appeared timid. But he could not quite tell; maybe the timid one was he.

To John's dismay, his vehicle required three key rotations to start, an embarrassing delay which he attempted to minimize by distracting with a few insubstantial questions. He had developed a fondness for his vehicle with its dicey origins, but it failed to impress at the moment. It must have harbored some sympathy for John's plight, as it finally started, humming smoothly, and they pulled out on the way to Santa Gertrudis.

"Where did you unearth this thing?"

"This Mercedes?"

"If this is a Mercedes, I'm from Tokyo."

"Hey, so claimed the farmer who sold it. And I still truly believe that at least one part, perhaps the mirror, is from a Mercedes."

"The mirror is broken."

An unnoticed crack lined its upper left corner.

"Those Germans never could make a good mirror."

It only took fifteen minutes to arrive at her friend's restaurant. The town of Santa Gertrudis was inland, settled between fragrant orange groves and carob farms. An unconventional town, if it could be termed a "town" at all, as it consisted of an inordinate amount of restaurants and not much else. While this was known as the finest location on Ibiza to dine out, few people actually lived there. John followed her animated directions as they circled the town aimlessly three times, but he refrained from commenting even though he had spotted the restaurant. This was her project, and he knew it best to let her captain it. In due time they pulled up in front of La Grenouille.

"Armand is my friend's name. Owned this place for six years." Apprehensiveness riddled her expression.

"Diana?"

"Yes?"

"Is there anything you would like to tell me about this Armand before we enter?"

"No," she retorted. "Not at all. Why ask such silly questions?"

"Just wondering."

"Well, I did inform you that he can be a bit of an ass."

"You did."

"Occasionally a tad abusive to others when I'm around."

"A tad?"

"Yes."

"I see."

"He also seems to have some sort of pet peeve with Americans."

John squinted.

"Yes. Thinks they lack culture. That they are vile creatures."

"Interesting. Sounds like he will love me."

She smiled.

"But he is always nice to me."

"Well, that's good to know."

"Look, Armand has a good heart, okay?" she shot back defensively. "His boyfriend lives in London, also a great friend of mine."

John always wondered about the ubiquitous classification of the difficult person who really has a good heart. A bizarre consignment. Essentially, it meant said person can be nasty or cruel, but deserves a free pass because that is not who he truly is. Allegedly, deep down he is wonderful. But, for reasons never explained, this wonderfulness remains latent.

An open-air terrace with a latticed roof fronted the restaurant. Vines of orange Bougainvillea flowers crept across and draped down the walls. Rustic wooden tables and chairs spread throughout, all filled with recent arrivals ordering wines from the esteemed vineyards of France. Inside, in a dimmer space, candlelit tables and oil paintings of provincial French scenes filled the room.

John had not anticipated the crowd, since most dined absurdly late on Ibiza. The common dinner time often passed ten o'clock. For John, eight qualified as a late supper, and ten o'clock classified as a nighttime snack.

No sign of this Armand. A relief, to be sure. Although curious, he worried about the impending interaction. Diana would witness all of this, and then form her impression of him based upon it. Thus, he likely would need to defend himself from being humiliated by Armand, yet do so without behaving brutishly or offensively. Not such an easy line to walk.

Diana whispered to a waitress, who disappeared into the kitchen. Tempestuous words escaped from the back, a piercing male voice amidst the clanging of pans.

"He'll be coming out now."

A short man emerged moments later, wearing a white shirt and burgundy vest. Purple veins cobwebbed his bulbous nose, and he toted a round, hard belly which caused him to sweat and inhale laboriously.

When he spotted Diana, his scowl vaporized, replaced by unadulterated delight.

He embraced her, his head barely reaching her neck. Squeezing her right hand, he scanned her dress, telling her what a magnificent choice it was and that she must absolutely reveal her source.

When she introduced John, the corners of Armand's mouth plummeted, and he nodded coolly, sans a word.

He hollered at a waiter in French, who leaped and furiously prepared a table in the corner. Armand guided them over.

"I will bring the wine," he said, rushing away.

"He used to own the premier restaurant in Lyon, critically acclaimed throughout," Diana whispered. "Clients from all over Europe. He was famous, in all the magazines."

"Used to?"

"Details are murky. They never really told me all," she said. "It's sensitive, but he was forced to sell everything after a drunken car accident with some politician. Got a bit ugly with the courts, and all that. His beloved place was everything to him, poor darling. After that, he vanished into heavy drinking for years. Rumor has it he made an attempt on himself."

"Horrible to hear."

"Oh, yes."

"That's a real shame. Especially after that rarefied success."

"After drying out, he journeyed here to Ibiza to try to restart his life. Believed in his heart that Ibiza would be the one and only place he could resurrect."

"That seems to be a common belief."

Diana nodded. "And lo and behold, he absolutely did it."

Clients continued to arrive, now waiting for tables.

"Most of his clients are French, which is a good sign."

"How did you connect with him?"

"His boyfriend. I've known him from London for years. Charming man, absolutely charming. Works for one of the large fashion houses. He's Italian." She laughed, clapping her hands together. "They only spend two or three months a year together, or they would murder each other. Believe me, I've seen it."

The soft leather menus were but a single page. A positive sign, as Armand sourced local ingredients and focused on preparing few dishes at the highest level. John had spent a week on a business trip in Lyon years ago, and recalled the superlative restaurant scene. The city was famed for its bouchons, which served local meats such as duck and pork, and for its freshwater fish from nearby lakes in Savon.

"So why do you think people from London and New York tend to get along?" Diana asked. Her long legs stretched comfortably beneath the table.

"Do they? You have far too many preposterous newspapers with outlandish headlines. That, I confess, I can never understand."

She smiled. "You don't smoke?"

"Smoke? No, no. Can't stand it."

"Do you mind if I do?"

"If you smoke? Well—"

"Don't have a breakdown, silly," she said, laughing. "Just teasing. We both don't puff away, thank heavens. A rarity, I must say. People here all tend to smoke something, heavens knows what."

"So I've noticed."

"And do you work, or just wander the island's beaches all day?"

"Wandering, at the moment."

"And before the moment?"

"Finance."

"Really?" She paused. "You don't seem the sort."

"I'll take that as a compliment. Anyway, I abandoned it."

Diana leaned forward. "Oh? What will you do now?"

"Now? I've considered pursuing a career in the deejaying field."

She laughed delightfully. "You just might be good at it."

"That, I highly doubt."

"I've traveled and been around, John. You do seem a bit of an odd sort."

"Oh?"

"I don't mean you linger in the attic and consume insects," she said. "You are just difficult to place."

"I like attics."

"Well, you don't seem like a club-goer from Ibiza Town, and yet you don't come across as a hippie, either," she said, smiling. "And you don't seem like one of the wealthy types hiding dark secrets up in their villas."

"Don't we all have our secrets?"

Armand arrived with the wine. "Chateau Montrose," he said, cradling the bottle. He smiled lovingly at Diana, then glared at John. "That's a French wine, not a brand of your American cola, if you are not aware," he added in his thick French accent.

Diana rolled her eyes.

"Ah yes, Chateau Montrose," John said. "One of my favorites."

"Is that so?" Armand asked with a smirk. "You get it in your vending machines in Ohio?"

"That, I don't know. But I did visit their vineyard in Bordeaux in the Saint-Estèphe appellation. Lovely town and chateau. Beau vignoble."

Armand fell silent.

"I believe they use nearly seventy percent Cabernet Sauvignon there, or in the mid-sixties, if I recall. I met charming members of the Charmolue family," John continued.

This, Armand had not seen coming.

It should be noted that although he maintained his scornful aspect, his left eyebrow rose, and his lower lip quivered ever so slightly. But as a seasoned batterer of others, he recouped rapidly, dismissed John's words as an anomaly, and said, in a slightly more cautious tone, that he would return for their orders.

On Armand's walk to the kitchen, he did momentarily peek back at John with a befuddled expression.

"He wasn't expecting that," Diana said. "His nasty little habit of showing off his expertise flares up occasionally." She peered at John with curiosity. "But how did you know all that mumbo about that wine?"

"A lucky guess perhaps?"

"A lucky guess? Come now. Is Mr. John actually a humble man, as well?"

"So, any career before your deejaying success?"

She gazed at him before responding, a surveying, amused gaze. "Not really. A few nonprofit positions mother thought appropriate for me, and from there came the music."

"Mom is in England?"

"Oh, yes. The old bat is up in our place in Yorkshire," she said, laughing. "She still maintains it with staff and all the pomp. Probably her only friends in the world, but they have no choice in the matter, now do they?"

"I suppose not."

"She loves it up in those hedged gardens. Less and less time in London."

John sipped his wine, an intense, complex vintage. "Are you in Yorkshire often?"

"She's a crazy old bat, but I'm there for a good portion of the year. The two of us dine on a table the size of this restaurant, each of us on one end," she said, shaking her head. "Better that way, as I can't hear a word she is saying."

John heartily laughed.

"The rest of the year I'm in London, or here."

Armand returned to personally take orders.

"What do you recommend for us, darling?" Diana asked.

"For you, my dear, I recommend our delectable lamb chops. We have a cognac-Dijon cream sauce."

She clapped her hands together in delight. "That's sounds absolutely lovely! And for John?"

Armand's mouth turned up in wry amusement. This was not going to be pleasant.

"Perhaps that most rare delicacy known as Big Mac? Would that satisfy our Ohio friend's needs?" He laughed in self-delight, placing his hand on Diana's shoulder. She sighed resignedly.

John waited, allowed him to laugh it out, as any comment delivered prematurely would be submerged by cackling.

"Sounds appetizing, but considering that belly of yours, I suspect there might be a Big Mac shortage on the island."

Armand's laughing halted, and he stared at John, trembling slightly.

Diana fell silent, and John made sure to avoid eye contact with her for the moment. He waited patiently through the thorny silence—harder to do than it sounds—allowing Armand to stabilize before continuing.

"But I truly do hope, monsieur, that your quenelles de brochet with Nantua sauce is even better than what I tasted in wonderful Lyon during my time there. Now that was a meal fit for a Roi Soleil."

Armand's mouth cracked open.

"Oh yes, I dined in fair Lyon," John continued. "Up in a charming place in La Croix-Rousse, two years ago. On the far end of Rue Villeneuve. And in another bouchon on Rue Jacquard."

His eyelids blinked erratically.

"And such superb summer vegetables from Bresse! The Piment de Bresse is consummate. Now if you can top that, maestro, if you can show me better than Lyon, then please, let me partake of that."

All of Armand's features darkened and twitched. In the furthest recesses of his mind, he had never fathomed anything proximate to this. This response, from a cretin American, moreover, supposedly from the depths of Ohio, shocked him through. And now raged a monumental battle as he combed through conflicting thoughts and emotions to find the suitable words to express them.

"Of course, my quenelles de brochet is premier! Do you

think I cannot top that which you ate in Lyon?" He looked toward his tiny leather loafers, shaking his head in disgust. "Probably in one of Daniel's new eateries. I know the non-sense he calls 'food.' Not as fabulous as he likes everyone to believe," he said bitterly. A few dining couples glanced over at the swelling volume. "Do you not think I get great freshwater fish here as well? We will see, monsieur!"

Armand strode off toward the kitchen.

Diana, with an expression of amazement, watched him scurry away. "What on earth did you do to him?"

"Meaning?"

"Wound him up. I thought spontaneous combustion was next."

"I simply ordered."

"You actually visited restaurants in Lyon?"

"The world capital of gastronomy, according to Curnon-sky, the Prince of Gastronomy. I would agree. A magnificent crossroads of regional cuisines."

"This is fast becoming an interesting evening. Very interesting." She sipped her Chateau Montrose. "And quite surprising."

"How so?"

"Well, truth be told..."

"Yes?"

"Well...I thought you might be a bloody fool."

John exploded in laughter. "What?"

"Yes. No offense, though."

"None taken. But why, then, invite me out in the first place?"

She stroked the ends of her hair.. "Well, it's not common to find someone who seems to have at least half a brain. And with good looks and fine manners. So, I thought I would settle for that."

"Half a brain is not a bad settlement."

"True. But your expansive knowledge has certainly been a pleasant surprise."

"I'm pleased to have provided you with a full, intact cerebrum, cerebellum, stem, pituitary, and hypothalamus."

"Is there anything you don't know, Mr. Erudition?"

"Plenty."

"Such as?"

"Whether or not there is actually a McDonald's open late night on Ibiza."

Diana laughed, dimples forming in her cheeks. He found himself absolutely delighted to witness her enjoyment.

The waiter served their dinners, with Armand on his toes, peering over his shoulder. But a marked transformation had now occurred. When arriving at the table, he attended to John first, inquiring about the food and wine. And although he did not ignore her, he no longer fawned over Diana.

They both relished their sumptuous dishes, complimenting each bite. Armand returned again only minutes later, most eager to know John's opinion of the quenelles de brochet, and how it compared to Lyon's offering. John was forthright. They were proximate, but Armand's tarragon tasted a tad fresher.

"Yes! Yes, it is. You noticed." He mopped his forehead with his sleeve. "I pick them in our gardens right outside. Not like those new chefs now in Lyon, using packaged herbs."

"They are probably using canned crawfish for their sauce as well, instead of the fresh ones from Savoy."

Armand laughed in gulping fits. His quilted hand rested on John's shoulder. "They probably do, they probably do." After composing himself, he looked to John. "Another bottle for you, monsieur?"

Diana observed this camaraderie unfolding in awe.

"What do you have from the Joseph Drouhin domain?"

Armand's widened eyes made momentary contact with John's, stunned one final time, as apparently repeated evidence was required to permanently alter his headstrong opinions about denizens of America. "I have from Côte de Nuits, Côte de Beaune. What do you desire, monsieur?"

"You have a pinot from Bonnes-Mares?"

Armand bowed. "Yes, yes, of course I do. I keep those specially downstairs, in the cave à vin for those au courant. I bring it up for you."

The remainder of the dinner unfolded splendidly as they savored their wine and traded anecdotes, and even engaged in a spirited discussion concerning which genre of fiction is the finest. Diana's encyclopedic knowledge of the romantic literary realm, coupled with her ardor for it, offered a formidable challenge for John, who was additionally distracted by her exquisiteness.

Armand checked with them twice more to assure all was exceptional. Unequivocally, it was. Truth be told, Armand impressed John thoroughly. In these last years he had developed a pet admiration for those who overcame debilitating adversity.

Somehow, this tenacious Armand had moved on from his thwarted life in Lyon. Instead of resigning to the role of a whining martyr, a diabolically seductive role, he had crusaded through the ruins of his felled restaurant and years of wine-soaked depression. He had found the resolve to successfully erect his second dream on the shores of Ibiza—a laudable accomplishment, considering the disheartening reality that realizing one's hopes even once in lifetime is often an unattainable goal.

And once again, this place—this Ibiza—served as the magical host for fulfilling dire aspirations.

As they departed, Armand informed them that he would serve Rosette de Lyon and Tablier de sapeur for his cultivated customers later next week. A table awaited John, if he would have it.

John thanked him for a dining experience that now made Lyon seem like backwoods Ohio, and Armand laughed uncontrollably. After accompanying them outside, unprecedented behavior for Armand, he embraced them and returned to his restaurant.

John opened the car door for Diana, and she slipped inside. With windows down, and a night breeze, it was pleasantly cool.

"I've never seen that in all my years with Armand. Never. I just need to tell Tony."

John turned left on a silent street; as the road lacked streetlights, he minded the sharp bends. "Never seen what?"

"Armand, so nice to a guest. He practically *served* you."

"It is a restaurant," John said. "That tends to happen."

"I know, but that was absurd," she said in an exasperated tone. "How did you manage it?"

"Are you disappointed?"

She swiveled toward him. "And what is that supposed to mean?" She had released her hair, which hung in twists over her shoulders.

"Could it be that you enjoy watching him picking on others, while fawning over you?"

"What is *that* supposed to mean?"

"It's simply a question," John said. "He's an admirable man, but has a comedic element, one must admit."

"Stop the bloody car."

John pulled over onto the dusty roadside beside a lemon orchard.

He expected her to speak, but she exited and strode a few

steps away, halting alongside a wooden, post and rail fence. John quietly followed. Apparently, he had misstepped. All fell silent, except for the steady beat of cicadas. The perfume of bitter lemon peels emanated from the encircling groves.

"You have a lot of nerve."

"I simply asked you a question," John said. "Some people enjoy the fawning and entertainment. It's amusing, admittedly. I've met many who like that."

"I don't know what type of people you've met, but I'm not one of them."

"Fair enough."

"Armand is a friend. Friends, for me, are not so easy to come by. From me, somebody always wants something. Always."

"I understand."

"Do you?"

"I believe so."

"That's why I enjoy my own company, nowadays. You might say I'm a bit of a recluse."

"Nothing wrong with that."

"But Armand doesn't want anything from me. I like that."

"I understand," John said. "With your beauty and talent, someone will always want something. That makes perfect sense."

She shook her head, focused on the brittle grass blades crunching beneath her feet. "Have you ever been married?"

"Married? Why ask about that?"

"Just answer the question."

He paused, nervous as to where she was headed. "I have not."

"Probably not engaged, either?"

"Never engaged," he said. "I was offered marriage, though."

"You mean proposed to?"

"No. 'Proposed' means a ring and romance and such. This was just a request."

"And?"

"I said no."

She perked, approaching with widened eyes. "Really? And how do you think that made her feel? Thought about that?"

"Yes," John said, gently. "I don't believe it was that important to her, in the long run. In fact, I don't think it mattered to her at all."

He did not see the fist coming. In John's defense, the heavy cloud layer made for a dark night, and he certainly did not anticipate it. Her fist landed squarely on the left side of his mouth. An admirable, crisp punch, well-placed.

"What the hell was that for?"

"Maybe you should have considered her feelings."

The blood tasted coppery. "Feelings?"

"How do you think your treatment of her made her feel?"

"Our relationship was not meaningful," John exclaimed, spitting out a bit of blood. "Money and society interested her. We acted as business partners who planned on merging finances. That's all. She was dating again two weeks later, someone else from my company. Doesn't that say it all?"

Diana said nothing.

"I believe you are making far more of it than warranted."

"That's what all of you say."

"'All of you?' Who is this 'all of you?'"

"Just drive me home."

She slammed the door shut, the thud echoing across the grove.

They rode in silence.

Evidently, John had made a horrific mess of the night.

He failed to anticipate her reactions, but he probably should have. Yes, he should have. Perhaps he had become imperceptive to the feelings of others during these last, emotionally parched years of his life. This thought terrified him profoundly, for it would ban him from forming meaningful relationships, something he desperately sought.

Diana gazed out her window, forehead pressed against the cool glass, remaining mute. While they climbed back into the hills of Siesta, he built up the nerve to inquire if she enjoyed her night. A painful question to ask, as the silence had morphed from an awkward cloud into a comfortable respite. Nonetheless, he felt it should be asked, as most of the night had been delightful, at least from his perspective. Even her jab to his mouth brought a lovely, histrionic element to the evening.

Obviously, from her fiery and unanticipated reactions, there was much about her he did not comprehend. Much he was missing. But, yes, he would like to know more. Very much so. In truth, he found her utterly charming. The thought of her brought a smile, although his injured lip pained at the stretch.

Just then, as they reached halfway up the final hill, and as John began uttering ameliorating words in a final attempt to salvage the evening, the car sputtered and jolted to a stop.

He rotated the key five times, each time with increased vigor, but no luck. Dead. Absolutely stupendous. What superb timing.

Diana exited the car and he rapidly followed, desperate for a moment to speak. The delicate night air was perfumed by the sweet scent of Clematis flowers.

"Goodnight," she said flatly as she began striding home, just up the hill, leaving a speechless John in her wake. Her steps were definitive and refined, and she did not turn back once.

He had ruined this precious night in the last few moments, all the more distressing after such a pleasant evening. Horrible.

A few clouds retreated, permitting moonlight seepage, and he admired her in her blue, flowing dress as she ascended the pale incline. An ethereal figure.

He wondered if his freezer contained ice, for his lip began to swell.

TEN

As June unfolded, far more people populated the beach in Santa Eulària than when John had arrived. Several mid-sized hotels lined the beachside, and most patrons of these hotels were of the stock who stayed for a week or less, spending the majority of their time on lounges imbibing cocktails. They never strayed far, good heavens, no.

John supposedly would meet Andre at 12 o'clock, but as he waited by the beach, he questioned whether Andre would actually arrive. Not due to a lack of want—as Andre seemed to enjoy his company—but rather because something, however trivial, might go wrong. Andre had forfeited control of the most important things in his life. This incensed John, as he sensed benevolence and a diligent nature in Andre, two traits he thoroughly admired. Rooting for Andre came naturally.

By 20 minutes after 12, a disappointed John prepared to depart. Just then, a reedy figure hustled down Carrer des Riu. Andre approached, waving wildly as if fleeing a war zone. He stopped in front of John, hands on thighs, stabilizing his breath.

"You are okay?"

"Yes, yes," Andre said, claiming more air. The gray strands of his partially tied hair swung freely. "Trouble with my van, and then couldn't find a parking. I knew you were waiting."

"Don't worry." John peered up the hills into sleepy Siesta, recalling his end-of-night fiasco with Diana. "It recently took me a full day to revive my car..."

"Listen, John. Can we just grab some food and take it on a ride? I need to pick up materials for my sculptures."

"Let's get something easy."

Along Carrer Pintors Puget, a sunny street lined with squat palms, they found a takeout restaurant offering sandwiches and falafels. A refrigerator with a cracked window contained brands of canned sodas rarely found, usually for excellent reasons. There was absolutely nothing appealing about the place, including the shady, mustached proprietor on the lookout behind the counter, but it would suffice.

"You can have our special," the proprietor instructed Andre, the gold of his teeth flashing. His heavy hips supported a tall figure, and he spoke forcefully, assuring that both John and his diminutive cook would hear.

"Special?"

"Yes, you get sandwich and soda all for thirty-five pesetas. That's all it costs." He stroked the grayish hairs of his heavy mustache.

"Thirty-five?" Andre said. "Well, I don't think I really need a drink."

The man haughtily laughed. "Don't worry so much. We all need to drink."

"Well—"

"Drink is life. Our drink is in the special. Reduced price. Thirty-five pesetas."

"Well—"

"Thirty-five pesetas."

Andre resignedly counted the money, coin by coin. The man repeated the order and the cook, cigarette dangling from his mouth, nodded without turning. The reused grease on the grill began to pop and sizzle.

After secreting Andre's money in a hidden compartment beneath the nearly bare upper money tray, he focused on John. "Special for you also, of course."

"No."

The man, surprised by the confident tone, paused, appearing almost childlike. But his sardonic smile snapped back.

"Your friend gets the special, you get the special."

"Just the sandwich."

"Get the special, young man, and your drink is reduced."

"Just the sandwich," John said. "Thank you."

"What, you don't drink? You are camel?" the man said, cackling, as he slapped his cook's shoulder in an attempt at solidarity. The skeletal cook convulsed from the force, ashes dislodging from his cigarette and drifting down onto the food, perhaps becoming the finest ingredient in this dubious meal.

"So what do you want, cola or orange?"

John did not reply.

"You are not too cheapskate, no?" the man said, the hairs on his mustache quivering as he bellowed.

John still did not speak. The first shreds of concern flashed across the owner's face.

"You are cheap with the ladies too, yes?" he tried, in a last-ditch attempt—which likely, within certain groups, had provided him much success.

Plunging this man's head into the falafel frier was tempting, and might even improve his appearance. But John could show Andre a little something here, and needed to seize the opportunity.

"I do not want to spend a single peseta of my money on a drink," John said, enunciating each word distinctly.

The proprietor's giddiness evaporated. He paused, staring at John's unflinching expression, and then knew any resistance would be in vain. This man, unappealing as he might be, was remarkably shrewd, and made his living instantly assessing situations. He knew the game was up, and moodily mumbled John's order. Twenty pesetas. As the food was prepared he spoke no more, sulking, but the cook's restrained smile, lacking in teeth, revealed some secret satisfaction at witnessing his employer's rare failure. No love lost, there.

As John and Andre received their bags, the proprietor veered his head aside and refused eye contact. From falafel hawker to spurned lover.

While walking away, Andre shook his head admiringly. "You sure put him in his place."

"Oh?"

"I just love how you told him you didn't want the drink. Did you see his face?"

"I did."

"And how you told him the reason: that you did not want to spend any money on it. That simple."

"So I guess you don't need to be a great talker to resist."

Andre considered this comment. "That guy did not expect that. No one ever just says the truth."

John motioned toward the yellowish can in Andre's hand. "Did you want that?"

"Not really."

"Not really?"

"No, I didn't."

"So why the hell did you order it?"

"Why?" Andre said. "I don't know why. He just said it, and I ordered it."

"You just told me you didn't want it."

Andre began to fidget, feet shuffling. "Maybe I was embarrassed saying no to him. He was pushy as hell. It's embarrassing, saying no."

"Yes, it is. And he knows that," John said. "He's probably been doing this for twenty years, and every bit of coin matters. It's all a sport to him. He instantly read your lack of confidence, and forced the soda on you."

"You're probably right."

"Now, if that mustached manipulator reads that meekness on you, don't you think others do also?"

Andre ground his molars as he wrestled with this galling thought. John braced for his next question. A flammable inquiry, but it needed asking.

"Don't you think your ex-wife does?"

Andre looked up with widened eyes, as if John had voiced the unutterable. "What business is it of yours?"

"None."

"Well then, forget about it."

"Okay."

"Just forget about it."

"I will."

John was sure to keep silent as Andre's veins popped on his temples. He shook his head and mumbled bitterly, gesticulating and pacing about.

Suddenly, his glare softened and fell resignedly down onto his unsought soda can.

"I suppose she *can* tell, can't she?"

John felt a wave of pity, observing his drooped posture.

"Look, I don't know the details," John said. "And I understand that in life, the devil is in the details. Believe me, I know that. But if you are sleeping in a rat-filled tent in the forest, after your ex-wife pilfered your apartment and your daughter—and in addition, she moved her boyfriend in—I think we can all agree something is askew."

"I know, I know." Andre tapped a smooth stone with tip of his sandal. A few strands of his gray hair flipped in the breeze. This silvery mass atop his head must be a recent development, engendered by the enormous stress and misfortune this good-hearted man had endured.

"To be honest," John said, "I enjoyed telling that bastard I didn't want his soda."

"Why?" Andre appeared most eager for an answer. "Why did you enjoy it?"

"A fine question. I suppose anytime someone is trying to obliterate your free will, you should be enraged. And as trivial as one soda sounds, it matters. Also, of equal or higher importance, I found that colossal mustache aggravating."

They laughed together as they strolled up to Andre's three-wheeled van. In the daylight it could be seen clearly, which was not necessarily a good thing. The lone wheel up front appeared impractically small, like something befitting a toy. With a trembling fit, it started. John felt as if he were inserted into a hollow, plastic tank with a faulty engine clanking around inside. Andre concentrated on the naked shift and the turns on the roads, his brow furrowed and expression grim, an aspect borne from innumerable tribulations suffered in this jalopy.

"Where are we headed?"

"Hills way above Portinatx, one of the most northern bays on the island. I know a guru there. Lets me take materials from an old temple. For my art."

"A guru?"

Andre shrugged, and tugged the shift, the flimsy walls of the van violently jerking as gears switched.

On the way, they passed fields rife with carob trees. Andre noted, with pride, that the carob tree was esteemed over the centuries on Ibiza for helping survive arduous times when rains were scarce and other plants faltered. Spanish farmers wearing white cowboy hats and jeans strolled through the groves and inspected this year's particularly vibrant growth. A massive harvest would come to fruition by late summer.

In the northern regions, the island's most isolated territory, they began ascending the loftiest hills on Ibiza. The terrain transfigured to more majestic vegetation as juniper and Aleppo pines gave way to grand Lebanon cedars and stunning views of the distant jagged coastline. Although a typically hot and arid day, in the upper hills it felt far cooler. Portinatx was the only northern bay with any tourists, and even there, few visited. The rest of the tiny, northern coves lay deserted, mutely pondering the expanse of blue Mediterranean.

Finally, on the peak of a mighty hill, they turned up a dirt road and made a last charge until Andre shut his three-wheeled creature down. It quivered from exorbitant toil.

"We've arrived?"

"We can leave the car here."

Although sunny with a brilliant blue sky, abundant branches filtered a fair bit of light. At this altitude the air was still, with moisture beading the lengthy grass blades.

"But where are we going?" The term "middle of nowhere" certainly applied here.

"Through the forest."

A tranquil aura enveloped them. Virginal scents of pine and cedar pervaded as they began traversing the forest's depths. They followed not a path, as none existed, but rather journeyed among trees coated with emerald moss. Rabbits darted at impossible angles before them.

John found himself relishing every moment as he inhaled and exhaled deliberately. His often-tensed shoulders relaxed. Andre must know where they were headed, and if not, it mattered not, as here lay a most magical place to be lost. Their steps made no sound on the damp earth, and they instinctively remained silent, as any noise would violate this sanctuary.

Eventually, after continuing through this scented forest, they emerged onto a flat clearing ending in a dramatic cliffside. John stepped back in astonishment.

Before them stood an immense Buddhist temple, finely constructed alongside the cliff's edge, beyond it only sky. At least twenty red-and-gold roofs of varying sizes, with curled, sharp corners, topped it like exotic scoops of ice cream. The gold glinted intoxicatingly in the sunlight, while walls were painted a pristine white. It all appeared something out of a hazy daydream, and John, viewing this amidst deep forest aromas, questioned whether he was immersed within one.

Outside wandered dozens of people in orange robes. All had shaved heads. A group of seven sat cross-legged and motionless along the cliff's edge facing the northern sea view, while others roamed the meticulous gardens before the temple. No one made a sound or noticed them.

"We should wait here," Andre said. "He will come soon."

"Who?"

"The guru."

"Who is this guru you are talking about?"

"An interesting guy. There is an older, smaller temple to the far side that collapsed. I get excellent wood and metals and trinkets from it; he allows me to take whatever I want. I bring him up some fruits usually."

"Oh? And what did you bring him now?"

He turned to John, mouth agape. "I forgot."

"We might have finally discovered a use for that lovely soda you purchased."

Andre laughed good-naturedly.

"So where is this guru from? India, or Tibet?"

"No, no. Sweden, actually."

"Sweden? What on earth?"

At that moment, a tall, thin man with a blond beard walked toward them along a path emerging from the temple's center. Andre whispered from the side of his mouth that the guru approached. Clothed in an orange robe, he moved smoothly as his free, blond hair dangled halfway down his back. He stepped delicately with pale, sandaled feet.

Andre introduced John.

This guru surveyed John from head to toe. He smiled, flawless teeth shining. Amidst all this conglomeration of hair and gleaming smile, his age was difficult to determine, but John felt he must be in his early fifties.

"Baba Bir Bahadur," he said.

Most probably not his native Swedish name.

"John."

"My Sanskrit name. Erik was my civil name. Our spiritual name identifies with our spiritual body, not the physical one." He looked toward Andre. "Feel free to search and find your latest goods. And do take your physical body with you." He smiled at John. "Our Andre likes to recycle for productive purposes. Who am I to stop his environmental ethic?"

Andre nodded to John and scurried to the side of the temple. The guru surveyed the gardens with John at his side.

"My yogis," he eventually said.

As John observed, he realized that most were female. With their shaved heads, it took a moment to distinguish. In fact, as he continued scanning, he did not locate a single male. He would deposit this particular observation for later use.

"We practice Tantric Buddhism," the guru said with a slight element of superciliousness. "Do you know anything of it?"

"Yes, I'm quite familiar with Vajrayana Buddhism."

The guru stepped back, eyebrows raised. "You were a practitioner?"

"No, but in an earlier chapter of my life, I studied many such things."

The guru nodded in approval, any remnants of haughtiness now vanquished. Knowledge impressed him.

"Our goal is to become fully awakened. That is our goal." He looked over the thriving gardens. "We do this through identifying with tantric deities. Our deities are not spirits to be believed in, as often is seen in the Western religions, but are representatives of the tantric practitioner's own inner nature."

"Yes, I'm familiar. The tantric path as opposed to the sutra path. You take the quicker path."

The guru placed his left hand on his heart, pantomiming offense. "But not a lesser one."

"That, I do not know," John said. "I do recall the sutra path is slower, following precepts and developing meditative concentration in order to develop the seeds of enlightenment as opposed to enlightenment itself. So, their enlightenment will be realized in the future."

"Very true. But we bring the future result into the present moment, by realizing oneself as an enlightened being." He walked a few steps, then turned to John. "At this level, John, dualities cease to exist, and one can discover that opposite principles are, in fact, one."

John nodded.

"Come, do stroll with me a bit." Clearly the breadth of John's knowledge pleased him, as he was eager to continue.

Wildflowers surrounded the soft dirt path. The guru pointed out the intricate herbal gardens cultivated by attending yogis, as well as the magnificent temple, which he personally founded after giving up his company and business life in Sweden. The maritime industry had been his trade, inherited from his father and grandfather before him. Initially he had been an extremely adept businessman and manager, diligent and reverent, not the prototypical spoiled rich man's son. Company's profits actually increased markedly under his watch. Unfortunately, the work itself did not engage. It gave him no satisfaction whatsoever, for although fiscally triumphant, he felt vacant. Near the end, he spent more time gazing out at the Norrström river flow by his sprawling Stockholm office than applying himself to their efforts. He wished not to be a detriment to the company of his father and forefathers, as he respected them, nor did he want to dishonor his own yearning. And so, he departed, despite facing heated backlash for his decision.

After vanishing for five years in Lhasa in Tibet, during which time his father temporarily disowned him, he eventually drifted to Ibiza. A special place for realizing dreams, he had heard. The guru had plenty wealth saved, as he never cared for material things. And he was not a drinker or partaker of drugs, oft the downfall of the young and wealthy. He and his father did occasionally speak now, as he had retired and lived comfortably in Uppsala.

The guru suggested to John, as they paused by pastel clumps of wild thyme flowers, that he should consider spending time here at the temple. This life might suit a man like him. Several of his yogis peeked over, then quickly looked away.

"It doesn't look like I would fit in."

"Don't let your outfit dissuade you. We all wore Western shorts and shirts at one time."

"It doesn't," John said. "But my gender does."

His eyes widened in surprise, and he then stroked his soft blond beard as his countenance relaxed in contemplation. "Most of my yogis are women. That is for sure."

"It seems more than most."

"We are open to all who wish to journey."

"Are you?"

"Women are more introspective, and far more interested in channeling divine energies than men these days."

"Interesting."

"Women are the future gurus."

"Fascinating," John said. "Now, much time has passed since my university studies. But if I recall, to be initiated into the upper levels of teachings in Vajrayana Buddhism, one must train with their guru."

"That is true."

"The esoteric teachings, they term them."

Erik—or Baba Bir Bahadur, if you will—smiled ever so slightly, with a droll aspect. A clever man, he anticipated John's trajectory.

"Now if I recall, and again, I confess it has been a while, but many of these upper level teachings are sexual in nature."

The guru remained quiet, his startlingly long fingers stroking his beard.

"Our goal is enlightenment, John. We use rituals, meditation, visualization, and everything needed to attain our goal. Sexual teachings as well."

His voice was measured.

"These are not my inventions, John, as you well know. They are reaped from the rich history of our Buddhist form."

"No doubt," John said. "And you must be quite the busybody, teaching these ancient lessons here."

The guru smiled, the sides of his eyes crinkling. In fairness, he took his jostling admirably well. Always a good sign.

Sharp snaps pierced the air as several of the nearby yogis clipped the lavender and basil plants.

"I've heard some say this type is so far from Buddhism, it is actually not Buddhism at all. That it's closer to Hinduism and Shaivism, worshipping Shiva."

The guru bowed. Billowy clouds glided across blue realms of the upper sky.

John rubbed his chin, endeavored to speak, and faltered. Another attempt, and again failure. The sense that this guru might possess information he desperately desired had suddenly overwhelmed him. He had suspected this since arrival, but now the need to ask reached a boiling point.

The perceptive guru absorbed his trying emotions.

"What is it you would like to ask?" he tenderly inquired.

"I must ask you, Baba Bir Bahadur..." John exhaled. "Did you ever encounter, in your time here, someone by the name of...Gunther?"

The guru surveyed the shifting clouds. "Many here I have met."

"I'm sure," John said, pushing forward. "But this man was about my age, a German named Gunther Djurgenson. A very knowledgeable man."

"Gunther?" He took a step forward, softly exhaling. "Yes,

yes I do believe I did, now that I recall. Most funny you should ask. A strikingly intelligent man. But this transpired long ago, about five years."

"Yes?"

"German, about your age. Gunther. Visited here early one bright morning."

John's throat tensed. His first substantial lead on his search for Gunther, and instead of experiencing jubilation, it terrified him. Gunther, after all these years, had morphed into an almost mythological figure, a gleaming, alabaster statue on distant display in a grand, Greek-columned hall. It was a detached and less painful way to remember him. Now, the alabaster cracked and he became palpable once again.

Gunther was real.

This epiphany struck sharply, like iced water hurled across his cheeks. He struggled to speak, but then words poured out. "And what did he say? Was he living on the island? Did he seem happy? What did he say?"

The guru observed John with pale, calm eyes. He seemed to be sharing John's anxiety. He looked aside, graciously allowing John time to compose.

"He did not speak much, but I do remember, quite similar to you, that he knew an enormous amount about our Buddhism. Surprising. That morning, I let him wander around."

"What else?"

The guru brightened. "Yes, one thing I do recall."

"Yes?"

"He cherished that view of the northern sea," the guru said, nodding at the faraway water. "And spent a few hours alone by that cliffside meditating. He thanked me profusely afterward, although in truth I did not know what I had offered him to deserve such gratitude. This is what I remember."

"He is a brilliant person, Gunther," John said, despondently. "And as kindhearted as you will ever meet."

The guru nodded, noting John's trembling voice.

"He never came back?"

"I have not seen him again."

John stepped forward and stared out beyond the temple at this distant view of the northernmost coast. A weaving coastline, intense and deserted. But what a stark difference from the populous and cocktail-laden southern coast, where pleasure reigned. Two alternate realms.

So, Gunther had gazed out from right here a mere five years ago. It was likely that he stood on this very spot of earth. John picked up a pale, smooth stone, the emanating heat warming the fate line of his palm. Here formed his first connection with Gunther in fifteen years. The hairs on his forearm came alive, standing erect. What had Gunther been contemplating as he stared out at this exact vista?

"Everything adrift can be found."

His voice startled John. The guru stood directly behind him.

"Do you really believe that?"

"Yes. But one must transform within, first," the guru said. "We are all searchers. All of us. But only if one is truly ready and seeks with a pure heart, can one find."

"Not to sound pessimistic, but those seem like impossible qualifications to achieve."

"Nirvana is never reached in a day."

John was astonished to discover himself so emotionally stirred once again, and although he plumbed, he found no befitting response.

Andre hustled back, chock-full of darkly stained chunks of juniper wood and an assortment of nails and rusted rivets. He grasped three gleaming copper rods, elated about his new stock of raw materials.

They thanked the guru and left, stepping carefully along the moist path.

A voice rang out.

The guru was beckoning John. The yogis in the gardens now paused to observe them, their diaphanous arms relaxing by their sides.

"Remember to consider joining us, John. You are most welcome here."

The yogis appeared to be all smiling with empathy, as if John were undertaking a journey they well knew.

"But no matter what, persist in your journey," the guru continued. 'I would like to see you finally find some measure of peace."

John's throat constricted at the compassionate tone, and he found himself elegantly bowing.

Back in van, they coasted down the hills without use of the accelerator, a method Andre had mastered to conserve fuel.

"What was that all about back there?" Andre said.

"Our guru is undoubtably an insightful man."

The vehicle slowed around a sharp turn, producing a horrific grating sound. These brakes begged for a bare investment in new pads.

"Many of my best materials come from up here. He owns the properties, but unlike others, who forbid you, his generosity and politeness never wanes."

John's breathing had still not steadied, as his initial discovery about Gunther left him deeply rattled.

"A fascinating person," John said. "Surrendered his Stockholm financial empire for this dream."

Andre's collection of new materials sprawled across the back seat.

"Now let us hope you create meaningful works from those."

ELEVEN

he lukewarm shower felt so superbly soft, John ignored the ringing phone. As he grabbed his towel, it sounded once again.

"Where have you been hiding?" A most frenzied voice. "Why aren't you answering?"

"Angela? Is everything okay?"

"I've an amazing guy for you to meet tonight. Bob is from Brooklyn originally. Your hometown." She instantly calmed from whatever bizarre panic wave besieged her. "He's hosting us for a special dinner."

"I'm from Manhattan." He balanced the phone on his shoulder while toweling off. "So, you want us to go see this Bob character?"

"Character! The nicest, most interesting guy. Been on the

island since 1971, so over fifteen years here. Knows the people. Plus, he's another American."

"Is that a good thing?" He continued his toweling. "Look, Angela, as long as you are happy to go, let's do it."

Silence again, and he suspected their connection failed.

"Can you pick me up at eight?" she eventually asked.

"Eight it is."

Angela wore a tight, sleeveless dress, fiery red and stamped with golden peace symbols, more an exoskeleton than garment. She kept in remarkable shape, possessing not an extra ounce of body fat. But never did she mention exercise, and seemed carefree about diet, so how she possibly managed all this remained an enigma.

When she hopped into his car, a vigorous citrus odor from her natural perfume exploded throughout. Anything synthetic she abhorred; tonics of the devil, she exclaimed. They pulled away, with Angela, as usual, spouting directions.

"Let me tell you something, and don't you forget it."

"Do tell."

"Bob is a genuine 1960s hippie who settled on Ibiza. Absolutely everyone adores him."

"That's a high percentage of adoration."

She turned with narrowed eyes. "Look, John, you're lucky for this opportunity, okay? You wanted these special chances to get to know Ibiza. Be grateful. He's the genuine thing."

John had the impression they were off to an interactive museum.

She informed him that Bob had left humble beginnings

in Brooklyn in 1963, when he moved to Los Angeles and then on to San Francisco. And there he was in San Francisco during the heyday of the hippie movement and the Summer of Love, relishing every moment of it. He eventually employed his Brooklyn wiles to start a designer denim jacket business, with all goods assembled in Southeast Asia. He was one of the first to do that. He amassed a fortune, purchased an estate on Ibiza, and remained here ever since. Much of the late autumn and winter he spent in Vietnam, but the rest of the year he was here, on Ibiza.

"When does he go to the United States?"

She stared at him blankly, as if his question lacked logical foundations. "He renounced his American citizenship. Never been back. After the Vietnam War, he washed his hands of the government and country."

After passing a series of bordissot and alcudia fig farms, the land cleared into dusty fields. She instructed him to pull aside before a ranch-style wooden fence in the middle of nowhere, where she bounced out and swung open a gate. As they pulled in, the tires scratched earth and stones.

They passed dry, open fields with isolated olive trees and clumps of red poppies.

"I imagined his house would be up in the hills, or beside the water."

"He likes the countryside. It's flatter and dryer here."

The smoothly worn tires sprayed clouds of dust into the air, and deep, orange tones streaked the horizon. Darkness was impending.

Something shimmered in the distance, like a dollop of trembling jelly. Gradually, it came into focus: a large, white, Spanish home, traditional, with flat roofs and gardens of colorful flowers exploding before it.

They parked beside a few other cars, all in the costly range.

An expansive terrace fronted the home, lined with dining tables and a series of grills. High beams crossed overhead, with purple and pink Rockrose flowers draped across. An enormous crowd could be hosted here.

Yet most impressive, which he had not immediately noticed, was what lay beyond the home. An immense vineyard, with darkened vines spanning as far as the eye could see.

"Do me a favor, John." Her fingernails dug into his shoulder. "Be nice."

"Now, what is that supposed to mean?"

She removed her glasses. The slight pouchy skin under each eye shined from some seed oil.

"You are both New Yorkers, both well-educated, so do not get snappy with him. He occasionally does that, I admit."

"Oh? I thought everyone adores him and he is so genuine."

"They do. He is. I just don't want the two of you snapping at each other."

"Of course not," John said. "But why deprive him of that essential pleasure?"

A middle-aged Asian woman wearing a tiny green dress greeted Angela with a hug. Lano, Bob's wife. As she guided them inside, she engaged them in small talk. Yet, something seemed a bit off. She produced soothing sounds that merged exquisitely with the rhythm of talk, giving the full impression of an ongoing conversation, but she had not spoken a single intelligible word. Just hums and chirps. A remarkable display.

A collection of oversized black-and-white photographs from the 1960s, images of San Francisco hills and billboarded protests, dominated the hallway. Poor design choice, as they were too large to appreciate in the confined space.

A grand, spacious area followed, serving as both dining

room and living room. It was replete with crammed bookshelves and more photographs. Glass panels faced the back, where outdoor tables and chairs awaited impressed guests on a patio.

And beyond it all sprawled the mighty vineyard, quite a sight to behold. Silhouettes of vines extended under the waning sun.

A balding man, his brown beard speckled with gray, strode into the room, looking about as if he were entering a cheering colosseum. He was on the shorter side, but thick, with a low, powerful center of gravity. He wore a pair of rounded glasses. One could feel his presence instantly, that much was undeniable. It felt as if he were stalking something, or searching for something to stalk.

He embraced Angela and, turning to John, unabashedly surveyed him.

"Angela told me so much about you."

"Well, I assure you it's untrue."

"The good or the bad?"

"There was good?"

Bob laughed hysterically, hands clapping together, and asked them over to the couches.

"Some superb local wine, John?"

Bob did not ask Angela if she wanted to partake. Come to think of it, he had not yet seen Angela consume a drop of alcohol.

Lano effortlessly guided in another couple. A well-dressed, middle-aged couple, bland as could be. They introduced themselves as Cody and Eliza from Wales.

Bob doled out the glasses of wine, sharply twisting the bottle after each pour.

"Did he happen to offer you the local vintage?" Cody

whispered to John. For some reason, his lower lip trembled, as he appeared on the verge of a laughing fit. He looked the fool.

"Why do you ask?"

He cleared his throat in a theatrical manner.

"So, tell us John, how do you find the wine?" he announced.

Everyone fell silent.

Bob paused, blinking behind his round lenses. Lano stood with her hand resting atop his shoulder; together, they appeared even shorter than when viewed individually. Cody smiled expectantly with Eliza, and Angela's expression stood out, as it burned with apprehension.

It took not a second to connect everything—partially due to the young and feeble taste of the wine, and partially due to the inordinate interest put on his opinion of said vintage. Might as well get this Bob feeling good.

"Superb," John said. "Only a master vintner could create a wine on this esteemed level."

Bob cackled, pointing at Cody to signal his victory on what was likely a prolonged debate, and everyone rejoiced with cheery laughter.

"Excellent answer John, excellent answer," Bob said. "We should get along quite well."

Bob explained he chose this wine from a prized vintage of three years ago. Downstairs a cellar housed fourteen consecutive years of his wines. He began naively, producing what his wife benevolently termed "pee-pee," but advanced over the years to what they currently sipped. Clearly he took pride in his wines, so John made a note to only compliment them. However, considering that the present "prized" vintage tasted like alcoholic grape juice, the lowly production from years ago probably did befit Lano's urination categorization.

At dinner, Bob sat majestically at the head of the lengthy

countryside table, with Angela next to him and John beside her. Across sat Cody and Eliza. Lano sat beside John, as she repeatedly darted from chair to kitchen to serve. A bit surprising, with this grand home, that no staff helped her in kitchen or house.

The food tasted splendid; they sampled freshly fried vegetable spring rolls and bowls of spicy salmon soup with pineapple and kale.

Through Bob and Angela's conversation, it seemed they might have a common friend in California. He could not listen properly, as for some reason they leaned in on each other and spoke in troublingly hushed tones. But had these two been acquainted outside of Ibiza? Eventually, Bob turned his attention toward John.

"Enjoying the meal, John?"

"Superb soup."

Bob sniffed contentedly. "I'm a pescatarian. Raising confined animals and then slaughtering them is inhumane, but I struggle surviving only on Brussels sprouts and bok choy. I discovered a nice compromise." He slurped his soup so fiercely that everyone, except Lano, cringed. "So, what do you think of Ibiza so far, John?"

An excellent question. In truth, John had never encountered, or even envisioned, any place remotely like this. How could he have?

"Incomparable landscapes. And I'm definitely discovering some, how shall I say this...*unique* people here."

Bob squeezed Angela's hand, exchanging triumphant smiles, as they appeared "in" on something. Cody and Eliza dutifully laughed along, about the only thing they seemed versed at doing. They served simply as filler for the evening.

"Now, if you really want to witness something, John, you

must attend my end-of-summer harvest party," he said, winking at Angela.

"Absolutely. The best party on the island. Only residents of Ibiza are invited."

Lano filled everyone's wine glasses again, save Angela's.

"Tell me, John, are you still an American citizen?" Bob removed his spectacles, revealing miniature, darting eyes. Pouches resided beneath them.

"Of course."

"That's not an 'of course,' John. I'm not."

"I see."

Bob recklessly flicked his spectacles onto the table.

"You are not required to stick with something when you don't believe in it anymore, John."

Although a self-contained statement, it beckoned for a response. Bob was already getting feisty and fishing for opinions to combat.

"Well, I am no nationalist. But I've always thought of country like family: it has its faults, but you must stand by it, and hopefully bring about some change. Not just abandon it."

"And have you?"

"Have I what?"

"Brought about this change?"

"No."

Bob sighed. "Good honest answer, John. That candor says something fine about your character. Most mumble some self-defensive rubbish when answering that question."

"So you ask this question often?"

Bob scoffed embarrassedly and returned his spectacles to his nose.

John stroked his chin. "Sadly, achieving that change escapes me."

"I understand. Nor do most ever achieve that, so please don't take it too personally."

Angela began conversing with Cody and Eliza so Bob could focus on John. Impeccable orchestration.

"Managing the basics of your own life is difficult enough," Bob said, laughing. "But in the sixties, we endeavored to enact change through a passionate movement. Real determination. We did not passively accept government and their decisions."

John nodded. Bob was rolling, so there was no reason to interfere.

"The true hippie movement was the outside expression of an internal desire for substantial change to a faulty system."

"Positive results came from that."

The comment pleased Bob. "I do hope so. I really do. And thank you for saying that, it means a lot to me, John. We protested with all we had, and we certainly changed people's view of war after that."

"An amazing effort."

Bob exhaled, growing somber, and appeared more youthful, like a dismayed child. "But sadly, the government ultimately did not change."

"To some degree, surely?"

"On the long term, I must admit, no. War is profitable, John. When something is profitable, it is impossible to exterminate. Simply consider drugs or prostitution over history."

Angela continued to work Cody and Elizabeth. She remained animated in exchanges with the couple, affording both lavish attention, while simultaneously, she captured each word Bob and John exchanged.

"So the question for you, John, is when will you stop jabbing on about it and actually go and make that difference?"

"A superb question."

"We are both from the same town, John. And I'll tell you, one of life's most challenging tasks is to make a lasting difference."

"Are you satisfied with your choice to come live here?"

Bob appeared surprised. "Certainly. I have met a great many people here." He perused the room with a distant smile, undoubtedly recalling grand parties of the past. "And I still spend time in Vietnam, as well."

"Still have your denim jacket business from the old days?"

"Absolutely! You've seen my jackets in photos of red-carpet Hollywood premiers. I sell a single jacket for over one thousand dollars," he said shaking his head, as if the purchasers suffered from insanity. "My masterpiece of marketing."

Angela seamlessly joined in. "Bob gifted me one of his jackets ten years ago. With the good old Hollywood sign on it." Bob glowed as she squeezed his hand.

"I'm still waiting for mine," Cody said.

"You don't deserve one," Bob said, roaring. Everyone joined the laugh, even John, as people tend to do in parties when the host jokes, although John had no idea of what the joke meant. He suspected no one did.

"Come, let us go sit outside in the back."

The night was warm, and the cadence of cicadas was emerging from the vineyard's depths. Bob sat in a wicker chair facing the vines, with Cody instantly sitting on one side, and then John on his other. Inside, the three women explored Lano's shipment of clothing that had arrived from Asia the previous day.

Bob poured wine without inquiring if they desired any, filling glasses markedly higher than during dinner. A bit splashed out of John's glass. He surveyed his fields as a lord surveys his estate.

"Cody spent time in Liverpool in his teens. Home of The

Beatles, my all-time favorite band. But he never even met one of them."

"True. But I visited all the landmarks, be sure."

Bob turned to Cody. "Cody, if I spent time there back then, I would be best friends with Paul and John, and I would be camping out on strawberry fields." He swirled his wine, staring at the revolving darkness. "Cody is also anti-war."

Cody nodded. "War is a bloody business."

"And you, John? How do you feel about war?" Bob asked.

An anemic question if considered, exceedingly wide in interpretation and scope. But dear Bob was feisty again, and in the process of vetting John for his deepest beliefs. This is why John was lured outside. His chief interrogator reclined comfortably within the bowels of his throne, with his minion poised beside him.

"What can I say? War is something best avoided at all costs."

Bob sipped his wine. "So you are saying there are exceptions, when war is okay?"

"I would not phrase it that way. War is never okay."

Bob nodded, maintaining his gaze on the vineyard. His features were indiscernible in the gloom.

"But I do think in certain instances, it is warranted."

Bob roused, back straightening. "Such as?"

"Well, let us see. If your country is invaded by foreign armies and is being overrun, I do believe it is necessary to fight these invaders off. Now that would be considered a war, and it would be warranted."

"Come on, John," Bob said. "There is always another way."

"In my example?"

"Of course."

"Such as?"

"Diplomacy."

"Diplomacy? In the example, the country has already been invaded and is in the process of being leveled."

Bob scoffed. "So? You can still negotiate."

John laughed heartily, perhaps slightly condescendingly. Bob veered toward him, clearly unaccustomed to this tone.

"That sounds lovely in theory," John said. "But to negotiate, one needs some position of strength to be taken seriously. And negotiations take time. So I fail to see what position of strength you will be in if your country is in the process of being ransacked, and you don't even fight back. And you certainly do not have the time."

Bob patted John's shoulder. "I've told you, John, war is a profitable business. As long as something is profitable, it is nearly impossible to rid of."

He was beginning to find Bob annoying.

Outgoing and certainly hospitable, Bob had offered a splendid meal, and they drank his laced grape juice liberally. But John was irritated. Perhaps Bob's refusal to acknowledge the complexity of certain situations vexed him. His phraseology relied too heavily on soundbites that would undoubtedly garner general approval, but lacked intricacy or subtlety. This lamentable development had likely evolved over his later years while pleasing his endless guests.

"As per your theory, using inordinately cheap labor is also profitable, and thus, like war, it is hard to exterminate as well," John said, placing his glass onto a coffee table.

Bob was silent.

"So your theory is sound," John continued.

Bob's body shuddered, and he gulped his wine to quell the tremors. Angela peeked out of the house.

"You do make your denim jackets in Vietnam, do you not?"

"They do."

"And those factories are paying the workers less than three cents an hour."

Cody leaned forward, squeezing the chair's arms. The breezy attitude he had carried throughout the evening vanished, and his eyelids stretched in alarm. Now he finally had a purpose besides serving as a laugh track.

"Come off it, John. We all know there's not much in those countries. At least he offers them something." He glanced nervously at Bob to gauge his performance.

"We are talking about exploitation of labor," John said. "And if you are making thousands of dollars on a jacket that someone gets a few cents to sew, that is exploitation. You could pay far more reasonable wages, and still make an enormous profit." John chose to preemptively prune justification attempts. "And this is a niche item. Not in general competition with similar products where price needs to be restricted to compete in the market."

Cody's features contorted and his neck changed to a darker hue, but he found no retort. Not a beacon of debating skills, certainly. He anxiously checked Bob, who remained silent throughout. He appeared asleep, deep in the shadows of his chair.

Silence reigned, save for the cicadas.

"You worked the financial sector—hedge funds, didn't you, John?" Bob asked, almost whispering. His face was obscured, but his pale hands and wine glass glowed in the light.

"I did."

"The investors in hedge funds are almost entirely the top one percent. That is correct?"

"It is."

"So you spent all your time making the already very rich, richer. Did you not?"

"When I did my job right, yes. I would say that is a fair statement."

Angela stood outside now, directly behind them.

"And did that serve as a commendable use of your time and intelligence?"

"Meaning what?" John said, exhaling.

"Well, a man of your talents could create things that help society. Instead, you dedicated your mind and precious time to ensuring a few more generations of the exorbitantly rich would never need to work. And that their kids would end up snorting cocaine in bathrooms," Bob said. "And you ruined yourself. Drained yourself of all inspiration in life." Bob's voice remained sedate, but firm. "Am I correct, John?"

Bob's acumen deserved admiration. Here was a skillful debater. He sveltely shifted the discussion from his own insidious business onto John's life, making searing points about John that demanded instant responses in order to salvage his dignity, responses Bob would rely on to deflect any further talk about malevolent jean jackets.

"Sadly, I agree with that, Bob. But do remember, I am not pretending otherwise. Thus, I have abandoned that part of my life." He stepped forward, scanning the vineyard. "Now, I do not know if you are pretending your business is legitimate."

No response from behind him. John proceeded, as he could not help it, although he probably should not have.

"But we certainly damaged Vietnam in the war that you so strenuously protested and renounced your citizenship for. And I agree with you that the damage from that war was devastating."

Bob remained buried in darkness.

"So I cannot fathom why you continue to despoil that very same country by exploiting those who survived it."

A cutting statement, admittedly designed to maim.

John closed his eyes. Statements of this nature have repercussions. Newton's third law of motion applied here, where for every action there will be an equal and opposite reaction.

Angela stepped forward with a contrived nonchalance that, although quite well-performed, was comical to witness. She inquired how everyone fared on this most pleasant of evenings. Bob simply ignored her, delicately placing his wine glass onto the table. He asked if John would be so good as to accompany him into the vineyard to survey his lovely grapes.

The vines stood in lengthy rows, with wooden supporting posts planted every yard. Soft moonlight silhouetted these vines into silky, dark columns, much like endless soldiers restlessly awaiting battle. Bob stepped erratically, breathing heavily, earth and rocks crunching under his thick sandals. His bloated big toes startled, but the corresponding digits appeared vestigial. John followed closely. They continued deep into the vineyard, inhaling cool night air.

Bob halted.

"Are you trying to humiliate me, John?" He still faced forward, back to John.

"That was not my original intention."

"So what the hell are you doing?"

He turned, sweat beads glistened along his deeply creased forehead. His fingers, uncannily resembling root vegetables, gripped his spectacles. This did not bode well.

"Look, Bob, you are the one discussing our lives. You placed me under the microscope. And I admit, you are an acute observer.

"Yes, I am."

"I admire that about you, and I conceded your points. But then I simply turned the microscope to you, and suddenly," John said, staring directly at Bob, "you become a sniveling little mess."

Bob swung his fist at John's jawline, but his flamboyant movements telegraphed this poorly thrown punch. John dodged it.

"I thought you genuine 1960s hippies don't believe in violence?"

Bob swung again, with identical results. He grunted and charged without a plan. They crashed into the vines. On a positive note, some of next year's inevitably awful vintage collapsed with them. Bob was burly, but unskilled, and John pinned him down. He cussed unintelligibly, something about unreliable New York subways and bad tuna, and he squirmed, but could not break free.

Eventually, John released Bob's quivering arms, backing off a few steps. Besides cicadas, only silence.

Bob gradually stood, wiping himself off. He took his time, slapping forearms and knees.

"Am I clean?" he asked, displaying his back.

John brushed reddish earth from Bob's shirt. "Looks passable."

"You're okay, also."

"Good to know."

"We don't want them knowing how well we behave."

Bob began walking, then waited for John, placing his hand on John's shoulder. A windless night.

"Just because we are bad in some parts of our life, doesn't mean we can't be good people, does it John?"

A surprising contriteness mellowed his voice.

"A difficult question to answer."

"Meaning what?"

"A question like that contains many elements."

"Can you just answer the damned question?"

John laughed. "Well, not to oversimplify, but if one is doing something gravely harmful and refuses to ever change it, then that likely corrupts fully," John said. "Sure, one can perform mitigating acts in the meantime, but one *is* overall a 'bad person,' as you say, in that scenario. The essential penitent heart is lacking."

"Meaning?"

"A vital element of penitence is the actual turning away from the wrongdoing."

"Interesting point, John," Bob said. "I do like the way you think. Not quaking in your boots at having an opinion, other than stating everything is subjective and relative. Don't see much of that, anymore." Bob cradled a clump of the pinot grapes in his palm, the yeast on the skins glowing in the silvery light. "Now it's just people kissing my ass, saying only things they believe I will agree with."

"Perhaps they fear you might take a swing at them?"

Bob's left eye squinted behind the round lense. For a moment it seemed Bob might charge in for round two, but he began laughing.John joined in.

"Bob, I have a question for you."

"Please."

"In all your events on Ibiza, have you ever come across someone named Gunther Djurgenson?"

"Doesn't ring a bell."

"A German guy. Educated. About my age."

"Many come to my parties." Bob peered at him. "Why?"

"Don't worry. An old friend."

Bob walked for a bit. "You'll find whatever you want on Ibiza, John."

"And how about what I need?"

He wore an admiring smirk. "Let's get back."

Everyone was pacing around the wicker chairs on the back terrace. Angela bounded forward upon spotting them, striving to feign a carefree demeanor.

"You gentlemen enjoy a nice stroll in the grapes?" She scanned their tarnished clothes, her left eyebrow rising, but prudently withheld comment.

Bob looked at John affectionately, patting him on the shoulder. "Absolutely we did. We discussed how difficult it is to do right in this world, no matter what your original intentions may be."

"That," John said, "I could not agree with more."

Cody and Elizabeth laughed on cue, although no one told a joke.

Everyone sat back down, and talk lightened instantly. A pleasant time ensued for the next hours. Bob kept the conversation flowing; he touched on wildly variant topics from Spain's emerging parliamentary monarchy to the lengthy gestation periods of elephants. In entertainment mode, he displayed flawless skills. Before they departed at fifteen-past-two, Bob reiterated to Angela, his forefinger stabbing the night air, that he expected John at his harvest party in September, and absolutely no excuses would suffice.

As they drove away, Angela's expression transformed from gaiety into somberness.

"Enjoy yourself?" John asked, bracing for the forthcoming outburst.

She whirled toward him. "What happened between you and Bob?" she demanded.

"What do you mean?"

"Don't act stupid."

"Maybe it's not an act."

"What happened?"

John suppressed a smile. "We are fine. Discussions get heated."

"I told you to behave yourself," she pleaded, straining outstretched fingers out the window toward the night sky. "I should have known better."

"He made good points, and I believe I did as well. People only get distressed when your points are on the mark."

"I had that feeling you two would clash."

John turned onto the main road, a deserted, two-lane street stretching through sleeping peach orchards.

"Good can come from clashing."

Angela mumbled sourly, staring out her window. The sweet smell of peaches drifted into the car.

"Hey, he still wants me at his harvest party, does he not?"

"That's true," she said, lurching up. "He did say that, didn't he?"

"Yes, he did."

"He was adamant about that."

"See?"

"Maybe he does like you after all," she said, enlivened.

"Maybe."

"Yes, I believe he does."

"Excellent."

"Bob has always been a forgiving man, John." Her voice quavered, and he could not prevent glancing over. Her warped features appeared on the verge of a tearful breakdown. "A very, very forgiving man."

A curiously specific description moored to absolutely nothing they had discussed. All quite bizarre.

"Forgiving?"

"Yes."

He best just agree. "I am sure he is."

"And his glorious harvest party! A place for making memories." Her voice became melodious. "Oh yes, John, such a marvelous occasion awaits us."

TWELVE

In Cala Llonga, the quaint port due west of Siesta, one can find a medium-sized hotel, a tiny Spanish tapas restaurant, and a bar and night club with live shows a block from the beach. The rudimentary posters for this bar, stapled on a few posts, advertised an "out of this world" song and dance routine for free that very afternoon.

Shows took place seven nights a week, at nine and midnight. Although it was only ten-to-twelve in the afternoon, the stage rehearsal was about to begin, as high season was imminent. The stage sat beneath an overhang, with tabled seating entirely outdoors. No indoor area except for a straight, stool-free bar to the left. Of the thirty tables, a single one was occupied. A tall man with sandy blond hair, mahogany pipe in hand, comfortably dozed in the back.

John ordered a drink from the portly bartendress. She could not have been more than twenty-one; despite her considerable mass, she moved with alarming rapidity, even harshness, as she prepared his drink. She appeared in the process of slaughtering heathens on the battlefield rather than readying a gin and tonic. John did not amuse her in the least, as she snatched his money without ever establishing eye contact.

The music began. A one-minute montage of rock and pop songs from the sixties, seventies, and early eighties. When it abruptly halted, the curtains parted. Two extremely tall women, dressed in skirts and bras, stood motionless, staring into the yonder. Black top hats sat upon their heads.

With a crack, the music restarted and they launched into frenzied dancing. They moved remarkably well to the first few songs, elbows swinging and legs high-kicking, wearing unwavering smiles throughout. How they simultaneously breathed so steadily while moving so frenetically was inexplicable.

It took John a bit of time, and a few chin scratches, to realize our dancers were not women after all, but men. A bit too thick in the neck. Between each song they changed outfits in seconds, directly in front of the audience, and then launched on a new skit-and-dance routine.

After another song, the curtains shut for intermission. In the audience, the man with the pipe roused with a start and clapped.

The charming bartender was now stomping across the floor, honing in on this man's table. She snatched his gin and tonic and raised it high above him, dumping its contents atop his hair, her lion's head tattoo roaring directly over his chiseled skull as she poured. Ice cubes cracked and shattered on the table's surface. He neither glanced at her nor flinched during this entire pouring process. She then strode contentedly back to the bar.

As liquid cascaded over his fine, aristocratic features, he remained markedly steadfast. When the flow reduced to a trickle, he began leisurely stuffing his pipe. Upon spotting John's confounded stare, the left corner of his mouth upturned a tad in wry amusement.

He raised his barren glass from the table and elegantly saluted.

Astoundingly, this man did not seem the least bit ruffled. Rather, he seemed quite at peace.

John was admittedly intrigued, as one does not witness such events on a daily basis. He strolled over, and the man offered him a seat with a smooth wave of his hand. A slice of lime nested in his soggy hair.

"Please, old chap, do take a seat."

The last of the tonic dripped down his cheeks. He continued stuffing his pipe.

"John is my name. John Balkus. From the States."

"Remarkable," declaimed the man in a jovial voice. "Graham. Graham Fogg. So you are from across the pond. Lovely to hear so. I'm a London chap myself."

He had a solid, handsome face, but red veins latticed his eyes and his white skin wrinkled beneath these eyes. Exhaustion came to mind. Although likely around forty, his affect was far older. Certainly, he had not tanned much for one on Ibiza.

"May I offer you a napkin?"

Graham observed it with curiosity, as if handed an ancient parchment. He smiled as he gingerly wiped himself. "Yes, thank you dearly, old sport. I almost forgot my new chapeau comprised a gin and tonic." He chuckled. "Hopefully that won't make the latest fashion pages. And what brings an esteemed chap like yourself to our peaceful cove?"

"You live here?"

He pointed to a two-story apartment building across the street. "We live there, top floor."

"We?"

Graham smiled. "Yes, the plural first-person usage was categorically correct. That delicately delightful being behind the bar, Samantha, and I reside there."

Things began to make some sense.

"So you've made her unhappy?"

"Incorrect, old chap," Graham said, with a wave of his index finger. The slice of lime plopped into a fizzy puddle on the table, bubbles flaring. "She was born unhappy. A limited mind, and a rather unsavory personality, and thus happiness is not readily available to her."

"I see."

"Undoubtedly, my failure to seek gainful employment and contribute to the rent and bills does not aid her on her quest for bliss. But such it is."

"Favorable though, that Samantha happens to work behind a bar."

Graham's eyes sparkled. "That it is, old boy. Awfully clever of you to notice. Awfully clever. She occasionally relieves the bar of an extraneous bottle of gin, or if they are burdened with excessive vodka, she assuages their unfortunate overload. Quite talented at it, she is." At the bar, Samantha chopped lemons on a wooden board with emphatic strikes. "She's not very old, only about twenty-three or four, I would guess, and I don't suspect she has ever read an entire book, but she does toil awfully hard back there. Says she can straighten me out, and eventually get me on the straight and narrow. I let her believe so," he said with a wink. "Keeps her inspired. She'll probably be off when the summer is over either way."

"Off?"

Graham extracted a flask from inside his crinkled white dress shirt. "I'm a photographer by trade. Top shelf magazines for a time: *Country Life, Cosmopolitan* and the such. Even hung a few solo shows in London, and all that nonsense."

"Congratulations to you."

Graham peered up at John with youthful, perk eyebrows aloft, then turned aside with flushing embarrassment.

"So you are still at it, I assume?"

"Not anymore. Not anymore." He held the flask at arm's length, squinting as he studied it. "The drink, as many sadly know, can be quite seducing."

"I see."

"My old agent Nigel, poor chap, still attempts to reach me on occasion. A most persistent little fellow. Haven't answered him in years. Can't endure the badgering."

He offered the flask to John. John's initial instinct was to refuse, as sharing a flask and its unknown contents did not tempt. But Graham passed it over with a spirit of genuine sharing. Inscribed on the front of the silver flask were the words "Dominus Illuminatio Mea." The coat of arms of the University of Oxford was below.

"The Lord is my Light."

Graham smiled with delight at John's translating talents. "Sit mihi deus dirigat in omnibus," he said, nodding with a wink.

John turned the flask's base upwards. The biting impact of straight gin tormented his tongue, and his eyes expanded.

The music cracked and the curtains parted, and part two of the cabaret show was underway. The dancers pranced and contorted without sweating a drop. Physical comedy seamlessly mixed in. An extraordinary show, really. Graham watched with a distant but admiring smile, all the while pulling from his beloved flask.

When the show ended, he steadily clapped. The dancers, whose concluding outfit consisted of bikinis and hats stacked with bananas and mangos, bowed as if a full house were hurling roses. They blew kisses into empty seats.

Hopping off stage, they placed their produce-ladened hats down on Graham's table and joined them. The cloyingly sweet scent of overripe fruits overwhelmed. Graham offered cigarettes all around.

"Now that was an exhausting bit," the first performer said. He introduced himself as Robert while exhaling smoke through his nostrils. He combed through his reddish-brown hair with slender fingers, a tad of gray revealing itself at the roots.

"You better bloody believe it," the second performer said, pulling from his cigarette. Todd, or "the Toddster," was his name.

Samantha materialized, wielding a tray of four gin and tonics. Robert and Todd stood and kissed her cheeks, kisses which she affectionately returned. She refused, of course, to acknowledge John or Graham as she placed drinks around the table. One drink she carefully kept separate from the others, and positioned said glass right before Graham.

Graham Fogg was now charged up in high spirits with company and drinks aplenty.

"This is my very good friend, John," he announced. "He came all the way over from the States just to see us."

Robert looked over in wonder. "New York, I hope? I would love to get my act over there in the future."

"*Our* act, not just yours, you bloody rag," Todd added.

"Do tell us, lovely John," Robert said whimsically. "We have never performed outside of Ibiza. How do you think our act would go over in New York?"

John had discreetly switched the drink intended for Graham

with his own. He sampled, and nearly spat it out across the table. Unadulterated gin. Samantha, however agitated with Graham's drinking she claimed to be, apparently capitulated and catered to his desires. "Enabling," was the term. Doing so was indubitably her tried-and-true technique to prevent him from straying too far.

"I don't see why you wouldn't be successful," John said, as they thirstily absorbed his words. "In New York, live theater rules. But competition is ferocious, so be prepared."

Robert clapped his hands together in delight. "See? John confirmed it. We need to just keep at it, and the big time is next."

"You both deserve only the finest," Graham said, his drink raised.

"Last Saturday, we finally made the big decision," Robert announced, focusing on John.

"What decision is that?"

"After ten years, we have finally decided..." he said, pausing while Todd imitated a drum roll, "...that we will take our act abroad and on tour. We leave this autumn."

Todd was beaming, struggling to hold back tears.

"So, what do you think?" Robert asked.

"Well, I suppose it is a grand idea."

Robert and Todd embraced.

"And do you think we will make it?"

Now, John had absolutely no idea whether they could succeed, or even why they bothered asking him. What did he know? But hope shown radiantly on Robert's and the Toddster's countenances, and he dared not extinguish that most precious thing.

"I'm no expert," John said, observing the two eager faces. "But I do not see why not."

Cheers and hoorays followed. Todd and Robert slapped hands together, and all four drank to the glorious future of the "Cabaret Now and Mostly Forever Act," as Graham officially named it. He promised T-shirts emblazoned with this title to celebrate this seminal moment. They concurred that the act would always center on Ibiza, but incorporate winter tours of Paris and New York—and, Graham added, after another fallen drink, that even the Far East would be explored.

Graham raised his glass to salute each new idea, and he even volunteered to manage their troupe if need be. When Robert inquired what experience he had in such things, Graham conceded that he had absolutely none, but his passion for their act would compensate for his dearth of experience. This earned perhaps the most emotional salute, with eyes moistening. It was even decided that John would oversee all American operations.

Eventually, as the drinks ran dry and Graham's arm fatigued from toasting, Robert and Todd hugged John, thanking him for his belief, and waved to Graham. They bounded backstage in high spirits. At nine that night, their show would debut.

Graham watched them depart with a distraught expression.

"Can't wait to see how they will be received abroad," John said. "You have to give them credit for deciding to risk it."

Graham gently smiled. "Nice enough chaps they are," he said. "Samantha absolutely adores them. Work themselves to the bone during high season, and never lose their good humor or hope." He stared at the wilted lime peel in his empty glass. "Poor old Robert."

John turned. "What's the problem with Robert?"

"Robert? Every summer it's the same."

"What's that?"

"Ends up dating some tourist. Usually some married guy.

Then comes the fights, hard drinking, and Robert shedding tears. Got a bit violent last year, poor old Robert. Broken jaw."

"Broken jaw? And Todd?"

"Todd? Lovely hearted. Would help anyone in need. A proclivity for flings as well, God bless him."

John wanted to keep things positive. "Well, nonetheless, it is inspiring they finally got organized this year and will tour."

Graham smiled wistfully.

"What?"

He began shaking his head.

"What is it?" John insisted.

He settled back in his chair. "Each year, they announce their same grand plans to tour the world. Say they are finally ready. Last year some older chap from Brussels with quite the bushy beard heard about it all."

John recalled their exhilaration, their zeal.

"But too much drama and drink, and they are left with naught every winter. It's been like this for the last eight or nine years."

So much for the big launch.

"That's disheartening to hear."

"Time passes swiftly, and then come the wrinkles and regrets. The poor chaps never quite got their act together to expand."

The gray backstage door was shut. The faintest whiff of decaying fruits remained.

Graham observed John as if for the first time. "By the way, what are you doing in these parts?"

"Living out here for a while, in Siesta around the bend."

"Lovely little place, Siesta is," Graham said. "I used to work out of London. Became a bit dispirited, if you want the truth. Eventually sailed away. The direction things were headed scared the soot out of me."

"Direction things were headed?"

"Couldn't stomach it. The fall of individuality. But fortunately, out here on fair Ibiza, it's a more pleasant game."

"What direction are things headed?"

"Consolidation old sport, consolidation."

"Meaning what?"

Graham glanced at Samantha's broad back. "Would it be uncivil to ask you to attempt to procure a few more libations, to ease the afternoon through? I fear my request would not be magnanimously received."

John waited for a time as Samantha furiously polished glasses. He released a few guttural sounds, but to no avail. Finally, a rudimentary "excuse me" prompted her to veer. A most intimidating sight.

"Two gin and tonics."

She failed to move. "For?"

"Sorry?"

"For?"

"For me."

"Now you're drinking two?"

"Well, no, actually."

She did not budge, and John relented.

"Well, one for me, one for Graham." He recovered some nerve. "So does this establishment require customers to explain who consumes their purchases?"

Her molars ground to powder. "That sod drinks too damned much." The glass in her hand trembled under pressure. "You are drowning him before it's even one-thirty in the afternoon."

"I see."

"I've enough problems with him."

John stroked his chin, feeling brash. "But did you not just serve him a glass of pure gin? Odd behavior for someone desiring to cure drinking maladies."

Her lower jaw dropped as if cables snapped. For the briefest moment she appeared terrified, pure animal fear. But she recovered awfully rapidly, her eyes darkening.

"I'm the one who needs to live and deal with that sod, not you. Remember that."

Tough statement to argue with. John took the single cup and returned to the table, handing it to Graham.

"Not drinking anything yourself, old stick?"

"Just taking a breather."

Graham pretended to believe him and stretched his legs while delicately sipping in full view of Samantha. John dared not venture a glance over to the bar.

"As I was saying," Graham said, "we have a consolidation problem."

"Is there a problem?"

Graham laughed good-naturedly and set about lighting his pipe. He scowled as he puffed at it, the tobacco glowing red and cherry-scented clouds wafting out. "Let's take a look at your country, shall we? Now most of your media, ninety percent, is only owned by around fifty companies. That means all the information your three hundred million Yanks receive is controlled by a mere fifty people."

"I see."

"I dearly hope you do, my old friend," he said, with intensity. "For in the next years, this number will plummet to less than ten companies. And what does that mean?" Graham said, as rings of smoke lingered. "It means seven or eight constipated autocrats will decide what the world believes. So if they want people to believe llamas are contagious disease carriers, people will believe that. If they want people to believe miracles are nonsense, people will believe that. And if they want people to believe that a life of purchasing goods and showing them off to others is the optimal way to live, people will worship that."

A chilling hypothesis.

"The era of governments and countries is finally closing. Supranational organizations are taking over and will manipulate our pliable gray matter on what to believe."

"And what can we do to avoid this?"

Graham drained the remaining drops from his glass. "A superb question. Identifying the problem is an essential step one. But solving it, chap, regrettably that's another game I've yet to master."

A familiar disquietude bedeviled John.

How long had Graham resided on Ibiza? For this Graham would hit it off with Gunther quite well. Yes, he could see that. They could be most marvelous friends. A real possibility existed that Graham had met Gunther at some point during these years.

"Graham, how long have you lived on the island?"

"It must be ten years on."

His sensed his hunch correct.

"Perhaps you met an old friend of mine, by the name of Gunther Djurgenson?"

Graham raised his eyebrows and lowered his pipe, exhaling smoke and words. "Gunther! Lovely chap, lovely."

"So you know him?"

"Certainly. A brilliant sort. We spend time together. Lovely kraut, Gunther is."

So here it was. Finally. The time had come. At times it all seemed mere fantasy, but now, the time had come.

John shifted to his chair's edge, pressing heels into floor. "Well, have you seen him recently?" he said, fumbling. "Will you see him soon?"

"Not seen him in a bit."

"Not in a bit? Did you see him in the last few days?"

"Funny, come to think of it, it's been a while."

"A while?" John asked with growing dread. "How long? A few weeks?"

"It must be a year or so."

His chest tightened in letdown. "Never get exuberant before something is sure," one of the truest of all adages.

Would life not be easier if he had just said Gunther was stopping by that very evening for the grand opening of the Cabaret Now and Mostly Forever Act?

Yet, at least here was someone who actually knew Gunther, who met with Gunther multiple times in friendship. The quest seemed more attainable now. John's fondness for Graham warmed, generated by his connection to his long-lost friend.

"Funny," Graham said. "I've missed him dreadfully. Clever chap. He would drop by here to see me. And always so polite to my latest summer girlfriend."

"Where do you think he went?"

"Went?"

"Yes, where is he?"

"Well, I don't just know," Graham said. "On Ibiza, one never knows where anyone lurks. Still on the island, I suspect. Quite difficult to locate people here. No phones, people shift and drift about."

"I see." A dejected sigh escaped.

Graham, remarkably cool up to this point, suddenly appeared to be wrestling with thorny thoughts, as his lower lip quivered.

"Perhaps he, well, he might have gone...."

"Yes?"

"Perhaps he is somewhere up north. It's quite fascinating up there."

"Fascinating?"

"Yes. Me, I don't journey up there anymore. No sir, not me."

"Why is that?"

"Why?"

"Yes, why?"

"Well…I don't quite know." He steadily exhaled. "The metaphysical, the spiritual. Up there along the coast are some, how shall I phrase this…some quite powerful places. Our blessed world contains holy locations."

"Powerful?"

"Yes, yes."

"What are you talking about?"

He began pulling at his pipe. His pale complexion had become translucent.

"Everything okay?"

"Okay? Yes, yes."

"You seem troubled."

"Do I? No, not in the least, old chap. And you?"

"So you were saying, about Gunther?"

"Was I? Oh yes, so I was. The old mind loses track a bit nowadays."

"So, you were saying?"

He patted his forehead with a yellowing napkin. "Yes, yes. That coastline up north. Told me he's fascinated with exploring that coastline up there. In full disclosure, I myself once went up there, and never will I—"

Graham's name was barked from behind the bar. Samantha motioned him over, viciously swinging her considerable limb.

"What were you saying about up north and Gunther?"

"I must go, old chap," he said. "You best depart, in the interests of your safety and well-being. I'm afraid when she runs short of mental recourse, she relies on her formidable flesh to doll out chastisement. Might even brandish her cherished cat o' nine tails, which I oft face the wrath of, and I must advise eluding that."

Just how much of this last portion had Graham meant in jest? On rare occasions, extremely rare, it is truly better *not* to know, and here John had arrived at one of those occasions. He shook Graham's soft and chilly hand, which felt like squeezing frozen custard.

"A pleasure."

"The pleasure is all mine," Graham said. "Don't be such the stranger. I'm usually here, or up in the apartment across the way. I never stray too far," he said, pausing. "If I did, she might think I'm up to nefarious doings," he added with a wink.

He moved toward the bar with a startling spring in his step.

THIRTEEN

Just before nine in the morning, while John jogged up the final hill toward home after six rugged miles, she swooshed by. Her long strides were a blur, and she halted atop the hill in front of his door, her back facing him. Seconds later, he arrived, audibly stabilizing his breath.

"Heavens, you are the sloth." Diana appeared barely winded.

"Am I?"

"I would say."

"Well, I best toil harder so I can evolve into the tortoise."

She turned and smiled. "Shall we walk a bit?"

They strolled silently through the moist morning air. Aleppo pines lined both sides of the street, and although already hot on the beaches of Ibiza, in the hills it would remain cool for another few hours. John considered speaking, but thought it wise to allow her to direct the path of conversation. He was simply relieved, and quite surprised, to see her once again.

"Perhaps I overreacted a bit the other night," Diana said.

The blue rosemary struggled through cracks in the sidewalk.

"That's fine," John said. "Maybe I didn't break up with my girlfriend in the most prudent way. Too absorbed in my own damned misery."

"I highly doubt that. As you mentioned, you never even got engaged. I'm just a tad sensitive on that topic."

"I understand."

"Do you?"

"Well, not really. It just seemed the proper thing to say."

She laughed. "No reason not to tell you. It's been bloody long enough." She gazed at the azure sea far below. "Humiliating enough also, I can tell you that."

"Oh?"

"I don't see a reason not to tell you."

"Whatever you feel comfortable with."

She exhaled. "Would you like to hear about it?"

"As long as you are comfortable talking about it."

"You are the polite one, aren't you?"

John smiled, abashed.

"So be it. If you absolutely insist," she said with a laugh. Her expression took a radical turn, aspect turning somber. "Two days before my grand wedding, the bloke called it off."

"What?"

"Left me out to dry. Almost fifteen years ago, mind you. I was only twenty-two."

"I'm sorry to hear that."

"All the arrangements were top notch. Dartmouth House in

London. Honeymoon in Saint-Émilion in Bordeaux. A major event in all the society pages."

"But why? Did you know him properly?"

"Unfortunately, no. But our families were well-known. His father was in the House of Lords, a hereditary member. They arranged us becoming a couple, and the wedding, of course."

"I see."

"He was twelve years older than I. Didn't know he had another woman hidden the entire time."

"Sorry to hear that."

"He telephoned me two days before the ceremony, mid-afternoon. Called it off. Call lasted two minutes. Told me I should 'take it in stride.' Said it in quite the dry tone."

Although she spoke composedly, this debacle did not sound at all like something recuperated from readily. Public humiliation scars deeply.

"Huge scandal. All over the papers."

"Astounding."

"And then came the disaster with my friends. *Supposed* friends, more like it."

"That doesn't sound promising."

"They all abandoned me. Abandoned me, not him! These were our dear 'friends in common.' Our society."

"What about the truth?"

"The truth?"

"Did they discover the truth about his behavior?"

She laughed, with a troubling ring of cynicism. "The truth? Sure, John, word got out about his other woman. But this woman was all my fault, supposedly. I'm to blame. I must have done something to drive him to her. I must be 'a bit too quirky,' they said."

"Absurd."

"That's their reality."

John shook his head in dismay.

"And so, I started avoiding public places. 'What a nasty thing happened, you poor girl,' the women would say with sneers. 'How on earth do you endure that type of humiliation with such dignity? So admirable,' was another favorite. They were enjoying it." She paused, staring at the dusty sidewalk. "Eventually, I stopped going out at all."

"Horrific."

"And then came the fleeing."

"Fleeing?"

"Escaped town. Made a run for it. Off to Rome, the Trieste neighborhood, and thankfully I was introduced to the deejaying scene. Then Tangiers. The rest is history."

"So it all worked out for you in the end."

"Is it already the end? That's a bit depressing."

John laughed. "But it did work out for you."

"I suppose one could see it that way."

"The world gained."

"That might be pushing it," she said, smiling with amusement. "But amazing, how naive we really are at that age. The fact that we even survive is a miracle."

"Did you love him?"

She halted, with a bit of rebound, as if crashing off of invisible wall. Beside a klaxon echoing far below, no sounds whatsoever.

"What did you ask?"

John coughed. "Did you love him?

"Love him?"

"Yes."

It's funny."

"What's that?"

"No one has ever asked me that question. Not once."

"Well. I'm asking."

Her brow furrowed. She treated the question deferentially, as her deliberation took time.

"Actually, no," she said at last. Dimples formed on the side of her cheeks as her large eyes brightened. "No, I did not love him."

"I'm glad to hear that."

"As am I. And it is most refreshing to finally say it aloud."

"Feel free to yodel it off the hill."

"As long as you play the alphorn beside me," she said, laughing.

The day's heat was gradually setting in.

"But I confess I never truly trusted a bloke since. Trust was gone."

John cleared his throat. "Well, I think he must have been insane."

"Oh?" she said, turning. "Why do you say that?"

Her golden hair twisted at the ends.

"Well, to let someone like you go when you were about to share a lifetime together. That requires a man to be insane."

She blushed, looking aside, and he was astounded at what had emerged from his lips. The words had just slipped out, without his usual analytical deliberation. He had not spoken in such a fashion in a long time. Perhaps ever.

"Let us go to Es Vedrà," she stated with conviction.

"Sorry?"

"Es Vedrà, you silly. One of the most magical places in the world. You, the genius man who knows everything, must have heard about it."

Es Vedrà, a dramatic rock outcropping off the western coast of Ibiza. Uninhabited. He had learned many startling things about it, including its stature as the most magnetic place on earth. The Phoenician goddess Tanit had been born there. It attracted pilgrims, but one could not actually step onto it. This was strictly forbidden.

"Supposedly a place of great healing."

John perked. "Healing?"

"And of transformation."

"Shall we change and leave in fifteen minutes?"

They took the road to Es Cubells. Pale yellow clouds lingered along the roadside from the steady stream of passing tires. Traffic congested as they passed Ibiza Town with Dalt Villa and the formidable Castle of Ibiza towering over the sea. After continuing westward for twenty minutes, they arrived at Cala d'Hort beach and turned onto a dirt road which ended abruptly, high above the coast. They then traveled by foot along an arid field dotted with straw-colored grass.

"I have been to Cala d'Hort," Diana said. "Marvelous beach. Lovely views of Es Vedrà. But I've heard if we take the trail this other way, we can get to Sa Pedrera de Cala d'Hort: Atlantis."

"The ancient sandstone quarry?"

"They say it's lovely. A dreadful bit of a climb down, though. Leads to the finest views of Es Vedrà."

Dust puffed as their sandals struck brick-colored land. The breeze carried the salty smell of sea far below. After strolling under the cloudless blue sky, they arrived at the cliffs high above Atlantis.

Looming out over the sea stood massive Es Vedrà. A jolting

sight, as it arose starkly to over one thousand feet above. An isolated mountain in the water. To venture down to the sea-level view, to this Roman sandstone quarry known as Atlantis, would not be easy. A steep trail snaked down sand-colored cliffs, and in certain areas this trail appeared to dissolve into sheer cliff. No one was climbing or descending.

"Shall we?" Diana said, jovially.

"Why not? At least if we slip and fall, we perish in Atlantis."

Diana led the way down. She moved swiftly but deliberately, saying nothing. Several times, they clutched the rocks for stability. The pale cliffs reflected the afternoon sun, increasing the already formidable heat.

Gradually, as they descended, the rectangular pools of the quarry became discernible. They resembled ancient Roman baths, filled with rain and seawater. Rocks were cut throughout this area, cut over many centuries, forming walls and sharp angles, creating the impression that a city once thrived here, now long desolate. As they neared the bottom, peculiar stacks of smooth, round stones grew like stalks over the landscape. How did these get here? After hopping down onto the first flat surface, they shared a sigh of relief.

"That was a bit of a quest," Diana said. Her eyes widened in delight. "Behold."

Before them, overlooking the sea, which still lay fifteen feet below, resided a lengthy, rectangular quarry hole, filled with chartreuse water dappling in sunlight.

Diana stripped off her shirt and shorts, revealing an indigo bikini underneath. She leapt in, a streak of light. Certainly, not one to hesitate.

John tested the water with his toe; warm as an evening bath. She asked him to jump in, but he politely refused, and watched her splash and enjoy the mossy water.

A myriad of pools beckoned, layered on various levels as the quarry meandered down to sea level. The countenance of a Roman soldier with galea helmet, carved into the rock wall, gazed at them. He wore an appalled look, as if eternally perturbed. With the stacks of smooth rocks, the enchanting emerald pools, and the blistering heat, John found himself dazed. Everything warped out of any semblance of life as he knew it.

As Diana examined a carving of a portly Buddha, John lowered himself to sea-level, to the rocky shoreline. He had expected a crowd, but save a single man seated alone on a rock alongside the sea, nobody was present. Es Vedrà towered above the sea, directly across. An irrefutably magnificent, yet unsettling image.

The seated man gazed unfailingly at Es Vedrà, as if it held hypnotic sway over him. His black, thin mustache curled with panache at both ends. John neared, and from this proximate view, he seemed gaunt. As the man appeared immersed in rumination, John turned away.

"You do not offend me, my friend," the man said.

John's neck tensed at the voice, for at this juncture he almost believed him another stone element of this unconventional landscape.

"Quite a view," John said.

"The view, my friend, is enchanting. But it is only a view."

"That's true."

"It is experiencing the actual thing that matters in life."

John began turning away again.

"My name is Jose Barracuda Marquez."

"Barracuda. Like the fish?"

"I know of no such fish," he said, crisply.

"I see."

"As I was trying to say, my name is Jose Barracuda Marquez. I am from a small village in the north of Spain called Santillana del Mar." he said. "It is known as the town of three lies."

"Three lies?"

Jose smiled, clearly pleased at the inquiry. "Yes, my friend. The town is not named after a saint, nor is it flat, nor is it by the sea. Three lies."

"You grew up there?"

Jose turned to John. His aquiline nose protruded between wide, wet eyes which exuded despondency. "Yes, I did. And I never left, until now," he said. "For now, I am dying."

A moment passed with nothing else added. So, this was not said in jest.

"What is wrong?"

He gently smiled, viewing Es Vedrà. "Well, many things can be wrong. Like Ms. Domingo stealing my tomatoes off the vine after midnight, and then insisting otherwise."

"Okay."

"Have you ever grown succulent, ripe tomatoes? The type that bend the vine?"

"No."

"Well, neither has she," he remarked bitterly.

"I see."

"But unfortunately, I also suffer from an incurable illness. The good doctor from my town says only a month remains in my life. That was three weeks ago. Maybe I deserve death, maybe not. These things, I have not yet worked out. But I have lost much weight, and much hope."

"What's the problem?"

"That matters not anymore, my friend. Here I am."

"Can I be of any help?"

Jose smiled. "That is kind of you, my friend. I can see, and feel, the special kindness glowing inside you. A gift from God. But what I need is far from easy to get."

John felt Diana's smooth hand on his shoulder. Her face was flushed from heat, and her hair frizzed at the ends from drying with briny water.

"I just need to show you some marvelous carvings I found." She noticed Jose for the first time. "Oh! Who is your friend?"

Jose gradually stood, stepped over in a few painful, rickety strides, and kissed her hand. "I am Jose Barracuda Marquez." He sat back down and sighed, resuming his seaward gaze.

John took Diana aside and explained both that his middle name was not fish-based (which prompted a befuddled glance) and that he suffered a grievous predicament. Aghast, she demanded to know more about Jose and what afflicted him. John suggested that they should leave him be, as he seemed to yearn peace. She staunchly refused, and John, observing her resolute expression, her eyes aflame, resigned to the fact that he had absolutely no choice in this matter. Her passionate concern certainly deserved admiration aplenty.

"So what is it you are doing here, Jose?" John asked.

Jose squinted as he looked out over the sea. "What do you see out there?"

"Es Vedrà."

"Yes, young man," he replied. "But do not obsess over the literal. This is what the fat man does when spotting the chicken."

As John attempted to unpack that, Jose spoke again.

"Now look once more, and tell me—what does that mean to you?"

He glanced at Diana, and she nodded, encouraging his reply. "I have heard much about it. Sirens and sea nymphs called from there, attempting to lure Odysseus from his ship. Might even be the tip of the lost world of Atlantis."

"Much truth to everything you said," Jose said. He slowly stood and pointed out to sea with his sinewy arm. The spiraling ends of his mustache fluttered in the breeze. "But most important is the Rondalles of the Giant of Es Vedrà. That is its true secret."

"What is that?" Diana excitedly asked, stepping forward.

Jose smiled, contented by her enthusiastic interest. He gradually sat down, grunting, interlacing his fingers before him. "Once, there were two brothers with an ill father. Incurably ill. They wanted to help him," he said softly. "But there was nothing to do. Nothing. Horribly sad they felt, at their lack of ability to help, as they loved their dear father." His voice rose. "Until, they learned, there existed one way to save him."

"And what was that?" Diana appeared stricken.

Jose's eyes narrowed, and his voice lowered. "On Es Vedrà, and on Es Vedrà only, grows a special rock samphire plant. It grows directly on the cliffside, at higher altitudes. Only by bringing that plant to their father, could they cure him."

"So what happened?" she demanded.

"They did it. They made their way out to the rock, tricked the giant who lived in the caves, grabbed the rock samphire from the cliffs, and returned. Their father instantly healed after consuming the rock samphire."

He sighed, exhausted from telling his story. Tiny waves splashed against the shoreline, foaming against the smooth stones.

Diana walked a short distance away, and John followed.

"Should we do something?" she whispered.

"Help him climb back up? We probably should. How he made it down here is a mystery, but in his condition, he cannot climb up alone."

"That's not what I mean."

John stared at her blankly. "What then?"

She stepped to the edge of the sea, hands on hips. Her toes stroked the water's surface, leaving a smooth trail.

"What is it? What is on your mind?"

She turned, wearing an aspect of defiance; he took a step back from its sheer force.

"Shall we go and get him the rock samphire?"

Interpreting her words required a few moments. "What are you talking about?"

"You heard what he said. On Es Vedrà grows that special plant. It can cure him."

"That is some sort of fairy tale. You don't believe that?"

"Most fairy tales are based in reality."

"Yes. But it's the moral element or life lesson that is true. Not literal facts, about giants and magical plants."

"Come on John," she said. "You've witnessed the power of Ibiza. This is a magical place. A unique place. You must be willing to acknowledge that by now."

"To be honest, I am not sure what I am willing to acknowledge anymore."

"And why have different people revered Es Vedrà for centuries? From all the sea nymphs and sirens to goddesses. Something dwells there. Let us go get him his plant."

John began to pace.

"I cannot believe we are even having this conversation. I cannot believe this. To think a few months ago I was analyzing spreadsheets," he said, exasperated, hands slicing air. "What do we really know about this character anyway? And how the hell are we supposed to go and get it? We have no boat. And people are forbidden on the island."

"We will swim."

"Swim?"

"Yes."

Es Vedrà was a mile and a half offshore. "That is not an easy swim."

"No, it certainly is not."

"And let's not forget the part that if we happen to make it there, without first becoming a relic at the Mediterranean's bottom, we're not allowed on it."

"I'm not worried about that, John."

"No," John said, exhaling. "I can see that you are not."

When John approached Jose Barracuda Marquez minutes later, and revealed their plans, he listened in silence, staring seaward the entire time. Subsequently, Jose struggled to stand. He took two lurching steps forward, and collapsed onto John, hugging him and kissing both cheeks, then hugged Diana, kissing her cheeks.

"I knew my prayers would be answered if I came here. I have been saying my rosary, Fatima prayer included, which was given to me by good father Lorenzo. And we always knew you would come," he said, his large eyes fastened on John.

"What does that mean?"

"Look for the little green plants with tiny yellow flowers," he said, ignoring John's inquiry. "A unique taste, unlike anything you ever felt. They only grow high up, on the sides of the cliffs."

Diana and John began walking to the sea.

"And be careful," Jose yelled. "Where God's good exists, great evil lurks as well."

At three in the afternoon, John and Diana stood at the water's edge. Jose watched from afar. John stretched his shoulders and neck, and Diana repeatedly touched her toes. Time for a swim.

"Are you such a good swimmer?" John asked. "You seem awfully relaxed about this."

"Not particularly. Are you?"

"I should have taken his rosary with me."

As they stepped into the water, John realized he did not know if her "not particularly" applied to being a good swimmer, or being relaxed. After reaching neck deep, they shared the apprehensive smiles of two embarking on a perilous, and perhaps foolish quest.

They began swimming. Initial strokes were smooth and effortless, as they customarily tend to be. Diana swam steadily with admirable form.

Then the water unanticipatedly darkened as it deepened. Temperature plummeted. A drastic transformation. It dawned on John that he faced a formidable swim, far longer than any multiple lap tryst he managed in a lifeguarded pool from his past. Panic blitzed him.

He and Diana popped heads up occasionally to survey if headed in the proper direction, and to check each other, and they pressed on. Stroke after stroke, they continued. After about half an hour, they floated on their backs, breathing deeply in an attempt to recoup. The depth of water could not be gauged due to its darkness. Diana seemed composed; she breathed steadily and they continued. After another twenty minutes, they almost arrived.

Es Vedrà rose harshly and audaciously upward from the sea. Viewed from the cold water, with a fatigued body, its dramatic angles and acute edges radiated a cruel air.

A landing point was desperately needed. Diana pointed to a slope that appeared flatter, where it might be possible to hoist oneself up. At this point, with his exhausted arms, John would try anywhere. As they placed their fingers on Es Vedrà's surface, it felt sizzling hot, as if grimly rejecting their presence. They struggled defiantly with weary limbs and collapsed onto the island. Odysseus would be proud.

"Now that was a swim," Diana said.

"You were unbelievable." John exhaled, catching his breath. "Unbelievable. How did you learn to swim so well?"

"Three times a week back in England at the pool. Laps. Doing it for twenty-five years."

"Twenty-five years of swimming? You omitted that minor detail before we left?" John stood, and squeezed the water out of his dark hair.

"Hey, you look fit enough. Besides, you run like a lunatic every morning for miles in those hills, so you seem like a chap who can handle it."

The parched mountain loomed above. Winds blew more severely out here, and the gusts begot moaning sounds: faint, yet consistent. Hopefully from the wind passing through coves and caves, and not from some long-tormented giant.

Not much soil for plant growth existed, though a few raggedy pine bushes grew in black patches of dirt. They began hiking up the initial part of the rock, a moderate slope, before the transformation into dramatic cliffs.

"What in heaven's name is that?" Diana yelled, pointing to the rocks, her mouth agape.

Three hideous heads peered at them from an outcrop thirty feet above. In the glinting sunlight, they appeared to be some sort of Luciferian demon heads. A jarring sight. The heads remained steadfast, glowering down at them, brimming with vitriol.

John thrusted leftward, out of the direct brightness.

He positioned for a clearer view, then realized, with cascading relief, that glaring down at them were not pernicious residents of the netherworld, but rather three black-and-white, horned goats.

"Goats, I believe."

Diana clambered over to John and ventured another peek. "My God, they appear so. Still, there is something quite odd about them." She looked to John with stretched eyes as if something unintelligible had dawned upon her. "But how in heaven did they ever get here? How is that possible?"

"Maybe they swam the breaststroke?"

They nervously laughed together. "Just remarkable," Diana said.

"Next thing, the giant will be coming around."

They agreed to start climbing, and as rocks slipped off their feet and clanked down the hill, the ghostly goats vanished.

The climb was undeniably fierce. They meticulously surveyed and stepped, knowing any slip would be costly. Through helping each other, working together, gradually, they ascended. Auspiciously, both wore rugged sports sandals that day, as the stone was jagged and unforgivingly hot.

"There," Diana yelled.

She pointed to a patch of tiny yellow flowers with succulent green stems growing sideways off of the cliff's surface.

"Could that be it?" John asked. "It fits Jose's description."

"Must be. It has to be." Her eyes stretched open in anticipation. "Just reach over and grab some. Then taste it."

"Taste it?" John said. "When did that become part of this deal?"

"What's wrong?"

"What's wrong? Maybe this plant makes deadly nightshade look like Pepto-Bismol. What do we know about this?"

"You worry too much, John. I thought I worried a lot, but you do far more."

"Well, I wouldn't be withering from worry either if someone else served as the Roman taster."

She laughed anxiously. John seized a clump and snapped it off the main plant. After observing the emerald stalk on his moist palm, he exhaled, smiled at Diana, then bit it and chewed. A refreshing, spicy taste flashed across his palate. Never had he tasted anything even similar. So Jose was...right.

"This must be it."

They held fast to the rock edges, and John leaned across to cull several handfuls. Diana gripped his left arm as he extended his right. Satisfied they had accumulated enough, they began the harrowing descent to the water's edge. Several pauses assured stability, and eventually, they reached bottom. John peered back up, hoping for a final confirmatory view of the diabolical goats, but only a refracting, blinding light greeted his gaze. The wind wailed longingly.

"I believe it's departure time," Diana said.

"You know, something just occurred to me."

"Yes?"

"How on earth are we going to get this back through the water?" He presented the clump of rock samphire before him.

She appeared stunned. "Well, aren't we the two geniuses of the year? Can you stuff it in your pockets?"

"After one hundred yards it will come right out into the water."

"Then hold it."

"Hold it? And swim for miles with a fist?"

"Well, I don't know. Shove it in your bloody bathing suit."

John could not help but laugh. "That's not very polite. Pulling it out of my shorts."

"Hey, he can't be too choosy. Let's just go."

After wishing each other the best of luck, they leapt back in.

Cold slapped them mercilessly. They forgot, as is common after warming up, the chill of the water. The swim back would be formidable, but knowing the shore of a familiar location awaited soothed a bit—but only a bit.

After nearly an hour of swimming and floating on their backs, and after three sleek bottlenose dolphins passed while leaping in and out of the sea, they at long last stepped back onto the shore. Diana walked out first, and offered her hand as John emerged. Both exhausted, they sat side by side in silence on the nearest stone.

When they approached Jose, he was on his knees, eyes closed, rosary draped over clenched fingers, lost in prayer. John offered the plants on a flat rock directly before him. It should be cited, in the name of prudence, that he extricated them from his shorts while still a fair distance away. Jose's lips fluttered rapidly in prayer, and then abruptly halted. He opened his eyes, and looked down at the rock samphire. Gradually, his lids widened as he smiled broadly.

"Thank you," he said. "With all of my heart. I am saved."

His eyes shut again, and he continued praying.

"Is he going to eat it?" Diana whispered.

They could not just linger and stare. "Let us leave him now. He needs his time."

Diana hesitated, but they slowly backed up, then turned away. When back alongside the green pools of Atlantis, they peered down at Jose. He still kneeled, the rock samphire glistening on the rock before him. After waiting for a time, John suggested they move on.

"Will he be okay?" Diana said.

"I hope so."

They ascended the steep trail on the cliffside overlooking Es Vedrà. After a few stumbles, they reached the top and peeked a last time at the coastline. Far below, Jose kneeled and prayed, hands pressed together, a figurine in the distance by the sea.

They headed back to their car. The weather, quite warm, would gradually cool as dusk arrived. The seats in the vehicle burned from a lengthy day baking in the unyielding sun. He sighed as they pulled away.

"Stop!"

He slammed the brakes, both lurching forward.

"What's wrong?"

"It's he," she said, pointing behind them. "Look."

John peered in the rearview mirror. Striding down the path was Jose Barracuda Marquez. He stepped sprightly while flicking his long hair out of his eyes. They exited the car.

"Jose," John yelled.

He turned with an enchanted expression and glided up to them. He embraced Diana, and then John.

"You are fine," John said.

"Yes."

"But how did you get up here so fast? I just saw you way down...how could you possibly move so quickly?"

Jose heartily laughed. "Of course I am fine. Did you think I would request you to journey all that way, through all that struggle and risk, for no reason?"

John looked toward Diana, and she shook her head in wonderment.

"How is this possible?" John said.

"But why are you surprised?"

"Well, let me give you a ride somewhere. Do you need something?"

Jose laughed cordially. "Perhaps my lovely tomatoes back from old Ms. Domingo."

John smiled in delight.

"My friend, my good friend, you have given me all I need. Now I will spend time enjoying the beaches here, laughing and swimming. And being thankful." He kissed them both, and clasping John's head in his tanned fingers, he locked eyes with him. "I am so happy you finally arrived," he whispered.

Jose walked off along the coastline cliffs, gradually melting into the golden distance.

As they drove away, returning to the main road, both sat in stunned silence. The traffic congested as they neared Ibiza Town, cars stopping and starting. Engines rumbled and growled. In time, Diana turned to John.

"What just happened back there John? Please do tell."

John sighed. To their right the indomitable Dalt Villa, its massive limestone walls obtained from the Atlantis quarry, reflected evening light in warm bursts.

"Whatever happened," John said, "every aspect of life appears a little different now."

"Is that a good thing?"

"I believe so," John said. "I believe so."

FOURTEEN

A week had passed since John dropped Andre into the hills, and he visited Las Dalias in hopes of finding him. Las Dalias market, which holds the title as the oldest on the island, started in the 1950s as a roadhouse with fruit and vegetable stands. Over the years, it blossomed into a thriving hippie market. An array of performers were on display, and local artwork, trinkets, Balearic food, and red wines overflowed every Saturday.

Locating Andre, with his Bedouin lifestyle and tent home buried in the bowels of the forest, was no easy task. Supposedly he peddled his artwork somewhere here amidst the many tables.

At ten-thirty in the morning, visitors already flowed in.

Finding Andre's table would be challenging, as the stalls meandered in a labyrinthian pattern, many hooded with byzantine cloths overlapping their neighbor's. Occasionally, these narrow lanes opened into tiny open courts, with shirtless musicians strumming Spanish guitars and cafes serving chilled glasses of emerald, Moorish tea. One easily vanished amid the endless winding paths lined with colorful Eastern clothing, the heavy smoke of incense obscuring each unexpected turn.

John felt providence on his side upon finding Andre's table within minutes.

There Andre sat, wheedling away at a chunk of driftwood. The site of John bewildered him, as if John had stepped forth from a parallel universe. He eventually made the earthly connection and sprang up, pumping John's hand.

"Sit down, sit down. What are you doing here? Sit down."

"I came to see how you are."

This concept flummoxed him, as he stroked his cheeks in bafflement.

"So how are you?"

Andre sighed, motioning toward his collection of curious sculptures. In the center sat a papier-mâché work of a single sinewy arm emerging from the earth, fist displaying an engorged and erect middle finger. "Need luck today, as my ex is on the warpath, demanding money from me."

"Why?"

"That's normal for her. But this time it's worse. Supposedly my daughter is in desperate need of school supplies"

"It's summertime, Andre. School is closed."

"I'm a bad father, she says."

"Hard to be a good one when she prevents you from seeing your child."

He glanced at John, on the verge of saying something confirmatory, but then surrendered in a head shake of dismay.

"Either way, she's inflamed. Screamed yesterday when I

called to speak to Laura. Said I'm withholding money. Hung up."

"When did you last donate to your ex-wife's causes?"

Andre weakly smiled. "Last week."

"Doesn't sound like an extensive withholding period."

"I do four markets a week. She takes it all, every peseta."

"All of it?"

"She comes, or sends the boyfriend."

"She ever come by with friends?"

Andre squinted, as if viewing an asylum inmate. "No. No friends. Never friends."

"I didn't think so."

"Why?"

John shivered from dispiriting memories. "Unfortunately, this all reminds me of my past. Certain fields attract certain types."

Andre stared at him for a time with glossy eyes. "Sorry you were exposed to that element for so long."

"As am I," John said. "I suspect your ex doesn't work?"

"Work?" Andre asked with a scoff. "Never. Never worked in the Netherlands, never here. Definitely likes others to work, though. Her new boyfriend receives some monthly family money. And they both live in my old place, so no rent to pay."

"Unbelievable," John said. "But why, right now, is she so particularly desperate for your cash?"

"Obsesses over buying ridiculous things. Always claims Laura needs the money, but she uses it."

Terming Andre's situation as deplorable was an understatement. And it was apparent it would further deteriorate until only singed remnants of his carcass remained.

"Hasn't the time come to organize a schedule of who pays what and when you see your daughter?"

"I really should."

"Disorganization inevitably leads to abuse."

He veered, piqued at the term "abuse." "You're painting it too tragically."

"Am I?"

"I fight back," he stated. "Well, I have..." He mumbled bitterly, kicking up a dust cloud, and John abandoned the subject for the time.

Andre's expression snapped into solemnity.

A woman with bleached-blond hair, and pretty but severe features, stood before their table. She was short and overly fit, as if she exercised excessively until burning away anything even hinting at softness. Her hair was strangulated into a ponytail.

Spotting John sitting aside Andre's table, she hesitated, concern flashing across her face. But she re-calibrated, apparently believing they could not possibly be associated, and faced Andre with her veined hands gripping hips.

"Laura has been crying."

Andre's head hung limply.

"A father's sacred job is to his daughter."

"I gave you all the money last week."

She scoffed. "You should see what her classmates' fathers do for their daughters! At Antonia's birthday party, Francois bought her a beautiful Losino pony."

Andre peeked at John with what seemed an element of imploring. No viable openings existed, so he had to passively witness the slaughter.

"Her classmates tease her about you being a loser," she said. "She was sobbing in bed last night about it."

So here she was, finally. His lovely ex-wife.

As she focused on Andre, her eyes protruded perversely, and

his head hung. It was excruciating to witness such a corrosive association.

"The money?"

"I need to make a few more sales today."

"She needs school supplies. You're destroying her education."

"Sales should go well." He swallowed. "So you brought her today?"

"She's with Rolf in the market."

Andre said nothing.

"Listen carefully—if you're capable of at least that. I'll stop by, one last time, in an hour for the money. If not, you won't see her until winter."

Her well-formed legs marched off.

Hard to fathom Andre was once a successful man in Amsterdam, with his own home and burgeoning career. How far a person, even after dedicating years of diligence to establishing himself, and doing things the right way, can plummet. Terrifying, as it unmasked the true fragility of our existence.

"So I met your ex-wife."

"Lotte is her name. Fabulous person, isn't she?"

"So what happened to all that 'fighting back' you claimed you do?"

Andre stared at his twitching big toes. "No one ever stands up to her," he said defiantly. "Not even her mother. So don't blame me."

"No one stands up to her?"

"No one ever dares."

"We shall see."

He peered at John, curiously.

"A true New York mafia shakedown," John said, jocularly.

"Intruding on businesses and threatening for payoffs. Finally, it's revealed why those films fascinate you so."

"Exactly like that, isn't it?" Andre asked, cheering up. "Well let's pray for a buyer in the next hour or I won't see my daughter 'til December."

For the next forty minutes, a steady stream of people passed. Several stopped and asked questions, but despite the exigency, Andre offered listless answers and they shuffled on. Some he failed to even acknowledge. A baffling display, an exasperating display. John found himself increasing tempted to both box Andre's ears with one of his bizarre sculptures, and to enter the sales fray.

Then, out of the chaos of bohemian passersby, a crisply dressed man in his thirties with a fresh haircut and thick-framed glasses emerged. He paused, methodically studying the sculptures. His pale, soft hands handled the works with care.

"Where did you find the materials for these?"

Andre stared straight ahead in a trance.

The man observed Andre's non-responding countenance with interest, as if studying one of the sculptures, and then repeated his question, slightly louder, but to no avail.

Intercession time, or the bells of the hour would toll without a single sale.

"From various deserted parts of the island."

The man's tiny, perceptive eyes moved to John.

"Fascinating," he said, now believing John the artist.

He handled the carving of a screaming nude man, hands above his head, looking down at his missing private parts. "I love the despair in these works. Might I inquire on your influences?"

Although Andre's head faced downward, his eyes peeked up rife with curiosity.

"I greatly admire Constantin Brancusi," John said.

"What do you like about Brancusi?" he asked, removing his glasses.

"The simplicity of his forms. The combining of his folk traditions from Romania with African wood carvings."

The young man reached out his hand to shake. "Dirk."

"Andre," John said. "The dadaists and the surrealists also affected me enormously. Expanded boundaries."

Dirk nodded his head, listening attentively.

"Probably my biggest influence is Henry Moore, though."

"Why?" Dirk asked, stepping forward. "Why is that?"

"The evolution and the materials. I saw his style develop from more traditional to abstract. And his harmonization of various materials, like wood, bronze, and stone, I found amazing." John chuckled. "He actually kept a collection of driftwood, pebbles, even skulls to help him with his forms. That reminds me of myself. Minus the skulls."

Dirk laughed and nodded gracefully. He introduced himself as a collector of unique sculpture, as he owned two galleries, in Amsterdam and The Hague. They were highly successful galleries, decidedly on the eccentric side, and he hoped to debut one in London in February. He always sought the nonconformist artist.

He returned his glasses onto his face, selected three separate pieces, and purchased them at prices reasonable for an undiscovered yet talented artist. John did not charge excessively, or he would sully the relationship, but enough to establish a base of respect. This was essential. For Andre, the wad of cash was more than he earned in a month.

Dirk inquired if John was normally found at this market, and he said yes, every week. He would return late in the summer to visit once again.

They waited until he disappeared into the crowds.

"Fantastic!" Andre said. "Fantastic job."

John handed him the pile of cash.

"But how did you know so much about sculpture?"

"A few art courses and a very good memory. A blessing and a curse. More of a curse, perhaps, in my case."

They laughed together, John patting Andre on the back.

"So are you familiar with the sculptors I mentioned?"

"Of course. I worked for the airlines, but studied art on the side for years. Anyone who uses collected objects, like Marisol Escobar, I love. My hoarder tendencies flourish, if allowed."

"Excellent," John said. "Excellent. Perhaps you can mention some of your knowledge to your more sophisticated clients. It helps."

"That's true."

"Because it's true doesn't mean you are going to do it," John said, with a flare of anger. "It is true you should speak up to your ex, and yet you do not."

"That's also true."

John could not prevent a smile. "So truth is just the start."

Andre folded the money into his pocket. He began laughing hysterically, bony shoulders shaking up and down.

"What is it?"

"I just thought of something. What if this Dirk guy returns one day, and you're not here? And he's asking for you, the artist?"

John chuckled. "Just tell him some unhinged guy joined you at the table, and you let him speak out of pity. Plenty of them on Ibiza."

Andre observed John for a time, squinting with amused deliberation.

"You're a fascinating character, John. I have never met someone like you."

"So odd am I?"

"No, no, not that. It's just, you are a knowledgeable guy and possess unique skills. You understand what makes people tick," Andre said. "Someone like you could do a lot of good."

"Well, I..."

"I'm just grateful to have you on my side."

To hear he was helpful for reasons other than fortifying massive fiscal portfolios deeply gratified John. A sudden buoyancy inundated him. Now, if only he could apply his talents to helping recover his own life as well. But that part, for whatever reason, is always trickier.

Sadly, Lotte soon returned, deflating any pleasantness. She possessed a knack for that. Although no direct sunlight shined, she severely squinted.

"Well?"

Andre sacrificed the cash offering on the alter before her.

She lunged for it far too abruptly to sustain her pretense of composure. Yet John was faster on the draw, intercepting the billfold. She veered in outrage.

"What—" She frowned at Andre. "Who the hell is this?"

Andre shrugged and stared at his dusty, tanned feet.

"So you would like this money?" John asked.

Lotte observed Andre gazing at the ground, neck limp, and knew very well he would not look up. For she was quite familiar with that posture, as she founded it within him. No alternative but to face John herself.

"That is my money."

"Andre would like to see his daughter first."

"Would what?" Her nostrils distended. "Who are you?"

"John of the Baskervilles."

She frowned in befuddlement. "John of...This is absurd. I'm leaving."

"Excellent. Then the cash is all mine." John inserted the money into his pocket, and began to step away.

"Hold on," she hollered. Andre was still locked in the same wretched position. Her jaw muscles pulsed in rumination as she weighed options.

"I'll bring Laura over for a second," she mumbled.

As she strode away, both waited in silence

"Have you lost your bleeping mind!" Andre exclaimed. "She will skin us both alive."

"Calm down."

"You damned New Yorkers are insane."

He paced around his table, gesticulating, noiselessly mouthing words, as if engaged in genuine argument. So here lay the forum where Andre rebelled and stood up for himself.

"I know what I'm doing, Andre."

"You don't know her. Now she will never let me see my daughter again. You've ruined everything."

"See your daughter?" John asked. "She doesn't even let you speak to your daughter on the phone now. You give her ninety-nine percent of your money. Things can't get worse."

Andre kneaded his hands as if warming them from a deep chill. Something had impressed him, for he suddenly appeared eager, even childlike. "You think she will come back? With Laura?"

"Trust me, she will be back for the money."

"You think so?"

"Well she's not coming back for your charming personality."

It certainly did not take long; within two minutes, Lotte had returned. A tall man with a swimmer's physique followed her, holding a small girl's hand. Her chestnut hair fell over her eyes, and one could appreciate the mix of races in her pretty face. When she spotted Andre, her expression brightened and she dashed toward him.

Andre hugged her and began presenting his latest sculptures. They giggled, enacting farcical scenes with them.

Responding to Lotte's grotesque jerking head motions, the man approached John with a comically resolute expression.

He introduced himself as Rolf, and flatly asked John, in an Australian accent, if he had Lotte's money. He did his best to maintain his austere expression, but it obviously did not befit him. His handsome face creased from years in the sun. Here stood a man who had not been serious often, a man who had once enjoyed a carefree existence. That life was long gone.

When John asked where in Australia he hailed from, Rolf perked. Hearing the answer, John remarked that the Gold Coast had a most wonderful reputation in America, and he had a colleague, Oliver, from Brisbane. (Now, Oliver really came from Staten Island, but we digress.)

Rolf loved the Gold Coast, and missed it every day. John followed his hunch and inquired about the legendary surf in that region. Any remnants of Rolf's gravity dissolved. Apparently he had been a professional surfer, but now only surfed for two brief weeks a year during winter, when Lotte begrudgingly permitted him to travel for the waves. John recounted his sole experience surfing, on a crocodile-sized longboard, which he flew off of in five seconds. Rolf boisterously laughed at this adolescent humor. It should be noted that Lotte observed all this unfold with an expression of disbelieving horror.

John stated that he always hoped to learn from a true surfer. Rolf's mouth began opening, but Lotte, who was staring a burning, unholy stare, released a chilling, artificial cough. Rolf, with a start, snapped back into his trance, and robotically requested the money again. Lotte would need to ask for it herself, John informed him. A hint of admiration seeped through his sober expression as he walked away.

After an assortment of hissing sounds passed from Lotte to Rolf, she approached John, jaw set, eyes askance.

"The money?"

Andre and Laura laughed spiritedly together.

"They are having a wonderful time, aren't they?" John asked.

Andre now looked over, scrupulously observing as if tuning into an anticipated television event.

"He's a pathetic loser who abandoned his daughter." An element of coquettishness existed within her smile. "I'm sure a real man like you can see that?"

"I see quite the opposite. I see a man unjustly forced out of his daughter's life."

Her lips set tightly, slightly bluish. "Whatever you are attempting to do, it is not working," Lotte said. "This whole bizarre little stunt."

"This is a stunt?"

"Don't you have anything better to do with your time?"

"Not particularly."

She hesitated. An unexpected response. She now abandoned any attempts at flattery, and shifted to more blunt methods.

"Take my advice. Learn to mind your business and not meddle in people's families."

"On Ibiza, aren't we all one great big universal family?"

"You're as pathetic as he is, aren't you?"

Her voice had thickened, and her flesh became progressively crimson and shiny as capillaries expanded to her mounting attack.

"Perhaps you are right," John said to the burning features before him. "But at least I'm not the one spending my entire day pressuring a homeless person to surrender his money."

Her frenzy screeched to a halt.

"That's not only 'pathetic,'" John said. "But it's also criminal. This should be reported to the authorities."

Her eyes flared at the fear of exposure, invariably one of the deadliest strain of fears. She said no more, seizing the cash and scuttling away with Laura. Rolf's dragging feet trailed behind as he prepped for the ensuing tempest.

Andre looked to John with wonderment, as if viewing a resident of the heavenly realm.

"In eight years, I've never seen my ex defeated like that. She verbally annihilates everyone."

"No. All just an illusion."

"Illusion?" he asked with incredulity. "So how do you explain it? Doug Henning?"

"Simply," John said, smiling. "She surrounds herself exclusively with those terrified of her. Easy prey. There you have it."

Andre said nothing.

"I've encountered many of these types in the high finance world, both men and women. This type grooms their slaves."

"And?"

"Terror of their retribution keeps them obedient."

Andre nodded.

"Besides Lotte's slaves, no one else is allowed near. She never works a job, unless she's the boss, so she doesn't have to take critique from colleagues or anyone."

"That's for sure."

"And I bet she never has lasting friends. So once again, no one to criticize her. I am right, am I not?"

Andre stared at his sculptures, fingers twisting his gray hairs.

"A completely monitored existence. Life in her deluded incubator," John added.

"It is true. Yes," Andre said, as if reaching a revelation. "And as I now recall, no one was ever allowed to visit us in Amsterdam. Any acquaintance she made, especially women, vanished within two weeks. Always horribly wronged her." Andre abruptly stood. "And any friend I made, no way! I brought Lukas home for dinner. A botanist, nicest guy. She insisted that he 'stared at her with disapproval.' Ridiculous. But how do you argue against that? She banished him from my apartment and my life."

"Sorry to hear that."

"And if they weren't disapproving, she claimed my friends viewed her with lust. Method number two. So if I tried keeping them as friends, I insulted her dignity." His voice lowered to depressing dreariness. "Before I realized it, everyone I knew, friends and family, dropped off the radar. It has been barren since."

John removed a lump of cash from his back pocket.

"What is this?"

"You didn't really believe I would sacrifice the entirety of your hard-earned money to the dark side, did you?

Andre gingerly received the cash into his palms as if handed an alien life form, examining it cautiously at a distance, and then finally counting it.

"That's a very good amount," he said. "This is very good."

"See? I held back money from her. No problem. Lightning from the sky didn't zap me dead."

Andre smirked. "She would consider that too quick and merciful an ending."

They shared a light laugh.

"If I did it, Andre, so you can, too."

Andre's eyes moistened. "I can really use this."

"Now hold on," John said. "I'm expecting some of that used for essentials."

"Essentials?"

"A few cervesas, perhaps?

FIFTEEN

John's illustrious strategy for finding Gunther consisted of driving to beaches along the mysterious northern coastline, chatting with people, if anyone could be found, and garnering relevant information. Thus was the grand plan; brilliant in its simplicity, he hoped, rather than inane in its bareness.

Venturing through the island's loftiest peaks was required to reach this elusive next area, and his car's engine already emitted ominous clicks while ascending the initial hills.

While coasting down a particularly high hill and viewing the distant turquoise world far in the distance, he realized the engine was silent. Gravity alone propelled the vehicle. After floating for another minute in neutral, he eased over onto a grassy bend on the roadside and exited.

The robust smell of forest pervaded the still air. A pair of Marmora's Warblers, bright red rings encircling their darting eyes, tweeted in the trees and hopped from branch to branch, peeking down with curiosity at John.

All seemed fine with the alternator and battery. Then with a resounding thud, he realized: the gas tank. Like a blithering fool, he had failed to fill it. And on Ibiza, petrol stations were a rarity. Emotions about his quest today had so overwhelmed him with the possibility he might actually find Gunther that he forgot cars require gas.

No options but to wait for help. And wait he did.

After listening for cars for nearly an hour, and shuffling a dozen sticky pinecones across the street, he finally detected the murmuring of a distant engine.

On the snaking roads above, a pale blue van gradually descended. When it made its final turn toward John, the VW sign shined. He waved his arm as it rumbled toward him. Light reflected off the windshield, obscuring the driver, but the van groaned and halted, the passenger window squeaking open. The face of a man with a deep, acquired tan peeked out, round spectacles sitting atop his thin nose. He enthusiastically requested John to join him.

"Would you like me to look at your engine?" he asked, with a strong French accent, after John sat beside him

"I'm out of gas. Hasn't happened since I was eighteen years old."

"Mine's almost empty also," the man said, while laughing good-naturedly as he pulled away. "But I store tanks at home. We can pick one up."

The man scrupulously observed the road, blinking behind his spectacles. A red bandana covered his head, and his long brown hair swung rhythmically with the shaking van. Only then did John notice—sadly, a bit too late. The man was completely nude, minus the bandana. In some sense, considering Ibiza, John was not entirely surprised.

"I'm Pierre."

"John."

"So where are you heading in these areas, John?"

"Just wanted to see some of the beaches."

"Really?" he asked with incredulity.

John could not help but feel a bit defensive. "Why? Is that so peculiar?"

"Yes. Yes, it is, in fact."

"I see."

"We get no visitors way up in this region. They are all obsessed with jamming into Ibiza Town and San Antonio for the heavy partying."

"Not my cup of tea."

Pierre glanced at John with a raised eyebrow.

"You live up here?" John asked.

"Been here a few years. Quiet."

"Where are you from?"

"Originally?" Pierre asked. "Domrémy-la-Pucelle. A tiny town in the northeast of France"

"1412."

"What?" He peeked at John with a furrowed brow.

"The birthplace of La Pucelle D'Orléans. Born in 1412."

Pierre clicked his tongue. "Amazing John. Très bon. I am impressed, truly."

"That impressed?"

"I meet few, if anyone, who know that anymore. It's the 1980s. People don't care." The creases around his eyes extended as he smiled. "I thought an American education didn't cover such things."

"I've never visited that region of France, but when younger I desperately wanted to go. Seems a magical place. Joan of Arc's biography occupied a prime place on my shelf."

Pierre's eyes moistened. "And do you not want to visit anymore?"

John had not considered that trip for many years. "I do," he said. "Perhaps even more now."

"Beautiful John. Beautiful. Then we should visit together."

The time to inquire had arrived.

"Pierre."

"Hmm?"

"I notice you happen to be driving without many clothes on."

"That is true."

"Do you normally drive around like this?"

"I do, John."

Not much one can respond to that.

"Do you see that in the back, John?"

Buried beneath stacked wooden boxes and empty burlap sacks lay a double kayak and oars.

"Ever been kayaking?" Pierre asked.

"About a decade ago."

"Well, I planned on a little launch off of Cala Xarraca. Join me?"

"I hoped to get the fuel and get going."

"John, it won't be the longest of trips. Just out onto the sea. Stunning cliffs in the region," he said. "Then we will get the petrol, and you will be on your way."

He harbored little leverage for negotiation. And the idea of kayaking in this northern region appealed enormously. Any reluctance was due to the fact that his companion on the seafaring voyage would be a naked van-driver from the land of the Franks.

"What do you say John?"

John scratched his chin. "Why not?"

Once in the water, Pierre took the lead seat and began paddling. The muscles on his back flexed and relaxed. The kayak moved fleetly through calm water, and they moved straight out to sea.

The details of their kayaking plan eluded John, adding to the oddity of the day, as he had not even bothered to inquire. Pierre steered the kayak westward as they exited the cove, and remained reasonably close to the shoreline, which transformed into stark cliffs plummeting directly into the sea. Without the inlet mollifying, the water roughened, and more thrust was required to maintain speed.

After a few minutes, Pierre pointed toward the shore. The curve of an immense cove unfolded before them.

"Benirrás." His wet hair clung to his back.

"That is the legendary sun beach?"

"Every week they celebrate the sunset. You must go. It is pure joy."

John found it peculiar to converse with someone without the luxury of observing his expressions—expressions which typically prove to be invaluable, often belying the literal words. He recalled speaking with taxi drivers late at night in his Manhattan days. At least in the car, a rearview mirror afforded brief but telling views of inquisitive eyes.

"You live alone on the Ibiza?" Pierre asked.

"I do."

Pierre digested his answer as his paddle infallibly dipped into the water. "So tell me, John."

"Tell you?"

Pierre was momentarily silent. "What are you really doing here on Ibiza?"

"Really doing?" John asked, momentarily indignant.

"Yes."

Embarrassment singed him. Yes, he had not lied outright about his purpose of his trip up north, but certainly had not been forthright or transparent.

"If I say I'm going for swimming lessons, would you believe me?"

"Your eyes reveal to me you are on a mission."

Water sprayed John's face as he plunged his paddle into the sea, his lips tasting of salted seaweed. He could not help but admire the astuteness of this man.

John exhaled. "I came to find and reconcile with an old friend, and get my life straight."

"Have you accomplished either yet?"

"Intertwined works in progress."

"It is good you are searching for things, John," Pierre said. "When a person stops searching, no matter the age, he begins to die."

Schools of razorfish, flat and deep red, streaked by the kayak.

"There," Pierre pointed.

A narrow point peeked out from the cliffs along the shoreline of Ibiza. They paddled to land and tugged the kayak onto the thin, rocky edge. Scanning the sea and spotting nothing, Pierre entered a slim canyon between the cliffs. A path winded upward, and they carried the kayak on their shoulders, the sides rasping against stone. The path eventually widened, and Pierre guided John behind hard, green shrubbery, where a tarp awaited them. He concealed the kayak.

"Just a bit more up here," Pierre said. "And we shall arrive."

John again found it astounding that he, who for years fastidiously monitored his itinerary on a minute-by-minute basis, did not inquire about their destination. He sensed the time to be led had arrived, and was pleasantly surprised that, since coming to Ibiza, he was learning to succumb to that sense.

They emerged beyond the cliffs onto a steep hill.

They pressed on, ascending rapidly. Junipers, pines, and occasional Lebanon cedars forested the area. Each breath rewarded, filling John with the potent combination of woodland scents and salty sea air. At the top, Pierre halted. His arm stroked before him, indicating with pride the view below.

The sight stunned.

Far below lay a round valley, like a crater, entirely concealed by encircling hills. On the gentle slopes leading downward were endless terraced fields of plants. Marijuana plants. In the center of this valley was a large farmhouse, constructed from gray stones. Wooden buildings stood to the sides of this central house, and a series of greenhouses lay on the western end. Figures glided along the slopes of the fields, attending to the rows of plants.

Truly, a lost world.

"Welcome to my home," Pierre said. "Please, come this way."

As they followed a mellow grass path into the valley, those in the fields paused their work to view John. It should be mentioned that all these people shared Pierre's aversion to clothing.

The fields were irrigated by a raised, wooden aqueduct, which guided fresh water all throughout the compound. An engineering marvel.

Beside the farmhouse grew dozens of rows of vegetable plants. Immense, ripe tomatoes burdened the vines. They entered the house through ancient wooden doors leading into a grand central hall with lofty ceilings and a lengthy wooden table surrounded by at least twenty chairs.

"We eat as a community here. We live as a community here."

"Apparently laundry duties must be the easiest job."

Pierre paused in befuddlement, and then laughed as he poured cups of red wine from a pitcher. The pitcher and cups were carved from wood.

"Do not let the nudity frighten you, John. We live free of any burdens."

"Well, I hope they are not burdened by the fact that I'm clothed," John said, motioning to the fields.

"You are free to live however you feel. Those who come here start with clothes, and often shed them in time. Do as you please."

Thick stone walls kept the spacious room remarkably cool. The clanking of plates and cups emerged from rooms in the back, and the immaculate scent of baking bread floated in.

"How on earth did you ever accomplish this entire operation? I confess I didn't think such things truly possible."

John's comments pleased Pierre. "Everyone here takes turns working different jobs. We alternate every two weeks, so everyone shares in the joys and the burdens."

"A fair system."

"And everyone comprehends the jobs others perform. This creates empathy, as opposed to specializing, which is one of the banes of modern society."

John nodded.

"But don't let it all fool you. We are not here to hoard profits," he said. "We grow and harvest and dry here, and then sell our product in Ibiza Town. Tourists demand local weed. And we help our own whenever they are in need."

Pierre looked out the window. "The rest we just give away. Philanthropy."

"Give away?" An alien concept to those he worked with in the Wall Street world.

"Don't be shocked!" Pierre said laughing. "Years ago, I set up a nonprofit in France, and annually we all choose our favorite charities. We give an enormous amount." He laughed and shook his head. "If only some of the stodgy recipients knew where the money really came from."

"You've done so much."

He surveyed the room. "Like many, I journeyed to Ibiza for positive change. Not all make it, but if you are dedicated and believe, you can."

"But what gave birth to all of this?"

Pierre swirled wine in his cup, as if armed with fine crystal.

"About ten years ago, I visited Ibiza. Was working as a business manager at that time in France, in Marseille, doing quite well," he said. "After coming here and experiencing the sunset festival at Benirrás beach, I wandered alone into the hills. Got lost in the middle of the night, for hours. It's not easy to be lost, John. Panic sets in that you don't understand unless it happens to you."

"What did you do?"

"Kept randomly walking, scratching myself on the underbrush. Losing hope." He paused. "Eventually, I found this hidden farmhouse. Abandoned. Only later I discovered pirates had used it a hundred years ago to stash their smuggled goods."

John drank the hearty, solid table wine. Tannins had stained the inside surface of the smooth cup.

"Exhausted, I entered and lay on the floor to sleep. A full moon shined that night and came through the window like sunlight. And in the middle of the night, I heard a voice."

"Don't tell me a pirate arrived."

"No one was here John. All abandoned and desolate."

"But you—"

"I heard a voice, and I heard it clearly. And it said I should establish myself here and help others in need. This was to be my new home."

"And that is what you did?"

"Hey, Joan la Pucelle listened, and she saved all of France. The least I could do is listen."

"Is there anyone from your town who doesn't hear voices?"

Pierre chuckled. "Does not anyone hear voices in Manhattan?"

"Yes, but it usually precedes someone attacking you with a vodka bottle from behind a trash bin."

Pierre refilled both cups as they laughed, the wine frothing.

"Three months later, I sold all I owned in France and purchased this land. No building permits are issued in this region, and no one knew about this magnificent old stone home, as growth covered it. And most importantly, I discovered a freshwater spring the house had been built beside hundreds of years ago. Started the farm with a few friends, and gradually we built an entire irrigation system from the spring."

"Astounding on every level. I don't know how you did it."

Pierre's shoulders broadened. "When a person is inspired by God, he can accomplish much. He can move forward without debilitating hesitation."

The clanking sounds from the back rooms heightened. A bell rang, softly echoing throughout the valley.

"They are bringing lunch in now. Please join us."

In the next minutes, twenty-five people filed in from the fields. They spoke animatedly amongst themselves, hands on each other's shoulders. Most were nude, although a few wore shorts. Working outdoors had tanned everyone.

They congregated around the table, and several people,

on kitchen duty, burst out with bowls of vegetable soup and piping chunks of fresh bread. A spirited, merry lunch with intermittent laughter erupted around the table. John sat by Pierre, who chatted with the woman next to him. On John's other side sat a man wearing shorts.

"You are joining us here now?" the man, probably in his mid-thirties, inquired. He had cheerful eyes, and his hair, unlike most, was not long, just a wild tussle atop his head.

"I'm just visiting for the day."

"Really? That's unprecedented."

"I would think so."

"Pierre does not often bring visitors. He must trust you," he said. "I'm Lukas, by the way."

For some reason, Pierre believed he could trust him with his considerable secret after such brief time together. In a life riddled with self-doubt, often justifiable, nothing is more reassuring to the soul than when a wise individual has faith in your character.

"How did you find yourself living here?"

Lukas swallowed a heaping spoon of stew. The scent of crushed herbs arose from the bowls. "I met Pierre about nine years ago in Ibiza Town. We talked through the night about life. And, of course, cannabis sativa."

"By the way, I notice you are wearing shorts."

"On and off. But I never got used to the nudity at mealtime, as I grew up eating all my meals with my grandparents. They would not approve, I assure you that." He laughed heartily. "But most enjoy it. Of course, in the colder months, we are all dressed."

"You are from Austria, are you not?"

His eyes widened in surprise. "I was a botanist at the Institute of Botany at the University of Innsbruck. Also worked for a time in Amsterdam. And as you see, I continue my work," he said. "Pierre, as knowledgeable as he is, did not realize cannabis is a dioecious plant."

"This effects cultivation, does it not?"

"I began growing the female plants separately from the male plants. This introduces parthenocarpy in the female fruits and increases the cannabinoid resins. Otherwise, pollination reduces THC."

"Your knowledge here is invaluable."

"It doesn't take long to learn," Lukas said. "Here, the conditions are ideal. Our soil pH is in the low sixes. Good humidity, adequate nitrogen. And everyone has learned to dry the plants in proper darkness and temperature."

"I'm curious about something."

Lukas squinted.

"Home. Don't you ever miss it?"

"Oh, I go. Each December, for a month, to see my father. But after one week, I'm eager to return."

"Why?"

Lukas smiled, seemingly embarrassed.

"I was a bit of a lone wolf before. But here, I have the beauty of community. This is home, now."

Pierre tapped John's shoulder, leaning back as he introduced a woman named Serenity. He asked if John might switch seats with him.

Pink oleander flowers were braided into her lengthy brown hair, and she smelled of the sweet petals. She concentrated on her soup, as if some word puzzle floated atop the liquid. Why Pierre wanted him to move here was unclear, as Serenity seemed occupied by thoughts.

"I'm glad you have joined our community," Serenity suddenly announced, dropping her spoon into the bowl. Her broad smile revealed a space between her front teeth.

"Just here for a visit."

Her palm pressed John's hand. "You have an awakening soul, John."

So she already knew his name.

"I can plainly see how much our Pierre likes and trusts you. A very good portent." She stared directly at him. "What is your sign, John?"

"Sign?"

"Astrological."

"Does that matter?"

"Nothing matters more. Each 30 degrees of celestial longitude on the zodiac belt is crucial."

"Aries."

"I felt it instantly. And I am Aquarius. We connect with the most superb pairing for love and excitement."

"I don't suppose Serenity is your real name?"

"Yes, it is, John." Her eyes had a glassy, faraway look. "You remind me of someone I met in a dream, many years ago. He was you and we aligned."

"At least it wasn't a nightmare."

She laughed, sipping her soup again.

"Might I ask what you did," he asked, "before you came here?"

"Agronomist," she said. "I still am. Just in direct practice, not lost in research."

"No wonder the soil is so productive. Is everyone here a scientist?"

"Three of us, and one doctor. Everyone else is from a variety of backgrounds. Alvaro, one of my lovers, was a stripper in Barcelona."

Lunch was finishing. All stood simultaneously and brought their bowls and cups into the back kitchen. Three large basin sinks were fastened to the wall, with a canal of spring water running above them. Faucets could be turned to pour the water. Like something from *The Swiss Family Robinson.* Ingenious.

Everyone drifted back into the slopes and it grew quiet again. John could not find Pierre. Someone grabbed his hand and squeezed. Serenity.

She led John outside into the warmth and sunlight, guiding him past rows of Padron pepper plants to one of the living quarters. The wooden buildings, square in shape, had immense windows which flooded the rooms with sunlight. Inside were raised beds, each separated by a network of brightly colored Eastern curtains. Dream catchers hung from the ceiling, an assortment of guitars and tambourines lay in a corner, and paintings of varying sizes and styles graced the walls. An astounding collection of colors and moods, of harmony and disharmony.

Serenity guided him to her bed area and pulled the indigo curtains. She stroked his cheeks.

"What are you doing?"

She smiled, the space between teeth seemingly widening, and kissed him.

John pulled back. "You don't know the first thing about me."

"I know I feel a cosmic connection with you. We are as one. The Aquarian Age has already commenced. That is all I need to know."

John discovered warm feelings for a certain deejay rising to his consciousness.

"I have someone else," John said. "Or, at least, I hope to."

She laughed as if dealing with a child. "That is wonderful. I have others as well."

"Yes, I believe you mentioned that."

"We love freely, here. Free love."

"That is a difficult concept for me to grasp."

She squinted, observing him with puzzled curiosity.

"Not a concept which works with me," John added.

"Oh? But why?"

"I suppose if I feel love for someone, I don't want to be with anyone but that person."

"Then that is a way for you," she said. "But the health of our planet matters also, does it not?" she asked, in an accusatory manner.

"I think that an irrefutable statement." An irrelevant one also, but he refrained from divulging that element.

"Absolutely. So, we must love and align ourselves with each other, don't you see? For if we don't, the next evolutionary step of our planet cannot be taken."

"I should have used that pickup line when I was a teenager."

She appeared baffled by John's attempt at humor.

"Shall we go?" he asked.

As they strolled outside, he mentioned that Pierre waited for him.

Dimples formed in her cheeks as she squeezed his hand. "I hope you return to us some day so you can progress. We must, all of us, awaken and evolve."

"Must we?"

"Yes. This is essential. Then, and only then, can we usher in the dawning of the New Age." She kissed him, and wandered off into the fields. Her tanned form blended into the plants.

Back at the main house, Pierre was tilting back a cup of wine.

"Ready to go?" he said, jumping up.

"So I met with your friend Serenity, as you wanted me to."

Pierre raised his palms before himself. "She was insisting to speak with you. But I can see your interest was limited."

"And does everyone here share Serenity's worldview?"

Pierre paused with an amused smile, as if anticipating the question.

"Serenity and a group have their certain beliefs. And quite strong ones, at that," he said with a laugh. "But each here is free to believe in their particular way. I am more of a traditionalist."

"You mean like your fellow townsperson, Joan?"

They laughed together. As they ascended the slopes of the valley, John admired the terraced fields and the figures floating about them. At the summit, he turned for a final viewing.

"What did you think, John?"

Breezes propelled the clouds over the hot sun, dispersing undulating shadows. The fields were emerald waves ceaselessly searching.

"I am astounded."

They returned to the kayak and voyaged through the choppy, late-afternoon waters, foam spraying as waves slapped. After returning the kayak to Pierre's concealed van, he pointed to dense shrubbery, where dozens of petrol cans hid within bramble.

"But why didn't you just tell me the gas was here in the first place?"

"Then you would have missed all of that trip," Pierre said. "When is extra effort not worth it?"

On the ride back up the hills, the van hummed along pleasantly. Pierre, in high spirits, whistled a fine rendition of the Toreador Song.

The time had come to ask. Of course, he felt apprehensive, but it was time.

"Pierre?"

"Yes, John?"

"Pierre, have you ever met a Gunther Djurgenson while living up here?"

Pierre whirled toward John, the errant tires popping over stones on the roadside. John smacked against the window glass as Pierre jerked the wheel back into position.

"You know Gunther?"

"Yes," John said, stroking his forehead.

"But how can that be?"

"We were best friends many years ago. Back in the United States."

"Incroyable." Pierre shook his head "I had no idea."

"So you know him?"

"Bien sûr," Pierre said. "But of course. When I originally built our community nine years ago, it was Gunther who helped me. Brilliant ideas. Without Gunther, I could not have done it."

"Let me guess: you have not seen him since?"

Pierre turned, fog coating his spectacles. "Of course I have."

"When?"

"He stops by to visit several times a year."

John swallowed.

"In fact, I just thought of Gunther the other day. I have not seen him in a while." Pierre appeared quite eager. "But you must be in touch with him, no? You mentioned you are best friends."

John looked away, shame hot on his skin.

"What is it?" Pierre asked.

The truth works best in compromising situations. "I'm afraid I betrayed our friendship."

Pierre drove for a time. When he finally spoke, his voice was mellifluous.

"So, here is your mission that I sensed when we met." He placed his warm hand on John's shoulder. "Misfortune befalls all of us. Thank heavens the Ibiza gives us a second chance."

John collected himself. "Where does Gunther live?"

Pierre laughed, shaking his head side to side.

"What is funny? What is it?"

"No one quite knows that."

"What do you mean?"

"I think Gunther likes to keep it that way," Pierre said. "I do suspect he lives farther north up the coast. Rough up there, even compared to here. But as you well know, Gunther marches to his own tune."

They emptied four cans into John's tank, the pong of petrol penetrating. John requested to pay, but Pierre dismissed his offer with a wave.

"You know you are welcome back anytime, John," Pierre said. "And if you ever want to join us, a place for you awaits."

"Pierre, I have spent years in a world where the obsession to have more elaborate ski vacations and more expensive coastal homes than your colleagues is the driving force. One's faith erodes. So it's beyond inspiring to know people such as you are active in this world."

Pierre bowed.

"Although I truly doubt there is another quite like you."

Pierre held his fingers out the window in the peace sign as he coasted down the hill. The van descended the winding road, transmission humming, the light-blue form becoming smaller and fainter, until finally vanishing from sight and sound. All was still. Two birds chirped in the trees.

SIXTEEN

he knock rattled him. Partially because the clock read 5:22 in the morning and he was immersed in dreams, but more relevantly because he had never received a visitor here.

A thin, tangerine strip trembled along the horizon. John shuffled to the door and checked the peephole. In New York, one never opens an entrance without looking first, often with confirmatory peeks, and his habit remained.

What on earth was she doing here at this hour?

He patted his hair down, adjusted his shorts to make sure all was concealed, and opened the door.

Diana stood before him. She wore white shorts and shirt, spotless running shoes, and her hair tied in a ponytail. A wonderful, if not unexpected, sight.

"Ready?" she asked brightly.

"Ready?"

"For our run."

He thought it best to invite her inside.

As she brushed by, the air tingled of delicate flowers. He placed the tea kettle on licking, blue, gas flames, and she relaxed on a wooden chair. After arming themselves with hot mugs, Diana scanned his nearly bare kitchen.

"I half expected a bunker of American Spam."

"Shall I open the cupboard?"

She laughed, her ponytail bobbing.

"So, what inspired this?" John asked.

"Inspired?" She appeared baffled by his question.

"Well, I'm certainly delighted to see you. That's for sure. But number one, we never ran together and had no plans. And number two, it is 5:30 in the morning."

Diana laughed lightheartedly. "Sometimes you are a bit serious, John. This is Ibiza, not Wall Street."

"Well yes, but..." Her expression radiated an effervescent pleasantness. He sighed. "Let me fetch my sneakers, and we'll be off."

The warmer colors of the spectrum slathered the distant sea. They ran by thick, dew-covered grass and wildflowers. As they ran, Diana chatted, and chatted a great deal. John was accustomed to jogging alone, so fortunately she did not appear to require responses. Rather, she commented on the superb weather and the startling terrain; in truth, just about any subject seemed fair game. She mentioned how startlingly different the flora was in England, especially in Yorkshire, where grew both the upland Atlantic flora and southern, more drought-tolerant plants. Her mother, by the way, telephoned and complained ceaselessly about their loyal service staff in Yorkshire. Diana always felt a certain sadness departing from Ibiza in the autumn—this was inevitable—but enjoyed returning to bustling London and, later, to the Yorkshire countryside. Certain locales in London she absolutely loved to visit, primarily her favorite bookstore in Notting Hill where the proprietor recommended Regency romance novels to her and then eagerly awaited her assessment. She did not lose her breath at all while running and speaking simultaneously. He uttered not a word the entire run. He was simply overjoyed she felt free to share her thoughts, and agreed with her reflections and opinions with affirming nods.

When they finished, she invited him to dine at indubitably the finest lunch establishment in the world. John laughed at her hyperbole, but she maintained eye contact with a deadpan expression and instructed him he should refrain from chuckling. After realizing she was serious, he most certainly did. If he learned to have a little faith, she said, he would soon discover the truth of her claim. So, John repeated he would gladly meet her, and would eleven o'clock be fine for the ride over to the planet's top afternoon eatery?

They parked on a flattened area in front of Cala Mastella, a tiny cove beach on the southeastern shore of the island. The clay content of the reddish earth surrounding the cove generated a sucking grip which left defined footsteps. Coarse, dark sand, like smooth glass, coated the beach. Hundreds of winding plants and vines draped the two sides of the cove, probing like tentacles deep into the bay's green water. No waves at all, just a still, emerald pool. The view seemed more a psychedelic trip than reality.

Visitors were rare, as it was a distance from the major cities, but two others, a man and woman, sat pressed together beside the water at the far end of the beach. They must have arrived by foot, as John's was the sole vehicle, yet he had not seen a single footstep on the clay. A breeze hosted the fresh scent of pine needles.

"A wonderful sight."

"Isn't it?" Diana said. "You don't want to ever get used to a scene like this."

"If you can't appreciate this, you know you're doomed."

At the water's edge, they dipped in their sandaled feet. Warm fluid seductively invited swimming, and the temptation swelled to forgo all arrangements. But they had plans.

"So, where is this esteemed place?"

She pointed to the rocky hill to the left. "Over that hill. On the other side is another cove. There, we shall find it."

The hill was steep. "How on earth do the customers normally get there?"

"By parking farther down the road and hiking through the forest. Or what we are doing."

"This place must be superb," John said. "Accessibility isn't even a consideration for the owner."

The hill baked from absorbing direct sunlight. Cream-colored lichens coated the rocks, and spotted wall lizards darted about, one directly over Diana's toes. She hollered in horrified delight.

"I can't get used to those bloody things."

"They're cute."

"Cute? I don't think in our planet's history has anyone referred to a lizard as cute."

"I feel quite the pioneer."

"Next thing you will want to adopt a Komodo."

Shuffling sounds emerged from behind a boulder, hopefully not from a member of the lizard species due to the considerable resonance. A small boy with blond dreadlocks popped up, clutching a stick with two clam shells fastened onto its branches—a cross between art and a weapon. Toobee, Klav's son.

"Toobee," John said. "I remember you."

His grin revealed an array of various-sized teeth. "You haven't visited Dad lately."

"You two know each other?"

John made the introductions to a thoroughly perplexed Diana.

"But where are your parents?" she asked.

Toobee observed Diana with curiosity, puzzled she bothered inquiring about such trite details.

"I'll explain later," John said. "A bit of an unorthodox family, let me put it that way. I forgot they live right around the bend."

Toobee was tanned from hours in the sun, his dark skin incongruous against pale dreadlocks. He began hurling tiny stones which plonked into the motionless water, producing gradually expanding circles across its green surface.

"What shall we do?" Diana asked.

"Do?"

"We can't just leave him here. He is what, seven years old?"

"Leave him here?" John said. "He lives here, nearby. His parents will be back."

"We can't just abandon him."

"Is there anyone you don't want to rescue?"

Diana laughed. "Let's bring him for lunch."

Toobee's tiny hands gripped his hips as he examined the ripples on the water.

"You don't think his parents would mind?"

"Mind?" she said. "We are taking him to eat."

"Well, yes."

"And they know you, so it's not like strangers are taking him." She surveyed Toobee. "The poor thing is probably hungry."

In truth, Toobee appeared fine. Obviously, simply inviting a seven-year-old to lunch would not be happening from where John was from. But, as John repeatedly learned, Ibiza is not like anywhere else.

"Shall we?" John said, pointing the way for Toobee to lead.

On the opposite side of the hill rested another cove, even smaller than the first but blessed with the same jade water. A long, wooden deck with tables and white umbrellas was planted alongside the shore. These plump umbrellas appeared as immense mushrooms reflecting sunlight in sharp bursts. Pale green forest surrounded everything beyond.

A narrow wooden dock extended into the cove, with a single bay boat bobbing beside it. The short boat's high sides and deep hull provided smooth passage in the shallow coves and coastline it trolled.

They descended the rocks to the tables, with Toobee deftly leading the way.

"And here we are," Diana announced.

Nine tables in total, all informal, wooden constructions, with eight fully occupied. The pungent scent of various burning woods emanated from a massive metal grill. The sole empty table was a large one, meant for eight guests. John's curiosity was certainly piqued, for he wondered how such informality could lead to such venerated dishes.

"The owner is coming," Diana said.

A tall, trim man dressed in slacks and a pressed, white-collared shirt greeted Diana. His magnificent head of hair was steel gray and he had pronounced cheekbones with a sharp nose. A sumptuously dignified posture. Upon spotting Toobee, shirtless, with his bathing suit and matted hair, the man's right eyebrow rose in surprise and disapproval, the corner of his mouth following upward, ever so slightly, in amusement. Toobee gazed at his own shuffling feet, revealing an abashed smile. Perhaps there existed some history between these two, as Toobee might have foraged the restaurant over the years for morsels.

Diana explained it was just the three of them, and yet he still offered the large table, positioned majestically alongside the water. Everyone had arrived in the last half-hour in a single grand rush, and no other table would be free for some time.

Toobee sat, absorbed with stacking flat stones and cockle shells. He was not a boy who bored easily, a talent he had doubtlessly honed over the years as his parents were occupied entertaining visitors or wandering about.

"Are they bringing menus?" John asked.

"No."

"Shall I fetch them?'

"You don't understand. This restaurant has no menus."

John looked searchingly at the other tables. No menus. An unconventional start for an establishment Diana held in such high esteem.

"That is the owner's fishing boat." Diana pointed to the bay boat gently bobbing in the peaceful water. "Every morning at 4:30, he's out for his catch. Whatever he pulls in is lunch. And there is no dinner."

"And I thought *we* went out early this morning."

She laughed, sweeping hair from her eyes.

"By the way, does this owner have a name?"

"Won't give it out."

"What?"

"I asked him last time," she said. "He held my hand and said 'Worry not, my name is unimportant.' No one knows it."

This owner knew precisely what he was doing. A wise man, indubitably. Restaurant clients infamously consider themselves entitled, as passing through the threshold of a restaurant tends to activate the narcissistic proclivities of a person. But without the owner's name, clients would struggle asking for the special indulgences they inevitably sought. The personal connection established from the employment of a first name is oftentimes the launching point for requesting favors. This owner desired to avoid these petitions at all costs, for no reservations existed here and it was first come, first serve.

"In truth, I've never heard of a restaurant like this. And I've been to hundreds in New York and beyond. Thought I had seen it all. But on Ibiza, once again, I'm learning how wrong I was."

"And there is no electricity here."

"Really."

"And no phone."

"Is there any food?"

Diana laughed. "Everything is cooked over that open fire."

Several men tended to a massive grill with crackling wood fire. "Astounding."

The owner approached. "You are ready?"

"Plates for three."

"Hold on," John said. "What are we ordering?"

The owner veered and Diana gasped. Of course, he regretted the question the moment the words had recklessly passed his lips, but the damage was already inflicted.

"Are you so skeptical?" the owner asked, smoldering.

A dash of self-flagellation would be the necessary ingredient for restoration.

"Quite the contrary. Sadly, I was just unable to control my curiosity."

The owner nodded, accepting the answer as sufficient. "I serve a mixed seafood grill. Some bacalao, mero, and rodaballo." He observed Toobee joyfully sitting by John's side, and his dark eyes mellowed. "You will like it, do not worry."

"I'm sure I shall."

He nodded and walked away.

"I came here last year. Superb, John. No chemicals, no additives, all pure."

"Like Spam?"

She laughed. "All the fruits, vegetables, and herbs come from his organic farm a few miles from here. Lovely place."

"Like a dream."

"And the fish. Fresh out of the Mediterranean just a few hours ago. Now consider this: even your old billionaire clients cannot get the same service while in New York or London, no matter how much they scream or spend. Somewhat empowering, is it not?"

Bright sunlight dappled off the bay, and although the umbrellas sheltered the tables from direct light, the heat was inescapable.

"You must admire his lack of advertising. Not even a single sign. And here they are, ensconced away, and every table is full," John said, shaking his head. "An original model."

"On this island, nothing surprises me."

The owner stood by the water, arms folded, lording over everything.

"Friends told me he has operated this place for over twenty years and nothing has changed. He's too stubborn to change."

"This type of stubbornness I've learned to admire."

"Oh?"

"Without people of his fortitude, nothing unique would exist," John said. "Everyone would just be bending to the whims of the masses."

"Have you no faith in their whims?"

"Certainly not when it comes to food."

"Such the elitist you are?"

"Shall I introduce you to the aforementioned and ever-popular canned Spam, available in over one hundred countries?"

Diana laughed lightheartedly, and waived dismissively at John. "And do you like it here, Toobee?"

"The swimming. The water is very warm."

"Perhaps we can all three go for a swim after lunch."

"At the other beach we can swim all the way out. All the way out to the sea."

"Don't tempt her, Toobee, she has fins and gills."

The seafood sizzled and popped on the grill. Diana's brow furrowed as she observed Toobee erecting a pyramidal shell structure.

"You never had kids John?"

The question surprised him. "No kids."

"Neither did I. Which I regret."

One needs to tread carefully on such topics. "Well, you're certainly still young enough."

Barely a ripple crossed the bay.

"But I don't know what kind of mother I would make. And you?"

"I wouldn't make much of a good mother. The breastfeeding part."

"Cut it out, silly."

John observed his own folded hands. "Sadly, I didn't think much about children these last bleak years. Adding another life to that tundra was the last thing on my mind.

But I suppose the most important thing a father can offer his kids is his time."

"Heaven knows I never met society's expectations," Diana said with a sigh. "But having a child seems extraordinary. I'd want to impart some wisdom in her that I acquired over all these ridiculous years. What in bloody hell was it all for, otherwise?"

"I agree. But let's not forget that knowledge is to enrich our own lives, as well."

"You believe so?"

"Absolutely. I'm always wary of those who willingly, and I emphasize *willingly*, allow their own lives to crumble for their children. It does not help anyone, especially the kids. Seems more of a masochistic indulgence."

"Well said. And quite directly." Diana laughed. "I remember Missus Bobbins. Her husband finally escaped her, disappeared off onto the moors with his walking stick, and I couldn't blame the poor man. She whined incessantly about their daughter, that raising her had destroyed her life. But lovely Jennifer was the only thing that ever held that mess together."

Toobee scuffled over to the water's edge. He had spotted a school of silver fish, and attempted to spear them with a sharpened stick.

Diana clasped her slender fingers, leaning forward.

"Now let us be honest John, shall we?"

"I had hoped we already were."

She observed him with a sly smile. "Are you afraid?"

"Of?"

"Marrying?"

"Afraid?"

"Yes, afraid."

He leaned back in his chair. "Well, perhaps I was."

"Men and marriage." Diana plaintively sighed. "But I do appreciate your candor."

"Perhaps you misunderstand me. Commitment to another woman in itself did not scare me. I actually always loved that idea."

"Oh?" Her eyebrows arose in surprised interest. "Now there's a first. You are a rarity."

"I find lizards cute, and I like commitment. A true novelty."

Diana's white teeth shown through her smile. "So what terrified you then? The rabid mother-in-law that came with it?"

"My life," John sad, with a dolorous smile. "I abhorred it. What I was doing with it. And I was terrified of being cemented in that place due to obligations to her."

The rumbling of a boat engine resounded across the tiny bay. A loud, invasive sound. A sleek, charcoal motorboat, containing four formally dressed men, the front two standing like sentinels, cruised toward the dock. The restaurant owner peered cautiously over his tables, sizing everything up as one does when checking his brood, before marching out onto the dock to greet the invading ensemble. Two of the men stepped out onto the creaky planks, and the owner greeted them with aloof handshakes. Far out, peeking in from bending pines on the western side of the cove's entrance, jutted the gleaming white and steel bow of an immense yacht.

"What's happening?"

Diana squinted. "It appears they think themselves important."

Toobee crept onto the dock, drifting beside the men, unnoticed. Amongst the numerous talents he possessed was the rare ability to become invisible whenever requisite.

The owner conversed with the two men. They were initially all formal smiles, accompanied by graceful waves of the arms, but after a time, their motions became more staccato. The owner shook his head side to side, yet the men continued to press some demand. The index finger of the taller man stabbed the warm air. This man suddenly revolved toward John and Diana's table, and he pointed accusingly at them.

He separated from the assemblage and strode in their direction. A white fedora sat atop his prodigious head, and he stared unfailingly at John's eyes his entire walk over, apparently not needing to heed the terrain.

He now stood before John, legs planted apart for stability, as if anticipating a rush.

"We need to ask you something," he announced, peering at John. His gaunt mustache seemed penciled, not grown.

"Please."

"We would very much like to use this table. We have someone waiting in the yacht of high importance."

Toobee arrived back at the table. He carried two purple mussel shells in his left hand.

"And why don't you just wait for a table?"

"Let's just say we cannot."

John smiled amusedly. "Well, I must ask my lovely guests first, of course." John turned to Diana. "And would you mind sharing our table, dear?"

"So considerate of you to ask, darling. I don't see why not."

"And how about you Toobee?"

Toobee just smiled.

"If you are in need of help, we don't mind sharing. Plenty of room. Please do feel free, if you want, to join us."

The man shook his head. "I'm afraid the person wanting to use this table needs it alone."

"Alone?"

"Yes."

Diana, growing uneasy, bit her lower lip as she watched John.

"Well then I'm afraid he won't be using it."

The man removed his fedora, and held it upside down before him. "You are American, no?"

"Yes."

"Well, I have a person of high importance. You Americans understand that."

John looked over at Diana and Toobee. "I have two people of high importance also."

The man glanced at Toobee and smirked. "I came over here because I believed I could talk reason with you. The owner said we cannot take your table. He said whoever is first is first. He is a stubborn old fool."

A surge of defensiveness for the owner inundated John. "He might say the same of you, and I don't know if I'd disagree."

The man exhaled through his nostrils. "Can I offer you five hundred of your American dollars for the table?" he said, a smile of derision smeared across his face.

"You can. You proved that by just doing it," John said. "But I refuse it."

He focused on his gleaming leather shoes. "Then a thousand?"

"A thousand?"

"Yes."

"You want to offer me a thousand dollars to use this table?"

"For the three of you to leave it. That is correct."

"Is the table that important to you?"

"I have a person of importance."

John pressed his palms and gradually exhaled. "The answer is no."

The man said nothing.

"But if you change your mind, you still may join us for free," John said. "And not only that, I will treat you. You seem such a warmhearted person that I would hate to miss out on your company."

Diana muffled her laughs with her cupped hand.

The man's eyes briefly shut, and he shuddered. Certainly he had done far more in the past, in the harsher sphere, to ascertain whatever his bosses desired. Rejection was unheard of. But unfortunately for him, the situation was unsuitable for his preferred methods. He returned his fedora to his mustached head and stomped away.

"What on earth was that all about?" Diana said when he had passed out of hearing range.

The men slid into the awaiting motorboat. The owner strode back to his restaurant, his head tilted in defiance, his mouth discreetly muttering. The boat roared away, foaming the peaceful waters as it exited the benevolent harbor. The four men never once looked back, nor did they ever return.

The owner guided his young assistant by his elbow as he brought over the wide plates of Parrillada de Pescado. Everything grilled to perfection, with heaps of onions and red peppers and cherry tomatoes roasted with them, and the scents of ginger and rosemary and charred pine enveloped the entire table. Bright slices of freshly picked lemons lined the sides of the plate. As the young man placed all three platters before them, the owner stepped back to relish the sight in its panoramic entirety.

"What happened over there?" Diana asked, pointing to the dock.

The yacht had vanished from the horizon.

"They thought they were special."

"Were they?"

The owner scoffed, his chiseled features growing stoic. His chest inflated as he studied the bay. "Whoever follows the rules is special," he said firmly. "I told them, first come, first serve. That is our policy. For decades. We don't bend for anybody. Once you do, even once, it is the beginning of the end."

They delighted in their meal, as the delectable grilled fish and vegetables tasted of crackling fire. Each mouthful was savored, as John experienced the marked difference of consuming seafood pulled from the sea and vegetables plucked from the field just hours before consumption. Toobee's eating ability defied natural laws, as he devoured the entire contents of his sprawling plate. He received adulation from both Diana and John. Diana consumed about three quarters before she dropped her fork in laughing surrender. John ultimately crossed the finish line, bolstered by their incessant teasing and prodding.

They departed in merriment, thanking the nameless owner. He peered sternly down at Toobee, before releasing a splendid smile. As he patted him atop his matted hair, Toobee's face reddened, the coloration undoubtedly induced from recalling past mischief. The owner winked at John as they walked away.

As they ascended the rocky hill back to the beach on the opposite side, they turned for a last view of the restaurant. It now appeared miniature, like a porcelain model, securely nestled in the still cove. Their table was already occupied by a new group, this one filling all the seats.

"Who owns that horrid yacht, anyway?" Diana asked. "What a pissy attitude."

"Probably another insanely wealthy businessman suffering from narcissistic personality disorder."

"The King," Toobee said

They turned to him.

"What did you say?" she asked.

Toobee cradled a dark purple mussel shell in his hand. He scraped it with a rock, producing a rasping sound.

"Why did you say, 'the King?'" John asked.

"I heard them."

"Heard them say what?"

"The King."

"What did they say, Toobee?"

"They said the King of Spain waited in his yacht, and wanted to come for lunch."

Diana looked to John. "Really?" she asked.

Toobee hurled the shell down the hill. "He told those guys that we have no open tables for His Majesty."

John and Diana exchanged looks of wonderment. They descended back to the Cala Mastella beach, the sultry green bay greeting them. Toobee jumped directly in, without a second of hesitation.

"John?" Her lower lip trembled, and she blushed. "I must tell you something. I'll be quite disappointed if I don't, and I'm desperately trying to change that utterly useless part of me which refuses to say things close to my heart."

"You really are a closeted Spam lover?"

"No, silly."

"So, what is it?"

"When you told that awful man that we were important," she said, "I was touched. I know it sounds silly to say this, but it meant a lot to me. Quite chivalrous of you."

John looked into her slightly watery, blue eyes. Such an enchanting sight. A particular warmth of soul inundated him, a peculiar, wonderful feeling he was unaccustomed to.

"And when you turned down a thousand dollars for the table, it showed me something about you."

"That I'm an idiot?"

"No," she said, hysterically laughing. She finally calmed herself. "It showed me that you have principles."

"Really?" John said, with a slight smile. "I was just holding out for the next offer. I still cannot believe he stopped at a thousand."

She playfully shoved John into the water, labeling him a scoundrel, and laughed as he splashed the warmth back over her. They ended up joining Toobee on that swim, and all relished in the wonders of Ibiza.

SEVENTEEN

Her voice was jarringly hoarse, but he answered composedly nonetheless, a skill honed from years of fielding desperate calls from palpitating investors who believed they might be an iota less wealthy after some mild market fluctuation.

"Yes, this is John."

"John?" Angela said. "Where in hell have you been these days?"

Since when did his whereabouts concern her so much? "Is everything okay?"

"Can you come and see me today? I'm not in the best of moods."

"You're sure you are okay?"

"Can you come by?"

The clock on the wall read nine in the morning.

"I'll see you in an hour?"

"Just come."

When John arrived at Angela's tiny, one-story home, lonely out on arid fields, the ubiquitous wind chimes performed softly in the breeze. A fine dust blew, imparting everything with an orange haze. He stood motionless by his car for goodness knows how long, hypnotized by this fuzzy view. After a time, she jutted out the doorway and motioned for him to enter before darting back inside.

The pong of rancid incense overpowered as he peeked in. Murkiness reigned as red hemp curtained the windows. Tiny tealight candles burned throughout.

For some reason, a black laced veil obscured her face. The kitchen flowed into a tight living room, and that was about it for this railroad car of a house. She tugged him by the hand and guided him onto a stiff, cushioned couch. A cramped, dark place, notably crowded with artwork of a decidedly unpleasant nature. Dour paintings of stormy coastal scenes and grotesque sculptures of what seemed to be demons populated the room. He yearned for the sunny cheerfulness outside.

Yes, he had sensed she might be a bit peculiar, but this gothic cave was unexpected. Although they spent time together on multiple occasions, he realized he knew absolutely nothing about her.

A framed black-and-white headshot of a man sat on a table, with candles forming a half circle before him. The man wore a wry smile, a slightly disconcerting grin, as if he knew something relevant that you did not. He really did look extraordinarily similar to John.

"What is going on here?"

She sat beside John and raised her veil, revealing heavily mascaraed eyes. The flesh beneath her eyes puffed from weeping. "Today is the anniversary of my husband's death. Each year, I mark this day to remember him."

"Ah, I see."

"Do you think me a fool, John?"

A sudden landmine of a question, with only one way to answer. "Of course not."

"I live a full life. You've seen that, haven't you? But one day a year I try to honor him, and it drags me into this foulness. I'm still haunted by how fast the cancer took him."

Her husband's smile seemed to have broadened upon a second viewing. Angela gazed at the image, her lower jaw dangling open.

"It's fine," John finally announced to crack the awkwardness. "Respecting the dead was commonplace in many cultures. Regrettably, these rituals are fading."

"Today, I will also visit him. And I want you to join me."

"Visit him?"

"Yes."

"He's interred on the island? I didn't know that."

"No, John, he's buried in Laguna Beach in California."

He waited for the explanation. None came.

"So how do you plan on visiting him?"

"We will visit Boyana. She's in the old city of Ibiza Town. She will help us."

"With what?"

"To visit Stephen, my husband."

"I see," John said, failing to see at all.

"She's the finest clairvoyant on the island. I've arranged a seance for tonight. We will talk to him."

She appeared entirely serious.

"And why would you want me present? What about Bob, or one of your other longtime friends?"

She seized his wrist, a constricting clutch. "I'm afraid." She focused on the photo. "Afraid of what he will think of me now. Afraid his skin is still polished, and I've aged into a corpse."

Although this did not quite answer his question, John let it pass. More pressing concerns beckoned.

"Angela, not to sully your big plan, but do you really believe in seances and clairvoyance?"

Her eyes narrowed in derision. Perhaps the wrong question.

"Certainly," she stated. "And your doubting self will also, after this evening. Boyana is from Bulgaria, originally. Part Gypsy. Some possess that ability, like other people are born with abilities to play pianos or win at Yahtzee."

"I can safely state I've never heard that analogy."

She abruptly stood. "Why so damned skeptical, John?" Her voice was shrill. "Why so insecure?"

"Calm down, calm down." In truth Angela had taken him out socially several times and introduced him to a number of local people, so helping her was the least he could do. "I will go with you, don't worry. I simply asked how you felt about this."

"And I told you."

"You went to her before?"

"No. Never."

"No? So what is the basis of all this confidence?"

"My friend Margaret. She connected with her first husband. Poor thing was shot trying to sneak over the Berlin Wall. Margaret said Boyana has the true gift."

Obviously, Angela was experiencing a taxing day, so she needed reassuring. Her husband's passing burned as a blistering memory, but the particulars, or even the overview of their relationship and his death, remained a mystery. John knew nothing, absolutely nothing. Angela possessed the remarkable ability to raise a subject multiple times and seemingly discuss it at length, all while imparting no actual information. She created the impression of openness, but revealed naught.

"It should be interesting tonight. Parapsychology was actually founded as a branch of psychology by Joseph Rhine."

"Just like my late husband, once again. Two peas in a pod. Always know too much for your own good."

Not the first time she had mentioned their similarities, which, according to her, went far beyond appearance.

"Your Boyana, I assume, will attempt to help you communicate with Stephen by having the spirit's voice speak through her, via automatic writing or other methods."

"I do hope it's his voice."

"I'm sure you do."

"The funny thing is I never really liked my husband's voice. Loathed it, actually. Nasal and grating." The first hints of buoyancy perked her demeanor.

She snapped John into an embrace. Her wiry strength startled as his breath left him. Her hair, which appeared thick and attractive from the sides, was actually disconcertingly barren on top, a veritable wasteland. He felt hotly embarrassed and looked away, as if sneaking a peek at a forbidden scene.

"Thank you for always supporting me," she announced.

An accolade he had not earned by any standard, considering he could not recall "supporting her," as she said, even a single time. Why she claimed this was yet another mystery in the growing pile.

"Tonight, she awaits us at nine-thirty. I expect you on time."

His attendance seemed crucial to her, for reasons he could not discern. At the very least, it would be amusing. A seance might be one thing, but a seance with Angela in old Ibiza Town, well, that smelled of something memorable.

"I'll be ready."

Ibiza Town impresses for many reasons, but foremost is its appearance. Perched atop a hill alongside the gleaming Mediterranean, it serves as an imposing sight whether arriving by land, sea, or even air for that matter. Founded by the Phoenicians, the massive walls arising from the water were built by Phillip II of Spain as a defense against the Ottomans and French. Although these threats dwindled over the centuries, except for an occasionally inebriated Frenchman wandering the streets seeking mischief, the walls still inspire awe.

The old part of the city, the Dalt Vila, sits atop this steep hill. It can only be explored on foot, as its cobblestone streets are far too narrow for vehicles. What one finds is a labyrinth of winding streets with seemingly no order, a striking contrast to those accustomed to Western, suburban grids. These streets are packed with cozy cafes, seafood restaurants, and numerous other establishments less easy to categorize. The town thrives day and night throughout the summer, attracting those exploring history and architecture as well as those seeking merriment and other sides of life.

Angela claimed that Boyana was located somewhere on the very top of the hill, which loomed above them like a winding Tower of Babel. The climb to the peak of the Dalt Vila was intimidating, as the remarkably steep streets gradually morphed from wider spaces teeming with boisterous groups to narrow, twisting lanes where a few lone stragglers suspiciously wandered.

They ascended without conversing, as Angela's repeated mumblings revealed mental strife. These struggles John dared not disturb for fear of backlash. As the concluding rays of sunlight submerged into the sea, the rose skies melted into darkness.

"Here we are," she finally announced, exhaling from the strain of the climb.

They had reached the peak of Dalt Vila.

Neglected two-story buildings hunched on either side of the narrow cobblestone road. The vanquished sun and derelict buildings, along with a naked high-altitude breeze, made for a foreboding atmosphere contrasting with the warmth and cheer below. Not a single soul roamed.

They stopped before a distorted wooden door with a dusty, peeling threshold. Above hung a bare iron lamp.

"This is it."

Now, how Angela located this place was a fair question, as she claimed she had never visited, and no signs or visuals existed. But it was not the time for interrogation.

She knocked. A hollow sound reverberated off the rotting wood. Unsurprisingly, no answer. She knocked again, with more force, dust puffing off the sides of the door. Distant group laughter echoed from the maze of crowded streets far below. Still no answer.

He questioned whether Angela was stable. Perhaps the strain of the day had deluded her. Reviewing the circumstances, he could not help but be appalled. Here they waited in front of an abandoned building, on the very top of the Dalt Villa, hoping a Bulgarian clairvoyant might answer so they could converse with Angela's dead husband. A faint laugh escaped as he realized just how far he had come from polished Wall Street board meetings. Angela, ears prickling, whipped her narrowed eyes toward him, rife with suspicion, and began opening her lips to admonish him.

The door cracked.

A short woman peeked out, squinting, but darkness prevented a clear view of her face.

"Boyana," Angela said. "We are here."

She ushered them inside.

Mustiness hung inside the poorly lit hallway, as if fresh air had dared not traverse through in decades. They followed her stout, hunched figure to the end. She wore layers of peasant's clothing, and each time she stepped with her left leg, something squeaked. John stroked his cheek, working to repress inappropriate laughter, for as dismal as everything seemed, something undeniably humorous and absurd existed to all this.

They entered a tiny side room. A round table covered with velvet red cloth was positioned in the center, with three smooth wooden chairs encircling it. Three candles burned on the table.

Boyana led Angela back out into the hallway, shutting the door after her. Hissing sounds passed back and forth, as if Boyana instructed and Angela questioned. John tiptoed to the doorway, straining to listen. More intensive whispering, back and forth. Was that his name he just heard? Moments later, a slightly flustered Angela entered, Boyana following.

John stole the opportunity to observe Boyana when she neared the candles. A dark bandana covered her head, and her face was ghastly pale. Most fascinating was her majestically long nose which curled down precipitously at its end, as if melting. Unfortunately, she caught John's horrified stare. Her eyes flared, and he looked embarrassedly away.

"May I ask everyone to sit down," Boyana announced. Her deep accent sounded as if it might originate from the Eastern European region, but John, usually adept at recognizing accents, could not place it.

John and Angela awaited instructions.

"Did you bring it?"

Angela handed a paper satchel to Boyana. She removed four cookies and placed them on a cream-colored plate which she positioned in the table's center.

"His favorites, yes?"

"Butter cookies. He always tried not to eat too many."

For some reason, Boyana was glaring at John. Faces were murky as it was dark, but fondness was certainly not the prime emotion in her expression.

"Now, we proceed. I must first ask, have any of you been drinking alcohol?"

They answered no.

She stared darkly at John. "Ever?"

"Ever?"

"Have you ever consumed alcohol?"

John looked to Angela. "Well, yes, of course. But..."

"Enough," Boyana said firmly. "We do not need your endless tales of drunken revelry. This session is not all about you."

He looked quizzically to Angela, but she focused on the plate of cookies.

"You must want to be here. Seances are only for those who want to attend."

Angela's steely gaze transmitted a clear message. He resolved to keep an open mind. Best to say nothing.

"Remember not to give me any information," Boyana said. "What you hear will come from the spirit we are contacting, not me."

Angela nodded.

"Also, this is important: you must trust those you are with. This can be a revealing experience, so be sure you trust each other. If not, information that is revealed could be exploited."

Boyana turned to John again, eyeing him beneath bushy eyebrows. "You've trusted her with everything?"

John looked to Angela, then back at Boyana. "I'm sorry? Have I what?"

"Revealed everything to her."

"Me? Everything about what?"

"Everything."

"What does my life have to do with anything here?"

"Your dating and love interest. Your fantasies."

"What fantasies?"

"I see. So we have a regular repressed sort. Devoid of all feelings?"

"No, not at all, but—"

"No need to babble on and on with lascivious tales," Boyana said, admonishing him with her thick finger. "As I told you before, whether you like it or not, this session is not all about you."

Making sense of this all was an insurmountable task.

Angela smiled. "I trust him. He's a bit droll at times, but he has a good heart."

"Then let us begin."

Boyana instructed them to link hands. They would chant until a response came. If a response did not come, it simply meant the spirit could not be contacted. Spirits, like people, are sometimes busy.

"Your husband's name is Stephen?" Boyana asked.

Angela gasped. "But how did you know?"

"I can feel it. He's close. Now let us begin."

Angela nervously glanced at John.

"All chant the following: Our beloved Stephen, we bring you gifts from life into death. Commune with us and move among us."

They began to repeat this mantra along with Boyana, a methodical performance. How this spirit, if not currently occupied with a full schedule, would manifest itself was unclear. Boyana's voice dominated, and Angela joined, but John never contributed to the chorus. Since Boyana and Angela's eyes were shut, he could not refrain from stealthily observing their determinedly earnest expressions through the flickering candlelight.

Boyana halted.

"What is it?" Angela said, opening her eyes.

John signaled with his expression for her to be silent.

Boyana's eyeballs rolled upward, unveiling veiny whites. Her head and nose swayed side to side, inexplicably in opposite directions. All hands remained linked.

"Angela," she said. Her voice was now far deeper.

"Angela, my dear," the voice said again. The former accent vanished, and it sounded like a native of Brooklyn.

Angela looked imploringly to John, and he nodded for her to respond.

"Yes?" she asked.

No response.

"Yes?" she tried again, more forcefully.

"I am glad you came for me."

Angela smiled gratefully, tears welling in her eyes.

"I've missed you," the voice said.

"Missed you too. So much."

Silence for a time. She panicked, looking searchingly toward John.

"Are you still there, Stephen? Are you there?"

"Are you happy?" the voice asked. Boyana's eyes remained rolled as she swayed in her trance.

"Not truly. Not without you."

"I want you to be happy."

"I am happy that we are talking. Now I am happy."

"Angela?" the voice said.

"Yes?"

"Don't feel guilty about anything. You did your best."

Angela's face wrinkled in torment. "I tried to get you to stop those cursed cigarettes. You wouldn't listen to me. You never listened to me."

Silence. Angela looked desperately to John. He nodded in encouragement.

"You never listened to me," Angela repeated.

"Angela."

"Yes?" she asked. "I'm here."

Silence followed.

"What did you want to tell me, Stephen?"

"You need to move on. I am fine. You need to move on now."

A tear fell. "But what about you?"

"Now, I am fine."

"Are you?"

"I am fine now. But it is time for you to move on and find someone new."

"Yes, but—"

"I insist. It is time."

"But—"

"It is time. You deserve that. And whoever he is, he will be a very lucky man. The luckiest man in the world."

Boyana's eyes dropped and her swaying halted. She appeared confused, as if awaking in a foreign landscape. Her hands relaxed and released, and John and Angela's followed. As Boyana exhaled, candlelight sparkled on sweat beads beneath her eyes.

"He appreciated your cookies." Boyana's voice had returned to its former timbre and accent.

They observed the plate. Empty. The butter cookies were gone save a few crumbs. Angela squealed in amazement.

At this point, it is important to note that John worked diligently to keep an open mind. He voluntarily attended, and obeyed the rules. But inevitably, incredulity lurked. Nothing particular in that conversation offered evidence of spiritual contact, nor was there any particular giveaway of falsehood. But where the damned butter cookies had vanished to was beyond him. The cookies were present moments ago, in the center of the table, and all their hands had been linked the entire time.

Boyana led them back down the hall to the doorway, her left steps still squeaking. No one spoke, as it was a time for contemplation. At the threshold, Boyana hugged Angela and winked triumphantly at her. She ignored John entirely. They walked past Boyana's protracted nose, which seemed to have melted more at its distant end, then returned to the dark street. Thankfully, a blast of nighttime sea air replaced the hallway's miasma.

Angela strapped her arm around John's waist, her fingertips probing uncomfortably into his pelvis, and tugged him along.

"So? Do you think Stephen correct?"

Apparently, they would now discourse about the opinions of a dead man.

"About?"

"That I should move on with my life."

"It seems you have."

"You know what I mean."

"Well, you do maintain a vibrant social life. You're out meeting people all the time. It's impressive."

Angela seized his shoulders, blocking advancement. Despite the warmth outside, her flesh felt clammy. "He meant moving on from him. Acknowledging a new love."

"That's a personal issue. Only you can decide that."

Her eyeballs seemed to be oscillating. "But you did hear him say that."

"I did."

"And you agree?"

Questions concerning dating and deceased spouses demand circumspect treading. Most answers, regardless of tact, lead to trouble.

"That is personal, and up to you."

"But do you agree?" she insisted, her jaw muscles pulsing.

"Well—"

"Yes or no. Just answer."

He detected rising anger, and needed to avoid an overflow. "Well, it has been some twenty years. You need—"

"I'm so happy you agree," she interjected. "Now, let's get back down into the town. We can celebrate together."

As they descended back into the busier, wider streets of Dalt Vila, her pace inexplicably alternated between sprinting to barely shuffling. A bizarre display. She turned, panting.

"Thank you."

"For?"

"For being such a help to me, John."

"I didn't do anything."

"And to the many others besides me," she said with a sudden harshness.

"Many others?"

A mawkish smile arose across her face. "You do perform so wonderfully when you're out attending to all those other lucky people, and ignoring me. A real good Samaritan."

Apparently, she preferred his attention focused solely on her.

"That said," she said, squinting. "If you could only apply some of that superb confidence to helping yourself..."

He nodded.

"Helping others resurrect is great." Her nostrils flared in a patronizing expression. "But perhaps you are compensating a bit for ignoring your own lonely life, my dear John? Hmm?"

Odd to hear this, since she had contacted him and demanded his help today, but in truth, some validity could exist to her theory.

"That wouldn't surprise me in the least."

His acquiescing response caught her off guard. She had possibly hoped for some sort of squabble in order to raise the temperature, but was now left dumbfounded. He simply walked away.

"No need to be lonely anymore, John," she said, catching up to him with a frantic dash. "You just need to acknowledge the love in your life, as well."

"Perhaps you are right."

"I am. And I'm so excited for our big Harvest Party at Bob's finca coming up. Remember? The best party of the year."

"I remember."

"The perfect time to create lasting memories," she announced with aplomb.

John nodded.

"Bob keeps asking about you since that first dinner date he hosted for us."

He had not considered the outing as a "date," but so be it. "Do tell him I say hello."

"You can tell him yourself at the party; it's only a few weeks away. He would absolutely murder me if I didn't bring you."

"Then I best attend, no?

EIGHTEEN

After politely informing Angela on the phone that he could not visit that day, painful silence followed. His inability to immediately meet apparently offended her, though he had just seen her the evening before.

But today, he had other plans: pick up Diana, meet Andre, and take them to the legendary Benirrás beach. Andre and many others raved about the weekly tribal drumming show to honor the sunset and peace on earth and any other cause one felt inspired to throw in. Supposedly, this beach was home to the world's finest sunset. At least, that is what John heard from multiple sources. Admittedly, not all these sources were sound, but it was a surprisingly consistent message nonetheless.

"Why can't you see me today?"

"Why?" John said. "I have plans. I just saw you last night. But tomorrow, Monday, I can drop by if you like."

Angela said nothing.

"You there?"

"What are you doing today?"

Always quite direct.

"Meeting with a few friends."

"Why?"

"Why?" John said. "To see who memorized mathematical pi to the most digits."

She did not laugh.

"The same reason most people meet with friends," he said with exasperation. "To enjoy the day."

"And who exactly are you meeting?"

"Well, I'm sure you don't know them." Her line of inquiry began reeking of entitlement, and he felt peeved. "It might shock you, but you don't know everyone on Ibiza."

"Men?" she said, disregarding his comment. "Or are you meeting with a woman?"

"What? Why ask these absurd questions?"

"No need to be rude."

Arguing logically was useless. Being correct—which, when one is naive, seems paramount—often matters not. In fact, correctness and truth often endangered a person. This perturbing revelation he had experienced over and over throughout the last years, and it had the lamentable effect of introducing an element of cynicism into his worldview.

"Okay, okay. Sorry for any rudeness. How about this: would you like if I stopped by tomorrow?"

"We'll see about all that," she answered dismissively.

"Up to you."

Two painfully synthetic coughs rang in his ear.

"By the way, where are you heading today?" she asked in a suddenly congenial tone, as if a different person inquired.

His lips, parting to answer, froze.

His instincts had twitched. Why he hesitated in divulging his destination he could not articulate, perhaps due to her increasingly erratic behavior. Regardless, something primal told him he should withhold it.

Complete silence on her side of the receiver. A trying struggle, but eventually he yielded. He failed to hold fast to his instinct.

"Benirrás beach."

"Oh?"

"Sundays are supposed to be memorable."

"Very nice choice," she said. "A flood of hippies pours into there Sunday evenings for drumming at sunset. Enjoy."

"Thank you."

"I'll call tomorrow morning so we can arrange our meeting."

Thank heavens she seemed to have stabilized. Did she not?

At ten minutes before two, John strode down the sunny block to pick up Diana. Apprehension reigned. Not a complete fool, he understood that his fondness for her caused this. With her, his grand plan had been to take things one step at a time. Superbly judicious—but he needed to be mindful that he did not take one step at a time until time expired. He had a tragic proclivity to do so, at least when he felt strongly about someone or something.

She greeted him by leaning her left shoulder against the door frame, her body angled most pleasantly. She wore a blue-and-white sundress, and her hair flowed freely over her shoulders. Her ebullient mood impressed as much as her fair appearance.

"Let me grab snorkeling gear," she said. "I just can't wait to catch a ride in your wonderfully reliable car."

As they pulled away, quite smoothly, Diana inquired about "this Andre chap" they were to meet. He informed her of the plans to extract him by the sea in Santa Eulària. Andre owned a Djembe drum and drummed at Bennirás occasionally, as many of his fellow market vendors also made the weekly trip. Not that Andre actually socialized much with any of them (heaven forbid), but rather it served as a Sunday jaunt that offered more thrills than his lone tent amidst the trees. After hearing of Andre's absentee daughter and chilly former wife, Diana became appalled, and as usual wanted to remedy everything instantly. But this time, this one time, John convinced her that a bit of patience would be wisely heeded. Not only bettering his income, but developing his ability to hold on to it and resist the sticky clutches of his ex would be essential to Andre's redemption.

Andre wore pirate shorts and a ripped shirt. A goblet-shaped wooden drum hung from his neck. With his gray hair flipping in the breeze, he looked the part of a genuine Ibiza hippie.

"Welcome aboard. This is Diana."

She turned and smiled. John, observing through the rear-view mirror, spotted Andre's eyes expand.

"Now, you look like a real Ibiza drummer," Diana said.

His face flushed and eyebrows lowered. Curiously, this designation displeased him when coming from Diana.

"Few know that only a couple of years ago I worked in Amsterdam as a manager for the airlines," he stated, a bit too hurriedly.

She detected his discomfort, and maneuvered to assuage it.

"Did you really? Fabulous! And how was it?"

"Wore a tie everyday. And my father is a career military man."

"And I'm sure you were wonderful at it."

They pulled away, heading north.

"How do you like it here on Ibiza?" Diana asked. She was caught in that awkward social situation, where one needs to feign ignorance about the new person present, although all know otherwise. In these circumstances, everyone must play along dutifully until the initial hump is traversed.

"I appreciate this island," Andre said. "But I could be doing better here."

"And why is that, dear?"

Perhaps it was the "dear," or the general merriment, but Andre proceeded to describe in detail his dire situation. Atypical, for the terse Andre. John's presence might have precipitated this change, as whomever John trusted, Andre now felt comfortable with. But he orated in a more impassioned form, and this invigorated version was likely prompted not solely by any formidable bond of trust, but also by the pulchritude of the inquirer. By the time they neared Benirrás beach, his lengthy tale of ignominy greatly affected them both.

They began their final descent.

Unlike most other beaches in the Northern region, which lay directly below cliffs, here the hills gradually sloped. As they flowed down, the massive horseshoe-shaped cove of Benirrás materialized. Immense, rocky slopes stretched on either side of the bay before finally meeting the sea several hundred feet out. Cap Bernat, a rock formation rising from the water where bay met open sea, appeared as a hand pointing heavenward. It was referred to by locals as "the finger of God."

Smooth, wet beach stones glinted in sunlight. Four yachts

already moored in the harbor, and twenty or so people collected on the far end of the beach. All was serene, as it was only mid-afternoon, hours before the celebration would erupt.

"That is where it all happens," Andre said with reverence, motioning to the beach's far end.

Drummers congregated around a dilapidated stone building with a porch and poles propping up a corrugated metal awning. The choice instrument was Djembe drums originating from West Africa. These loud, goatskin-covered drums with leather neck straps are played bare handed. The name "Djembe" originated in Mali and came from the mantra "Anke djé, anke bé," meaning "everyone gathers in peace." Unsurprisingly, Ibiza wholeheartedly embraced them. The other drums, the Dunun, were smaller gathered in clusters of three, and are played with sticks. Most of the drums hailed from the island itself, lovingly crafted by artisans in their secluded workshops tucked into forested hills.

It would not be imprudent to state that all those in this drumming clan appeared remarkably similar. Although from different lands, the extended list of similar traits included lengthy and unkempt hair, absence of shirts, sun-beaten skin, wiry physiques, and blithe attitudes. Andre checked all points save the final characteristic. They tolerated him, though he did not integrate much. This association did not possess any indoctrination regulations besides an openness to participation.

The real drumming occurred closer to sunset, when the visitors flooded in. For now, these early arrivals played sporadically, chatted, and smoked tobacco and marijuana. A handful of men and women danced by themselves on the beach.

Andre dashed over. "You must meet this guy. He's ninety-seven, and still loving drumming. You two will get along."

A tanned man sat in the center of the other drummers. He seemed to consist solely of bone and tendon.

"Reynaldo, this is John and Diana."

Reynaldo turned to them. Irises and pupils in his dark eyes were one. He observed each of them in turn without hurry.

"You have come for the drumming and the sunset, no?"

"We have," John said.

"I do hope we are not disturbing you," Diana quickly added.

Reynaldo smiled, his wrinkled skin stretching over prominent cheekbones. He rested his bony hand onto Diana's.

"Do you know what Tolerancia Ibicenca is?"

She looked searchingly to John, and he shook his head.

"No?" Reynaldo said. He laughed pleasantly for a time. "Then let me tell you. You see, natives on this island are very tolerant people. How did they develop this way?" He grinned, many of his teeth still intact. "From invasions. The Carthaginians, Romans, Moors, the Catalans, the Spanish all invaded Ibiza. You understand?"

They nodded.

"And now is occurring the latest invasion and the most difficult of all."

Everyone glanced at each other, eager for him to continue.

"The tourists!" he said, laughing heartily. The drummers chuckled and patted each other's backs and nodded in assent.

"All of these groups came here over hundreds of years, while we, the natives, have always been here. We, over time, developed a patient tolerance of other cultures." He winked at John. "Mostly out of necessity."

Diana smiled in admiration.

"Now notice," Reynaldo said, "Ibiza never invaded anywhere."

"Yes," John replied. "That's true."

"Do you know why that is?"

Diana looked to John.

"Why is that?" he asked. The true answer could only originate from Reynaldo.

"Because none of us ever wanted to leave here!"

His joy infected, and all joined in laughter. The giddiness clearly pleased Reynaldo, as his face beamed with pleasure. Here sat a man whose remarkable youthfulness undoubtedly stemmed from a lifetime of relishing in the mirth of others. He began to drum, the rest instantly joining his rhythm.

Since it was mid-afternoon and hot and they happened to be standing on a gorgeous beach, Diana suggested they capitalize on this propitious situation. She would fetch snorkeling gear from the car.

"So, how well do you know her?" Andre demanded, the instant he gauged she had departed from hearing range. Increased patience might have facilitated a more accurate estimate, as she threw back a coquettish glance at John.

Andre lowered his eyes, embarrassed. But he recovered with surprising rapidity, and awaited his answer with mouth open.

"Well?"

John stalled his response, mostly to irk him, let him stress a tad. Childish curiosity from an adult invites a bit of teasing.

"So?"

"What? What is it that you need to know so desperately?"

"Are you two dating now?"

"Good heavens," John said. "You are the little eager beaver. Suddenly your infamous reticence vanishes?"

Andre waited resolutely.

"We have spent time together this summer. She's astounding. Okay?"

"Yes, yes. But are you dating?"

His persistence impressed. "No. Not dating yet."

"Yet? What are you waiting for, Armageddon?" His brow furrowed, palms facing the clear sky. "You usually know how to do everything." He seemed acutely disappointed.

"I wish."

"Well, what are you waiting for?"

"What am I waiting for?" John said. "I don't know what I'm waiting for."

"No?"

"Just seeing how things progress. I need to take care of things in my life, as well," he added testily.

The drummers struck a more powerful beat.

"Does everything need be set before you date her? Maybe she can help you along."

"Everything needs...well, no. No. But I need to take care of things in my life."

"And she can help you with that."

"Well, I suppose."

"I can see she likes you."

"Can you?" John asked brightly.

"Getting someone like her to be interested in anyone...such things I thought impossible. But here you are. Just like those Hollywood guys."

"You are absurd."

"By the way." Andre's grave tone was a jarring shift from the levity moments ago. "There are times when it's *not* good to think too much. Even for someone as clever as you," he added grimly.

"I'll consider that."

"Opportunities slip away forever."

Diana returned with snorkeling gear, and Andre announced he would join the drumming.

"Shall we?" Diana held out a mask and snorkel. "Or are you off to pound a drum as well?'

"Don't tempt me."

They traversed the rocky slopes on the eastern side of the bay, past the aged wooden boat houses built on rock, and found a flat launching point halfway out to sea. The water's bottom, entirely visible, was rocky, not sandy, which contributed to the water's transparency as it offered no sediment. The sea beckoned.

"Are you a proficient snorkeler?" she asked.

"Why do I have the distinct feeling I'm not as good as you?"

"If done properly, it's one of life's most rejuvenating experiences."

"Well, seventy-one percent of the earth is covered by water," John said, as he lowered himself into the warmth. "Let us spend some time with the majority."

"A bloody know-it-all."

Below existed an alternate world. Dark seaweeds flourished, and colonies of yellow-tubed sponges grew on the rocks, appearing like clusters of chimneys. Slender seagrass swayed in underwater currents. They moved along the rocks and encountered seahorses, picking away at plankton floating by.

As they swam farther into the bay, schools of silver gilthead fish passed, and several large dusky groupers swam along. Diana motioned vigorously, finger flashing in the water, and initially John could not locate what she so ardently pointed out. Then, with a start, he spotted two sea turtles, each three feet long, with heart-shaped shells. A wondrous sight. They swam nimbly, pausing occasionally to consult with one another as they headed farther out. Diana gracefully dove underneath. Both turtles remained unfazed as she swam beside them, as one even peeked and acknowledged her. She stayed alongside for such a remarkable length of time it seemed she had mermaid descendants.

Nearing the rocks again, John detected rapid movement along an outcropping and identified an octopus. While it lay camouflaged against the sandy rock's color, the flailing of its tentacles revealed it. With a twitch, it vanished into a crevice.

John and Diana floated on the bay's surface, the sun tanning their backs, intermittently plunging into the coolness below.

In due course, they climbed onto the baking rocks, reclining in the shade beneath a cluster of Mediterranean pines. Diana closed her eyes, breathing rhythmically. Her exquisite presence was as soothing as the natural beauty surrounding them. John peered out to the sky through the web of green needles vibrating in the breeze, a mellow but persistent buzzing sound. Clouds moved smoothly across blueness, smoothly and steadily on their journeys, steadily, each on its own journey, and John drowsily joined them. Life seemed limitless.

When they awoke, a dozen more white yachts had moored at the harbor's edge.

The sunset preparations had begun. Those aboard the yachts would celebrate in an alternative manner, as gin and tonics with slivers of lime were more likely to be found than communal flasks of local hierbas, but all would revel in the same perfect sunset.

Back on the beach, a throng had amassed. Everything moved intensely as fervor pervaded. Andre found them instantly, as if waiting the entire time.

"How was it?"

"Simply lovely," Diana said, sharing a furtive smile with John.

A mass of dancers shook before the drummers. Not an organized gathering by any means, as shirtless men and topless women congregated around the old building. They danced, hopped into water, kissed, or practiced the Vriksasana and

Balasana yoga positions along the shoreline. Clouds of marijuana smoke hung low in the air and dissipated whenever a breeze blew off the bay, soon to be replaced by the next billows.

Andre offered his drum to John.

"I'm not a drummer."

"So? Just bang away at the rhythms and enjoy."

While John considered this, Diana snatched the drum from Andre's outstretched hands, smiling as she strapped it around her shoulders. "I'll go, if you are too much of a scaredy cat." She seized John's arm and tugged him into the drumming group.

Diana started tapping, imitating the man seated in front of them. Vertebrae protruded along his back. His long black hair remained perfectly steady, but his elbows, sticking out like chicken wings, methodically rose and fell as he rolled a beat. She tried her first rolls with a fixated expression, and played awfully well for an amateur.

The sun, the reason all had come, now commenced its descent.

Bodies throbbed before the drums. This collective zeal evidenced appreciation and awe for this honorable maintainer of life. John now understood why many deemed the Benirrás beach sunset the perfect one. This massive, red-and-orange gas ball known as the sun descended precisely in the middle of the bay, framed perfectly by enormous rocky crags on either side, serving as velvet curtains on a sumptuous stage. The stage itself was the venerable Mediterranean sea, and the sun swelled as it began immersing into these tranquil waters.

The dancers now directly faced the enormous and trembling sun, which melted into the stage and slowly slipped away. The sea turned crimson. An overwhelming sight, a sensory overload, having the beneficent effect of causing all participants to abandon their tribulations and needs, as they witnessed their triviality in comparison to the cosmic majesty of all things.

While Diana drummed, already improving markedly, John detected something deep within the crowd.

He noticed something peculiar—which is saying much, in a group of this nature. A discordance existed. Nothing overwhelming, but a form attracted his attention, presumably due to its lack of motion, an anomaly among the pulsing bodies. He disregarded this form, and jumped into a few more rifts, as he now was armed with a drum. Yet once again, he detected this stationary form behind others, more a silhouette than a person.

The sun finally dipped below its stage. Its concluding layers of fiery warmth quivered on the sea's surface.

In the amassing purple darkness, he focused on this unsettling person, standing steadfast between two dancers who moved left and right like reeds in shifting winds. This form, directly facing him, felt familiar. The sloping of shoulders, the slightly oversized head, even a whiff of the vigilant demeanor.

Angela.

She stood on the beach watching him. Staring. She had come after all. He should have kept his bleeping mouth shut when they had last spoken.

John poised to approach her, but something prompted him to wait a bit, perhaps what we term "instinct." If she desired to say hello, she would have already done so.

Diana still drummed, and with Andre planted beside her, lost in music, the moment was opportune.

"Can you stay with Diana for a while?"

Andre turned with a contorted expression, appalled that John would dare leave fair Diana for even a moment. A scandalous concept. "Where are you off to?"

"I'll return in a few minutes."

In the growing darkness, John worked through the moisture of bodies.

He arrived at Angela's side. She seemed shorter than usual. She now busily moved side to side, facing the drumming. Surely she knew he waited directly beside her, yet she refused to turn and acknowledge him.

A horrific awkwardness persisted.

"Angela."

She did not bother to look.

"Angela," he repeated, louder. "How are you?"

Her head rotated, gradually, a smile rising.

"What are you doing here?" John asked in as lighthearted manner as he could muster.

She surveyed him for a time, amused. A dancer swirled around, grabbing at John's hand with slippery fingers, but he held fast.

"Are you alright?"

"I came to enjoy the sunset," she said in a musical voice.

"I see."

"When you informed me of your little upcoming trek to Benirrás, I remembered just how much I cherish it here." She giggled wildly, establishing eye contact for the first time. "Why John? What else would I be doing here?"

John felt relieved. Mostly. Or partially. She appeared in high spirits, if not a bit askew. Maybe his initial disquietude, mysterious in that he had not diagnosed the exact cause (rather just experienced its aggravating effects), was frivolous. Maybe.

"She's your friend?" she asked, pointing in the direction of Diana.

Diana drummed, her hair curled at the tips from their salty swim. Other drummers smiled at her, admiring her, attempting to initiate insouciant conversations. Andre sat nearby, frowning at all suitors.

John felt intuitively protective of her. "Those are a few of my friends."

"And what is her name?"

"Andre is his name. She is Diana."

"Where did you meet her?" she insisted. "She is a beautiful one, John."

"I met him at the market, and her around."

"Yes, I saw him earlier this afternoon when I arrived here. Drumming." She looked into John's eyes. "I saw him. But not her, and not you. Off somewhere together?"

"Around."

She grinned, eyes so narrow the whites vanished. The rank smell of perspiration and musty seaweed wafted off her.

"You were awfully careful never to mention this Diana to me. Never once."

This interaction was increasingly unpleasant, and he now felt determined to keep her from meeting Diana, at all costs. Just had to be smart about it.

"Never came up."

"Very good answer, John, very good." She shook her head with a scoffing laugh. "I do remember discovering you on your first day on Ibiza months ago. Lonely at that cafe. So badly I felt for you. How I wanted to help you."

She oscillated and hummed to the music. Her humming swelled in volume, and her dance rose in energy, but they were incongruous, unrelated to each other. Unintelligible lyrics emerged.

"Are you sure you are okay?"

She looked up at him sharply. "Why do you keep asking that?" she asked in a piercing voice.

The party continued around them.

"Who are you, the judge and the jury?" she demanded. "Come to convict and send me away?"

"What are you saying?"

"Come to smash down the gavel?"

"Just asking if you are okay."

"Bringing the chains and cuffs."

Time to switch course, as this was leading to nowhere but perturbing bizarreness.

"So how did you get here?" She did not possess a car.

"A friend," she said, her tone lightening. "He's lost somewhere in all that crowd and darkness. I won't be able to get home."

"Shall I help you?"

Her chilly fingers gripped his forearm. "Always so considerate, John. My dead husband incarnate."

"How can I help?"

She searched his face, then peered up and down the beach. "You can check for him one way, I the other."

"Whom am I looking for?"

She hesitated, for whatever reason. "You remember Bob, of course? Our dear Bob."

"Bob's visiting out here tonight? Really?"

"Don't be so surprised."

John scanned the lengthy beach.

"That's the longer end," she said, pointing to the eastern portion of Benirrás. "You canvas that one. You're much faster."

"Am I? Okay, let's meet right back here."

"And I will leave right now to check the other end."

The core of the celebration had passed and many were leaving. This did not result in an instant departure, but most lived many miles from Benirrás beach and public transportation did not exist. Uninhabited forests surrounded. Thus, people searched, often fruitlessly, for their initial rides, or attempted to charm their way into new ones.

John foraged for Bob through shifting groves of people, but could not locate him. After scouring all the way to the rocks, he turned. No sign of him on the way back, either.

Back at the meeting point, no Angela. Curiously, he could not locate her anywhere in the vicinity. Diana and Andre were gone, as well. Everything seemed to be spiraling awry.

"John? Is that you?"

A familiar voice. In darkness against the sea stood Pierre. His silhouette was purple as the water. They embraced.

"So good to see you again, friend," Pierre said. "So, you visited Benirrás! I hoped you would. Enjoy the show?"

"Quite an experience."

"Yes, I still come once in a while." He examined the cloudless sky, focusing on the brightest star in the multitude glimmering above, seemingly taken aback by it. "They have been asking about you at our community. 'When is John returning?' they ask me," he said with laughter. "You are well?"

"I'm fine."

"Yes? But something troubles you I can see."

Was he that transparent?

"I'm fine," John said. "A fascinating night. Your kayak is here?"

"Beyond the rocks. I go back now."

"You decided to wear clothes?"

"In the crowds it can be helpful," Pierre said with a smile. "But I will strongly consider your suggestion."

"I hope I will see you again soon."

"John?"

Something about the way he addressed him, the tentative tone, unsettled.

"Yes?"

Pierre hesitated.

"What is it?"

"You know, I've not heard from our good friend Gunther in a while. A long time now."

John's chest tightened. "Do you think he is fine?"

"It's unusual of him not to visit for so long."

"Well last time I saw you, you did not seem worried."

"I did not wish to worry you also. But it is very unusual for him to stay away so long."

"I see."

"As I mentioned, I know of no way to contact him. And then you came along."

"So, you feel something is not okay with him?"

"I find it troubling he does not visit for such a length of time."

John found himself growing frustrated, as he could not decipher what exactly Pierre desired from telling him this. Where he fit into all of this. But he wanted something.

"Why are you telling me all this, Pierre?"

Pierre surveyed John's vexed expression. "Because after meeting you, it is my true sense that you can find him."

"Me? What does that mean?"

Pierre peered at the brightest star once again. "You have journeyed all the way from America to Ibiza to find Gunther, have you not?"

Hearing this stated aloud struck him profoundly, as if he had not quite realized the truth of it until now.

"Yes. Yes, I have."

His warm hand rested on John's shoulder. "You possess the heart to find him."

He said farewell, squeezing John's shoulder and vanishing

into the darkness along the rocks. John gazed out to sea, working through all Pierre had said.

Only two drummers remained from the initial brigade, both languidly tapping their drums. Their drumming sounded flimsy in the night. No Diana, no Andre, no Angela, no Bob. The remaining groups moved toward cars.

The beach was nearly empty, as the dissipation rate at such events grows exponentially, and everything shifted to silence.

The piercing smell of the sea now pervaded, finally releasing its scent after an exhausting day baking in the heat.

In exasperation, John jogged toward his car, desperate for answers.

There she was. On the hood sat Diana, legs outstretched. Fascinating how just the sight of her induced such instant solace. But perhaps he had worked himself up over nothing. Andre stood to the side, by the mirror.

"Couldn't find you, man," Andre said, rushing over. "Where did you disappear to?"

"I told him you probably swam out to sea," Diana said. She cradled his hand, searching his eyes. "Everything fine?"

"Yes, yes, it is. Shall we go?"

He surveyed the area a final time, but no Angela. And certainly no Bob. The beach was dark and naked, a desolate strip compared to the exuberance of an hour before. Sturdier gusts blew in from the sea, and dried seaweed strips flapped across pebbles.

With a few engine revs, they departed. Ascending the hills, John checked his rearview mirror, and the bay below was an obscure matte pool.

"Now that is what I call a wonderful day," Diana said. Her skin flushed from extended time in the sun. "Nonstop action."

"Marvelous time," John said.

"I think she will call me."

His hands tensed on the wheel.

"Call you?" John turned to Diana. "Who will call you?"

She frowned. "Your friend."

"What friend?"

"Angela."

John swallowed once, but held steady. "You met Angela?"

"Yes," Andre said, interjecting. "I saw you two talking. That Angela watched you leave down the beach, and then immediately stomped right up to Diana. Bragged what great friends you two are. Certainly wasn't shy."

"Two American buddies," Diana said. "So cute. And she asked for my phone number."

"Your phone number?"

"Yes."

John swallowed noisily, a coppery taste in his mouth. "And you gave it?"

"Certainly."

Just wonderful.

"Even asked for my address."

"What?" This was fast turning horrific. "But you didn't give that, did you?"

"Said she wanted to stop by sometime, so I gave her that also. Don't normally do that for anyone, but she was pushy, like a good American, and said we could all get together."

He could not swallow again.

"Odd type. Wrote everything I told her with a pen across her forearm." Diana rested her hand on John's shoulder, her thin fingers massaging him. "You really are the charming sort, darling. That old American from Beverly Hills seemed quite taken by you."

John made sure to smile. "So it seems."

The road inclined. "And where did she go afterward?" he asked.

"Don't know," Andre said. "Just strolled away alone toward the forest."

John continued into the hills, relying on the headlights in the growing darkness.

NINETEEN

At ten in the morning the next day, John returned to Cala Llonga.

Lines of bodies baked on the beach. Down the road, in the corner of the Cala Llonga Club, at the same back table, sat Graham Fogg. Had he not bothered moving in the weeks since their first meeting? Samantha, the portly bartender and his latest dear, busily readied for a bustling Monday. During summer, no off days existed for bars on Ibiza.

Graham, on John's first visit, had mentioned he was friends with Gunther, good friends, yet had not seen him in a year or more. But this Graham, although disheveled in presentation, seemed a man of a particular perspicacity. John carried a lingering suspicion he knew more of Gunther's whereabouts than had yet been divulged. Dexterity would be required to procure this information though, as Graham possessed a talent for charming but elusive answers.

Time to determine if his hunch was correct.

When Graham spotted John approaching, he appeared muddled, as if harboring a murky recollection, but was unable to moor it. Then the bulb of identification flashed with raised eyebrows. He arose, and motioned John over with a grandiose smile.

"Old sport, how are you?" He wore a T-shirt bearing the words: "Cabaret Now and Mostly Forever."

He shook John's hand as they sat. The deep, high-quality cologne he wore layered over a stale liquor pong.

"Good to see you, Graham. How is the cabaret act going? Finally joined in?"

Graham chuckled good-naturedly, peering at the vacant stage. "I simply don't possess the talent, sadly. Otherwise, I would be the headlining with boa draped."

"How are they doing?"

"Robert and Todd? Busy bees those two. Twice an evening they're up there giving it their all. Troopers they are."

"They certainly are."

"Poor old Robert had a blackened eye last week. Nothing to do with your American Cajun cuisine, mind you. Needed Samantha's makeup to cover it up, poor chap."

"What happened?"

"To whom?"

John paused. "Robert, of course."

"Started dating some tourist. Sizable fellow from Newcastle. Said Robert should stop prancing in front of everyone like a tart. Funny thing, this chap actually met Robert while in the audience. Next thing you know, after only two days of romance, he demands Robert drop everything and stay chained up at home. No more showing it off on the stage."

"What did Robert say?"

"Told him he couldn't do that. Dancing is his livelihood. The big chap went off the handle, divvied out a few shots. But Robert's a trooper."

"What happened to that Newcastle guy?"

Graham turned to John. "Only visited for a week's vacation, like most of them. Went home of course. Wife and kids back there."

A single cube melted dolefully at the base of Graham's empty glass. He was keenly aware John noticed this lamentable circumstance. With his nimble hands, which trembled slightly, he unveiled his mahogany pipe, and took his time lighting it. Wisps of cherry smoke floated into the atmosphere.

"You look a bit parched, old stick."

John smiled, aware of Graham's trajectory.

"Why don't you pilgrimage to the bar and help yourself to a cool gin and tonic," Graham continued. "Wet your gizzard. I'm sure lovely Samantha won't withhold from you, although one never knows with a being of that disposition."

John summoned a most cheerful tone for ordering two gin and tonics. Unsurprisingly, she received it without eye contact or words. Snatching his money, she stamped the change on the damp bar a fair distance over, requiring a stroll to obtain it.

"You shouldn't have, old bean, you shouldn't have," Graham said, artfully feigning surprise, as John placed the drinks onto the table.

Although seemingly a typical sun-soaked day, far in the distance an ominous cluster of lead-colored clouds aggregated. Graham squinted off at them, deep creases lining his forehead.

"Might see a bit of rainfall today. Quite rare for this time of year. Quite rare."

John tasted his gin and tonic—only bitter tonic and lime.

A key ingredient had been, shall we say, forgotten. Graham detected angst in his expression, and alarmingly sampled his own.

"It seems dear Samantha has forgotten the key ingredient of a gin and tonic. It's all quite Gordian to her." He pulled out his flask with a wink, and poured lavishly into both cups. Samantha, wiping the bar with a tiny cloth, observed them from the distance, her hand moving in circles, head static.

"That's more like it," he said after a deep taste.

John had patiently waited with his question since arrival. The time was ripe to pounce.

"Graham, did you ever run into Gunther again?"

His hand jerked, gin fizzing over the glass's side. After a few coughs, he sipped at the cascading fluid.

"Gunther? Heavens. Forgot you know him as well. Lovely man. I haven't seen that charming old kraut for a year or so."

"Yes. But I do recall you said he probably lived up somewhere on the northern coastline, correct?"

Graham, eyes appearing exhausted as ever, peeked at John. He had detected, despite John's feigning calmness, the exigency of this inquiry. He puffed his pipe, gathering thoughts.

"You know, I used to get out more, when I first came to the island."

John nodded, as it was a time to listen.

"Over time, I based myself right here. Presently, what I need is here," he said, saluting with his drink. "But I myself explored up north back then. Many forget, but quite the photographer I was. Learned my trade while in Oxford." He sipped. "Photographed the entire coastline of Ibiza years ago. All around. Was going to have quite the show."

The gin burned John's tongue.

"Old Gunther is a lively sort. A man with grace," Graham

said. "But he likes a little time on his own. The contemplative type. My father was a similar sort."

"What did your father do?"

"The old man was a minister. Studied at Oxford as well. I always felt a bit jealous of that sumptuous lierne vaulting on their old Divinity building, mind you. Graduated top of his class. Traveled to southern India and Africa, bringing the good news. Evangelii."

"He sounds impressive."

"Spoke seven languages, so he got about quite well. Could even order a gin and tonic in nineteen languages. 'One must be prepared for dire situations,' he always said."

"Amazing."

"A charming man. Ultimately went to the Belgian Congo for his work. Much success there. Even Kimbanguism spread, though the origins of that are a bit suspect."

"I recall. Founder supposedly came down straight from Mount Zion."

"That's it, old stick. Other than that, rather surprisingly Puritanical in outlook."

"Where is your father now?"

"Caelum, I would presume." The base of his pipe glowed as he tugged on memories. Portentous clouds continued coalescing in the distance. "Disappeared in the Congo during his work. All quite mysterious. Those Belgians over there never trusted the Brits. Never heard from him again. We all took it hard."

"Sorry to hear that."

Graham saluted John. "Kind of you, old sport. He passed doing what he cared about, which is more than ninety-nine percent can say."

"A frightening yet superlative observation."

Graham relished the compliment. "Certainly was the

introspective sort. Would spend months alone by the shore hiking, reading, always thinking and sorting things out." He tilted his drink. "Old Gunther reminds me of father."

"You think Gunther is living alone up north?" John asked. "That is what I now also believe."

"Father spent time living alone on a beach in Kerala. Ascetic side flourished. This sort of thing appeals to them, so it seems. I'm too fond of a comfortable bed, but God bless them both."

"There are many beaches up north."

"And much forest."

"How to ever know where he might be located?"

"Just between us," Graham said in a confiding voice, "during my photographing, something strange occurred. Something happened one day."

"Yes?"

"It sounds a tad odd, but one beach struck a particular chord in me."

"Oh?"

"Yes, old stick."

"Which beach was that?"

Graham puffed his pipe, wistfully eyeing their empty glasses.

"Would you mind if I grabbed another drink?" John asked, grasping the meaning of Graham's forlorn gaze.

"Not at all. Please. Never one to interfere with a chap's thirst."

This time, John reminded Samantha that he strongly suspected gin to be one of the ingredients in a gin and tonic. She fitfully tilted the bottle's neck into the tall glasses as the ice clicked in appreciation. Her glare sizzled his shoulder blades as he returned.

"I hope you don't mind," John said as he placed the two drinks on the table.

Graham was aglow. "Not at all. A philanthropic sort, you are. Sensed it the moment I first saw you. We never should have taxed you Yanks so much back then," he said, laughing. "At least, not without a bit of representation."

They saluted with raised glasses, tonic still fizzing. Graham winked upon tasting gin.

"As I was saying," he said in his hushed voice, scanning the empty room. "A particular beach caught my attention. It felt distinctive, to put it mildly." He pulled on his drink, eyes tenderly closing as he savored the flavor and plumbed sunken memories. "Was only there one day photographing. But something struck me deeply."

"And what was that?"

"I've been endowed with an acute intuition, if I might humbly add. Inherited it directly from father. Sense impending things, hear things others cannot. A blessing in some ways, but a curse as well."

"Fascinating."

"Wrote many things down. Old Gunther read through much of them for me. He cherished my scribbled pages."

"Sounds like some sort of a prophet."

"Been a burden to me much of my life. Made living the normal life, as they say, impossible. Had no choice but to flee all that and found myself here."

The slightest perspiration coated his brow. He appeared ghostly.

"So what did you sense on that beach?"

Graham turned, focusing his normally fatigued eyes directly on John. They smoldered with a ferocity unexpected from a man of his genteel demeanor.

"Emptiness," he said. "And everything."

John could not summon a response.

"Never experienced that before, and never since."

Graham shuddered dramatically, then deflated into his chair. He now appeared a much older figure, stooped into the bowels of his seat. The room was silent.

"So what do you think happened there?"

"Not fully sure, old boy," he said softly. "Not fully sure."

"What beach was it?"

Graham looked up with startled unease, as if John should never voice that question.

"The beach. What beach was it?" John repeated.

"You want to know the name of the beach?"

"I do."

"Are you sure about that?" His moist eyes searched John's face.

"Yes."

"Quite sure?"

"Yes. Yes, I am."

He feebly smiled. "Very well then. So be it," he said exhaling. "Cala d'en Serra is the name."

"Cala d'en Serra."

"Yes. That's it. The northernmost point of the island. The final peak of Ibiza."

"Cala d'en Serra...odd. I've never even heard of it, in all my exploring."

"Who has? And a trek to get there. Hidden far away. No roads."

John removed his worn map from his pocket. "Can you mark where it's located?"

Graham perused the map, and then pulled a stubby, knife-sharpened pencil from a back pocket. He winced as he marked the spot on the coast with an "x."

"Have you been there since?"

"No, no. Absolutely not," Graham said vigorously. "Get the jitters at the very thought of returning."

"Why?"

The cubes had nearly melted in his glass.

"Perchance the truth terrifies me, old boy."

They finished their drinks while discussing lighter fare. John asked Graham to give Robert and Todd his best, and he hoped to return for another cabaret show. As he stood, and glanced at the bar, Samantha swerved, assuring her broad back faced him during his entire exit.

"Good luck, old sport," Graham said. "If you find what you're searching for, don't be shy. I'd be delighted to hear about it."

"I'm no longer exactly sure what I'm looking for."

"A good sign."

John's brow furrowed. "Now how on earth could that be a good sign?"

Graham released a perfect smoke ring, gradually ascending before fading into softness. "Isn't honesty always a good sign?"

Back home, rising winds flipped the cream curtains. John moved swiftly; no more delay. Time for the journey to Cala d'en Serra.

The phone rang.

He stared at the black receiver. The ringing seemed hollow, as if the room were empty. Louder than usual. The ringing continued, the phone shaking on the small wooden stand. He picked it up and said nothing.

"Whatever happened to you last night?" Angela finally asked.

"Happened to *me?*" John said, tone spiking. He made an effort to calm himself. "I should be the one asking that question."

"You disappeared."

"I disappeared?" His jaw tensed. "I scoured my side of the beach for Bob, per your request, and returned promptly. That is not classified as 'disappearing.'"

"We must define 'promptly' differently. When you never returned, I went off into those crowds looking for Bob."

"I see. And what happened?" How she would answer would be intriguing.

She waited for a time. "Fortunately, I found him. We left. A mess of cars and people, but we took off. I figured you'd be fine."

"Is that so?"

"What is that supposed to mean?"

"I notice you happened to omit certain parts of your story."

"Well, I am sorry if I left you there," she said. "I figured you would be just fine, as you seem to get on very well on your own, don't you now?"

"Cut it out. You've left out things."

"Like?"

"Like when you approached my friends the instant you sent me on your ridiculous errand. And like when you took Diana's phone number and then her home address. Did those minor details slip your recollection?"

A pause ensued, albeit a very brief one. But a pause, nonetheless.

"And?" she asked.

"Why do that?"

"Why not? We can all get together. Go to a party."

John listened.

"I've taken you to meet my friends, haven't I?" Angela said, her voice regaining momentum. "I brought you to my friends' parties and to their houses, no?"

John needed to concede that. "You did."

"Of course. So why turn irate if I acquaint myself with a few of your friends? Is this friendship a one-way street?"

John exhaled.

"Can't you see I have a social personality? Is that not obvious enough yet?"

"You do like to socialize."

"And I've not been secretive with my friends. You're welcome to talk or visit them any time. So why so defensive?"

Her arguments were sound. Something still perturbed him from deep within, something amorphous, but no time to sift and analyze it. She spoke logically. No reason to prolong this.

"So you found Bob and got home fine?"

"Busy again today?"

She had not bothered answering, but he wanted to end this call. "Yes, but we can get together soon."

"Sure. And John?"

"Yes?"

"Don't worry yourself crazy. I won't contact any of your friends."

"That might be a slight hyperbole."

"When you're ready for me to meet them, just say so. If not, I'll never speak to them. I do solemnly swear." She boisterously cackled, the phone shaking in his hand. He listened in horrified fascination, and joined in an attempt to finish things. But her laughter did not cease. Eventually he simply hung up.

One o'clock. Any remaining strokes of blue had been vanquished from the sky, leaving behind a gray palette. The winds blew in intentional gusts. Time to go. He put on his bathing suit and T-shirt and departed, the curtains still snapping into the room.

Diana was relaxing on her rooftop when John arrived. At the seaward edge sat her tiny table with not one, but two wicker chairs. A porcelain pot of tea steamed from its gently curving neck, and an open novel lay beside it. Diana arose and stood by the table's side, her long blue sundress and hair flapping in the wind.

"A scene that belongs in a painting. Seurat, perhaps."

"No Chagall, please," Diana laughed good-naturedly. "Marvelous paintings, but those cubist faces aren't overly flattering. Having two eyes is my preference."

"The more the merrier on you."

Diana smiled slightly while surveying him. "You seem primed for a journey today."

"Observant as always."

"Well today doesn't seem like the nicest weather. Odd for Ibiza. I was just headed inside."

John pointed to the chair. "May I?"

She peered, a bit nervously, at the dark clouds amassing in the distance. He waited for her to sit, then followed.

"So," she said, "what's on your mind?"

"Why do you ask?"

Her skin crinkled alongside both eyes. "You're wearing quite the determined expression. Very becoming, I might add."

Diana poured the tea, the level perfectly aligned in both cups. She ignored the loose hair strands blowing across her face.

"Did you ever deeply regret anything?"

"Regret?" She looked up, eyebrows lofty in surprise. "Well certainly. Plenty of things. Impossible to count them all."

"Of course," John said. "But major things. Directions your life went."

Diana raised her tea, staring at the amber fluid as she leaned into the cup and silently sipped. Whatever she did, no matter how simple, radiated elegance.

"Not particularly, to be honest with you."

"Interesting."

"When I look back, I'm grateful I didn't get married when twenty-two."

"So you are pleased with how your life proceeded?"

She considered the question. "I would say so, yes. Ups and downs, but no major regrets."

"That's refreshing to hear. It really is."

"And you?" she asked. "Major regrets?"

"I remember once finding this charming little cafe, and regretting choosing the espresso over the Earl Grey."

"Stop that, silly," she said, laughing.

John relaxed in his chair, exhaling steadily. Whitecaps began foaming across the sea. "I regret throwing the last fifteen years of my life away."

"And I thought the espresso an unfortunate situation."

"It's true," John said, smiling wistfully. "And fifteen lost years is a long run. Not a few-months jaunt."

"Sounds bloody awful, John."

"It was." The remnants of his cream spiraled into the dark tea. "No help at all to society. Hurting it, in full truth. And each year, I distanced myself from humans more and more. In time they became figurines, that's all."

"Thank heavens you are out of all that rubbish now."

"Maybe so."

"Why maybe?"

"Who knows what I've become? What permanent damage has been done."

"Meaning what?"

"Who knows?"

"Cut it out John," she said, standing. "Stop that morbid nonsense. I have seen plenty of good from you here on Ibiza. Plenty. Otherwise, I would not permit you to be standing here with me."

"I'm sitting."

"Don't try to be funny. I see the goodness in you."

"We will see."

"Will we?" she said. "So are you now dedicated to doing good?"

"Am I what?"

"You heard me."

"Come on now."

"You heard me," she repeated emphatically.

She was undeniably a rousing force.

"Yes," John said. "Yes. Now, I am. I can finally say that."

"You are what?"

"I am dedicated to doing good."

As he looked upward, her slender hand viciously greeted his cheek. His teacup fell, porcelain shattering on the ground. Tea coursed in amber veins across the white roof.

"What was that for?" he exclaimed.

"In my country, when they made a knight, they slapped him across the face after his oath so he would remember it. Perhaps you will, too."

"Now I'm a knight?"

"If you journey with a noble purpose."

He massaged his stinging cheek, a slight smile lingering beside it. "I believe you enjoy slapping me. It's becoming a habit."

"It offers its pleasures."

John arose and peered directly into her eyes, eyes which observed him intensely; turquoise pools resembling the eternal sea all around them. "I'm off, now."

"I know, John. I hope you find him," she said. "Please be careful with yourself."

"I will."

"Don't deliberate. It's okay to trust your hard-earned feelings."

He looked at her with curiosity. "You seem to know me awfully well."

She hugged him, for the first time. His eyes widened in surprise. She held on for several moments, and he breathed summer roses. How intensely warm her entire body felt, from her forehead to her very toes. How utterly remarkable. If only she never let go.

He returned to the street, opening his car door. Time to head north. The mysterious Cala d'en Serra awaited. Two bulbous drops plopped onto his cheek and forearm, but no steady rain yet. Before entering the car, the impulse to wave a final time overwhelmed him.

She stood at roof's edge. Her expression was unclear, as from this distance her face blurred and became one with the expansive sky.

TWENTY

Openings of rainfalls are like the start of symphonies: the initial notes seize your attention. The first spate of raindrops splashed against John's windshield with emphatic pangs. Distracted by this music, he forgot to turn on the wipers. Already submerged in contemplation about what lay ahead that afternoon, the liquid cadence deepened his hypnotic state. Being able to see, though, is universally agreed upon as beneficial while driving, so before John veered off the hillside to become a permanent part of the Lebanon cedar grove below, he providentially switched on the wipers.

This rainfall was the first since he had arrived on Ibiza months ago. Not ideal timing, but Cala d'en Serra could not wait. He finally felt ready, ready as he would ever be. Was

Gunther living there? In truth, he had not the foggiest idea. But he had gleaned over the last months that Gunther most likely lived secluded in the North along one of its beaches. Pierre, who lived in the same general region, also strongly suspected so. And when the gifted Graham mentioned Cala d'en Serra, the farthest northern point, and revealed his poignant feelings, the answer seemed deliciously obvious. It all seemed to fit.

Unblemished hills populated this region. No towns, no hotels, not even lone villas. Just junipers, Aleppo pines, Lebanon cedars, and bursts of wildflowers. Wild sage and rosemary flourished. Unlike the southern coast, no flatlands were found here, as steep hills plummeted directly into the sea.

The rain continued to fall, and the slate sky and darkened plants all melded into a somber impressionistic landscape.

Just past Portinatx, he traveled one of the last paved streets in the region, and then headed farther north to the land of dirt roads. The steady rain began creating traction problems. John's map, now ripped into worn halves, did not mark a single road leading to Graham's penciled "x," the supposed spot where Cala d'en Serra was located.

Instinct time, something necessary to thrive on Ibiza, had arrived yet again.

After twenty minutes of adventurous driving, with branches clawing at the dripping car windows, his chosen road abruptly terminated into a wall of trees. He climbed atop his car and stood on the slick hood, wiping rain from his eyebrows.

Down the hills he spotted, with elation, the not-so-distant sea. According to Graham's "x," and his best estimates, that should very well be the mystical Cala d'en Serra.

He proceeded on foot through forest. Trees and brushes lost density as he neared the coast. Growth was stunted, as salt and sea gusts had unremittingly tamed them. Now completely soaked through, the rain was inconsequential. As rivulets dripped from his limbs, he recalled a debate he and Gunther had engaged in one autumn in Connecticut many years ago. Outside the university library, between classes, the topic was whether a one-world government was inevitable. The debate was intense, so much so that when the chilly New England rain began falling, they did not seek shelter. A group of classmates stayed to observe. They chose sides and cheered them on, which reminded Gunther of coal miners from his home region in Germany cheering lunchtime fistfights among workmates. None of the students left, because the search for truth was the most important thing that could ever be. What an idealistic time that was.

Venerable Gunther sought conversations. And he sought them with just about anyone. For all of his profound intelligence—and he was the cleverest person John had ever encountered—he possessed not an iota of snobbishness. Perhaps this stemmed from his modest upbringing in the north of Germany, where his father worked as a civil engineer and his mother as a seamstress. Gunther did not limit his conversations to the academic spheres amongst fellow students and professors, but he would wander out to disfavored parts of the city and talk with those he randomly encountered at bars or parks. John found this peculiar, but how they all relished Gunther's humor and wittiness, his very presence! Knowledge must be foraged everywhere, Gunther often said, as one never knows where the true gems would be unearthed. How correct dear Gunther was.

The sea view sharpened as he descended the hill. Gone was the alluring, blue, Ibizan water he had become accustomed to. Rather, his eyes were slapped by a lead-colored mass with whitecaps brazenly marching through.

Passing a bend, he froze.

Along the path stood a wooden arrow sign, letters hand-painted in red, pointing toward the sea: "Cala d'en Serra."

Graham's haunting recollection of his experience on this beach struck John. So determined he had been to get here, he failed to truly consider what he neared. Maybe it would be best to wait for more affable weather before exploring this. It might be best to wait.

Nice try. No more delays. Press on and find Gunther.

The bay below unveiled; it was a narrow, horseshoe-shaped cove, tucked in, surrounded by steep, wooded hills. Was Gunther actually here? Could it really be? He tempered his excitement by preparing the appropriate words of salutation. Perhaps an embrace would be better.

The radical drop to the beach, with slick rocks and wet, orange-tinted earth demanded John contain his rising fervor. Aleppo pines, pale branches heavy with water, slapped at his arms like drenched mops.

Finally, sand beneath him.

After barely catching his breath, he frantically commenced searching. Gunther could be but minutes away.

He scanned both sides of the beach. No one. But perhaps he was missing something.

He jogged up and down the sand, each footstep fracturing the dark caking formed by rain and revealing the paler and warmer sand beneath. On the eastern side of the cove, built atop flat rocks, sat a series of weathered, wooden, fishing boat shelters. The corrugated metal roofs were rusted completely through, and not a single boat was found within.

He checked around the hillsides surrounding the cove, but nothing.

He returned to the beach. No Gunther.

Not a single soul, for that matter. Just a lonely, desolate beach. The sheets of raindrops relentlessly pattered the sea.

A tsunami of disappointment crashed over him.

For so long, he had anticipated this moment. Foolishly, he had dared to allow illustrious visions of a poignant reunion with Gunther to flicker through his mind like an old celluloid film. What a grand spectacle, complete with fireworks and a chorus line of celebratory dancers.

He dropped to the coarse sand. Briny odors were pungent. No end in sight on the horizon, as gray water met gray sky and melded into an interminable plain. The innumerable failures of his life began stabbing viciously. What wonderful opportunities he once had, how blessed and fortunate he had been, and how he had burned all of them at the stake. Rain and warm tears slid down his cheeks.

Weeping felt therapeutic. Decades had passed since his last tear had fallen. For the last years, the goal in life was to bridle emotions so one could function at maximum efficiency without interruption. He forgot he could cry. What an odd mechanism of the human being, shedding water through eyes when inundated with emotion.

One can be regretful, and wallow in pools of perpetual pity, but never blame oneself in the least. This is the path of choice for most, as it is delectably guilt-free. John avoided this seducing path, fully acknowledging that the tears cascading were due to his foolish and selfish mistakes.

The horizon before him seemed measureless, as everything warped through aqueous lenses. Just slate unfolding forever.

Then, a crisp, flashing dot in the sky.

Just a dot, mind you, but it moved erratically, at sharp angles.

He followed it, zigzagging, attempting to identify it, transfixed by its discordance. A bird. Difficult to tell, but it seemed white. A seagull. Perhaps a dove. Peculiarly, the only bird in the sky. Usually they travel in flocks, or in duos at least, but this bird ventured alone. In fact, it was the sole evidence of life in view.

The bird flew around the cove for a time, circling above, then landed on an extreme rock outcropping at the eastern entrance where sea met cove. It took off again, circling and dipping, then landed in the identical place. It launched and flew high above, plunging and landing once again in the same place. John stood and observed as the bird repeated this purposeful cycle over twenty times, like a spinning forty-five record. He began, without consciously realizing, to stride toward this end of the beach.

Leaving the sanctuary of sand, he climbed along the rocks toward the seaward end of the cove where this bird repeatedly perched. Something motivated it.

When at last he stood five meters away, he deduced that the performer was a dove. Extraordinary, with a cream beak and a smooth head and full white feathers. It perched on a flat, reddish rock. John stepped closer and, to his surprise, it failed to budge. Birds inevitably flutter off when approached. In youth, this feathery explosion had often been prompted for amusement, but never once did he consider just what to do if one remained unfazed.

He moved one step closer, but the dove remained steadfast. A meter away. The dove watched him, not warily, but with amused curiosity. John knew the obfuscating drizzle, the strain of the day, and the bird's anatomy counted against his proper judgement, but he verily believed the dove smiled at him. He wiped the rain from his lashes to be sure. It damned well appeared to be smiling. Imagine recounting this anecdote to his old work colleagues! Uneasy laughs and a rapid change of topic would inevitably follow.

How long they remained frozen John did not know, but this dove's company enthralled as a warming, peaceful presence. Whether this feeling intimated John's profound understanding of deeper things, or commented on a fracturing of his mental soundness, was unclear. He took one more step toward it, almost within reach, and it launched.

The dove flew out to sea, fading into the gray. It did not, as he hoped, return for more interaction. Apparently, it did not share his desire for mutual quality time.

He turned away, shaking his head with a smile, thoroughly amused at the fantastical scenarios one's mind can conjure when desperate. Time to return to the shore of Cala d'en Serra, and then back to his car. Let us face it: Gunther was nowhere here. So, Graham's fabled intuition was incorrect.

Well, tomorrow he would canvas another area. And he could do so far more efficiently when the weather returned to the usual, sunny Ibiza.

A resounding splash, as if something massive plonked into the water.

He veered and checked, but nothing.

The sea far out here certainly was a choppy mess. The many coves and inlets on Ibiza pacified any turbulence, leading to the calm, glassy water he was accustomed to. But out here, away from the cove's shelter and on the northern peak of the island, waves smashed frothy protests against the cliffs.

Heading eastward, these jagged cliffs formed a majestic wall along the coastline for as far as the eye could see, with no beaches or shore whatsoever. Cliffs meet water. The waves exploded against these rock walls in a mesmerizing beat.

John was on the verge of turning away, he actually began to, but a certain discordance in the water lingered in his mind and he turned back.

This white chaos of waves pounding against cliffs was not continuous. Not far in the distance, the foam entirely vanished. The water was purely smooth for this strip, maybe for one hundred feet—a tranquil pond—and then beyond it, the foaming and tumult instantly recommenced. Something, somehow, tempered those waves in that specific region.

What could possibly explain this phenomenon?

John became intrigued of course, and his disappointment in the day's results provided extra incentive to explore, as he yearned to recoup something. But these were sheer cliffs alongside the sea. No traversing along pebbly beaches was possible, as none existed.

The solution proved elementary. He lowered into the water, waded fifteen feet straight out, and then swam parallel to the shore. He felt quite reckless, after all. Hopefully, he swam far enough out so the waves would not dash him against the bluffs. Swimming in stormy weather, even if the sea is not greatly affected, is always a challenge. The tenebrous water and sullen sky tap deep into the instinct of humankind, unveiling some profound terror from long ago.

He swam a toilsome thirty meters along the coastline, then stood to observe the coast. Water bobbed at his shoulders and the floor, pebbly and smooth. But only cliffs were on the shore.

He swam, against substantial resistance. Looking up once again, salt water cascaded over his lashes. Something was there...or was not there. With the back of his hand, he wiped water away for a clearer view.

Stunning.

The cliffs had entirely vanished.

He had not noticed from the former, but here existed a second, smaller cove which was utterly impossible to spot from the first cove, since the cliffs curved in a gentle, convex fashion.

The rain was ceasing. He swam directly toward it.

He kicked and pulled inside with lengthy strokes, the water instantly calming. Tucked peacefully inside this elongated cove was a beach. His legs fatigued due to mounting excitement. The shallow water permitted him to wade toward the tiny, sandy beach. Precipitous, forested hills surrounded, with no paths or any signs of visitation. A secret beach.

Then he spotted it.

On this beach, on the western end near the hill's base, sat a hut constructed of wood, dried palm leaves, and thatch. Two windows were visible.

And wisps of white smoke emanated from a copper chimney.

TWENTY-ONE

As John stepped onto the beach's coarse sand, dripping from sea and rain, he scrambled to contain his fervor while deliberating the most sensible approach.

Who lived inside this hut? Gunther? Some random hippie? Certainly, there was no dearth of those on Ibiza. And does he simply holler a "hello," hands cupped around mouth? Or perhaps he should risk peeking inside first? What is the Geneva international statutory regulation for huts: is knocking requisite?

No sounds, only the gentle splash of the minuscule waves behind him. His initial rush of elation morphed into trepidation as he realized whoever dwelled inside was not accustomed to receiving visitors for afternoon tea and crumpets.

He approached the hut, senses alert.

No sounds from inside, yet the white smoke billowed industriously from the pipe. At least the rain had slowed. This hut was a most impressive little construction, crafted from wood and dried leaves, secure from rain, and evidently housing some sort of fire.

His attempted "hello" received no response. In fairness, he voiced it so faintly that even someone beside him would hear nothing. But let us call it a test run. He tried it again, slightly louder. No response. One more time, at a respectable level, and still nothing.

Time to knock.

The construction of this hut was a mystery. Materials must have been hauled down the treacherous hills, or arrived by sea. The door, made of horizontal planks, was attached with metal hinges. It would be judicious to refrain from peeking through the windows, as the view from the inside, if he were spotted, would be far too jolting.

He knocked, knuckles scratching on splintery wood, and the door shook hollowly. No response. He waited more than was necessary, then knocked again. Disappointingly, no answer.

Now came that inevitable moment. Does he attempt to open the door and enter, or does he respect privacy? As he discovered his trembling hand rotating the wooden door handle, apparently the former option triumphed.

He pushed the door inward and it creaked painfully. Inside, it was dimmer. He swallowed, tasting salt. Two windows lit the slightly musty smelling rectangular room. Shelves to the ceiling lined the walls, overwhelmed with rows of books and precipitous stacks of more books resting upon these rows. A narrow cot lay on the right side. A copper kettle sat atop an antiquated wood burning oven with a pipe leading through the ceiling. Visible through the grill, a tiny orange fire burned.

No one was home.

John remained in the doorway, only his eyes moving, scanning the walls of books. A substantial collection. Everything from Sartre, Kafka, collections of DC and Marvel comics, Bertolt Brecht, Sigmund Freud, C. S. Lewis, Saint Augustine, Kierkegaard, and hundreds more. Such a trove of knowledge before him! He found himself transfixed, stepping gingerly forward. He reached out, extended fingertips nearing the volumes.

"I miss *Almira*."

He froze.

The voice came from behind him.

As odd as this might sound, he did not turn, despite the compelling temptation. The primary reason why is that he recognized the voice. And perhaps he did not believe in it, or considered it fragile, terrified it would evaporate if he viewed its source.

"You mean the opera, *Almira*?" John asked, unmoving.

"Exactly."

"Handel's first, was it not? 1705, I believe."

"Excellent. I see you are not overly senile yet, although I strongly suspected otherwise."

John could not resist any longer.

He veered, and behind the door sat a bearded man. Or half-bearded. One side of his face was covered with full beard, the other only stubble. He wore shorts and a tattered shirt, and was very thin. Faintly smiling.

Gunther.

Yes, Gunther. Right before him. Lord, God, it was Gunther.

Sometimes, during rare intrepid moods, John enacted this moment in his mind, only to quash the thought for fear it would never transpire. It is treacherous business, imagining your deepest hopes coming to fruition, for if they do not, the heartbreak only intensifies. But here he sat, incarnate.

"You just like him, because he was born in Halle."

"Nonsense. I'm not from Halle," Gunther said. "Although nearby, to be fair. I ran away there once when I was eight, after an argument with my mother. She was correct and I wrong, of course. But please do remember, *Zadok the Priest* was composed by Handel, for the coronation of George the Second in 1727. And during every subsequent British coronation it has been performed. So he is more of a hero to the Brits these days."

"Why *Almira*, of all of his works, do you miss?"

"There is an innocence to it I admire. I miss innocence. Don't we all?" He pointed to the chair in the other corner. "Please, sit."

John hungrily studied Gunther, attempting discreet data harvesting by adopting a most ridiculously nonchalant expression. Although thin, he seemed in fine spirits. He was shorter than John remembered, but he was always on the short side. His enormous forehead shined, and his wide-set eyes scanned John. And of course, he wore a chestnut beard on only one side of his face. Although this would shock most, John was not, considering the eccentricities of this man.

Where does one start?

"What are you doing here?" John asked. Not the scintillating opening he had hoped for.

"Ahh. A question which has plagued humankind since the dawn of time."

John laughed, and tapped a few volumes from the collection of Wharton novels. "Don't forget I introduced you to her."

Gunther perused the books. "True. And admittedly, I was skeptical at first. Now I'm quite interested in the effects of class on consciousness."

"Have you been here all this time?"

"You believe I've been an anchorite in this hut?"

John smiled.

"All what time, by the way?"

The first pointed question. He was talking to Gunther, he must remember, and he was out of practice jousting with his razor expertise. Precarious conditions lay ahead.

"The last fifteen years."

Gunther heartily laughed. "Any coincidence that fifteen years ago is when we last saw each other? Thus, my entire timeline revolves around you?" Gunther asked. "A bit presumptuous, no? Copernicus could help you with your perverted worldview."

"Presumptuous? Not in the least."

"And why not?"

"From my particular perspective, the fifteen years is naturally the initial part I am curious about. But that does not mean that I believe your timeline, from your subjective, or even objective perspective has anything to do with me whatsoever. I might be an insignificant flea. But my question was predicated upon my personal interest, not what I believe your person revolves around. Thus, an accusation of narcissism, although inaccurate, would be more apt than an accusation of a presumptuous nature."

Gunther smiled broadly. "Fine answer. I see that whatever you've been doing all these years, which you have been so secretive about, so very secretive, has not entirely eroded your famous acumen."

The repeated "secretive" induced the hot rush of embarrassment.

Gunther, detecting John's flustered state, gently laughed in amusement. "Now why doesn't your little self take that nice kettle off the stove and make us tea, like you used to? I have Earl Grey, your favorite."

Two cups awaited, with teabags already draped inside them. He lifted the steaming kettle off of the stove and poured, handing Gunther his mug.

"I assume you enjoy Ibiza?" John said.

"Because I live here?"

"You seem free to choose where you live, so I assume you enjoy it here."

"I've made many intriguing friends here. A Byzantium of ideas and thoughts. But do know I also traveled much these last years."

"Wonderful."

"My language cache is expanding."

"Oh?"

"I've added Vietnamese, Malayalam, Basque, Finnish, and more."

"Now all that is left is English."

Gunther smiled. "I've had wonderful chances to explore."

"Have you?"

"Far too many places to mention in their entirety. But our fair Ibiza functioned as my base."

He wanted to divulge, and John wanted to hear. "How about a sampling?"

Gunther chuckled, stroking the smoother side of his face. "Almost too endless to discuss. Peru, for a time. Farming purple potatoes on a high-altitude commune with some superb people. Eventually a rebellion broke out, though."

"Rebellion?"

"Yes. The owner of the commune, who dressed up as an Andean condor each morning at five, wanted everyone to start the day by lining up and kissing a potato. Some rebelled."

He took a moment to digest the information. "And you?"

"I find the purple strain of potato quite alluring."

John rubbed his chin.

"Worked for months down in the La Boca neighborhood of Buenos Aires in an art gallery. Vapid works. Utterly vapid. But I was required to feign my love of them. Fired after a time."

"Fired? Why?"

"I kept telling the customers they would be far better off painting their own."

"I wonder why the gallery didn't retain you."

"Went to Nepal and helped with jute. Strolled around beautiful Galilee for a while—enlightening. Spent time in Vietnam on a tea plantation. Not that easy picking those leaves as you might think."

"I would not think that easy."

"Well, I did. Not supposed to pinch the tea buds with fingernails. Made a bet on my first day that I could out pick their top person, a woman in her sixties."

"What was at stake?"

"Eighty-seven dollars, which was my entire savings, and my clothes."

"And?"

"Let's just say a naked and penniless man was spotted later that evening wandering in the Lam Dong region of Northern Vietnam."

John heartily laughed. Just listening to Gunther again was delightful.

"Also climbed around Calabria. A marvelous time in Liverpool working in a pub for locals near the docks. Imbibed a bit much during that time though, and found myself spinning some fanciful yarns at the bar."

"Did they enjoy them?"

"Enjoy them? Yes. Believe them? Absolutely not."

John laughed.

"Spent time as a nude model for an artist in Aix-en-Provence."

"You? Come on now! A nude model."

"What's the problem with that?"

"The resulting artwork," John said. "Let me avoid the French art scene for a while."

Gunther placed his hand over his heart.

"Even lived with the Geraizeiros in Minas Gerais in Brazil. There I really learned about balancing. Taking from nature but preserving cycles and limits. In the mangaba harvest, they only take the fruit fallen to the ground, nothing more."

"How long did you stay with them?"

"One month."

"That's all?"

"Jelly doughnuts aren't native to that area."

"You really have been around," he said, smiling with enjoyment.

Gunther squinted in derision. John had somehow just misstepped.

"'Being around' means absolutely nothing," he stated emphatically. His intensity level had abruptly spiked.

"And why not?"

"Plenty of people have 'been around', as you so love to keep saying."

"Keep saying?"

"The imperative question is, are you learning wherever you go? Am I clear?"

"I believe so."

"Look," Gunther said, taking a moment. "I met a financier from Nebraska who had worked in nine countries and did not evolve in the least. Only ate rare steak and potatoes with a glass of milk wherever he went. Spoke to no one. Existed within his bubble and his bubble travelled with him. Yet, I met an old fellow in Liverpool, in his early eighties, who barely left the city his whole life but thought in remarkably flexible ways. And he operated off of a single testicle."

"I'm sorry?"

"He only had a single testicle."

"And this you know how?"

"The first thing he told me when we met."

"But of course."

"As I was saying, an open-minded and remarkably flexible thinker. Often dined on ika somen or masala dosa for lunch. So let us not praise travel too much, unless it is properly used."

"Jute?"

Gunther looked to John. "What?"

"Jute. You said you worked with Jute in Nepal?"

"Yes. Yes I did."

"Who is Jute?"

Gunther chuckled. "Jute. The vegetable fiber. Second only to cotton in production and uses. Affordable and comfortable. You're never allowed to hear of it around America."

"Some monopolies are too large."

"Many things are too large and unregulated. My dear uncle Fynn's diet comes to mind. Shall we test your knowledge?"

"Proceed."

"Please tell me, dear John: what is the largest organism in the world?"

"Are you referring to Professor Jerguson's brain?"

Gunther joyfully laughed. "No, but a worthy guess."

"The giant sequoia?"

"No, it's not."

"So what is it?"

"The largest organism on Planet Earth is all around you, right here on Ibiza. Right here, John. And you, for all your talents, did not even realize this during your time here. A crying shame. But please do not think yourself a complete imbecile, as almost no one knows or observes this."

Gunther certainly could be quite direct. That quality, he had not lost.

"So what organism is this?"

"You must realize John, the most challenging task in life is to truly see. Even the most immense things, truthful things, can be invisible right before you if your mind is not open to discerning them. Frightening but true."

"The organism?" John demanded.

"The *Posidonia oceanica.* Also known as Neptune Grass. The magnificent, dark seagrass in the sea all around us. The largest organism on our fragile planet, yet everyone just swims past it and terms it seaweed. They don't realize it is one single organism, spanning almost ten miles, nor that it is responsible for the crystal-clear quality of the waters around this island, and enriching the sea with oxygen. It is also over 100,000 years old, making it the oldest organism as well."

"Absolutely astounding."

Never had he even heard of it. Shocking, if not disturbing.

"And numerous species live and mate in this organism, raising their young there. *Posidonia oceanica* is the heart of Ibiza. It is Ibiza, yet so few humans know it exists."

"Astounding," John said. "And to think I had no idea."

Gunther brandished the particular smile of satisfaction he unveiled when imparting valuable knowledge.

"By the way, I used to love your jute blanket," John said.

"Which?"

"Back in your dorm room, the purple one. You kept it folded on your desk. So proud of it you were."

"You remember that?" His eyes narrowed. "Then why on earth did you just feign ignorance about jute?"

"Always worth it to lure you into one of your rants."

They laughed heartily together, heads tilting back, just like in old times.

"I must ask you something," John eventually said.

"Frage mich."

"So all these journeys. All these books." John exhaled. "What is the point in the end? Why do it all?"

Gunther stroked his half-beard with thin fingers.

"You really have suffered a dry spell these last years, for you of all people to ask a question like that."

John licked his salty lips and cleared his throat attempting to compose, but shame is a tricky emotion to mask. "Yes. Yes, I have."

"Very well," Gunther said. He peered out the window at the somber sky. "People say things are easier than they look, but I believe the opposite. We need to ceaselessly learn and amass wisdom. Only by doing this can we expand our perspective, expand and stretch it so we can think lucidly enough to find the solutions to assist us all."

"But do such solutions even exist?"

"Oh?"

"Well, do they? For years, I've doubted whether they do."

"Doubted?" Gunther scoffed. "Genuine, hard-earned doubt? Or just a convenient way to ease your nagging conscience due to your lack of effort or success, like our beloved fox and the grapes?"

John paused. "The latter, now that I think of it."

"Good answer."

"But I have begun to feel more hopeful since coming to Ibiza."

"Oh?"

"So, what are some of your newest ideas after all this time? I would love to know."

Gunther smiled ever so slightly, stroking his beard half, saying nothing. John had reached for a bit too much, too soon.

"Or perhaps it is time to explain your beard."

"What to explain?"

"Your beard. It's only half."

"How observant. Holmes reincarnate."

"Well?"

"For me it represents a life half-lived."

"In duration?"

"No," Gunther said. "In passion. I failed to do what I originally hoped."

"Which was?"

"Create the world's perfect organic beard oil."

John laughed, savoring Gunther's wit. Thank heavens that was alive and thriving. How profoundly one can miss intangible qualities.

"To find the best ways to help others. I haven't gotten there yet." Gunther sighed. "Trendy concepts I felt sure of, that I was even passionate about, I then completely reversed my opinion on. At the time, I would never, ever believe this possible. But it happened. Many times."

"I see."

"It made me wonder whether I had actually been searching for the truth, or just convenient so-called truths to satisfy my needs at that particular stage in my life. Painful self-doubt then creeps in and haunts you. I've been greatly humbled, John."

"I can fully relate to that."

"What is trendy versus what is eternal has become my real interest."

John steadied himself. Although nervous to ask, exhilaration flared. His fingertips were sparklers. The precious chance to finally get to what racked him for years.

"After your trip to New York that summer…when we never ended up meeting and launching our journal…"

Gunther cleared his throat. John paused, and continued.

"Well…did you ever go on to complete your graduate studies? Did things work out for you?"

Gunther studied him with a blank expression, "sizing him up" as they say. This was not going to be enjoyable.

"Ahh. I believe you are referring to when you completely and inexplicably abandoned our hard-fought plans and entire future without bothering to let me know?"

Silence.

"Is that what you are referencing?"

John struggled to salvage himself. Gunther definitely did not dance around the issue, oh no, he did not. He snapped his whip resoundingly, but as always, veraciously.

"Yes."

"Yes what?"

"Yes. I mean that."

"Okay."

"So did you go on and at least complete your graduate studies?"

"No."

A terse and terrible answer. John was culpable of not only derailing their beloved journal, but Gunther's advanced studies as well. A rarefied mind, which would have contributed greatly to our common good, had been sabotaged by John's foolishness.

"But why not? What went wrong?"

"I started. Even sent you a letter updating you. Of course,

I never heard back. You probably burned it, for all I know," Gunther said with a laugh.

John looked aside.

"And then I eventually gave it up. Or more accurately, other projects and trips distracted me from my goal. You certainly know how that works, don't you, John?"

John observed his twitching big toes. "That I do."

"You see John, once you start a gig as a nude model, everything else pales in comparison." He shook his head with a wisp of a smile. "In truth, I was unsure what would serve as the best use of my time. I was 'wasting my life,' as they say. An existential panic set in, the deadliest strain. So after a few semesters, I dropped and went searching," Gunther said. "But I still do believe solutions exist for people. In this life and beyond."

"Do you really?"

"Yes. Absolutely. I never abandoned the faith."

John's skin warmed with gratitude. "That is one of the most reassuring things I've ever heard."

John lowered his teacup, which clanked uncomfortably on the metal stove. Gunther, sensing something, quieted and looked up expectantly.

He decided to ask, even though it was clearly too soon to do so.

You see, patience is not always a virtue. It is absolutely true that John never dreamed he would dare ask about this, but seeing Gunther again inspired a surge of ambition, and a touch of lunacy. This could be a life changer. He methodically exhaled, a tad too dramatically.

"Yes?" Gunther said, watching him.

"Yes what?"

Gunther's face shined with amusement. "Your contorted

visage is obviously pining to ask me something. So just spit it out."

"Not necessarily—"

"Spit it out."

John cleared his throat. "Maybe we can, well..."

"Yes?" Gunther looked up, eyebrows raised.

"Perhaps we can finally launch our political and theological journal. Perhaps we still possess the wit and will to do it."

There. He had asked him, or "spat it out," per his request. With that came a modicum of cathartic relief, but he now hungered for the redemptive affirmative answer.

"A second chance," John continued. "Ibiza is the blessed island of second chances."

"Is that so?"

Gunther observed him with a perturbing cocktail of inquisitiveness and humor, avoiding any response John could moor onto. A dose of torture.

"I have thoughts, many dormant for the longest time. I've learned much since coming here," John said.

And then Gunther began to cough. A wheezing cough, deep and coarse, and it persisted.

"Everything okay?" John asked, alarmed.

"With?"

"Your health."

Hot tea splashed from Gunther's mug over his attenuated fingers while suppressing his next cough. "Regrettably, no."

"What do you mean?"

"Please don't be distraught, as you tend to get, or start making sounds of a clucking hen."

"Sounds of a—"

"But I have been dropping weight for some time. This cough, relentless."

"For how long?"

"Months."

"Months?"

He observed Gunther more objectively now.

He attempted to expel the old Gunther's image from his mind, inculcated there for a decade and a half. As it faded, and as the actual Gunther came into focus for the first time, the vexing details arrived. Dark semicircles under his eyes. The coat of sweat on his brow and prominent cheekbones. Hands and feet, bluish. Lower legs slightly swollen. Gunther was a mess.

"Months? Well, let's take you to a damned doctor and discover what's wrong, in addition to your tonsorial judgement, that is."

Gunther laughed, gently. "I'm not that stubborn a nitwit. I went a few months ago, to three different doctors. Couldn't identify the problem. Went in for tests. Nothing. No disease of any sort, no cancer. Just baffled them."

"That is why you haven't been out at all in these last months?"

Gunther raised an eyebrow in curiosity. "Yes. That is why."

"Well, we need to act immediately."

He scoffed patronizingly. "Oh? And do what, tote me over to the old campus nurse Missus Hearst? Like we took Oliver all those years ago when he imbibed Sambuca like well water?"

"Hey, it helped him. Even when he kicked you between the legs while we lugged him down the dorm stairs, it was worth it."

Gunther looked down. "Are you sure?"

"Seriously, we need to act. You look like Ichabod Crane after a Lenten fast."

Gunther smiled, shaking his head.

"Why don't we take you back home to Germany to see someone?"

He reclined in his chair, sighing. "One of my doctors here was German. From Leipzig. There is nothing else to do. I tried for months. Let us just see what unfolds."

"This is absurd."

"What?"

"After fifteen years I finally find you, and you are dying?"

"'And the dust return into its earth, from whence it was, and the spirit return to God, who gave it.'"

"Ecclesiastes?"

"Well done."

"You and your beloved Douay-Rheims version."

"Straight from the Vulgate."

Gunther's composure in the face of this crisis, although estimable, began irritating John. After all this time, he needed fanfare to cope with this debacle—everyone weeping and wailing, with a scoop of gnashing of teeth.

"You know, you sound resigned." John's brow furrowed as anger seeped in. "You sound like you have forsaken yourself."

"Do I now?"

"Yes, you do."

"Perhaps I have," he said. "Don't take it personally."

"Damn you. That is not the Gunther I know."

"How flattering."

"It's true."

"Come now, John, my dear. Don't snap into your little quasi fit. Fifteen years. What do you really know anymore?"

"I know enough to recognize when action is required."

"I see," Gunther said. "So then. What does our dear John the Dynamic suggest?"

An excellent question.

And embarrassingly, despite his indignant fervor, no answer came to mind.

How in the world had their winding roads ultimately led to this abominable demise? Gunther would perish, and John would dissipate from anguish. And all this after finally reuniting, after fifteen excruciating years! Impressive, in that it was just about the worst thing he had ever heard.

Remarkably, Gunther still harbored some faith in him. No matter how Gunther toiled to conceal it, he detected that faith in tone and expression. This was tremendously heartening, in that he did not wholeheartedly consider John a desiccated fish.

But was his faith misplaced?

John froze. Atop the bookshelf, with a worn, burgundy leather cover, sat Gunther's weathered Bible. That diagonal scratch, on the upper right corner. The very same Bible, many years ago, on which they had placed their youthful hands and boisterously sworn to launch their journal.

He trembled.

An idea.

This idea became clearer.

A terrifying prospect, one which he would have, in life before Ibiza, ruminated and deliberated before ultimately dismissing. Or more likely not have considered at all. But he now knew what he needed to do.

And yes, he would actually do it.

He abruptly stood. "Before you pierce the firmament to heaven—or, considering your foul disposition, before you descend to Gehenna—I have an idea."

"And that might be?"

"I believe I now know how to help you."

Gunther coughed. "You brought a bottle of Sambuca?"

"Unfortunately, no. But I learned something while on Ibiza."

"How to trespass into people's homes?"

"Yes, now that you mention it," John said. "But something else, as well." He neared the door, then swerved. "I shall return."

"Who are you, General MacArthur?" Gunther said, coughing spasmodically.

Although Gunther's voice was convivial, desperation was aflame in his eyes. Fleeting, but John spotted it. Never had he witnessed anything proximate on stalwart Gunther. The image slashed savagely and a long-standing security crumbled to dust, as it tends to when witnessing the mortality of a hero. John shuddered, but worked to display the equanimity needed.

"Do me a favor," Gunther said. "Just don't take another fifteen years to return this time."

TWENTY-TWO

The car skidded through puddles, spraying the sides of the road on the way to Cala d'Hort. Rains dissuaded most tourists from venturing far, as it never took much to do that, and he navigated to the opposite side of the island without delay. He dashed to Pedrera de Cala d'Hort and descended slick stones to the Atlantis rock quarry. The Roman soldier carving, darkened from rain, observed him with augmented disdain. Minutes later, John stood before foaming waves facing the distant and towering island of Es Vedrà.

Yes, as terrifying as the prospect was, heightened by rain and somber sea, he needed to launch once again. He would swim to Es Vedrà.

Only on that isolated locale grew the legendary rock

samphire plant which saved Jose Barracuda Marquez. Of course, lovely Diana had been the impetus for that journey. Her faith in Jose's tale and her burning concern for him propelled them on what seemed a reckless and cockamamie quest. John thought everyone deranged that day, himself included, before witnessing the results. But one learns.

Now, it would be delightful to announce that his swim to Es Vedrà proceeded smoothly, that his experience from the first journey served him readily. But sadly, this was not the case.

Simply put, John struggled. Mightily.

Without Diana swimming beside him, setting the pace in her deliberate manner, the swim rapidly devolved into a titanic struggle. Certainly, it did not help that the rainfall intensified, and the sea thrashed. Intimidating factors when in fathomless waters.

He swam with force, halted, peeked up, was shocked to see Es Vedrà far, far away, and swam more. Tiring, he searched again, but confoundingly the island was not closer, as if he had been circling. How had he possibly completed this brutal journey the initial time? It was as if someone else had done it for him.

Time could not be gauged. He attempted to rest on his back and float, but the unforgiving rain droplets felt like ice as they pelted his eyes. He pressed on, using various strokes (including a few inefficient versions created on the spot) in his frantic attempt to reach this stark island. Limbs burned.

In time, he got closer, but found himself lightheaded, floating on his back once again, and, as odd as this might sound, belting out a few renditions of Broadway tunes. If spotted, his very sanity would be fair territory for debate. Ultimately though, somehow, some way, he finally reached the edge.

He struggled up, planting both feet on Es Vedrà.

All was gray and wet and lonely. A ghastly place.

But he felt Diana's warming presence, as he heard her compelling voice exhorting him to press on. He climbed the jagged rocks. The Luciferian goats were nowhere to be seen. No sounds, as the persistent moaning from his former visit, whether caused by wind rushing through caves or a long-perturbed giant, had ceased.

His reddened eyes widened upon finding the rock samphire in the same location, high on the cliff. Yet something had drastically changed. Far less was present than he remembered. Just a precious few emerald clumps remained on the black rocks.

He culled these last bits, but was sure to leave behind a single stalk, trembling in the wind against the palette of gray sky.

Back to the water's edge. It should be mentioned he once again forgot a satchel, and needed to shove the rock samphire back into his bathing suit, but such things happen when one is inundated with emotions and existential thoughts.

The water thrashed against rocks, generating thick foam. An ominous sea, and he was enervated throughout. In all candor, his chance of making it back to shore one more time seemed slight, but what choice did he have?

He lowered himself into the coldness and bobbed out, an insignificant speck in the vast sea.

He rashly chose a strategy of blind attack, which one does in times of desperation, by swimming forcefully, if not, insanely. Too insanely, burning oil reserves.

Repeatedly, he convinced himself the shore must be proximate, that his landing impended, yet reality stabbed him each time when observing an indiscernible sliver off in the distance.

Limbs became cardboard cutouts. The bottom was no

longer more than thirty feet below, but still the endless journey to shore.

Complete exhaustion had now arrived.

The game was up. A watery grave would be his fate after all. Not a pathetic fate in the least, a rather romantic denouement, but for he did not desire to end it all here. Three months ago, he would have acquiescently joined the other relics at sea bottom. Now, meaningful work lay ahead, and people he desperately wanted to see again, to spend a lifetime with. Reasons to live.

Nonetheless, his limbs could battle no more.

A tugging force.

He began to sink. He yearned to resist it, but the water offered tranquility. Underwater. His tongue tasted of seaweed. The end was not as epic a struggle, full of panic and yellowed-tinted, slow-motion, childhood memories, as he always envisioned. He continued to seductively sink, and all was placid. A most peaceful end.

But something lurked below and surrounding. Immense, with dark, vivid colors, swaying elegantly on the sea floor all around him.

Could it be?

Posidonia oceanica, in all its grandeur. So, old Gunther was correct, once again.

For over 100,000 years it reigned here, silently and majestically protecting and enriching these waters, and contributing to everything around it. It swayed rhythmically, back and forth, back and forth.

Gunther was privy to all this, but well knew John had failed in his life to acknowledge the obvious.

He sank toward it, closing in. The water muffled his screaming.

Then his heel made contact. A force pulsed through, constricting and releasing his heart.

John surged upward, bubbles trailing his sides.

He shattered the water's surface, coughing out fluid, greedily inhaling air once again. Another chance, precisely what he needed.

He kicked zealously, sea frothing behind his toes. Freestyle stroke for a time, and then bobbing on his back licking the rain. Legs and arms were hot with activity as he swam again.

Ultimately, the water shallowed. He attempted to stand, and slipped on a stone, splashing right back in. So, he crawled. Rocks and shells scraped both knees, and the briny water burned as he bled brightly.

Shore. At last. On his feet, once again.

He ascended the steep hill back to his car, blood dripping down shins, and roared off once again for the North and his fate.

Dusk when he returned.

The hut's flimsy door violently banged open and shut, open and shut in the wind. A drizzle still fell. A scene reminiscent of a long-abandoned ghost town.

He rushed inside. Gunther was spread on his cot, forearm over his face. No movement.

"Are you all right?"

No response. John's entire body tensed.

"Gunther?"

"Am I all right?" Gunther asked with a cough. "Let's just say Dante's ninth is in clear view."

Just hearing his voice offered relief.

"I have something for you." John stepped forward, displaying a handful of rock samphire plant.

"You went all that way for my funeral flowers? Is it not the universal consensus that one waits until after the person is deceased?"

John pulled a chair beside the cot. Sweat glazed Gunther, and he coughed fitfully. His lips were pale coral and his half-beard was matted. He observed John, whose drying hair flew in all directions.

"Wow," Gunther said. "And I thought I looked awful."

John displayed the rock samphire. "Just eat this."

Gunther observed it amusedly. The corner of his mouth arose. "So you've finally gone entirely insane?"

"'Entirely' might be an exaggeration."

"John, what the hell is that?"

"Just have a little faith."

"Are you sure this isn't some form of Ibizan hemlock, and you're not giving me a Socratic exit?"

"It is a thought."

Gunther grasped a palmful of the plant with his slender fingers.

"You want me to eat this?"

"I do."

He released a pained laugh. "Why?"

"Gunther?"

"Yes?"

John paused, looking up at the wood-slat ceiling as he collected himself.

"I'm sorry for abandoning you all those years ago in New York that summer. I know you needed me."

Gunther was silent.

"And I'm sorry for abandoning our beloved journal. I truly let us, and those who would benefit from it, down."

Gunther looked at John, his eyes flickering. "I understand."

"Do you? I'm not so sure that I do." John swallowed, began to speak, and swallowed again.

"Go on."

It would be best to confess all to Gunther now. Let him know the abhorrent truth.

"Since that summer," John said, palms beginning to perspire, "I have discarded all our interests and all our humanitarian pursuits. I threw them all away."

"Go on."

"You see…I must finally confess this; what really happened to me." John stared at the floor. "I actually went to work for a major hedge fund that summer. Plotting for the ultra-rich, and razing all in their path. Ruthless financial behavior in weakly regulated markets, not good, solid financial planning for families that needed it." John collected himself. "And I never left. I confess that's where I've been all these years, a traitor to our causes." He released an extended, anguished breath, attempting to expel the despicable feelings lingering to the depths of his alveoli.

The door banged shut in the wind.

"Fifteen Broad Street, Manhattan," Gunther said. "An impressive office you had back then."

John peered up, startled. "What?"

"Your office. Quite swanky."

"But…how do you know about that?" His mouth hung open.

Gunther managed a smile. "This might shock you, but I visited your workplace one morning that August, before I left."

"What?" John said, aghast. "That's not possible."

"I did."

"But how? I had lied to you. I told you I was working a summer job managing a clothing store."

He coughed. "You avoided me, said you couldn't meet because you were too busy. Completely unlike your usual reliable self. Limited deduction skills were required to know something was terribly amiss, and it was not about an extraordinarily high demand for designer garments."

John shook his head in disbelief. This could not be possible.

"So, I snuck into your office with some fatuous pretense. Impressive place, polished leather everywhere. Smelled like lemon cleaner."

"I cannot believe this."

"And there stood our John, with his three-piece charcoal suit. Never thought I would see that," Gunther said, his laughter turning into coughing. "Quite the unctuous professional."

"But why didn't you walk up and say hello? Or say anything?" John asked. "Why did you not approach me?"

"Why?"

"Yes. Why?"

"There you stood, talking with two suits in that glass room. A fish tank. All so grave of expression, as if the fate of the world rested on that frivolous discussion," he said, laughing and coughing. "And one with a white beard..."

"Jenkins."

"Jenkins. He was patting you on the back as you spoke and pointed to papers on the table. And he winked behind your back at another colleague, a bald rather hideous one. Both their eyes burned."

John listened quietly.

"They were so proud of the brilliance they found in you. And then I understood."

"What?"

"You were marooned. Engulfed, while trying to pay off your debts. And, mind you, I'm not naive to the allure of the perks of the rich. I'm not a fool; I understood you succumbed. But you would need to find your own way out."

"Dammit."

"What is it?"

"You could have just strode over and pulled me out by the ear," John said, raising his voice. "Everything would have then worked out for us. We wouldn't have had to go through hell."

"That is not true, John."

"Why not? You could have slapped me across the face. Heavens knows I needed it."

"And ruin that slick hairdo? No way."

"You could have."

Gunther coughed in a fit, then peered out the window.

"Some things in life need to unfold, as interminable as the path might seem. No one can set you free except yourself. I know."

"Do you?"

"That is our personal journey."

Raindrops pattered against the roof.

"My lord, my lord," John said, hands stretching his cheeks. "I didn't think I would ever get out."

"But, as you see, you did."

"And here we are, fifteen years later." His eyes widened. "Probably to the very date, from that morning. Astounding."

"Here we are."

"And all these long years, I believed you had absolutely no idea of what I was doing. That you didn't understand my situation." John scoffed. "How completely wrong I was. I was so embarrassed about my choices."

"Well, you still should be embarrassed. Profoundly embarrassed."

He looked at Gunther with surprise, and then they shared a laugh.

"I miss everything before that mess. Life seemed simpler then."

"As do I," Gunther said. He roughly coughed and wheezed. "As do I."

John gently nodded toward the rock samphire plant. "Have a little faith in me. Like you once did long ago."

Gunther remained silent for a time, gazing at the pale green stalks in hand. "Well, you used to be the person I trusted." Streaks of red slashed the darkening sky. "Seems as if the world were entirely another place back then."

"How easy it is to let the best of ourselves slip away."

Gunther placed the rock samphire on his pale tongue. He chewed. Eyebrows arched.

"Never tasted anything like that."

They waited without words. Darkness outside. Eventually Gunther rolled over, moaning softly, and slept. John's eyes were closing as well. He waited to see if something transpired. Nothing, but Gunther sleeping and coughing in dire fits. He continued waiting, hoping. Exhausted everywhere, his muscles throbbed. Blood had caked in streaks down his knees and shins. Eyes closing. Rain pattered on the ceiling in gentle, rolling rhythms.

Eyelids slowly warming...now, hot. John opened them to white, blinding sunlight. Squinting in an attempt to see, he sat up, and found bookshelves all around. He was inside the hut, on the cot. Morning time.

Gunther. No Gunther. John leapt up and dashed outside onto the beach. Outside was only warmth, with expansive, blue, Mediterranean skies. No one around. The bright morning sunlight dappled upon the water's surface. All so beautiful.

"How did you sleep?"

John veered and spotted someone standing by a campfire beside the hillside. Gunther.

His half-beard had vanished; he was cleanly shaven, skin luminous in the sunlight. A pot hung on a tripod over an open fire.

"What is this?"

"I'm cooking a bouillabaisse. Clams, mussels, shrimp, razorfish, fennel, thyme, saffron threads, garlic, onion, a few tomatoes. You will love it."

Although thin, Gunther appeared fine. Beyond fine. Not coughing, and moving sprightly about, fully engaged in his task.

"How do you feel?"

"Wonderful. Cooking, which I always enjoy. This concoction is like the ones I ate while in Marseille. I learned to prepare bouillabaisse from a chef named Gaspard. Nasty at first, he identified your weaknesses in seconds, but I worked in his kitchen chopping vegetables and eventually made friends. The nastiness remained, but at least we were friends. I have rouille for this bouillabaisse, thank heavens. Gaspard told me a bouillabaisse without rouille is like Marseille without sunshine. He also used a cruder analogy, but let us leave it at that."

John watched in awe. "Your health?"

"Superb."

John's head flowed back and forth in wonderment. "You don't seem surprised," he said. "You don't seem surprised in the least. Why?"

"Surprised the bouillabaisse is coming along nicely? Now, why should I be. Trained from the best. Yes, he was crass at times, but a true artist, nonetheless."

"No," John said, laughing delightfully. His eyes welled with tears. "Your health is restored. Why are you not surprised?"

Gunther focused on the bubbling tomatoes, creases lining his brow, as he stirred with a lengthy wooden spoon.

"Because you finally found your way."

TWENTY-THREE

And so, the time arrived. The revered harvest party at Bob's villa would launch that very night.

Angela had been waxing lyrical about it since Bob invited John on their initial visit to his finca, and she telephoned him each of the last three afternoons, repeatedly inquiring whether he was "prepared."

After asking if he might bring friends along, a hollow silence followed. He glanced at the mute receiver.

"Why?" she finally asked.

"Why? To share the party. Why else?"

"Bob invited you, John. You alone. Not some seething hoard."

He laughed. "Well, I'm sure old Bob won't mind, even with

the attack of the 'seething hoard.' With him, the more lemmings listening to his lecturing, the merrier."

Angela did not laugh. "Are you bringing that Diana woman?"

Always she seemed to return to that. "Andre, also."

"I fail to see the need. We planned everything for months for our big night. Why bring her?"

"Her?" John said. "So it's okay if I bring Andre?"

Might Angela be jealous? But he had known Angela for months, and never had she mumbled anything romantic toward John. Certainly she had had ample opportunity. And besides, a colossal thirty-year gulf separated their ages. She also had encouraged him, multiple times, to find a girlfriend, and had advised him on properly doing so.

"Forget both of them. This is our night."

"Angela, it is the final party of the season. It would be nice to get a group together."

"Are you dating her?"

Sometimes the most reasonable inquiries can stun a person.

"Diana?" John eventually said. "Well, no. No, I am not."

How he wished the answer were in the affirmative! A "yes" would make her back off, and more importantly, it would mean he had actually followed through on his feelings. So, he rather bitterly added: "Not yet, at least."

A time of silence.

"You deserve better."

"What?"

"You heard me. You deserve better."

Where was she mining these outrageous opinions? A direct insult to Diana.

"And what do you know about her?" he asked in snippy fashion.

"That you deserve better. Someone who will love and adore you for all of your life."

"Maybe she deserves better."

"Okay. So why aren't you dating her after all this time? Hmm?"

John paused, stroking his chin. "I suppose I have been delaying."

"Delaying what?"

"Telling her how I feel."

"Delaying?" Angela cackled in a cringeworthy manner. "A man who delays professing love does so because he does not feel love. And he never will. Period."

This statement, meticulously crafted to sound like a truism, was meritless garbage.

"We'll see about that," he said shortly.

A freshly determined John proclaimed that he would be unable to chauffeur her, but would happily meet at Bob's. She had become increasingly pushy and privileged with him, and yes, he was guilty of indulging that, but this needed to change now.

Late that afternoon, John weaved toward the eastern hills where Andre resided in his infamous, rat-friendly tent. After retrieval, they would relax and talk for a time, as is always pleasant to do before parties. They would then stop for Diana, and journey to the main event.

The early September sun baked the island. The main beaches were sardined with tourists, the hotel rooms crammed, and the restaurants and bars desperately sought extra help which often came from stranded tourists who had spent their limited funds too lavishly while inebriated. The island creaked under the incessant demand for pleasure. Yet, in a few more weeks, all this fervor would vaporize, and Ibiza would once again return to a soporific state. But not yet.

"What do you think?" Andre asked as he entered the car.

He had emerged from the forest wearing jeans and a long-sleeved collared shirt with tan, leather shoes. John had never seen him with long sleeves, long pants, or even shoes for that matter.

"You appear a fairly serious person."

"'Appear?'"

"Until a conversation commences, and then the mirage fades."

Andre had been flustered when John invited him, as he had not attended a residential party for years.

"Rolf is gone."

"Your ex-wife's boyfriend? What happened?"

"Not sure."

"So how do you know this?"

He shrugged. "Lotte came by the market the other day, crying and screaming. Said he had abandoned her, and moved back to Australia."

An inevitable outcome.

"And still she demanded money from you, amidst the flow of tears?"

Andre nodded. "Brought my daughter though. While my ex bawled about Rolf, and how unfairly he treated her, I spent time with Laura."

"And I suppose with Rolf vanished his monthly stipend as well?"

Andre nodded again.

John stroked his chin. "So her demand on you will increase."

"I believe the time is ripe for me to make some demands on her."

His response pleasantly surprised. "Finally, you are talking some sense."

"I'm excited to set some things." He spoke with an uncharacteristically resolute tone. "There she was, bawling about Rolf, me pathetically agreeing, and my daughter acting the adult, instructing us to calm down. Humiliating. But I know what it will take to change things."

"Do you?"

"I do."

"If you say so."

"Don't sound so damned skeptical."

"I'm not."

Andre was impassioned, his shoulders spread like a concupiscent peacock's feathers. His feelings had apexed, and although against his nature, he would welcome a little conflict. His zealous state was something new.

"I'm not. At least mostly not," John said, placatingly. "I'm listening."

"I'm going to set a schedule with my daughter and money, like you once said. You were right."

"You need to establish a home to see her."

"I have my place."

"A tent lost in the forest full of half-empty bean cans won't qualify."

"I always finish my beans."

Smiles could not be prevented.

"More money is needed though," Andre said. "I just need that elusive lucky break they always get in your Hollywood movies." His shining eyes appeared melancholic.

"Hey, those movies must be rooted in some truth, right?"

They pulled up before Diana's. Fortunately, Diana had seemed enthused by his invitation. Parties must be treated as most fanciful affairs, she had said, and she announced she would get "all decked out."

Already late evening, the fragrance from rosemary plants lining the sidewalk intoxicated. John crushed their dark, narrow leaves between his thumb and forefinger, intensifying the piercing aroma. He ascended to Diana's front door while Andre waited in a curiously anxious state in the car.

Perspiration dotted John's forehead, and not due to the precipitous climb. On the second-to-last stair he paused, and chose to undertake that most arduous of tasks: to be honest with oneself. He dared wonder if tonight might be their night. He confessed that her captivating image invaded his mind randomly, and he even detected verses from medieval love poetry meandering through his thoughts. Only the befitting moment was needed tonight.

He just needed to remain amicable and relaxed.

She answered his knock instantly. Her sleeveless, pale blue dress hugged her body, which was tanned golden from time on the beach and her beloved reading roof. A white cockle shell necklace draped from her slender neck. The air smelled of orange blossoms.

"Are you ready?" Diana asked.

"For?"

"The party, of course," she said with a mischievous smile.

When their car arrived at the entrance to Bob's massive property, the gates were tied open. They drove through arid fields, tires scratching parched earth, passing aged olive trees with dusty leaves. In the distance, before Bob's finca, were clustered scores of vehicles and shining lights. A strip of marmalade slathered the horizon as darkness was impending.

A general order existed to everything, but at first glance, it sure appeared to be chaos. All the barbecues on the front porch were aflame, and the smoke of roasting Iberico pork and zucchini wafted over the property. Euro disco music blared from camouflaged speakers. Spirited guests arrived in bouncing clumps, hands secured on each other's shoulders. Boisterous voices and laughter echoed. An electric atmosphere by any metric.

"Tonight is the special moon. The Harvest Moon, they call it, because it's a time of reaping," John said.

"With that cloud layer," Diana said, looking heavenward, "we won't see, let alone reap, a thing."

"Let me find Bob."

"In this pandemonium?"

Inside, only denser. Strikingly, no consistency of dress whatsoever existed. While one might have experienced black-tie dinners, dress-in-white parties, or at least casual gatherings where all possessed vaguely similar tastes, in attendance were those wearing three-piece tweed suits, another with roller skates and a bikini, and another dressed as a tie-dye Merlin.

Inside the living room, Bob stood by the bookshelves at the far end, his left elbow resting comfortably on a shelf. As usual, he lectured with his booming voice, surrounded by his covey of listeners. Noticing John, he halted mid-sentence.

"Well, well," he said with a patronizing smile. "So, the prodigal son finally returns."

He hugged John, his sparse hair smelling as if he were secreting stale wine from scalp pores. After noticing Diana, and realizing she accompanied John, his eyes widened.

"And who might this be?"

"Diana," John said. "And Andre, a sculptor friend of mine."

Bob nodded, prudently making equal eye contact with both of them.

He cupped and kissed Diana's hand. "Delighted," he said, before turning to Andre. "And where can I find your sculptures?"

"Markets." Noting John's admonishing stare, he padded his barebones statement: "Las Dalias and the hippie market. I sell weekly."

"Fantastic," Bob said. "I always admire an artist. The true pioneers of our society, not the politicians. Please show them to me sometime."

Bob's thick hand plopped atop John's shoulder like a burger tossed onto a grill, and it guided him beside the bookshelves.

"What's with the beauty?" he inquired, head lowered, in a conspiratorial tone. His eyelids twitched as he awaited his answer.

"Diana?" John said. "A friend of mine."

Bob scanned the crowd with a furrowed brow of concern. "Does she know?"

What he referred to was unclear, but it seemed something surreptitious.

"Does Diana know what?"

"No, no. Does *Angela* know?"

"Angela?"

"Yes."

"Know what?"

He smiled slyly, and then winked at John. "Just be careful. I behaved the same at your age, but be careful. Be a little more discreet about it, my father used to tell me. If they find out, they always get enraged." He returned his padded hand onto John's shoulder. "And women can be dangerous."

A befuddled John prepared a question to lift this fog when a couple, laughing drunkenly and declaring their insane envy at Bob speaking with others, swept him away.

With Diana immersed in spirited conversation with another

woman, discussing something about the future of the East End of London, John chose to wander. She should enjoy herself, and soon he would reveal his feelings. When the time seemed just right, that is.

Dozens of bottles of wine, indubitably from Bob's beloved vineyard, were uncorked in the dining room and released a pong more akin to vinegar than vino. The main table was adorned with platters of grilled meats, soft goat cheeses, grilled octopus, and trays of fried spring rolls with orange dipping sauces.

"My dearest friend, I thank you for inviting us."

Klav and Natalia.

His green shorts hung over his knees, and a collection of Tibetan bead necklaces accrued over his chest. Natalia wore a bikini top and jean shorts. Both wielded loftily loaded food plates. As he had invited them specifically so they could satiate themselves, and perhaps find opportunities amidst the guests, their bravado greatly pleased John. Klav kissed John's cheeks, relieved at the sight of him. After spotting Andre, another friend, he confidently smiled, as multiple allies were now present, which galvanized him for his inevitable antics.

"You invited Klav here?" Andre whispered. "I suspect a few wealthy guests will be hearing about his brilliant art and literature."

"Why do you think I invited him?"

This concept momentarily stunned Andre, but he soon beamed with glowing admiration. "You're not shy. You don't let much stop you, John."

"They need this opportunity."

"That is true. Yes. That is true."

"I will be bitterly disappointed if at least one unwitting guest doesn't end up investing in his latest tour de force."

Andre and Klav began chatting while heading toward the back terrace. John considered Andre's comment about not being shy. Generally true. Unless, of course, it came to Diana. Then that cursed hesitancy set in and destroyed everything.

A warm hand draped his shoulder. Natalia stood behind him. She studied each of his eyes as if vital messages were inscribed upon them.

"Do you remember what I told you that night at the camping?" she asked.

Klav and Andre conversed by the back terrace.

Of course he remembered. "Told me?"

"That I love you."

John bit his tongue while chewing his roll. "Yes, yes, I do recall that. Yes."

"I meant it."

"Thank you," John said. "I care about you also."

She smiled understandingly. "I said 'I love you.' And thank you for taking Toobee to the restaurant that day. He repeats the story constantly."

"My pleasure entirely."

"Plenty of this food will go back to him." She observed John with curious admiration. "You are a special person, John."

"Don't give me too much credit. Believe me."

"Never have I met anyone who would be invited by the rich owner to a private party, and then turn around and invite us also," she said with an amused giggle. "People just don't do that. But you do."

John bowed.

"Now, I must go help Klav work his magic on these guests."

"If he needs a little assistance, for old time's sake, just summon me."

A cloth shoulder bag, garnished with indigo beads sewn into

the peace symbol, dangled from Klav's shoulder. Undoubtedly this satchel would be laden with victuals upon departure. Already he was conversing, his hands darting animatedly before him, with a sharply dressed man who seemed fully taken by his fanciful tales.

Natalia smiled, dimples forming, and walked away, heading toward Klav. A wistfulness flowed as he watched her go. He hoped she and her little family would always be safe.

Fingernails sank into John's forearm. Angela.

Her tight black dress barely reached her knees, and black talons encased her eyes from unrestrained mascara use.

"Where have you been hiding?" she demanded.

"Enjoying yourself?"

She pressed her wetted lips to his for several protracted moments. The tip of her tongue probed, before she broke away with a smacking sound. "I missed you my dear."

This kiss stunned him. "Apparently."

She had never, ever done this before. Although unnerved, he chose not to react negatively. The party atmosphere might be affecting her, and no one desired a scene on a night like this.

"So did you bring all those whining friends of yours?"

"Now they are 'whining?' Not long ago they were 'seething.'"

"I saw you brought that Diana."

"I did."

"And the other guy. The hippie sort."

"That's not narrowing it down much."

Angela cackled. "Your friend."

"Andre."

She snatched John's arm. "Come, let us go see Bob together."

On the back terrace, which faced the vineyard, Euro disco music blared and cobalt strobe lights flashed. Many danced en masse in the center of the expansive terrace. The dancers' passionate expressions, the whites of their eyes, flickered in the light. Angela dragged John into the group, brazenly shoving aside others. She began closely dancing. Her hands waved in the air and she screamed with unbridled glee. She pulled and pushed an astounded John, mouth agape, forward and back. She seemed inebriated, but Angela normally did not drink nor did she smell of alcohol. Her savage dancing persisted, as she seized John's hips while rising and falling. Eventually he grabbed an opportune pause in music to flee and secure refuge at the crowd's side.

"Where is Bob?" he desperately asked, as she pursued closely.

"By the edge of the vineyard," she said huskily. "Let's go."

Bob stood with his back to the vines, encircled by admirers. His voice reverberated and they laughed precisely during pauses, like a laugh track in a television show. At the sight of Angela and John, he instantly cut off.

He lifted Angela's red-painted toes off of the ground with a hug, all the while gazing at John.

"Well, will you look at the two of you," he said. "Perfect together."

She blushed. "John didn't reveal that he dances so well. He keeps his little secrets."

"That's the thing about secrets." He peered at John. "They all come out eventually. Don't they John?"

John found himself growing uneasy, and attempted to politely excuse himself. Angela was having none of it, as she snatched at his arm. "And where are you off to in such a big hurry, dancing man?"

Whatever foul concoction was brewing here needed to be flushed.

"To talk to Diana," he announced.

Bob and Angela's faces transformed into blank sheets. Not what they expected to hear.

"I've been wanting to convey my feelings, and as you so correctly pointed out, Angela, I have been delaying," John said, making firm eye contact. "No more delays."

Her grip collapsed limply off his arm.

He broke away and strode inside, as an instinct akin to Lot himself told him not to turn back around.

Inside, he sought Diana. She stood exactly where he had last seen her, conversing by the bookshelves, laughing blithely. His time had come.

"Lovely to see you darling." She fluttered his hair. "How is our Andre faring?"

"Joined a few friends of ours."

"I met that other friend of yours again. Certainly cordial."

"Other friend?"

"Angela. Your fellow American yankee. So, you are teaching her how to drive a stick shift car? How generous of you."

John swallowed. "Teaching her to drive?"

"Yes. Lessons three times a week, and she prepares home-cooked dinners afterward to reward you."

"But—"

"I was absolutely famished listening to her delectable meal descriptions. Seafood paella! You're so kind to that woman. You never cease to surprise me."

He struggled composing himself.

"Diana, this might sound odd, but I have never given her a single driving lesson. Since that night on Bennirás beach, I have not even seen her."

Diana laughed, swirling wine in her glass. "Don't be silly. It's a nice thing you are doing, darling. Don't be embarrassed about helping the old bird."

He wanted to further explain, or attempt to comprehend, but then a frantic Andre appeared, short of breath.

"Guess who's here?"

"Who now? Amelia Earhart?"

Andre paused. "She landed on Ibiza?"

"That wouldn't surprise me. So who is it?"

"Dirk. That gallery owner from The Netherlands. You convinced him to buy my sculptures from Las Dalias market that day, remember?"

"Wonderful! Now is your opportunity. Talk to him."

Diana had resumed her conversation. She laughed good-naturedly with her friend, appearing more captivating than ever.

Suddenly it all seemed so simple and easy. Why on earth had he not done this earlier? He felt free.

He was now ready to take her aside and announce his affection.

"Let me be and I'll catch up with you. I want time with Diana," he said, while admiring her.

Andre's eyebrows elevated. "Did you forget? He thinks you are the artist. He thinks you are me! Remember? He's asking for you."

John vigorously polished his cheek. "I did forget that detail." His head shook in mounting frustration. "Where the hell is Dirk?"

"Out front, by one of those raging barbecues."

Diana busily conversed. She would certainly still be here when he returned momentarily. Already he had waited this long, why would a few more minutes matter?

"Okay, okay, but let's make this brief."

Dirk's thick-framed glasses shined in the firelight. His reserved manner fractured at the sight of John as he unleashed a grandiose smile. Stepping forward, he pumped John's hand.

"Andre," Dirk said to John. "I had planned to come by Las Dalias market on Monday morning to see you."

"When did you return to Ibiza?"

"Two days ago. And I am the bearer of good news."

"Oh?"

"I displayed your works at my gallery in the Hague."

"Excellent."

"All sold. Remarkably fast. All of them."

The rush of pride flushed on Andre's skin. Mouth open, tongue trembling, he narrowly reigned in the temptation to speak.

"I informed you that I wanted to open a new gallery in London. In February," Dirk said. "And so I will."

"Congratulations."

Dirk nodded, exhaling. "I want to headline your work."

"Mine?" Even John was caught off guard, in the most pleasant way, of course.

"It will excel in London, as the Brits have, how shall I say this...somewhat peculiar tastes. Let us discuss supplying a steady amount. And of course, I will pay more than the first time."

Andre appeared ready to rupture in jubilance.

Time to tell Dirk the truth, as awkwardly painful as that would be. The intelligent approach would be the truth now.

"Fantastic news," John said. "But let me introduce you to the genuine Andre. I'm John. My friend here is Andre. He's the artist."

Dirk's head oscillated observing them. "I'm confused."

"Andre is a fine artist, but selling his work is certainly not his forte," John said with a laugh. "That day we met you in Las Dalias, I tried to help him a bit."

Dirk frowned. A businessman, he abhorred being fooled

as it exposed his weaknesses, which can be costly. But let us give Dirk some credit, as he recouped rapidly.

"Well, you sure did a good job of it."

"He's the artist. Been making these works for years. Works of that level need the proper publicity."

Dirk grinned wryly. "Any other secrets? The sculptures are really made in Taiwan?"

"They are mine."

Dirk turned to Andre. "Well, let me take care of publicity and sales. I just need you to do the creating."

John stepped away as they began discussing in detail the reactions in the Hague to his work. Andre flashed a grateful smile as he departed.

John next maneuvered through the crowd back to Diana. A few random grabs at his arms, but he ignored them and moved determinedly toward her. He had to profess his feelings for her, and he had to do it now. Enough bizarreness had occurred, and certainly enough delays.

How exactly would he broach this? No matter, he would just talk and let it flow. He did it for others, and now, he could finally do it for himself. Finally.

He halted.

No Diana.

He scanned the throbbing crowds, but did not spot her.

Perhaps illogically, he twinged with panic. Where had she vanished to?

Before him, two closely conversing men wearing khakis and navy blazers parted like stage curtains, and none other than Gunther strode forward between them. His hair was combed back over his head, he was cleanly shaven, and he wore a white T-shirt which read "Cabaret Now and Mostly Forever Act."

"You made it," John said. They hugged. "I wasn't sure if you would come."

"Sounded like too much fun to miss," Gunther said. "And I know many guests here from one part of the island or the other."

"Lovely T-shirt."

"Isn't it?" He wore a most amused smile, the smile of one who knew John far too well. "So whom are you looking for?"

"Why do you ask?" John said, startled.

"Perhaps your darting eyes and rattled composure? You appear to have sipped from the potion of Brangaine."

A slight laugh escaped. "I was searching for my friend Diana. She was here a moment ago."

"The blond damsel. Yes, I saw you talking with her before."

"How long have you been here?"

"You must care for her a great deal."

John swiveled to him in surprise. "And why would you say that?"

Gunther laughed. "Because, dear John, I know your expressions. And that stricken face cannot be induced by apathy. You appear like Tristan in Iseult's presence."

His perceptiveness never ceased to surprise.

"Your fair maiden Diana was just here a minute ago. Conversing with an American woman named Angela."

"Oh, fantastic. Not again. Now Angela probably told her I'm giving her daily parcheesi lessons and receiving tapas lunches," John said. "Wait." He veered to Gunther. "You know Angela?"

"I know of her." He raised an eyebrow. "And you know Angela as well?"

"The first person I met on this island." John gazed at the intricate patterns on the blood-red oriental carpet. "Ever since, she calls, inviting me to dinners and parties. Looking back, I believe I've only actually called her one single time, the first time. I didn't realize that until now."

"Interesting."

"Lately, I've been plagued by a foreboding feeling about her. And she seems to have an intense dislike of Diana. I believe it's best to avoid Angela for a while."

"You always acted gracious with people like that."

John peered at Gunther. "People like what?"

Gunther's expression contorted into the quizzical. "Know you nothing about her past?"

"Past?"

He snatched two glasses of wine from a nearby table and handed one to John as he gulped from his own. Bob's puerile vintage burned the throat.

"I felt sorry for her," John said. "She told me about the death of her husband multiple times, and the trials of widowhood. Seems lonely after all that horror. We even attended a seance to meet him."

Gunther laughed.

"What's so funny?"

"You."

"Why me?"

"You didn't believe all that?"

"Seances? I gave it a fair chance."

Gunther turned stern. "No. Her husband. He is alive and well in Beverly Hills."

The bitter wine seared John's tongue.

"What do you mean?"

"What I said."

"Stop it."

"I'm serious."

"You've lost it. She showed me photos of the two of them before he died. Photos by a tennis court. He died of cancer."

"I'm sorry, John. But her husband is alive and well in Beverly Hills. Some big hedge fund guy. You two could relate."

John's thumb and forefinger furiously stroked at his chin. "So what is she doing on Ibiza alone? Why the hell would she make all that up for?"

Gunther stared into John's eyes. "John, I don't know how to tell you this, so I just will." He secured a firm hand on John's shoulder. "She spent twelve years in jail, and then in an asylum for psychiatric treatment."

"What?" John said, uneasily laughing. "What are you talking about?"

"I just told you. Jail and an asylum."

"For what?"

"For murder."

"Murder?" A warm queasiness began to engulf him.

"Her husband was having an affair in Los Angeles. Angela discovered this and went crazy, as I heard she was insanely possessive. Obsessed with him. Stalked the woman, then stabbed her seventeen times in the face and neck with a pen up in the Hollywood Hills. Apprehended immediately."

"This cannot be true."

"It is true."

"It can't be."

"It is. She came to the island about eight or nine years ago to escape her past. To start again where no one knew about her. But I met her once with a friend of mine from San Diego who was privy to her true story. Had followed her trial. Dreadful details."

"Does anyone else know?"

"On Ibiza, you can hide your past without a problem."

John felt stripped naked. The crimson depths in his glass were bottomless.

"When I met her at a cafe, on my very first morning on Ibiza, she said she thought I was the ghost of her husband," John said, almost whispering. "I remember that now. Yes. His ghost, she said. Said I looked identical to him. Even acted like him. I saw photos; we are very similar." John looked toward Gunther. "She stabbed the cheating woman seventeen times?"

"Yes."

"Good heavens."

Gunther's expression turned grave. "Where is your friend Diana right now?"

"I have no idea," John said. "Wait. Wait a second." His chest constricted. "You said you saw Angela talking with Diana."

"Yes."

"Did...did they leave together?"

"I believe Angela led her out back."

They hustled to the back terrace where the dancing mass throbbed in pulsing lights. It now moved as one malleable blob greedily sopping up those foolish enough to venture into its orbit. No Diana or Angela anywhere.

Bob stood by the far edge, waving John over with harsh arm strokes. Purple stains littered his white shirt, and he was unsteady. He smelled of rancid wine. Although shorter than John, he fastened his burly forearm around the back of John's neck, crushing against his vertebrae.

"I just saw your girlfriend Angela. With your pretty thing-on-the-side," Bob said, winking. Redness latticed both eyeballs.

"'Girlfriend Angela?'"

"Yes."

"Angela and I are just friends."

He chortled, and began coughing. "Don't be ridiculous."

The record needed to be set straight, right now.

"She is only a friend."

He struggled suppressing his cough. "That's ridiculous."

"Why?"

He peered at John as if he were psychotic. "When you first came here a few months ago, to our couples' dinner, she announced she was bringing her new flame. Said you had flirted and picked her up at a cafe."

"Absurd."

"Absurd?" Bob said. "Angela informs me. Said your relationship progressed wonderfully. That the thirty-year age difference is but a pittance to you."

Blinding outrage swelled within John.

"This is absurd."

"You two are living together now, sharing her home, so how dare you talk like that? Shame on you."

"Living together?"

"In fact, John," he said, stabbing John's chest with an overgrown fingernail, "she expects you to propose tonight."

"Propose?"

"That's right. Marriage."

This one took extra time to process.

"Marriage?" John asked with incredulity.

"Yes. Tonight is her most special night in forty years. She's hysterical with excitement at her second chance at marriage."

John's throat constricted. Swallowing was no longer possible.

"A second chance, John. Don't we all deserve that?"

His mouth was cotton.

Bob's eyebrows lifted in supercilious fashion. "You should propose tonight, John, you really should. She deserves that. She deserves that, after all the poor soul has endured."

This Bob, he must know everything. Must have even known her from many years back in California, before all the trouble.

"You know all about her past," John said, flatly. "Don't you?"

Bob did not respond.

"Yes, you do. And," John continued, "you know all about the murder."

Bob's back jerked upright.

"Don't you?"

Silence. Although Bob had vanquished his American citizenship, he still fancied the fifth amendment approach.

"Where did she take Diana, Bob?"

He remained a statue.

"Bob, it's time for truth. Like you once pursued the truth with all your might in the 1960s. It's that time again."

Bob looked up at him, stunned by this reference to his glorious past. He swallowed.

"It's your time once again, Bob," John said. "Where did they go?"

Bob swiveled and looked over the dark, flowing fields of the vineyard. The leaves undulated in the breeze, forming black waves that journeyed into an infernal eternity. His expression transformed from shocked to vacant.

He pointed to the fields.

"Out there."

TWENTY-FOUR

John and Gunther moved swiftly between rustling vines. The vines maxed at shoulder height, so Diana and Angela should be visible, but condensed clouds concealing the full moon produced swaths of darkness.

They chose not to shout out the names, the commonplace technique in shows and movies, for approaching by stealth always seemed to be the far wiser course.

In essence, once the adrenaline of their initial brash charge into the inky vines petered, reality set in: they faced a convoluted, seemingly impossible hunt. An expansive vineyard, stretching endlessly in all directions, and two of them could only canvas so much. Which way to even go?

They listened for voices or footsteps, but with breezes blowing, the rustling vines and leaves dominated the soundscape.

They seemed to be whispering, mocking them from the darkness. Haunting sounds. The sickening, queasy sensation one feels when all is lost began to warmly set it. How easy it would be to succumb to this desperation.

They decided, rather rashly, to split up. Is not that the classic mistake they also make in all those lovely films?

Gunther and John wished each other the best of luck. They agreed, if they found them, to remain calm and simply lead everyone back to the party. Oh yes, it all sounded so feasible when discussing it. Plans usually do.

John ran up and down the paths between the vines. He stopped and listened but heard only the diabolical whispering, and discovered nothing but stirring leaves. Several times, he believed he spotted them, he was sure, but it turned out to be vines curving into human silhouettes. Would he be spotting zebras if searching for them?

He continued dashing about, looking in all directions, twisting in erratic circles. The harvest party had now transformed into an orange globe shimmering far in the distance.

And Gunther, absolutely no sound of his footsteps. He had joined the vanishing club as well. Apparently disappearing was in vogue.

Some sort of sound.

Giggling, a mocking laugh. He frantically searched all directions. A surging breeze revealed only flapping, heart-shaped leaves.

He continued sprinting through the lengthy rows, soft dirt giving beneath his feet, fatiguing his calves. But no Diana.

This grand rescue operation could be deemed a pathetic failure.

Finally, he halted and fell to his knees.

The rich smell of fertile earth dominated. Waves of rage

overcame him. Why had he not seen the truth about Angela? So blind an ignoramus was he? And why, why had he hesitated to tell Diana how he felt about her? All of this debacle could have been easily avoided had he just spoken earlier, and oh yes, many ripe opportunities had existed to do so. He had no slippery excuses; he had seized zero opportunities, and now everyone had to pay.

When he looked back to the sky, a few clouds began shifting.

The narrowest sliver of moon revealed itself. Not much light, but something. He arose and ran.

His feet pressed into yielding earth.

And then he heard something.

A sound nearby. Not whispering, but a harsh note, a command. Frantically, he searched. Was that hair? The top of a head behind a row. He slowed, steadied his breath, and stalked toward it. Through the vibrating vines into a clearing.

Angela.

She loomed over Diana.

Diana kneeled, her forearm bleeding.

John, for all his supposed cleverness, dashed blindly toward them like a blithering fool. At the sound, Angela revealed a silver scalpel and pressed it against Diana's throat.

The three stayed silent for several moments, each assessing. Diana remained impassive. The right side of her face was muddied, but she breathed calmly and watched John. The serrated grape leaves rustled.

"What are you doing?" John asked, as casually as could be managed. It should be mentioned that beyond his question's banal nature, his nonchalant tone sounded excruciatingly satirical considering the circumstances.

Angela, almost unrecognizable, extended a chilling grin. Her hair exploded in myriad directions, and her teeth seemed tinier and spaced farther apart.

"Saving us."

"Saving us? We are just fine."

"No!"

John breathed steadier. "Everything is fine."

"This tramp," she said, exhaling shortly. "She will come between us."

Beyond anything, he needed to assure the scalpel remained steady. "She won't come between us."

Angela laughed derisively. "I see the way you look at her. Oh, I do. My husband used to drool at that other blond tramp the same lustful way. That look I know far too well, my John."

"Let's just relax."

"Relax? Don't dare condescend to me. Both you and my husband are unfaithful at heart."

"Don't we need to begin our relationship before you call me unfaithful?"

Angela snorted. "Begin?" she said, in a contemptuous tone. "Begin? You and I have been together since you first called me up for our date. I didn't call you, you called me. Is that not true?"

Much he could contend with, which he burned to refute, but not the prudent course at the moment.

"Yes, I called you."

Her smile reeked of satisfaction. "And you rushed over to pick me up at my house that day. So impressed with my beauty you were."

John held his tongue, admittedly with monumental effort. She was quickly gaining momentum.

"Endless Ashtanga yoga and colonic cleansing for the last decade gave me these looks. Your jaw dropped at the sight of me. Don't you dare deny that."

The scalpel gleamed in a seepage of moonlight. He needed to tread circumspectly.

"I don't deny we spent time together. I've always had an interesting time meeting your friends. And even attending the seance to meet your dead husband."

Shock flared across Angela's face.

"But that's not a relationship yet," John continued. "We are friends, and moving forward from that." Of course, he furiously desired to brand her deluded, but he dared not expunge the possibility of a romantic future for them in her mind, or the scalpel would slice. That hope must be kept alive.

"I take things slowly," John said.

Angela's taut cheeks drooped slightly. "I know you do, John. You're a gentleman that way. I appreciate that, I really do," she said in an almost kindly voice.

This tender voice caught him off guard, he relaxed a bit, but her expression quickly hardened.

"But this one needs to go, or she will butcher what we have. I can't endure that pain again. I vowed, never again."

The clouds began retreating, and bleached light shone through. All countenances turned ghostly.

"So just let her go."

"Let her go?"

"Yes. She won't get in the way."

"Just let her go?"

"Yes. Don't harm her though, or you will get in trouble and be taken away. Then I will lose you forever."

John edged closer, and Angela reacted not.

"Just let her go," he repeated. "She will return to England. I will remain here with you."

Angela squinted in deliberation. Her face then became expressionless as she stared into the vines. Her thoughts were unreadable. The leaves rustled in the breeze.

"Stephen spoke the same way to me," she said, faintly,

seemingly talking to herself. "My poor, poor husband. So deluded by that horrific tramp. He was susceptible to her powers, poor man. And I believed every little word he said to me."

She tensed. The scalpel pressed against Diana's neck.

"But all he did was lie. Again and again. Do you know what it is like to be lied to John? Do you?"

"I have been lied to."

"But by the person you trust most? The person you stake your future with?" she said, her molars grinding. "A nauseating feeling. You actually start to believe *you* are the wrongdoer, no matter the logic. No matter that you are a faithful wife. You feel like *you* are the guilty one."

"I'm sorry about that."

"A goddamn coward," she said, her voice raspy. "Just tell me the truth like a man. But no, he wanted it all. That goddamn coward cheated on me for years, after I loved him with all my heart. He got away with everything, and I have suffered all these years. Where is the justice in that?"

"He should not have done that," John said. "He was a coward."

"You think so?" Her voice perked.

"I don't think so. I know so."

"You're just saying that."

"No. That, I'm not." John spoke firmly. "He was a deceiving coward, and he wronged you. I see no reason to deny that fact."

Her flesh contorted in deliberation. Tears trembled on her lower eyelashes, and she peered down at Diana. "Now, I will end this."

Just then Gunther burst through the vines.

His left foot struck a stone, and the man was airborne.

Angela looked up in astonishment, and Diana seized her wrist, twisting and plunging the scalpel into Angela's thigh. She howled, and John leapt atop her, restraining her writhing form. He tore off his shirt and used it to securely fasten her hands behind her back.

The breeze ceased and all the leaves stilled.

Back at the finca, two police officers discreetly escorted a hobbled Angela away. Her shoulders hunched and her head bobbed, as if a hen, pecking grain. John watched from a distance, their earlier meetings playing before him, the hollow clinking sounds of the wind chimes lining her lonely house rustling across his memories. He shook his head and pitied her.

Bob appeared stunned, and said not a word. He eschewed eye contact with John. Everything unfolded with remarkably little fanfare. Within minutes, Bob returned to recounting his innumerable anecdotes to another captivated group. The music resounded and dancers frolicked amidst laughter. The party, like Ibiza in summer, never even paused.

Obscuring clouds had completely moved on. The full Harvest Moon was now on grand display over all of Ibiza.

"You came for me, my darling," Diana told John when alone by the side of the finca. Her arm was washed and bandaged. "Quite chivalric of you."

"Of course I did. I would never let anything happen to you."

"But you did let me get dragged into the vines with a maniac," she said with her charming smile.

"Well, nothing much beyond that, I mean."

They both laughed and clasped hands.

"Darling, I'm not the complaining sort," she said, gazing into his eyes. "But in our future, do vet your friends a little bit better. Could you do that for me?"

John laughed, and promised he would. He would promise her anything. After considering something witty to say, and producing quite a fine line, he halted. He spoke not.

He gently placed his hand on her warm cheek, leaned forward, and he kissed her.

TWENTY-FIVE

Within a month, by early October, the weather had changed. Certainly, it was still warm, and the midday sun occasionally burned brightly. But evening winds gusting from the northeast were cooler, sometimes even bristling, blowing the remnants of summer out to sea. These evenings demanded a long-sleeved shirt or a sweater, and darkness fell conspicuously earlier each night. The rains had just started, a few times a week, dropping in short bursts, creating muddy rivulets cascading down steep hills.

The population of Ibiza transformed drastically. In a matter of weeks, hundreds of thousands left the island. A constant flow of air flights, red wing lights fading into the upper sky, had returned the freneticism to all corners of Europe. Now the airport stagnated.

The formerly throbbing streets of Ibiza Town were deserted. A few local children wandered about, kicking dented metal cans across cobblestone surfaces, the hollow clanging echoing through empty plazas. Most of the exhausted shops and restaurants were shuttered. They needed repairs and painting over the quiet seasons.

The multistoried cruise ships that once lined the main harbor, crammed with restless tourists craving to pour into Ibiza Town, had all sailed away. The harbor was quiet. Only the swooshing sound of wide brooms along the docks, wielded by elderly Spanish workers with cigarettes dangling from their mouths, filled the air. A few sailboats, white sails distended by the wind, slipped through the harbor with barely a trace in their wake, out to the wide-open sea.

All throughout the island, sereneness descended. The fruit orchards, once sagging with ripe apricots and pomegranates and peaches, bees buzzing about, had dropped their sweet fruits, and now bare branches remained, latticed above hushed fields.

The bustling markets, replete with hundreds of vendors plying their artwork just weeks ago, were deserted. Many vendors disappeared to other parts of the world, searching for more lively locales to hock their wares. Some would return at the start of next summer, and some would simply fade into the tapestry of distant lands, never to be heard from again.

Even the legendary nights were subdued. The pulsing music and magical parties dwindled into a few wandering guitar solos and respectable dinners. And although the island was pleasant, a bittersweet feeling enveloped all aspects of life, the feeling which inexorably exists when a mighty and terrible and wonderful summer, bursting with possibilities and dreams, has finally come to a close. There would be other summers, and hope arose from this prospect, but deep inside one knew none could ever surpass this one.

John drove them with his faithful car to Cala Salada on his final day on Ibiza. Here nestled the first beach he had visited upon his arrival, when his ripped map was still intact. For some reason, he had never returned all summer. But he remembered this cove as his favorite. Of all the beaches, none were as visually arresting as this one, as the shapes, the hues, and the clear water formed a whimsical amalgam. At two in the afternoon, the blue sky was cloudless and pure.

Lovely Diana snorkeled, searching for loggerhead sea turtles, while Gunther scoured the rocks on the cove's side, examining flora and seeking rare blue wall lizards. John anticipated meeting Diana's mother at their Yorkshire estate the following week. Diana informed him that in romance novels, a woman in love required her man to meet Mother. He responded that while he might hesitate using those books as a compass for life, he promised to read any of her choosing. Diana also warned that her mother qualified as an odd bird, and that she tended to "speak directly." He found it amusing that those whom "speak directly" tend to use this directness for derogatory remarks, and curiously, never employ this direct manner to compliment. They laughed heartily, and Diana told him, with an accompanying kiss, that he was absolutely on target when it came to her mother.

Gunther planned to visit John in London in a month. Finally, after over fifteen parched years, they would launch their political and theological journal. A dream cometh true. And using Diana's connections, a radio show as well. Thus, they could "expose the unsuspecting public to their perpetual debates," Gunther had said with a laugh.

Both had learned much from Ibiza. Perhaps in the process

itself, in the enduring quest for the Holy Grail, meaning could be found. The future scintillated. And with Andre's sculptures headlining the February gallery opening in the West End of London, a memorable reunion lay ahead.

With everyone occupied, John reclined on the beach, grinding coarse sand in his palms while inhaling salty sea air. Above, vastness. These vivid blue heavens over Ibiza were the finest he ever encountered. Forever he would be beholden to this island.

He experienced a compulsion to sprint over and ascend the long, flat rock which jutted out from beach into the water. A wave of warmth crashed across his soul as he recalled jumping from that exact spot into the Mediterranean all those months ago, when summer was born.

The heated amber rock rose ten feet above the beach. Would the water be deep enough to leap into at the far end? He stepped deftly along the rock's surface, and peered down from the seaward edge. Clearness to the sandy bottom, where cream cockle shells lay. But he could not gauge its depth.

"Magnificent, no?"

John veered, flummoxed by the penetrating voice.

There he sat. Yes, it was he. Miraculously, it was he.

The aged, vanishing man from the rock he had encountered months before.

Curiously, he had forgotten about him, yet the memory lingered and was somehow always present.

He sat cross-legged with an immaculately straight back, and still wore his necklace of brown seeds and golden nose ring. But he appeared different as well. The sun shone powerfully on him; his face reflected brightness, features barely visible and skin deeply bronzed.

"It is you," John said. "I remember you said you came from Norway. Stavanger, yes?"

His eyes glowed. "You appreciated that view of the water when we first met," the man said.

"You remember that?" John said, astounded by his retention.

He did not respond.

"I did appreciate it," John said. "But now, much more. I appreciate it so much more."

"You were distraught. But you freely admitted your mistakes."

John's eyes moistened.

"You also had patience." His voice rushed through John. "And you believed."

John smiled gratefully, a single teardrop sliding down his tanned cheek.

He turned back to the sea.

Without any hesitation, he leapt.

Moments in the air, silence, and then warm, reassuring waters encapsulating him. The sun, golden liquid shimmering above the water's surface, finally within reach.

KEEP IN TOUCH WITH THE AUTHOR

JustinKurian.com
Goodreads: Justin Kurian
Facebook: justin.kurian.54
Instagram: @justinbkurian

Printed in Great Britain
by Amazon